James Fitzmaurice-Kelly, James Mabbe

Celestina or the Tragicke-Comedy of Calisto and Melibea

James Fitzmaurice-Kelly, James Mabbe

Celestina or the Tragicke-Comedy of Calisto and Melibea

ISBN/EAN: 9783337007690

Printed in Europe, USA, Canada, Australia, Japan

Cover: Foto ©Andreas Hilbeck / pixelio.de

More available books at **www.hansebooks.com**

CELESTINA

OR THE TRAGICKE-COMEDY OF

CALISTO AND MELIBEA

ENGLISHED FROM THE SPANISH

OF FERNANDO DE ROJAS BY

JAMES MABBE

ANNO 1631

With an Introduction by

JAMES FITZMAURICE-KELLY

LONDON
Published by DAVID NUTT
IN THE STRAND
1894

INTRODUCTION

A PARENT source of what is called realism,
the *Celestina* has for its most striking
characteristic a quality of perennial fresh-
ness, beside which the most of Calderón,
howbeit a hundred and fifty years younger,
shows withered and scentless and stale.
The book, indeed, is near four centuries old, but its youth
is well-nigh unabated; and so much will be admitted even
by those ' rigid reprehenders '—if any there be left—whose
censure Mabbe encountered with defiance. Its vogue,
immense from the outset, is wofully diminished now; but
its authority rather waxes than dwindles with time. '*Le
'fruict que produict ce livre,*' said the old French translator, '*pour vieillir ne perd iamais saison*'; and he said
true. Fernando de Rojas belonged to no existing school,
nor did he found one: his distinction lies in his having
given coherency and impulse to certain tendencies which
he found scattered and inert. He brought into letters
not so much a new theory as a new intelligence and a
new method; and, from simple adequacy of execution, he
endures not only as an influence but also as an artist of

vii

high accomplishment. His survival is justified by the possession of qualities which do not age—as delicate analysis, ¶
acute observation, severe felicity of phrase. From the event
of his appearance in 1499 (if that be the real date) is to be
noted the entrance into literature of a treatment which,
despite the freaks and the eccentricities of its practitioners,
has grown continually in completeness, in serviceableness,
and in charm ; so that, from this point of view at least, his
achievement remains imperishable.

I

Novel or
Play ?

The questions of ascription and classification are hard to
answer. The very form of the *Celestina* has varied more
than that of most. In its earliest edition, as in its second,
the thing is but sixteen scenes long. In its final shape it
consists of the twenty-one divisions here 'put into English
'cloathes' by James Mabbe ; but at least three sixteenth-
century reprints present an additional scene for Traso and
his bezonians—discarded, probably, as the work of another
hand. Critics have argued about this matter and about :
these holding the book a novel, those a drama. But a
novel in dialogue, a novel without narrative, is almost a
contradiction in terms ; and though the length of the
Celestina makes it impossible to play, the spirit of the
dialogue, the transitions of incident, and the build of the
plot are essentially dramatic. All the same, its imitators
and its plagiaries apart, its effect is marked to far stronger
purpose in the Spanish novel than in the Spanish drama.
The work of Lope de Rueda and Juan de Timoneda is an

viii

CALISTO AND MELIBEA

exception; but after Timoneda's time the Spanish theatre drew its chief inspiration from such lofty sentiments as honour, loyalty to the King, devotion to the Church; and even where it was more in touch with life, as in the case of Moreto or the greater Tirso, its adoption of verse as the general vehicle of expression helped to check the advance of the *Celestina's* master-tendency, at least at home and for the time. On the other hand, the book's survey of life is wider, its range of emotion and its intensity of passion are ampler, than the scope of the picaresque novelist allows. And the controversy does not end with these tithes of mint and anise and cummin: there are weightier matters of the law. The authorship of the first act is variously ascribed to Juan de Mena, to Rodrigo Cota de Maguaque, and to Fernando de Rojas aforesaid. In an unsigned prefatory letter (omitted by Mabbe), the last named says that the first act was attributed by some to Mena and by some to Cota, but the remainder was written by himself; and with this curt report he passes on. Now, Mena, *Príncipe de los Poetas de Castilla*, holds much the same position among the courtly makers grouped round John the Second as Ronsard, *Prince des Poètes*, among the writers of the Pleiad. With all the ingenuity and much of the extravagant emphasis of the Cordovan school, his elaborate Latinised style is as unlike as may be to the luminous, idiomatic brevity of the Tragic-Comedy, which—assuredly—he would have banned as written in the *humilde y baja lengua*. The flaccid, pompous hyperbaton of such of his prose as remains to us exaggerates the defects of his verse, and is still more remote from the concentrated energy and the austere sim-

Marginal notes:

INTRO-
DUCTION

The First
Act

Juan de
Mena

b   ix

THE TRAGICK-COMEDY OF

plicity of Rojas. Only by a literary miracle could one
man be master of two methods thus essentially and dia-
metrically opposed ; nor would it be less marvellous that
Mena, in his endeavour to foist a set of obsolete Roman
models on his native tongue, should have hit as by a happy
accident on the terse, entirely autochthonic style of fifty
years later. He could not if he would ; and, as to do so was
to renounce his own ideals, he would not if he could. The
Rodrigo Cota claim set up for Cota is more embarrassing, partly because so
little is known of him and his writings. A converted Jew,
suspected of backsliding, he is one of three reputed authors
of the *Coplas de Mingo Revulgo* ; but his sole authentic
piece is the beautiful and famous *Diálogo entre el Amor y un
Viejo*, a lyric incomparably better than the tags of verse im-
bedded in the doubtful fragment of the *Celestina* ; while
of prose by him on which a judgment might be formed no
jot nor tittle is extant. That he may have written this first
act is possible : that he has left nothing at all resembling it
is certain. Moreover, the work has such a unity of language
and design as wholly discredits the theory of divided authorship. Juan de Valdés, indeed, upheld that theory ; but the
weight of his name and opinion is more than balanced by
the combined authority of Wolf and Blanco White, and
of late his hypothesis has been demolished by the most
learned and the most brilliant among living experts,
Señor Menéndez y Pelayo. Last of all, it has been argued
Fernando de that Fernando de Rojas never was in the flesh. But the
Rojas Solar Myth School of criticism has had its day, and it may
be taken as positive that Rojas wrote more than three-
fourths of the *Celestina* ; while it is much more than pro-

x

CALISTO AND MELIBEA

bable, on internal evidence, that he wrote the initial act.
Unless it be assumed that he rewrote that act, and so
metamorphosed it as to make it entirely his own, his so-
called continuation shows an identity of conception, develop-
ment, and language unique in literary history; for it is a fact
that no parallel to such an exploit can be found in any
other second part avowedly from a second hand. Nor need
we take too literally the man's own utterances in the contrary sense. His statement, that he wrote his share of the
book during a fortnight's holiday, leaves it doubtful whether
he should be held to mean the fifteen acts which follow in
the earlier form or the twenty-one of the book as we have it
now. The only existing copy of the first edition—which,
moreover, is of doubtful authenticity—lacks the title-page.
This may, or may not, have set forth a prefatory letter on
the reverse of the leaf; but in its absence the point must be
left unsettled. It matters little: for the lesser performance
would still be incredible, even were the work the merest
improvisation, instead of being the model of condensed,
deliberate form it is.

The vague reference to Mena and to Cota was doubtless
intended as a blind; but the trick is less baffling than discreet. Indeed, the mystification is obvious: no reader could
mistake Mena's style for Cota's; the two are poles asunder.
But though the example was not happily chosen, there was
clearly need for precaution, when such a man as Vives was to
be found denouncing the book as *nequitiarum parens, carcer
amorum :* a work as pestilent as *Amadís,* or as Pope Pius the
Second's *Euryalus and Lucretia !* Years later the philosopher revised his opinion, and, unphilosophically enough,

THE TRAGICK-COMEDY OF

found praise for the *Celestina's* moral teaching. But, once
started, a hue-and-cry goes on : there must always be, in
Mabbe's phrase, 'some detractors, who like dogges that barke
' by custome, will exclaime against the whole worke ' because
some part chances to be freer 'then may sute with a civill
' stile.' The hubbub helps to explain the author's silence
after his unexampled success. Unlike Mabbe, who testily
compares the cavillers to 'nothing better then the Scarabee,
' who over-flying the most fragrant flowers, chooseth rather
' to settle in a Cow-shard, then to light upon a Rose,' Rojas
paid no heed, and, his book having taken its definite form,
contented himself with amending here and there. From

some prefatory acrostic verses, reproduced by a *tour de force*
in the Italian and French versions of Ordóñez and Lavigne,
and rightly unattempted by Mabbe, it is gathered that he
was a Bachelor of Laws and a native of Montalbán in the
province of Toledo. With this announcement of ' *su nombre,*
' *su tierra, su clara nación,*' he vanishes out of literature as
suddenly and furtively as he came into it. The old legend of
his being in orders is now disproved : thanks to Gallardo, it
is known that he became Alcalde Mayor of Salamanca, and
that he married, was the father of a family, and died at
Talavera de la Reina. He wrote no more : there was perhaps
no special reason why he should. He had given a permanent
impulse to all European literature after him, and his work
was done. Yet to this day no personality of any time
remains more interesting and more enigmatic than that of
the Spanish country lawyer who took up his pen to write a
masterpiece, and, having written it, having seen it canonised
as a classic in his own lifetime, buried himself behind his

CALISTO AND MELIBEA

writs, fathered a part of his great achievement on two dead poets, and courted obscurity as strenuously as the most of men court fame.

II

Some touches he borrowed from Ovid's *Amores*, some from His Origins the *Satyricon* of Petronius ; and his ruffian Centurio springs from the loins of the Plautine bully who served under Bumbomachides. A fuller suggestion of his story as a whole has been traced to the *De Amore* of an Auvergnat monk of *De Amore* the tenth or twelfth century, called Pamphilus Maurilianus. But the nationality, the date, the name of this clerk are all uncertain ; and it would seem that here is the case of an author's being confounded with one of his own personages. In this comedy—for comedy it is—the characters of Pamphilus, Galatea, and Anus correspond closely to those of Calisto, Melibea, and Celestina. But if Rojas did not read it, he may have found the germ of his story in the *Libro de Cantares* of Juan Ruiz, who names his sources with Juan Ruiz characteristic candour : *lo feo del estoria dis Pánfilo e Nasón* : indeed the Trota-conventos of the Archpriest of Hita, mentioned by Parmeno in the second act, is as surely the rough sketch of the Bawd as Don Melón de la Uerta and Doña Endrina de Calatayud are anticipations of the lovers. And from the *Corbacho* of a second learned cleric, Alfonso Martínez de Talavera, Rojas not merely lifted some passages Martínez de bodily but, further, conveyed the usage of popular proverbs and catchwords, which he developed with a skill and a profusion unsurpassed by Cervantes himself. But Rojas, if he lack equally the debonair gaicty of Ruiz and the

splenetic wit of Martínez, is a sounder craftsman than
either. Ruiz outshines him as a lyrist and in richness and
variety of temperament, but Rojas has a rarer mastery of
his instrument than Ruiz, and, though he work mainly in
prose, he produces a deeper, rounder tone. A great but
unequal artist, he is better in execution and expression than
in composition and invention. He eliminates, but in such
frugal measure that there is warrant for Moratín's remark:
that you might remove every fault from the *Celestina* without
adding a syllable to the text. At times the writer in him is
mastered by the pedant: as when Parmeno talks of 'Apuleius
' and the Asse,' or when his fellow-varlet, Sempronio, babbles
on end of Alexander, Minerva, Virgil, and Seneca. But this
ostentation of learning is a darling vice with writers, great
and little; and Rojas was no more free from it than Balzac.
Also, what lettered Spaniard could avoid the reference to
Seneca, and what reader would not miss it, were it away?
What mediæval writer could resist the mention of Virgil,
and ' how in a wicker basket hee was hung out from a Towre,
' all Rome looking upon him '? Melibea fortifies herself with
a host of historic instances, 'gathered and collected out
' of those ancient bookes, which for the bettering of my wit
' and understanding, you willed me to reade '; and Celestina
and her apprentices are scarce less copious. But these are
concessions to the pseudo-cultured taste of an age which
loved to example each digression by some weighty precedent:
they are in no wise essential to the method of a writer whose
self-restraint is exceptional for his time. And if the man's
learning be mostly second-hand, superficial, and popular, the
man himself had thought much and suffered more, while his

CALISTO AND MELIBEA

picture of life is given in definite and unfaltering outline
with an impersonal ease, a certainty, an amplitude which
mark the entrance of a new ideal. His prudent parsimony
of epithet adds greatly to his translator's difficulties, and
lends force to Mabbe's rueful avowal: 'Yet have I made it
' as naturall as our language will give leave, and have more
' beaten my braines about it in some places then a man would
' beate a Flint to get fire.' Still, Rojas never condenses to
excess, never overcharges his weapon, never tries to impose
upon words a heavier burden of meaning than they can
bear. His dialogue, compact and trenchant, contrived
to illuminate the situation and the characters of his
personages, follows the steady current of his story without
haste and without stay. He avoids exceptions or eccentricities: his central theme is the elemental passion which
throbs through the general life of man; and, from sheer
truth of drawing, his creations pass beyond the stage of
types to become individual, representative figures of all
kinds and degrees—lovers, parents, nobles, servants, bilks,
decoys. '*L'artiste doit s'arranger de façon à faire croire*
' *à la postérité qu'il n'a pas vécu,*' says Flaubert; and in
Rojas's case the consummation has in fact been wrought.
Still, no piece of art is so impersonal as to dissemble
utterly the cardinal features of the artist. In Rojas's pre-
sentation, workmanship apart, the dominating qualities are
sincerity and creative power; the humour is of the dry
Spanish savour; there is little verbal wit, and there is still
less seeking after effect. The work is the product of a
mind vigorous, grave, lucid, shackled by few prejudices or
opinions, alert to impressions, stored with a large experi-

THE TRAGICK-COMEDY OF

ence of life and of men, their occasions, foibles, and pitfalls.
Synthetic in its present application, but innately critical,
the writer's talent is that of a man whose gaze is firmly
fixed upon the present, whose intelligence is prompt with
checks upon imagination. Richly dowered with the sense
of the romance, the mystery, and the passion of existence,
Rojas stands apart from the buoyant hope of youth and
from the ecstasy of love: he describes and analyses from
without. As in the great Catalan poet of the generation
before his own, his tear is readier than his smile—*amich de
plor é desamich de riure.* Perhaps it is to this attitude of
sombre reserve that he owes that unaccountable reputation
as a moral teacher which Mabbe labours with superfluous
antithesis: 'Her life is foule, but her Precepts faire; her
' example naught, but her Doctrine good; her Coate ragged,
' but her mind inriched with many a golden Sentence.' All
this is beside the mark. Rojas's end is distinct: there is no
other-worldliness in him: he is an artist, not a moralist.
He aims at giving an impression of very life, and by his
accomplishment he stands or falls. The writer nearest akin
to him in modern literature is Guy de Maupassant. Both
are too thoroughly disillusionised to believe in men, are
too far detached to hate them; both have the same precision of form, the same intuition of motive, the same
intellectual disdain, the same plangent note of pessimism,
the same retrospect of desires turned to regrets; both
brood from the same angle upon the comedy of human
action and the tragedy of human hearts; and as the
mechanism of each is consciously simple, so the performance
of each is, after its kind, complete.

CALISTO AND MELIBEA

If the learned be right in connecting *All's Well That Ends Well* with Accolti's *Virginia*, the relation between Rojas and Shakespeare is but once removed. In any case it is scarce an exaggeration to say that, after the creation of Calisto and Melibea, the appearance of Romeo and Juliet was but a question of time. Where in the Plautine and Terentian comedy there was appetite, where in their late derivatives there was rank lubricity, where in the writers who immediately preceded Rojas there were symbolism and mystical transport, the *Celestina* strikes the note of rapture, passion, the love of love. A famous living poet, a countryman of Rojas, has summed up the modern doctrine in two striking lines :—

> Es propio del amor, si es verdadero,
> compendiar en un ser el mundo entero.

The idea is comparatively new. Love in its later sense, love, the most puissant of sentiments, the focus of emotion, comes into literature, as M. Gaston Paris has shown, with the story of Tristan and Ysolt ; and it may be claimed for Rojas that he brought it forth from the fantastic dusk of romance, the home of shadowy kings and queens, into that light of common day which shines on men and women. That he did thus much in the creation of his sad-starred lovers were of itself enough for fame ; but his other personages are no whit less imposing. The fine unscrupulousness, the liberal mendacity, the splendid brag of Sempronio and Parmeno and Centurio are given with such vivacity and truth that no picaresque writer has ventured to depart from the model. Elicia and Areusa and Doll Tearsheet are worthy sisters, while Celestina herself, the daughter of Dipsas and the mother of

c

xvii

THE TRAGICK-COMEDY OF

Macette, eclipses the creations of Ovid and Régnier by virtue of a power which compels conviction. Even in the conjuration scene, weird almost as the orgy of apes in the Witch's Kitchen, her natural quality remains constant. So preeminent is she among her compeers that the original title of the Tragic-Comedy of Calisto and Melibea has been supplanted by the name of the great wise Bawd. Last of all,

His Art
the writer's craft is on a level with his material. His note is reticence: the fire in him throws off few sparks; there is little waste, there is no sort of love of the conceit for its own sake. As befits him who may be styled the father of his country's prose, his passion is centred rather on the capture of the just expression, the exact shade, the inevitable word. Master of his means, equal to any stress, he superseded the unreflecting profusion of Ruiz by an art no longer local, no longer even national, but universal. He cannot, perhaps, be called a great man of letters: his credentials are too few. But he is a commanding literary figure. He comes before the world, not of his own seeking, but reluctantly and coyly, a single small book in his hand. But that small book is a study of the tragi-comedy of human life—its heats and agues, its strength and weakness, its exaltation and despair: it is instinct with observation and with art; and, as its interest is permanent, so its influence has proved more fertilising than that of not a little greater work.

III

James Mabbe
In the diffusion of its lesson of loyalty to truth, to life and to distinction of form, no man, in the measure given to a translator, has played a braver part than its admiring

CALISTO AND MELIBEA

lover, Don Diego Puede-Ser. Much of the vigour, the passion, the fire of Rojas, much of the *gravitas et probitas* which stirred Barth's transports, is successfully transfused in his copy; and if its colours be not in all respects the same as his original's, they are of uncommon brilliancy and beauty. The ideal translator of a masterpiece must be of the same mould and of well-nigh the same metal as his original. In default of this supreme endowment, it may be said of Mabbe that he possessed the main qualification upon which Dryden insisted: 'a mastery of the language he ' translates out of and that he translates into.' 'A trans-
' lator,' says Glorious John, 'that would write with any force
' or spirit of an original, must never dwell on the words of his
' author. He ought to possess himself entirely, and perfectly
' comprehend the genius and sense of his author, the nature
' of the subject, and the terms of the art or subject treated
' of; and then he will express himself as justly, and with as
' much life, as if he wrote an original; whereas, he who copies
' word for word, loses all the spirit in the tedious transfusion.'
Mabbe would seem to have anticipated this canon. As a
translator he holds a most distinguished place; and in the
present instance his triumph is the greater since his manner
and the manner of Rojas are parasangs apart. Judging from
his prefaces, Mabbe's style was deeply tinged with both *culter-
anismo* and *conceptismo*: tendencies, or, if you will, defects,
most incident in a student of contemporary Spanish letters.
Nor was the magnificent Armado himself more charmed with
'ostentation, or show, or pageant, or antique, or firework.'
His love of the 'congruent epitheton' breaks out in his eulogy
on his text, wherein, as he pledges himself, 'you shall find

THE TRAGICK-COMEDY OF

' Sentences worthy to be written, not in fragile paper, but in
' Cedar, or lasting Cypresse, not with the quill of a Goose, but
' the feather of a Phœnix; not with inke, but Balsalmum;
' not with letters of a blacke tincture, but with Characters of
' Gold and Azure; and deserving to be read, not only of a
' lascivious Clodius, or effeminate Sardanapalus, but of the
' gravest Cato or severest Stoick.' Not Guevara, not Góngora

Euphuism himself, could better it! For an interpreter of Rojas, the
omen is disquieting; but Mabbe, dear as the effort must
have cost him, strove manfully to follow Sempronio's counsel
as to style. 'Leave off' these circumlocutions; leave off
' these poeticall fictions,' is easily said; but if he never quite
mastered the lesson, it was simply that his temperament was
too strong for him. His conscience is in his work; and,
when he turns to his author, his metaphors sit shy, and
much of his bizarre *cultilatiniparla* disappears. And if his
self-effacement be not absolute, he yet approves himself a
master in his art by fastening on the salient points of his
original, by distilling from it the essential secret of its meaning, and by rendering the close construction of a Spanish
phrase through some happy 'quillet or quirke' of his
own devising. He rarely blunders; still more rarely are his
blunders bad; at the worst, he is guilty rather of perversity
than of defective scholarship. Partly from an invincible

Scruples foppery, partly from sectarian scruples more or less respect-
able, he constantly puts a pseudo-classical gloss on the
simplest phrase. Where Rojas writes '*Por cierto los gloriosos*
' *sanctos que se deleitan en la visión divina,*' Mabbe turns it by
' Certainly, if sublunary bodies can give a celestiall reflection or
' resemblance.' Again, where the Spaniard speaks of '*estaciones,*

CALISTO AND MELIBEA

' *procesiones de noche, misas del gallo, misas del alba y otras*
him into 'Their most mysterious celebration of the feasts of
' their Vesta, nay, and that most strictly solemnized day of
' Bona Dea, where it is death to admit men.' Rojas makes
Celestina beg for Melibea's girdle, which has touched the
relics at Rome and at Jerusalem : whereby Mabbe is provoked to ramble into mythology, and to travesty the
passage into 'That same admirable girdle of yours, which is
' reputed to have beene found and brought from Cumæ the
' Cave there, and was worne, 'tis thought, by the Sibilla, or
' Prophetesse of that place.' With the same narrow consistency, he will convert a visit to Saint Mary Magdalen's
church into 'My wonted retirement to the Mirtle-grove,' an
Abbot into a 'Flamin,' nuns into 'Vestalls,' a saint into
' Venus sonne,' *soberano Dios* into 'Cupid.' Nay : with a
stroke of the pen he transforms you Guadalupe from a place
to a person ! His consistency, moreover, is purely superficial.
If he drew the line at admitting the existence of saints,
relics, monks, and nuns, it might pass as an amusing pre-
judice ; as it is, the line is not drawn straight, or, at least, is
drawn so capriciously that a reference to 'that fat Fryers
' wench' is rendered with all the precisian's sourness. (It is
diverting to find that in the hands of Rojas's French translator, whose pious scruples work from the opposite pole, the
fat friar becomes a *bon officier*.) These and a score of such
passages Mabbe misconstrues, not from carelessness but
from conscientious motives. Such rigid orthodoxy, ob-
jectionable only inasmuch as it destroys the atmosphere of
the original, is the more surprising in one who, two years

earlier, in his version of Fonseca's *Sermones de Quaresma*, had lulled his reader's qualms with the assurance that 'there ' is not so great a distance between Hierusalem and Samaria, ' as some imagine.'

In transplanting a proverb or resolving an idiom, Mabbe seldom stumbles. Such renderings as 'These papers with ' all ages' for *Estos papeles con todas las edades*, or, 'This ' foole is fallen into his thirteenes' for *En sus trece está este necio*, are the exception with him; just as such mistranslations as 'needles' for *aguijones* and 'injuries' for *injurias* are simple oversights. Still more seldom is the *nuance* lost; as where a *varonil*, a 'lusty' wench, is set down as 'manly.' At times a droll social distinction intrudes itself: the expression *mala landre te mate*, uttered by Elicia and Celestina, is given with a violent crudity which forbids quotation, but in the mouth of a great lady like Melibea's mother, it is refined demurely into

'beshrew thy fingers.' But with all his love for vehement antithesis and grandiose rhetoric, Mabbe never shrinks from homeliness if it but lend a glint of colour to his prose. He will as lief write 'treacle' as balm, nor will he shrink from saying 'Our solace is in the suds.' On occasion he will overstep the bounds of mere quaintness and will plunge into the banal and the grotesque: as in 'To fry ' in the liveliest flames of love.' A like lack of humour follows him when he allows Melibea to lament 'that powerful love ' of that late deceased gentleman.' Again, in transcribing the heroine's wail over 'the onely Patterne and Paragon of ' courtesie, of gallant inventions, of witty devices,' the nixie of interpreters drives him to add, as a translation of the

xxii

CALISTO AND MELIBEA

words, *de atavíos y bordaduras*, the stupefying anticlimax 'of
' neatnesse and decency in his cloathes.' As an example of
his oddity of expression, his Melibea 'hurling and rowling
' her eyes on every side' will serve. Of coining words he is
more chary: perhaps because his author's own sobriety in the
matter gives him few openings. ' Pompeans,' ' retchles,' and
' Fistick-nuts' are no doubt printers' variants; Sempronio's
determination to forbear till Calisto's 'angry fit be over-
' past, and that his hat be come again to his colour' may
perhaps be explained in the same way; but ' Copes-mates'
and ' similiancy' are possibly inventions. Exquisitely sus-
ceptible to the rhythm of prose, in his verse Mabbe scarce
troubles to distinguish assonant from rhyme. Rojas's songs
have a certain mannered note of simplicity which has won
them a place in the anthologies; and like most good things
they are better in their context than out of it. But they
clearly failed to interest Mabbe, who, with dogged adherence
to the Spanish, rhymes ' colours' with ' odours' as equi-
valents for *colores* and *odores*.

The gravest objection which can be taken to Mabbe's
version does not concern his delightful bizarreries so much
as his dilution of his original's concentration. It is very
doubtful if this could have been avoided at any time; but,
however this be, the exuberance of Mabbe himself, and of
Mabbe's epoch, made it inevitable. In amplifying, he is
not shirking a difficulty: he is conforming, not only to his
personal standard but, to the taste of the Elizabethans,
Jacobites, and Carolines, to whom the Spaniard's unadorned
directness must have seemed bald. It is to Mabbe's credit
that he withstood so stoutly as he did the strong tempta-

tion which he had to deform his text with arabesques, and to stifle it in wreaths. As it is, his virtue cannot be pressed too far: he is constantly expanding, now on compulsion and now from choice. Where Rojas writes the two words ' *Convidan, despiden*,' Mabbe uses two dozen, and beats the ore into the thinnest leaf: 'They will give you rost-
' meate, and beate you with the spit. They will invite you
' unto them, and presently send you packing with a flea in
' your eare.' Again, where the original gives ' *Anda, pase,*'
Mabbe translates: 'Well, let the world slide, and things be
' as they may be, when they cannot be as they should be.'
At whiles the redundancy becomes fanfaronade. Celestina, speaking of fate, says simply, ' *no me será contraria* ': but Mabbe—in the very spirit of the tenor who adds a long roulade to the coda, not because it is fitting, but because he wants to show off his technique—spins out her utterance into 'It cannot but goe well with us; it is impos-
' sible wee should misse of our purpose; All is Cock-sure.'

A kindred fault is his tendency to pleonasm. In such parisonic combinations as ' thy disdainnesse, thy pleasing coy-
' nesse,' 'affiance and confidence,' 'curses and maledictions,'
'diminished and lessened,' 'lessen and mitigate,' 'force and
' strength,' though a distinction of some subtlety may be established between each member, the general effect is to sacrifice the intensity of the original to the caprice of a virtuoso. In some instances the expansion degenerates into interpolation bordering desperately near the ludicrous. ' *Yo no sé nada
' de mi arte,*' writes Rojas ; and Mabbe, after translating correctly by, 'I am no body in this my Art,' adds cheerfully, ' a
' meere bungler, an Idiot, an Asse.' Celestina's declaration that

CALISTO AND MELIBEA

'Every strong sent is good: as Penny-royall, Rue, Worme-
'wood, smoake of Partridge, of Rosemary,' is completed
by a prescription of Mabbe's own—'of the Soles of old
'shooes.' Equally whimsical, though much more infrequent,
are his ellipses. Where Rojas speaks of '*un torzal para*
'*el bonete,*' Mabbe drily sets down 'a hat'; '*los devotos*
'*de templos, monasterios, iglesias,*' shrivels into 'your penny-
'fathers'; and the details of '*con todos cumple, y á todos*
'*muestra buena cara, y todos piensan que son muy queridos,*
'*y cada uno piensa que no hay otro, y que él solo es el*
'*privado, y él solo es el que le da lo que ha menester,*' are
curtly dismissed as 'and yet hath given good satisfaction
'to them all.'

But Mabbe can better afford than most translators to have
his shortcomings microscopised; and when all that man can
do in the way of carping has been done, his slips remain
astonishingly few and unimportant. His understanding is
as clear as his utterance is happy. The fine simplicity, the
rhythm and the music of his version are pregnant with
the amplitude and the urbanity which stamp the prose of
the heroic age. No man excels him as a writer of direct
description; no man has an ear more subtly attuned to the
ripple and the cadence of a phrase: 'Looke on the Moone,'
he writes, 'and see how bright shee shines upon us: looke on
'the Cloudes, and see how speedily they racke away: harken
'to the gurgling waters of this fountaine: how sweet a
'murmure, and what a pretty kind of purling they make,
'rushing along these fresh herbes, and pleasant flowres:
'harken to these high Cypresses, how one bough makes peace
'with another by the intercession of a milde, gentle, and

d

THE TRAGICK-COMEDY OF

' temperate wind, which moves them to and fro.' It would
be impossible to convey with loftier distinction and rarer
precision the subdued melody of the original; and the
achievement might be matched from page on page. Mabbe
had grasped, indeed, the essential principle of translation:
that a translator's chief duty is to translate. So far as the
Celestina was concerned, the examples he may have had
before him were mostly bad, and there were plausible reasons
for following them. Lavardin, the best known of the
French translators, plumes himself on his impertinent im-
provements: ' *Le repurgeant en plusieurs endroicts scandal-*
' *eux*,' he says, ' *qui pouvoient offenser les religieuses oreilles,*
' *et y adioustant du mien en plusieurs endroicts qui me*
' *sembloient manques.*' Mabbe has a higher and a juster view
of his office. Apart from omissions made on principle, his
respect for the substance of his original is complete. He is
singularly free from the vanity which leads the translator to
imagine that he knows an author's intention better than
that author himself. With Puritanism rising everywhere
round him, it would not have been strange had he tampered
with Rojas's natural candour; yet he stands staunchly by
his text, nor suffers himself to be dismayed by any ' Criticall
' companions, being of a depraved disposition, and apt in
' themselves to be evill.' His adoption of the pseudonym of
Diego Puede-Ser may look like a concession to vulgar pre-
judice, a desire to avoid open responsibility; and it is
probably true that he had no very special vocation for
martyrdom. The fact, however, is that he had taken the
name eight years before, and its transparency left his
identity an open secret. His Spanish *apodo* would come to

CALISTO AND MELIBEA

him recommended by its own conceit, for a conceit was
always infinitely attractive to his mind. As in his preface
he talks of ' unsavory meates mended by their own sauces,'
and hastens to add, ' I am too saucie in my desire,' so his
delight in a quip is irrepressible in his text: ' Why
' what,' says his Parmeno, ' were all the joy I now injoy, did
' I not injoy her ?' Again and again his respect for Rojas's
meaning is helped out by gusts of fine fearlessness, triumph- His Victories
ant in the result. ' *La cruda y rigurosa muestra de aquel*
' *gesto angélico* ' is admirably turned by 'that cruell and sterne
' looke of that impious face ': yet one can imagine the horror
of the stickler for exact scholarship, spoon-fed from Percival
and dandled by Minsheu, on seeing *angélico* construed
' impious.' In this way, time upon time, Mabbe equals, and
even outshines, his text. The movement and sound of
Elizabethan speech ring back from line on line. ' *Cuál fué*
' *tan contrario acontescimiento ?* ' writes Rojas ; and ' What
' contrarious accident,' Mabbe echoes him, ' what squint-ey'd
' starre ?' His verbal resource, his opulence of epithet, his
variety, his capacity for reproducing the effect of his original
by the simplest means, may be judged from such a passage
as that where ' *rincón de mi secreto y consejo y ánima mía* ' is
delivered as ' Thou that art the Clozet of my secrets, the
' Cabinet of my Counsell, and Councell of my soule.' His
faults themselves are turned to virtues when his hyperbole
answers to his call : as when the commonplace ' *Increible cosa*
prometes ' becomes ' Thou speakest of Matters beyond the
' Moone.' In both the severer and the lighter vein he is ever
prompt with a word of happy rarity. Thus, in his hands a
jerkin grows glorious as a ' Mandillion '; thus where Rojas,

describing a servant's lot, writes, '*Y tras esto mil chapinazos,*'
'Besides all this,' Mabbe tells you, 'her pantofles shall
'walke about her eares a thousand times a day'; and thus
you shall hear him talk of 'that great Captaine Vlysses'
who strove 'to shunne the Trojane warre, that he might lie
'dulcing at home with his wife Penelope.' He delights in
his list of 'lustrifications, clarifications, pargetings, fardings,
'waters for the morphewes, and a thousand other slibber
'slabbers'—in his mysterious catalogues 'of Axenuz or Melan-
'thion, of Lupines, of Pease, of Carilla and Paxarera.' Long
as the *Celestina* is, he never wearies of it, never flags like the
common hack. To the end he still esteems it, in his own
words, 'as Gold, amongst metalls; as the Carbuncle amongst
'stones; as the Rose amongst flowers; as the Palme amongst
'trees; as the Eagle amongst Birds; and as the Sunne
'amongst inferior Lights.' To the end he does his part by
keeping an almost unbroken level of adequate and numerous
prose. The passages of declamatory eloquence show him at
his best and stateliest, his solemn music lending dignity to
the commonplaces of death: 'There is not any thing that
'flyes so swift, as the life of man: Death still followes us,
'and hedges us in on every side; whereunto we our selves
'now draw nigh. Wee are now (according to the course of
'nature) to be shortly under his banner; this wee may plainely
'perceive if wee will but behold our equals, our brethren and
'our kinsfolke round about us; the grave hath devoured
'them all; they are all brought to their last home. . . . Let
'us therefore prepare our selves, and packe up our fardles,
'for to goe this inforced journey which cannot be avoyded.
'Let not that cruell and dolefull sounding trumpet of death,
xxviii

CALISTO AND MELIBEA

'summon us away on the sudden and unprovided.' In such
flights, where no differences of temperament separate the translator from his author, Mabbe recaptures and almost overtops the force and dignity of the original. His identification with the I. M. of the First Folio of Shakespeare is
conjectural; though the conjecture carried conviction with it to Dyce's mind. Still, were it proved that he did not write the verses attributed to him by Bolton Corney—' Wee 'wondred (Shake-spere) that thou went'st so soon'—his intimacy with Shakespeare would be suggested by the marked influence of the melody of Shakespeare's prose on his own at its highest level.

IV

According to Wood, Mabbe came 'of genteel parents in 'the county of Surrey and diocese of Winchester.' His father, James Mabbe, was the son of John Mabbe, a jeweller who carried on business in Goldsmiths' Row until the eve of his appointment as Chamberlain of London in 1577. Born in 1572, the younger James Mabbe (the name is also written Mab and Mabb) matriculated at Magdalen in the Lent term of 1586-7, was elected to a Fellowship in 1594, and served the usual round of college offices. In 1605 he is found speaking 'an eloquent oration' before Henry, Prince of Wales, on the occasion of the Prince's matriculation at Magdalen, when 'the gates and walls were covered with 'verses.' Four years later he begged the congregation of regents to admit him to the degree of Bachelor of Civil Law; 'but whether he was really admitted, it appears not.'

THE TRAGICK-COMEDY OF

In 1611 he was attached as Secretary to the Spanish embassy
of Sir John Digby, afterwards Earl of Bristol; and, on his
return to England, some two years later, he became a Lay
Prebendary of Wells. As late as 1630 he was Bursar of Magdalen for the sixth time; but three years after that he seems
to have left Oxford and to have settled with the family of
his friend, Sir John Strangwayes, at Abbotsbury in Dorset-
shire, and here he is thought to have died, and to have been
buried about the year 1642. He left the reputation of 'a
'learned man, good orator and a facetious conceited wit.'
On Wood's authority,—'being then in orders,' he says in con-
nection with the Wells appointment,—Mabbe is thought to
have been a clergyman; but a Lay Prebendary, who is also
a priest, is something of a monster, and it seems possible
that the word 'not' has dropped out of Wood's description.

His Prebend What is known is that Mabbe was Prebendary of Wanstrow,
near Frome, in 1613; that at the visitation of Bishop
Montague to Wells Cathedral in July 1615, opposite the
name of 'Iacobus Mabb artium magister prebendarius de
'Wanstrow,' the clerk has written the word *dispensatus*;
that on December 11, 1638, Mabbe resigned his 'canonical
'house' to Roger Wood; and that on December 7, 1642,
Anthony Madox was instituted to the Wanstrow prebend in
his room. This agrees with the account of him which was
given to Wood—evidently by Colonel Giles Strangwayes;

His Death but the date of his death cannot be more exactly determined,
inasmuch as at Abbotsbury, for the years 1637-1666, the
parish registers have been destroyed, while the cathedral
records at Wells are blank from 1641 to 1660. The
absence of any record of his institution to his prebend

is, so far as it goes, against the theory of his being in orders.[1]

His earliest published writing is a copy of Latin verses prefixed to Florio's Italian dictionary, called *Queen Anna's New World of Words*, issued in 1611, and here his ancient love of a conceit is shown by his anagramatising 'Ioannes 'Florio' into *ori fons alieno*. His visit to Spain gave him a new source of interest in Spanish literature: an interest which was stimulated by his friendship with Leonard Digges of University College, an Oxford man, 'highly esteemed as a 'perfect understander of the French and Spanish,' and now best remembered for his version of the once popular *Gerardo* of Céspedes y Meneses. With Digges he would seem to have contributed eulogistic verses to the First Folio of Shakespeare in 1623. In a surviving manuscript entitled *Observations Touching some of the more solemne Tymes and festivall Dayes of the yeare*, dated December 1626, 'From 'my chamber at St. Mary Magdalen College,' 'I dare 'promise you,' he says, addressing his 'worthy frend, Mr. 'Jhon Browne,' 'that this hand of myne, hath beene so 'carefull in the Limning of this little peece, that there is 'very little odds betwixt the Originall, and yt.' The same pleasant note of self-complacency is struck in his Spanish preface to *The Rogue*: '*El picaro està trasladado. Plega 'à Dios, que de mi mano no sea mal tratado. Traducido, 'si; Si traslucido bien està.*' In his introduction to the *Celestina* he seems for the first time wanting in self-confi-

---

[1] For help in verifying these details I have to thank the Earl of Ilchester, Canon Church of Wells, and the Rev. W. D. Macray, Fellow of Magdalen College.

THE TRAGICK-COMEDY OF

**INTRO-
DUCTION**

**His Achieve-
ment**

Cervantes

dence : 'nor am I any whit ashamed that any worke of 'mine should not be absolutely perfect.' If he piqued himself on his performance, he had good reason ; and if he knew his powers, he also recognised his limitations. He never attempted original work, but went on thriving on the results of his one great expedition. The taste for Spanish mirabolanes never left him. Besides the *Celestina*, the third in order of his printed versions, he translated *Guzmán de Alfarache* in 1623, under the title of *The Rogue* ; six years later he gave in English the Augustinian Fray Cristóbal de Fonseca's *Devout Contemplations Expressed In Two and Fortie Sermons upon all ye Quadragesimall Gospels* ; and in 1640 he published a rendering of Cervantes' *Exemplarie Novells*, eulogised by Godwin as 'the best translation in the 'English language.' Short of Godwin's superlatives, the work undoubtedly deserves the highest praise ; yet, as it happens, Mabbe's dealings with Cervantes are unlucky. No translation of the *Novelas Ejemplares* can be satisfactory which omits such masterpieces in their kind as *Rinconete y Cortadillo, El Licenciado Vidriera, El Casamiento Engañoso*, and *El Coloquio de los Perros*. A still worse omission than that of Cervantes' six best novels is that Mabbe in his preface tells us nothing of Cervantes himself. He would seem to have lived in Madrid for at least two years without setting eyes on the immortal whom he styles 'one of the 'prime Wits of Spaine for his rare Fancies and wittie 'Inventions.' The curiosity of the French embassy as to all that concerned the famous writer and hero is historic ; and Mabbe's friend, Ben Jonson, in *The Silent Woman* and elsewhere, shows that the interest extended to England.

CALISTO AND MELIBEA

But the Secretary of the English Envoy is blind and deaf in
Spain, or in England he is dumb and dull. On the other
hand, from internal evidence, we should never know that
Mabbe had visited Spain. He was reserved in all that
touches himself. His friendships can be divined only from
his dedications, and from the names of those who wrote
him laudatory verses; and with the exception of the
Celestina, all his publications are dedicated to some member
of the Strangwayes family.

V

The popularity of the *Celestina* is shown by the number
of editions in the original, and of translations in divers
tongues. A great thinker like Vives might denounce it and
repent; the Inquisition might frown on it; a charlatan like
Cornelius Agrippa might join the hue-and-cry; Vanegas
de Busto might jape and dub it the *Scelestina*. But at
home and abroad its reputation grew until it rivalled the
Decamerone in favour. Whole pages of a catalogue might be
filled to overflowing with the names of stage arrangements,
versified versions, continuations—a Second, a Third, perhaps
a Fourth, *Celestina*—the work of Sedeño, Urrea, Silva, a host
more. Sancho Muñón's *Lisandro y Roselia*, one of the rarest
of books, is one of the best among imitations. Lope de Vega
condescended to exploit the *Bawd* in his *Dorotea*. Its
partisans did not lack courage. Urrea publicly dedicated
his fine version of the first act to his mother; and Ordóñez,
boldly signing himself ' *Familiare della sanctità di nostro*

e

' *signore iulio papa secondo*,' did the whole book into Italian at the request of a great lady, ' *Madonna gentile*,' Feltria di Campo Fregoso. Clément Marot, as good a security as Bardolph, ironically goes bail for it :—

> Or ça, le livre de Flammette,
> *Formosum pastor*, Celestine,
> Tout cela est bonne doctrine
> Et n'y a rien de deffendu.

Hurado de Mendoza
The famous soldier and diplomatist, Hurtado de Mendoza, journeying as Ambassador to Rome, cut down his travelling library to two books — the *Amadís* and the *Celestina*. Bonaventure des Periers, in the sixteenth tale of the *Nouvelles Récréations et Joyeux Devis*, completes the list of his young Parisian's accomplishments by adding : **Some Foreign Translators** ' *Et avec cela il avoit leu Bocace et Celestine.*' The best known of the French versions is that made from the Italian by the Tourangeau Jacques de Lavardin, Sieur du Plessis-Bourrot ; and it seems certain that when Mabbe was in difficulties he consulted Lavardin. Dutch and German renderings were followed by Kaspar Barth's excellent Latin translation, *Pornoboscodidascalus Latinus*, issued with prolegomena, commentaries, all the bedizenments of a Greek tragedy. ' *Liber plane divinus*,' says Barth enthusiastically : unconsciously echoing the ' *Libro en mi* ' *opinión divi*'—the phrase wherein Cervantes records his verdict in the clipped verses which precede *Don Quixote*. **Robert Burton** Robert Burton was plainly a fervent admirer, but though it is hard to believe that he was ignorant of Spanish, he seems to have read the *Celestina* in Latin only : he quotes it

xxxiv

CALISTO AND MELIBEA

for the first time in his third edition, issued in 1628, four years after the publication of Barth. Clearly there was need for an Englishing of the book. As far back, probably, as 1530 a versified English adaptation of the *Celestina* was anonymously published ' with a morall conclusion and ' exhortacyon to vertew.' This wretched and lying piece of work fell dead on the town, and, like the first edition of the Spanish original, is believed to survive in one sole copy. On October 5, 1598, William Aspley of ' the Tigers Head in ' Saint Paul's Church-yard, afterward at the Parrat,' took out a licence to print ' a book intituled *The Tragicke Comedye* ' *of Celestina.*' But it was never issued, and no more is heard of the book until February 27, 1630, when the following record was made in the Register of the Stationers' Company under the name of ' Ralph Mabb,' our translator's brother : ' Entred of his copie under the handes of Sir Henry ' Herbert and Master Purfoote, A play Called The Spannish ' Bawde vj^d.' In 1707 a dramatic arrangement in five acts, filched from Mabbe by John Savage, was published and forgotten. In the same year Captain John Stevens, a famous pirate and botcher of other men's work, did his worst in a compilation called *The Spanish Libertines.* And as late as fifty years ago Germond de Lavigne and Eduard von Bülow issued new translations, the one in French, the other in German, faithful and inglorious both. Published in 1631, Mabbe's work appeared at an unlucky moment. It was not that the king sought any more to ' put a hook in ' the nostrils of Spain ': it was that the public interest had turned from letters to internal politics. As *Émaux et Camées* almost perished in the crisis of the *Coup d'État*, so

CALISTO AND MELIBEA

Mabbe's venture—a most comely folio—foundered in the
storm of the Civil War ; and in 1634 the remainder copies
were bound up with a third edition of *The Rogue*.   He
must have thought it worthy of a happier fate ; and pos-
terity has ruled with him.   **J. F.-K.**

THE SPANISH BAWD
REPRESENTED IN
CELESTINA
OR, THE TRAGICKE-COMEDY OF
CALISTO AND MELIBEA

WHEREIN IS CONTAINED, BESIDES THE
PLEASANTNESSE AND SWEETENESSE OF
THE STILE, MANY PHILOSOPHICALL
SENTENCES, AND PROFITABLE INSTRUC-
TIONS NECESSARY FOR THE YOUNGER
SORT : SHEWING THE DECEITS AND
SUBTILTIES HOUSED IN THE BOSOMES
OF FALSE SERVANTS
AND CUNNY-CATCHING BAWDS

1631

To my worthy and much esteemed friend

SIR THOMAS RICHARDSON

KNIGHT.

IR, I now send you your long since promised CELESTINA, put into English cloathes; I shall intreate you to give her a friendly welcome, because she is a stranger, and come purposely out of Spaine into these parts, to see you, and kisse your hands. I would not accompany her with my letters of recommendation, whereby she might finde the better reception. For, I must ingeniously confesse, that this your Celestina is not *sine scelere*; yet must I tell you withall, that she cannot be harboured with you, *sine utilitate.* Her life is foule, but her Precepts faire; her example naught, but her Doctrine good; her Coate ragged, but her mind inriched with many a golden Sentence: And therefore take her not as she seemes, but as she is; and the rather, because blacke sheepe have as good Carcasses as white. You shall finde this booke to

3

THE TRAGICK-COMEDY OF

be like a Court-Iack, which though it be blacke, yet holds as good liquor as your fairest Flagon of silver or like the Rod that Brutus offred to Apollo, which was rough and knottie without, but within, all of furbusht gold. The barke is bad, but the tree good.

Vouchsafe then (gentle Sir) to take a little of this coorse and sowre bread ; it may be, your stomack being glutted with more delicate Cates, may take some pleasure to restore your appetite with this homely, though not altogether unsavoury food. It is good plaine houshold-bread, honest messeline ; there is a great deale of Rye in it, but the most part of it is pure Wheate.

Our Author is but short, yet pithy : not so full of words as sense ; each other line, being a Sentence ; unlike to many of your other Writers, who either with the luxury of their phrases, or superfluity of figures, or superabundancie of ornaments, or other affected guildings of Rhetorick, like undiscreet Cookes, make their meats either too sweet, or too tarte, too salt, or too full of pepper ; whence it hapneth, that like greedy Husbandmen, by inlarging their hand in sowing, they make the harvest thin and barren. It is not as many of your Pamphlets be, like a tree without sap ; a bough without fruit ; a nut without a kernell ; flesh with-

4

CALISTO AND MELIBEA

out bones; bones without marrow; prickles without a Rose; waxe without honey; straw without wheate; sulfure without Gold; or shels without pearle. But you shall find Sentences worthy to be written, not in fragile paper, but in Cedar, or lasting Cypresse, not with the quill of a Goose, but the feather of a Phœnix; not with inke, but Balsalmum; not with letters of a blacke tincture, but with Characters of Gold and Azure; and deserving to be read, not only of a lascivious Clodius, or effeminate Sardanapalus, but of the gravest Cato, or severest Stoick.

All which, though I know to be true, yet doubt I not, but it will meete with some detractors, who like dogges that barke by custome, will exclaime against the whole worke, because some part of it seemeth somewhat more obscene, then may sute with a civill stile: which as I do not deny; so sithence it is written reprehensively, and not instructively, I see no reason why they should more abstaine from reading a great deale of good, because they must picke it out of that which is bad; then they should refuse Pearle, because it is fisht for in a froathy sea; or contemne Gold, because it is drawn from a dirty myne; or hate honey, because it is hived in straw; or loath silke, because it is lapt in soultage. Which kinde of men I can

5

THE TRAGICK-COMEDY OF

liken to none better, then those of whom Plutarke complainth, who are of so nice a delicacie, that they will not drinke a wholesome potion, unlesse it be given them in a Golden cup, nor weare a winter garment unlesse it bee woven of Athenian wooll.

The Lacedæmonians, who were as strict livers, and as great lovers of vertue, as any Nation whatsoever, would make benefit even out of vices. But these Criticall companions, being of a depraved disposition, and apt in themselves to be evill, I can compare to nothing better, then the Scarabee, who over-flying the most fragrant flowers, chooseth rather to settle in a Cow-shard, then to light upon a Rose: or Noahs Crow, which flew forth of the Arke, and preying upon carrion, returned no more. Howsoever therfore these rigid reprehenders will not sticke to say of Celestina, that she is like a Crow amongst so many Swans; like a Grashopper amongst so many Nightingales; or like a Paper-blurrer amongst so many famous Writers; yet they that are learned in her language, have esteemed it (in comparison of others) as Gold, amongst metalls; as the Carbuncle amongst stones; as the Rose amongst flowers; as the Palme amongst trees; as the Eagle amongst Birds; and as the Sunne amongst inferior Lights; In a word, as the choisest

6

CALISTO AND MELIBEA

and chiefest. But as the light of that great Planet doth hurt sore eies, and comfort those that are sound of sight: So the reading of Celestina, to those that are prophane, is as poyson to their hearts; but to the chaste, and honest minde, a preservative against such inconveniences as occurre in the world.

And for mine owne part, I am of opinion that Writers may as well be borne withall, as Painters, who now and then paint those actions that are absurd. As Timomachus painted Medea killing her children; Orestes, murthering his mother Theo, and Parrhasius; Ulysses counterfaited madnes, and Cherephanes, the immodest imbracements of women with men. Which the Spectators beholding, doe not *laudare rem, sed artem*; not commend the matter which is exprest in the imitation, but the Art and skill of the workeman, which hath so lively represented what is proposed. In like sort, when wee reade the filthy actions of whores, their wicked conditions, and beastly behaviour, wee are neither to approve them as good, nor to imbrace them as honest, but to commend the Authors judgement in expressing his Argument so fit and pat to their dispositions.

Nor doe I see any more reason, why a man should prove a Villaine by reading of other mens

7

THE TRAGICK-COMEDY OF

villanies, then a man should grow hard-favored, by looking Thirsites in the face, or a foole, for viewing Will Summers picture : But might rather grow as the Lacedæmonians did by their slaves drunkennesse, to a detestation of so foule a sinne. When therefore thou shalt reade of Celestina, as of a notorious Bawd; of Sempronio and Parmeno, as of false servants ; of Elicia and Areusa, as of cunning queanes and profest whores; of Centurio, as of a swaggring Ruffian, and common whoremaster; of Calisto and Melibea, as of undiscreet and foolish Lovers. And so in the rest, learne thereby to distinguish betweene good and bad, and praise the Author, though not the practice ; for these things are written more for reprehension, then imitation. And the minde that comes so instructed, can never take harme ; for it will take the best, and leave the worst : But he that reads all things alike, and equally entertaines them in his thought, that Reader shall easily shew himselfe obnoxious to many vices : And it shall happen unto him, as it did unto those who imitated Plato's crookednes, or Demosthenes stammering. But when a Reader shall light upon unworthy lines, I would have him cry out as a Philosopher adviseth on the like occasion; *Male hoc, et inconvenienter.* But when he meets with good ; *Rectè hoc et decorè.* As the Bee

8

CALISTO AND MELIBEA

feeds upon flowers, and the Goat on the tops of herbs ; so would I have him that reades Celestina, graze like a horse on that which is sweet and wholesome grasse ; and not like a hungrie dog, which snatches and bites at every thing that comes in his way. Socrates, when he saw a dishonest woman, would either turne his head aside, or cover his eyes with his cloake ; taking whores to bee like coales, which either blacke or burne. Indeede, it was the wisest way for Socrates ; for though he were a Philosopher, yet withall he was a wanton : and therefore, for such as cannot looke, but must offend in viewing of the looser Lines, I would have them imitate the Lightning, which vanisheth, before it scarce appeares ; or your Abortives, which die, before they be borne. But for as those that are truely honest, and of that perfit temper of goodnes, that nothing can make them decline from the rule of vertue, I would wish them to do with some pieces in this booke (yet to reade all, and where they finde any thing unseemly) as the Priests of old were wont to do, who in their sacrifices unto Iuno, took forth the garbage of their beasts, and threw it behinde the Altar. If any phrase savor of immodesty, blame not me, but Celestina. If any Sentence deserve commendation, praise not the Translator, but the Author ; for I am no more to be repre-

B

THE TRAGICK-COMEDY OF

hended, or commended, then the poore Parrat, who accents but other folkes words, and not his owne.

If there be any, that is either a Parmeno, or a Sempronio, an Elicia, or an Areusa, a Celestina, or a Centurio, I would have them to behold themselves in this glasse; not doubting, but that as Narcissus, viewing himselfe in that pure cleare Fountaine, wherein he saw his own most beautifull Image, dyed overcome with a φιλαυτία, or self-love; so these men will either die, or their vices in them, through an αὐτομισία, or hate of themselves; at least make other mens miserable ends, serve as so many sea-markes, that they may not run themselves upon the like rocks in the sea of this life; wherein all they are miserably drowned, who strike against them.

But to leave Celestina to a favourable censure, I must now come to intreate some favor for my selfe, who am so farre from pleading my excuse, that I must wholy submit my selfe to your favourable interpretation; for I must ingeniously confesse, that I have in the undergoing of this translation, shewn more boldnesse then judgement. For though I doe speake like Celestina, yet come I short of her; for she is so concisely significant, and indeede so differing is the Idiome of the Spainish from the English, that I may imitate it, but not

10

CALISTO AND MELIBEA

come neere it. Yet have I made it as naturall, as our language will give leave, and have more beaten my braines about it in some places, then a man would beate a Flint to get fire ; and, with much adoe, have forced those sparkes, which increasing to a greater flame, gave light to my dark understanding ; wherein if I have been wanting to give it it's true life, I wish, my industry heerein may awake some better wit, and judgement to perfect my imperfections, which as I shall alwaies be willing to acknowledge ; so I desire to have them mended by some better hand ; nor am I any whit ashamed that any worke of mine should not be absolutely perfect. For it is the Statute and Decree of Heaven, that every composition heere beneath, as well framed by the hand of Art, as fashioned by the helpe of Nature, should sustaine some imperfection : For Glasse hath it's lead ; Gold it's drosse; Corne it's chaffe ; Helene her mole ; the Moone her spots, and the Sunne its shade. My expression is but like a picture drawne with a coale, wanting those lively colours, which others more skilfull might give it ; and might better it as much, if they would undergo the paines ; as bad faces are bettered by painting, and unsavory meates mended by their sauces. But I am too saucie in my desire ; howsoever, I will notwithstanding shew

11

THE TRAGICK-COMEDY OF

my selfe a good Christian; that though my workes
doe not merit any reward, yet my faith and assurance is such in you, that I make no question, but
my workes shall be well accepted by you. In requitall whereof, I will ever love you, and rest

Your friend and servant,

DON DIEGO PUEDE-SER.

CALISTO AND MELIBEA

THE PROLOGUE

T is the saying of that great and wise Philosopher Heraclitus; That all things are created in manner of a contention, or battell. His words are these, Omnia secundùm litem fiunt. *A Sentence in my opinion, worthy perpetuall memorie; and, for that most certaine it is, that every word of a wise man, is pregnant, and full; of this it may be said, that through too much fulnesse it is readie to burst, shooting forth such spreading, and well-growne boughs and leaves, that out of the smallest Sucker, or least Sprig thereof, fruit enough may be gathered by men of discretion and judgement. But because my poore understanding is not able to doe any more, then to nibble on the drie bark and rugged rinde of the wise sayings of those, who for the clearnesse and excellencie of their wits, deserved to be approved; with that little which I shall plucke from thence, I will satisfie the intent and purpose of this short Prologue. This Sentence did I finde to be strengthened by that great Orator, and Poet Lauriat Francisco Petrarca, who tells us,* Sine lite atq; offensione nihil genuit natura parens : *That Nature, who is the mother of all things, ingendred nothing without strife and contention. Furthermore saying,* Sic est enim, et sic propemodun universa testantur ; Rapido stellæ obviant firmamento ; Contraria invicem Elementa confligunt ; Terræ tremunt ; Maria fluctuant ; Aër quatitur ; Crepant flammæ ; Bellum immortale venti gerunt ; Tempora temporibus concertant ; secum, singula ; Nobiscum omnia. *Which is as much to say ; Indeede so it is, and so all things almost in the world doe witnesse as much. The*

13

THE TRAGICK-COMEDY OF

*Starres incounter one another in the whirling firmament of
heaven; your contrarie Elements wage warre each with other;
the earth, that trembles and quakes, as if it were at oddes with
it selfe; the Sea, that swels and rages, breaking it's billowes
one against another; the Ayre, that darteth arrowes of lightning, and is moved this way and that way; the flames, they
cracke, and sparkle forth their furie; the windes are at perpetuall enmitie with themselves; times with times doe contend;
one thing against another, and all against us. We see, that
the Summer makes us complaine of too much heate; and the
Winter, of cold and sharpenesse of weather. So that this,
which seemeth unto us a temporall revolution; this, by which
we are bred up, and nourished, and live, if it once beginne to
passe above it's proportion, and to grow to a greater highth
then usuall, it is no better then open warre. And how much
it ought to bee feared, is manifested by those great earth-
quakes and whirle-winds, by those ship-wrackes and fires, as
well in the ayre, as the earth; by the sourse of water-courses,
and violence of inundations, by those courses, and recourses,
those rackings to and fro of the Clouds, of whose open motions,
to know the secret cause from whence they proceed, no lesse is
the dissention of the Philosophers in the schooles, then of the
waves of the Sea. Besides, among your bruit beasts, there is
not any one of them that wants his warre; be they Fishes,
Birds, Beasts, or Serpents; whereof, every kinde persecuteth,
and pursueth one another: The Lyon, hee pursues the Wolfe;
the Wolfe the Kidde; the Dog the Hare. And if it might
not be thought a fable, or old wifes tale, sitting by the fire
side, I should more fully inlarge this Theame. The Elephant,
that is so powerfull and strong a beast, is afraide, and
flies from the sight of a poore silly Mouse; and no sooner
heares him comming, but hee quakes and trembles for feare.
Amongst Serpents, Nature created the Basiliske, so venomous
and poysonfull, and gave him such a predominant power over
all the rest, that onely with his hissing, he doth affright them;
with his comming, put them to flight, and disperseth some one
way, some another, and with his sight, kills and murders
them. The Viper, a crawling creature, and venomous Ser-
pent, at the time of ingendring, the Male puts his head into*

14

CALISTO AND MELIBEA

the mouth of the Female, and shee through the great delight,
and sweetnesse of her pleasure, straines him so hard, that she
kills him. And conceiving her young, the eldest, or first of
her brood, breakes the barres of his mothers belly, eates out his
way thorow her bowels, at which place all the rest issue forth;
whereof she dies; hee doing this, as a revenger of his fathers
death. What greater conflict, what greater contention or
warre can there be, then to conceive that in her body, which
shall eate out her Intralls? Againe, no lesse naturall dissention can we suppose to be amongst fishes; for most certaine it
is, that the Sea doth containe as many severall sorts of fishes,
as the earth and ayre do nourish birds and beasts; and much
more. Aristotle and Pliny doe recount wonders of a little fish
called Æcheneis; how apt his nature is, and how prone his
propertie for divers kindes of contentions, especially this one;
that if hee cling to a ship or Carrack, he will detaine and
stop her in her course, though she have the winde in the
poope of her, and cut the Seas with never so stiffe a gale.
Whereof Lucan maketh mention, saying,

> Non puppim retinens, Euro tendente rudentes,   LUCAN. *lib.* vi.
> In medijs Æcheneis aquis.   *iuxta finem.*
>
> *Nor Æcheneis, whose strength, though Eurus rise,*
> *Can stay the course of shippes.*

O naturall contention! worthy of admiration, that a little fish
should be able to doe more then a great ship, with all the force
and strength of the winds. Moreover, if we will discourse of
birds, and of their frequent enmities, we may truly affirm,
that all things are created in a kind of contention. Your
greater live of rapine, as Eagles and Hawks; and your
craven Kites presse upon our Pullen, insulting over them even
in our own houses, and offring to take them even from under
the Hens wings. Of a bird called Roque, which is bred in
the East Indian Sea, it is said to be of an incredible greatnesse, that the like hath never bin heard of; and that with
her beake, she will hoyse up into the ayre, not only one man,
or ten, but a whole ship laden with men and merchandise;
and how that these miserable passengers, hanging thus in
suspence in the ayre, till her wings waxe weary, she lets them

15

THE TRAGICK-COMEDY OF

*fall, and so they receive their deaths.   But what shall we say
of men, to whom all the foresaid creatures are subject ?   Who
can expresse their wars, their jars, their enmities, their envies,
their heats, their broyles, their brawles, and their discontentments ?   That change and alteration of fashions in their
apparell ?   That pulling downe and building up of houses ?
and many other sundry effects and varieties ; all of them proceeding from the feeble and weake condition of mans variable
nature ?   And because it is an old and ancient complaint, and
used heretofore time out of minde ; I will not much marvell, if
this present worke shall prove an instrument of war to its
Readers, putting strifes and differences amongst them, every
one giving his verdict and opinion thereupon, according to
the humour of his owne will.   Some perhaps may say that it
is too long ; some too short ; others to be sweet and pleasant ;
and other some to be darke and obscure : So that to cut it out
to the measure of so many, and such different dispositions, is
onely appropriate to God ; Especially, since that it, together
with all other things, whatsoever are in this world, march
under the standard of this noble Sentence ; For even the very
life of men, if we consider them from their first and tender
age, till they grow gray-headed, is nothing else but a battell.
Children with their sports, boyes with their bookes, young men
with their pleasures, old men with a thousand sorts of infirmities, skirmish and warre continually ; and these Papers, with
all ages.   The first blots and teares them ; the second knowes
not well how to read them ; the third (which is the cheerefull
livelihood of youth, and set all upon jollity) doth utterly dislike of them.   Some gnaw onely the bones, but do not picke
out the marrow, saying there is no goodnesse in it ; that it is
a History, huddled, I know not how, together, a kind of
hodgepodge, or gallimaufrey ; not profiting themselves out of
the particularities, accounting it a fable, or old wifes tale, fitting for nothing, save only for to passe away the time upon
the way.   Others call out the witty conceits, and common
proverbs, highly commending them, but slighting and neglect-
ing that which makes more to the purpose and their profit.
But they for whose true pleasure it is wholy framed, reject
the story it selfe, as a vayne and idle subject, and gather out*

16

CALISTO AND MELIBEA

*the pith and marrow of the matter for their owne good and
benefit, and laugh at those things that savour onely of wit,
and pleasant conceite, storing up in their memorie, the sentences
and sayings of Philosophers, that they may transpose them
into such fit places, as may make, upon occasion, for their
owne use and purpose. So that when ten men shall meete
together to heare this Comedy, in whom perhaps shall happen
this difference of dispositions, as it usually falleth out; who
will deny, but that there is a contention in that thing which
is so diversly understood? the Printers, they likewise have
bestowed their puncture, putting Titles, and adding Argu-
ments to the beginning of every Act; delivering in briefe,
what is more largely contained therein; a thing very excus-
able, in former times being much used, and in great request
with your ancient Writers; others have contended about the
name, saying, that it ought not to be called a Comedy, because
it ends in sorrow and mourning, but rather termed a Tragedy.
The Authour himselfe would have it take it's denomination
from it's beginning, which treates of pleasure, and therefore
call'd it a Comedy. So that I seeing these differences, between
their extremes have parted this quarrell, by dividing it in the
midst, and call it a Tragick-Comedy. So that observing
these contentions, these disagreements, these dissonant and
various judgements, I had an eye, to marke whither the major
part inclined, and found that they were all desirous, that I
should inlarge my selfe in the pursuite of the delight of these
Lovers; whereunto, I have been earnestly importuned; in so
much, that I have consented (though against my will) to put
now the second time my Penne to this so strange a taske, and
so farre estranged from my faculty, stealing some houres
from my principall studies, together with others allot-
ted to my recreation, though I know, I shall not
want new Detractors for my new Edition.*

C

17

THE ACTORS

IN THIS TRAGICK-COMEDY

CALISTO, A young inamoured Gentleman.

MELIBEA, Daughter to Pleberio.

PLEBERIO, Father to Melibea.

CELESTINA, An old Bawd.

PARMENO,
SEMPRONIO,
TRISTAN,
SOSIA,
} Servants to Calisto.

CRITO, a Whoremaster.

LUCRECIA, Maide to Pleberio.

ELICIA,
AREUSA,
} Whores.

CENTURIO, A Pandar, or Ruffian.

A COMEDIE

OR TRAGICKE-COMEDIE

OF CALISTO AND

MELIBEA

THE ARGUMENT

CALISTO, *who was of Linage Noble, of Wit Singular, of Disposition Gentle, of Behaviour Sweete, with many gracefull qualities richly indowed, and of a competent estate; fell in love with* Melibea, *of yeeres young, of blood Noble, of estate Great, and only daughter and heire to her father* Pleberio, *and to her mother* Alisa; *of both exceedingly beloved. Whose chaste purpose conquered by the hot pursuite of amorous* Calisto, Celestine *interposing her selfe in the businesse, a wicked and crafty woman, and together with her two deluded servants of subdued* Calisto, *and by her wrought to be disloiall, their fidelitie being taken with the hooke of covetousnesse and pleasure; Those Lovers came, and those that served them, to a wretched and unfortunate end. For entrance whereunto, adverse fortune afforded a fit and opportune place, where, to the presence of* Calisto, *the desired* Melibea *presented her selfe.*

20

ACTUS I

THE ARGUMENT

CALISTO *entering into a garden after his usuall manner, met there with* Melibea, *with whose love being caught, he began to court her: by whom being sharply checkt and dismist, he gets him home, being much troubled and grieved: he consults his servant* Sempronio, *who after much intercourse of talke, and debating of the businesse, advised him to entertaine an old woman, named* Celestina, *in whose house his said servant kept a Wench, to whom hee made love, called* Elicia: *Who,* Sempronio *comming to* Celestines *house about his masters businesse, had at that time another sweet heart in her company, called* Crito, *whom they hid out of sight. In the interim that* Sempronio *was negotiating with* Celestina, Calisto *falls in talke with another of his servants, named* Parmeno, *which discourse continueth till* Sempronio *and* Celestina *arrive at* Calisto's *house.* Parmeno *was knowne by* Celestina, *who tells him of the good acquaintance which she had of his mother, and many matters that had past between them; inducing him in the end to love and concord with* Sempronio.

INTERLOCUTORS

Calisto, Melibea, Parmeno, Sempronio, Celestina,
Elicia, Crito.

CALISTO. In this, Melibea, I see heavens greatnesse, and goodnesse.

MELIB. In what, Calisto?

CALISTO. Greatnesse, in giving such power to nature, as to endow thee with so perfect a beauty; goodnesse, in

21

affoording me so great a favour as thy faire presence, and a place so convenient to unsheathe my secret griefe; A grace undoubtedly so incomparable, and by many degrees far greater than any service I have performed can merit from above. What inhabitant heere below ever saw a more glorious creature then I behold? Certainly, if sublunary bodies can give a celestiall reflection or resemblance, I contemplate and find it in thy divine beauty: had it perpetuity, what happines beyond it? Yet wretch that I am, I must live like another Tantalus; see what I may not enjoy, not touch; and my comfort must be the thinking of thy disdainnesse, thy pleasing coynesse, and the torment which thy absence will inflict upon me.

MELIB. Holdest thou this, Calisto, so great a reward?

CALIST. So great, that if you should give me the greatest good upon earth, I should not hold it so great a happinesse.

MELIB. I shall give thee a reward answerable to thy deserts, if thou persevere and goe on in this manner.

CAL. O fortunate eares! which are (though unworthily) admitted to heare so gracious a word, such great and comfortable tydings.

MELIBEA. But unfortunate, by that time thou hast heard thy doome. For thy payment shall be as foule, as thy presumption was foolish, and thy entertainment as small, as thy intrusion was great. How durst such a one as thou hazard thy selfe on the vertue of such a one as I? Goe wretch, be gone out of my sight, for my patience cannot endure, that so much as a thought should enter into any mans heart, to communicate his mind unto me in illicite love.

CALISTO. I goe; but as one, who am the onely unhappy marke, against whom adverse fortune aymeth the extremity of her hate. Sempronio, Sempronio, why Sempronio, I say, where is this accursed Varlet?

SEMPRONIO. I am heere Sir, about your horses.

CALISTO. My horses, (you knave) how haps it then that thou comst out of the hall?

SEMPRONIO. The Gyrfalcon bated, and I came in to set him on the Pearch.

22

CALISTO AND MELIBEA

CALISTO. Is 't e'en so? Now the divell take thee; misfortune waite on thy heeles to thy destruction; mischiefe light upon thee; let some perpetuall intolerable torment seyze upon thee in so high a degree, that it may be beyond all comparison, till it bring thee (which shortly I hope to see) to a most painfull, miserable and disastrous death. Goe, thou unlucky rogue, goe I say, and open the chamber doore, and make ready my bed.

SEMPRONIO. Presently Sir, the bed is ready for you.

CALISTO. Shut the windowes, and leave darkenesse to accompany him, whose sad thoughts deserve no light. Oh death! how welcome art thou, to those who out-live their happinesse? how welcome, wouldst thou but come when thou art call'd? O that Hypocrates and Galen, those learned Physicians were now living, and both heere, and felt my paine! O heavens, if yee have any pitty in you, inspire that Pleberian heart therewith, lest that my soule, helplesse of hope, should fall into the like misfortune with Pyrramus and Thisbe.

SEMPR. What a thing is this? What's the matter with you?

CALISTO. Away, get thee gone, doe not speake to me, unlesse thou wilt, that these my hands, before thy time be come, cut off thy daies by speedy death.

SEMPRONIO. Since you will lament all alone, and have none to share with you in your sorrowes, I will be gone, Sir.

CALISTO. Now the divell goe with thee.

SEMPR. With me Sir? there is no reason that he should goe with me, who stayes with you. O unfortunate, O sudden and unexpected ill; what contrarious accident, what squint-ey'd starre is it that hath robbed this Gentleman of his wonted mirth? and not of that alone, but of it (which is worse) his wits. Shall I leave him all alone? or shall I goe in to him? If I leave him alone, he will kill himselfe. If I goe in, he will kill me. Let him bide alone, and bite upon the bit, come what will, come I care not. Better it is that hee dye, whose life is hatefull unto him, then that I dye, when life is pleasing unto mee, and say that I should not desire to live, save onely to see my Elicia, that alone is

23

motive inough to make mee looke to my selfe, and guard
my person from dangers: but admit he should kill himselfe
without any other witnesse, then must I be bound to give
account of his life. Well, I will in for that, but put case
when I come in, he will take neither comfort nor counsell:
mary his case is desperate, for it is a shrewd signe of death,
not to be willing to be cured. Well, I will let him alone a
while, and give his humour leave to worke out it selfe; I
will forbeare, till his angry fit be over-past, and that his hat
be come againe to his colour. [For I have heard say, that it
is dangerous to lance or crush an Impostume before it bee
ripe, for then it will fester the more: Let him alone awhile,
let us suffer him to weepe who suffers to sorrow, for teares
and sighes doe ease the heart that is surcharged with griefe;
but then againe, if he see mee in sight, I shall see him more
incensed against mee: For there the sunne scorcheth most,
where he reflecteth most: the sight which hath no object set
before it, waxeth weary and dull, and having its object, is as
quicke. And therefore I thinke it my best play, to play least
in sight, and to stay a little longer; but if in the meane while
he should kill himselfe, then farewell he. Perhaps I may get
more by it then every man is aware of, and cast my skinne,
changing rags for robes, and penury for plenty: But it is an
old saying, He that lookes after dead-mens shooes, may
chance to goe barefoote: Perhaps also the divell hath
deceived me. And so his death may be my death, and then
all the fat is in the fire: The rope will go after the Bucket:
and one losse follow another; on the other-side your wise
men say, That it is a great ease to a grieved soule, or one
that is afflicted, to have a companion, to whom he may communicate his sorrow. Besides, it is generally received, that
the wound which bleedes inward, is ever the more dangerous.
Why then in these two extremes hang I in suspence what I
were best to doe? Sure, the safest is to enter: and better
it is that I should indure his anger, then for feare of his displeasure to forbeare to comfort him. For, if it be possible
to cure without Arte, and without things ready at hand,
farre easier is it to cure by Arte, and wanting nothing that
is necessary.

24

CALISTO AND MELIBEA

CALISTO. Sempronio?

SEMPR. Sir.

CALISTO. Reach me that Lute.

SEMPR. Sir, heere it is.

CALISTO. Tell me what griefe so great can be,
As to equall my misery.

SEMPR. This Lute, Sir, is out of tune.

CALISTO. How shall he tune it, who himselfe is out
of tune? Or how canst thou heare harmony from him,
who is at such discord with himselfe? Or how can he do
any thing well, whose will is not obedient to reason? Who
harbors in his brest needles, peace, warre, truce, love, hate,
injuries and suspicions; and all these at once, and from
one, and the same cause. Doe thou therefore take this
Lute unto thee, and sing me the most dolefull ditty thou
canst devise,

SEMPRONIO.

{ Nero, from Tarpey, doth behold
How Rome doth burne all on a flame;
He heares the cries of young and old,
Yet is not grieved at the same.

CALISTO. My fire is farre greater, and lesse her pity
whom now I speake of.

SEMPR. I was not deceived when I sayd, my Master had
lost his wits.

CALISTO. Whats that (Sempronio) thou muttrest to thy
selfe?

SEMPR. Nothing Sir, not I.

CALISTO. Tell me what thou saidst: Be not afraid.

SEMPR. Marry I said, How can that fire be greater
which but tormenteth one living man, then that which
burnt such a Citty as that was, and such a multitude of
men?

CALISTO. How? I shall tell thee. Greater is that
flame which lasteth fourescore yeeres, then that which endureth but one day. And greater that fire, which burneth
one soule, then that which burneth an hundred thousand
bodies: See what difference there is betwixt apparencies,
and existencies; betwixt painted shaddowes, and lively
substances, betwixt that which is counterfet, and that

D

which is reall. So great a difference is there betwixt that fire which thou speakest of, and that which burneth mee.

SEMPR. I see, I did not mistake my byas; which, for ought I perceive, runnes worse and worse. Is it not inough to shew thy selfe a foole, but thou must also speake prophanely?

CALISTO. Did not I will tell thee, when thou speakest, that thou shouldest speake aloude? Tell me whats that thou mumblest to thy selfe.

SEMPR. Onely I doubted of what religion your Lovers are.

CALISTO. I am a Melibean, I adore Melibea, I beleeve in Melibea, and I love Melibea.

SEMPR. My Master is all Melibea: who now but Melibea? whose heart not able to containe her, like a boyling vessell, venting it's heate, goes bubbling her name in his mouth. Well, I have now as much as I desire: I know on which foote you halt, I shall now heale you.

CALISTO. Thou speakest of matters beyond the Moone. It is impossible.

SEMPR. O Sir, exceeding easie; for the first recovery of sicknesse, is the discovery of the disease.

CALISTO. What counsell can order that, which in it selfe hath neither counsell nor order?

SEMPR. Ha, ha, ha, Calisto's fire; these, his intolerable paines: As if love had bent his bow, shot all his arrowes onely against him. Oh Cupid, how high and unsearchable are thy mysteries! What reward hast thou ordained for love, since that so necessary a tribulation attends on lovers? Thou hast set his bounds, as markes for men to wonder at: Lovers ever deeming, that they only are cast behinde; and that others still out-strip them: That all men breake thorow, but themselves like your light footed bulls, which being let loose in the place, and galled with darts, take over the bars as soone as they feele themselves prickt.

CALISTO. Sempronio.

SEMPR. Sir.

CALISTO. Doe not you goe away.

CALISTO AND MELIBEA

SEMPR. This pipe sounds in another tune.

CALISTO. What dost thou thinke of my malady?

SEMPR. That you love Melibea.

CALISTO. And nothing else?

SEMPR. It is misery inough to have a mans will captivated, and chained to one place onely.

CALISTO. Thou wot'st not what constancy is.

SEMPR. Perseverance in ill is not constancy, but obstinacy, or pertinacy, so they call it in my countrey; how-ever it please you Philosophers of Cupid to phrase it.

CALISTO. It is a foule fault for a man to belye that which he teacheth to others: for thou thy selfe takest pleasure in praysing thy Elicia.

SEMPR. Do you that good which I say, but not that ill which I do.

CALISTO. W[h]y dost thou reproove mee?.

SEMPR. Because thou dost subject the dignity and worthinesse of a man, to the imperfection and weakenesse of a fraile woman.

CALISTO. A woman? O thou blockhead, she's a Goddesse.

SEMPR. Are you in earnest, or doe you but jest?

CALISTO. Jest? I verily beleeve she is a Goddesse.

SEMPR. As Goddesses were of old, that is, to fall below mortality, and then you would hope to have a share in her deity.

CALISTO. A poxe on thee for a foole, thou makest mee laugh, which I thought not to doe to day.

SEMPR. What, would you weepe all the dayes of your life?

CALISTO. Yes.

SEMPR. And why?

CALISTO. Because I love her, before whom I finde my selfe so unworthy, that I have no hope to obtaine her.

SEMPR. O Coward, baser then the sonne of a whore: why, Alexander the Great did not onely thinke himselfe worthy the dominion of one onely, but of many worlds.

CALISTO. I did not well heare what thou saidst, say it againe: repeate it againe before thou procced any further.

27

THE TRAGICK-COMEDY OF

SEMPR. I said Sir, Should you, whose heart, is greater then Alexanders, despaire of obtaining a woman? wherefore many, having beene seated in highest estate, have basely prostituted themselves to the embracements of Muletteeres, and Stablegroomes, suffering them to breathe in their faces, with their unsavory breaths, and to imbosome them between their brests : And othersome not ashamed to have companied with bruite-beasts. Have you not heard of Pasiphaë, who plai'd the wanton with a Bull? and of Minerva, how she dallied with a dogge?

CALISTO. Tush, I beleeve it not, they are but fables.

SEMPR. And that of your Grandmother and her Ape, that's a fable too: Witnesse your Grandfathers knife, that kill'd the villaine that did cuckold him.

CALISTO. A poxe of this cocks-combe, what gird's he gives!

SEMPR. Have I nettled you (Sir ?) Reade your histories, study your philosophers, examine your poets; and you shall finde how full their bookes are of their vile and wicked examples, and of the ruines and destructions whereinto they have runne, who held them in that high esteeme as you doe. Consult with Seneca, and you shall see how vilely he reckons of them. Hearken unto Aristotle, and you shall finde that all of them to this agree : but whatsoever I have, or shall heereafter speake in them; mistake mee not, I pray you, but consider them as words, commonly and generally spoken: For many of them have beene, and are holy, vertuous and noble, whose glorious and resplendent crownes blot out this generall reproach. But touching the other, who can recount unto you their falschoods, their tricks, their tradings, their truckings, their exchanging commodities, their lightnesse, their teares, their mutabilities, and their boldnesse and impudencies : For whatsoever they conceit, they dare to execute without any deliberation, or advisement in the world ; their dissemblings, their talketivenesse, their deceits, their forgetfulnesse, their unkindenesse, their ingratitude, their inconstancy, their ficklenesse, their saying and gaine-saying, and all in a breath ; their windings and turnings, their presumption, their vaine-glory, their base-

CALISTO AND MELIBEA

nesse, their foolishnesse, their disdainfulnesse, their coynesse, their pride, their haughtinesse, their base submissions, their prattlings, their gluttony, their luxury, their sluttishnesse, their timorousnesse, their witcheries, their cheatings, their gibings, their slandrings and their bawdry. Now consider with your selfe, what idle gyddy-headed braines are under those large and fine cob-web veiles; what wicked thoughts under those gay gorgets; what pride and arrogancy under those their long, rich and stately robes; what mad toyes under their painted Temples.

CALISTO. Tell me, I pray, this Alexander, this Seneca, this Aristotle, this Virgil, these whom thou tell'st mee of; did not they subject themselve[s] unto them? Am I greater then these?

SEMPR. I would you should follow those that did subdue them; not those that were subdued by them. Flye their deceits. Know you (Sir) what they doe? They doe things that are too hard for any men to understand; they observe no meane; they have no reason; nor doe they take any heed in what they doe. They are the first themselves that cause a man to love; and themselves are the first that beginne to loath. They will privately pleasure him, whom afterwards they will openly wrong, and draw him secretly in at their windowes, whom in the streetes they will publikely raile at. They will give you roste-meate, and beate you with the spit. They will invite you unto them, and presently send you packing with a flea in your ear; Call you, and yet exclude you; seale you her love, and yet proclaime hate; quickly be wonne, and quickly be lost; soone pleased, and as soone displeased; and (which is the true humour of a woman) whatsoever her will divines, that must bee affected. Her apprehensions admit no delayes; and bee they impossible to bee attained to, yet not effecting them she streightway censures it want of wit or affection, if not both. O what a plague? what a hell? nay, what a lothsome thing is it for a man to have to doe with them any longer, then in that short pricke of time that hee holds them in his armes, when they are prepared for pleasure!

CALISTO. Thou seest the more thou tell'st me, and the

29

more inconveniences thou settest before mee, the more I love her. I know not how, nor what it is, but sure I am, that so it is.

SEMPR. This is no fit counsell I see for young men, who know not how to submit themselves to reason, nor to be governed by discretion ; it is a miserable thing, to thinke that hee should be a Master, who was never any scholler.

CALISTO. And you Sir, that are so wise, who I pray taught you all this ?

SEMP. Who ? why, they themselves, who no sooner discover their shame, but they lose it. For all this, and much more then I have told you, they themselves will manifest unto men, Ballance thy selfe then aright in the true scale of thine honour, give thy reputation it's due proportion, it's just measure, and thinke your selfe to be more worthy then in your owne esteeme you repute your selfe. For (beleeve mee) worse is that extreme, whereby a man suffers himselfe to fall from his owne worth, then that which makes a man over-valew himselfe, and seate himselfe in higher place then beseeme him.

CALISTO. Now, what of all this ? what am I the better for it ?

SEMP. What ? why this : First of all, you are a man ; then, of an excellent and singular wit ; To this, indewed with those better sort of blessings, wherewith Nature hath endowed you, to wit, wisedome, favour, feature, largenesse of limbes, force, agility, and abilities of body. And to these, fortune hath in so good a measure shared what is hers with thee, that these thy inward graces, are by thy outward the more beautified. For, without these outward goods, wherof fortune is chiefe Mistresse, no man in this life comes to be happy. Lastly, the starres were so propitious at thy birth, and thy selfe borne under so good a Planet, that thou art belov'd of all.

CALISTO. But not of Melibea. And in all that, wherein thou dost so glorifie my gifts, I tell thee (Sempronio) compared with Melibea's, they are but as starres to the Sunne ; or drosse compared to gold. Doe but consider the noblenesse of her blood, the ancientnesse of her house, the great estate

CALISTO AND MELIBEA

she is borne unto, the excellency of her wit, the splendour of her vertues, her stately, yet comely carriage, her ineffable gracefulnesse in all that shee doth; and lastly, her divine beauty; whereof (I pray thee) give mee leave to discourse a little, for the refreshing of my soule. And that which I shall tell thee, shall be onely of what I have discovered, and lyes open to the eye: For, if I could discourse of that which is concealed, this contestation would be needlesse, neyther should wee argue thereupon so earnestly as now wee doe.

SEMPR. What lyes and fooleries will my captived Master now tell mee?

CALISTO. What's that?

SEMPR. I said, I would have you tell mee; for I shall take great pleasure in hearing it, so fortune befriend you Sir, as this speach of yours shall be pleasing unto mee.

CALISTO. What saist thou?

SEMPR. That fortune would so befriend mee, as I shall take pleasure to heare you.

CALISTO. Since then, that it is so pleasing unto thee, I will figure foorth unto thee every part in her, even in the fullest manner that I can devise.

SEMPR. Heer's a deale of doo indeede: This is that I looked for, though more then I desired, it will be a tedious piece of businesse, but I must give him the hearing.

CALISTO. I will beginne first with her haires; Hast thou scene those skaynes of fine twisted gold which are spun in Arabia? Her haires are more fine, and shine no lesse then they; the length of them is to the lowest pitch of her heele, besides, they are daintily combed, and dressed, and knit up in knots with curious fine ribbaning, as shee her selfe pleaseth to adorne and set them foorth, being of power themselves, without any other helpe, to transforme men into stones.

SEMPR. Into Asses rather.

CALISTO. What saist thou?

SEMPR. I say that these could not bee Asses hayres.

CALISTO. See what a beastly and base comparison this foole makes!

SEMPR. It is well Sir that you are so wise.

CALISTO. Her eyes are quicke, cleare and full; the hayres

31

THE TRAGICK-COMEDY OF

ACTUS I — to those lids rather long then short; Her eye-browes thinnish, not thicke of hayre, and so prettily arched, that by their bent, they are much the more beautifull; Her nose of such a middling size, as may not be mended; Her mouth little; Her teeth small and white; her lips red and plumpe; The forme of her face rather long then round. Her brests placed in a fitting height; but their rising roundnesse, and the pretty pleasing fashion of her little tender nipples, who is able to figure foorth unto thee? So distracted is the eye of man when he does behold them. Her skinne as smooth, soft, and sleeke as Satten, and her whole body so white, that the snow seemes darknesse unto it; Her colour so mingled, and of so singular a temper, as if she had chosen it her selfe.

SEMPR. This foole is fallen into his thirteenes. O how hee overreaches!

CALISTO. Her hands little, and in a measurable manner, and fit proportion accompanied with her sweet flesh; Her fingers long; Her nayles large and well coloured; seeming Rubies, intermixt with pearles. The proportion of those other parts which I could not eye, undoubtedly (judging things unseene, by the seene) must of force be incomparably farre better then that, which Paris gave his judgement of in the difference betweene the three Goddesses.

SEMPR. Have you done, Sir?

CALISTO. As briefely as I could.

SEMPR. Suppose all this you say were true, yet in that you are a man, I still say, you are more worthy then shee.

CALISTO. In what?

SEMPR. In that shee is imperfect: Out of which defect, shee lusts and longs after your selfe, or some one lesse worthy. Did you never reade that of the Philosopher, where he tells you, That as the matter desires the forme, so woman desires man?

CALISTO. O wretch that I am, when shall I see this betweene mee and Melibea?

SEMPR. It is possible that you may: and as possible that you may one day hate her as much as now you love her, when you shall come to the full injoying of her, and to

32

CALISTO AND MELIBEA

looking on her with other eyes, free from that errour which
now blindeth your judgement.

CALISTO. With what eyes?

SEMPR. With cleare eyes.

CALISTO. And with what I pray doe I see now?

SEMPR. With false eyes; Like some kinde of spectacles, which make little things seeme great; and great little. Doe not you despaire; my selfe will take this businesse in hand, not doubting but to accomplish your desire.

CALISTO. Iove grant thou maiest: howsoever, I am proud to heare thee, though hopelesse of ever obtaining it.

SEMPR. Nay, I will assure it you.

CALISTO. Heav'n be thy good speed; my cloth of gold doublet, which I wore yesterday, it is thine, Sempronio. Take it to thee.

SEMPR. I thanke you for this, and for many more which you shall give mee. My jesting hath turn'd to my good. I hitherto have the better of it. And if my Master clap such spurs to my sides, and give mee such good incouragements, I doubt not, but I shall bring her to his bed. This which my Master hath given mee, is a good wheele to bring the businesse about: for without reward, it is impossible to goe well thorow with any thing.

CALISTO. See you be not negligent now.

SEMPR. Nay, be not you negligent; For it is impossible, that a carelesse Master should make a diligent servant.

CALISTO. But tell me, How dost thou think to purchase her pitty?

SEMPR. I shall tell you. It is now a good while agoe, since at the lower end of this streete, I fell acquainted with an old bearded woman, called Celestina; a witch, subtill as the divell, and well practis'd in all the rogueries and villanies that the world can affoord; One, who in my conscience hath marr'd and made up againe a hundred thousand maiden-heads in this Citty: Such a power, and such authority shee hath, what by her perswasions, and other her cunning devices, that none can escape her; shee will move hard rocks, if she list, and at her pleasure provoke them to Luxury.

CALISTO. O that I might but speake with her!

E   33

SEMPR. I will bring her hither unto you; and therefore prepare your selfe for it, and when shee comes, in any case use her kindely, be francke and liberall with her; and whilest I goe my wayes, doe you study and devise with your selfe, to expresse your paines, as well as I know shee is able to give you remedy.

CALISTO. O but thou staiest too long.

SEMPR. I am gone, Sir.

CALISTO. A good lucke with thee. You happy powers that predominate humane actions, assist and be propitious to my desires, second my intentions, prosper Sempronio's proceedings and his successe, in bringing me such an Advocatrix as shall, according to his promise, not onely negotiate, but absolutely compasse and bring to a wished period, the preconceived hopes of an incomparable pleasure.

CELESTINA. Elicia, what will you give mee for my good newes?

SEMPR. Sempronio is come.

ELICIA. O hush; peace, peace.

CELEST. Why? What's the matter?

ELICIA. Peace, I say, for here is Crito.

CELEST. Put him in the little chamber where the besomes bee. Quickly, quickly, I say, and tell him a cousin of yours, and a friend of mine is come to see you.

ELICIA. Crito, come hither, come hither quickely; O my cousin is come, my cousin is beneath; What shall I doe? Come quickely, I am undone else.

CRITO. With all my heart: Doe not vexe your selfe.

SEMP. O my deare mother, what a longing have I had to come unto you! I thanke my fate, that hath given me leave to see you.

CELEST. My sonne, my king, thou hast ravish'd mee with thy presence, I am so over-joyed, that I cannot speake to thee; Turne thee about unto mee, and imbrace mee once more in thine armes. What? three whole dayes? so long away together, and never see us? Elicia, Elicia, wot you who is heere?

ELICIA. Who, mother?

CELEST. Sempronio, daughter.

34

CALISTO AND MELIBEA

ELICIA. Out alas; O, how my heart rises! How it leaps and beats in my body! how it throbs within me! And what of him?

CELEST. Looke heere, doe you see him? I will imbrace him, you shall not.

ELICIA. Out, thou accursed traitor: impostumes, pocks, plagues, and botches consume and kill thee.] Dye thou by the hands of thine enemies, and that for some notorious crime, worthy cruell death, thou maist see thy selfe fall into the rigorous hands of Justice. Ay, Ay me!

SEMPR. Hy, hy, hy! Why, how now my Elicia? what is it that troubles you?

ELICIA. What? Three dayes? Three whole dayes away? And in all that time not so much as once come and see me? Not once look upon me? Fortune never looke on thee; never comfort thee, nor visit thee: Wo to that woman, wretched as she is, who in thee places her hope, and the end of all her happinesse.

SEMPR. No more (deare Love.) Thinkst thou (sweet heart) that distance of place can divorce my inward and imbowelled affection from thee? Or dead but the least sparke of that true fire which I beare in my bosome? Where-e're I goe, thou goest with me; where I am, there art thou. Thou hast not felt more affliction and torment for mee, then I have suffered and endured for thee. But soft; Me thinkes I heare some bodies feete moove above: Who is it?

ELICIA. Who is it? One of my sweet hearts.

SEMPR. Nay, like inough, I easily beleeve it.

ELICIA. Nay, it is true: Goe up and see else.

SEMPR. I goe.

CELEST. Come hither (my son) come along with me, let this foole alone, for shee is idle-headed, and almost out of her little wits; such thought hath she taken for thy absence. Regard not what she saies, for she will tell you a thousand flim-flam tales; Come, come with me, and let us talke. Let us not spend the time thus in idlements.

SEMPR. But I pray, who is that above?

CELEST. Would you know who?

SEMPR. I would.

THE TRAGICK-COMEDY OF

CELEST. A Wench recommended unto me by a Fryer.

SEMPR. What Fryer?

CELEST. O, by no meanes.

SEMPR. Now, as you love me, good mother, tell mee what Fryer is it?

CELEST. Lord, how earnest you be? you would dye now, if you should not know him; Well, to save your longing, it is that fat Fryers Wench: I need say no more.

SEMPR. Alacke (poore wench) what a heavy load is she to beare!

CELEST. You see, wee women must beare all, and it were greater, wee must endure it: you have seene but few murders committed upon a woman in private.

SEMPR. Murders? No, but many great swellings, besides bunches, blaines, boyles, kernels, and a pockes, what not?

CELEST. Now fie upon you, how you talke; you doe but jest I am sure.

SEMPR. If I doe but jest, then let mee see her.

ELICIA. O wicked wretch, doest thou long to see her? Let thy eyes start out of thy head, and drop downe at thy feete: for I see that it is not one wench that can serve your turne; I pray goe your waies, goe up and see her, but see you come at me no more.

SEMPR. Be patient, my deare, thou that art the onely Idoll of my devotion; Is this the gall that wrings you? This your griefe? Nay, if this make you so angry, I will neither see her, nor any other woman in the world. I will onely speake a word or two with my mother, and so bid you adieu.

ELICIA. Goe, goe, be gone, ungratefull, unthankefull as thou art, and stay away three yeeres more if thou wilt, ere ever thou see mee.

SEMPR. Mother, you may relye upon what I have told you, and assure your selfe, that of all the women in the world, I would not jest or dissemble with you: Put on your Mantle then, and let us go; and by the way, I will tell you all. For if I should stay heere dilating upon the businesse, and protract the time in delivering my minde, it would

36

turne much to both our hurts, and hinder thy profit and ACTUS I
mine.

CELEST. Let us goe then; Elicia, fare well; make fast
the doore; fare well, walls.

SEMPR. So law. Now (mother) laying all other things
apart, listen unto me, be attentive to that which I shall tell
you; let not your eares goe a wooll-gathering; nor scatter
your thoughts, nor devide them into many parts: for hee that
is every where, is no where: and cannot, (unlesse it be by
chance) certainely determine any thing, I will that you
know that of mee, which as yet you never heard. Besides,
I could never since the time that I first entred into league
with thee, and had plighted my faith unto thee, desire that
good, wherein thou mightest not share with mee.

CELEST. And Iove (my good sonne) share his good
blessings with thee, which (if so it please him) he shall not
doe without cause; because thou takest pity of this poore
wicked old woman: say on therfore, make no longer delay;
for that friendship, which betwixt thee and mee hath taken
such deepe rooting, needeth no Preambles, no circumlocutions, no preparations or insinuation to winne affection: Be
briefe therefore and come to the point; for it is idle to utter
that in many words, that may be understood in a few.

SEMP. It is true: And therefore thus, Calisto is hot in
love with Melibea, he stands in need of thine and my help.
And because he needs our joynt furtherance, let us joyne
together to make some purchase of him. For to know a
mans time, to make use of opportunity, and to take occasion
by the foretop, and to worke upon a man whilst his humour
serves him, why it is the onely round, by which many have
climbed up to prosperity.

CELEST. Well hast thou said: I perceive thy drift.
The winking, or beckning of the eye is inough for mee;
for as old as I am, I can see day at a little hole. I tell thee
Sempronio, I am as glad of this thy newes, as Surgeons of
broken-heads. And as they at the first goe festring the
wounds, the more to indeare the cure, so do I meane to deale
with Calisto: For I will still goe prolonging the certainty
of his recovering of Melibea, and delay still the remedy.

37

THE TRAGICK-COMEDY OF

For (as it is in the Proverbe) Delayed hope afflicteth the
heart. And the farther he is off from obtaining, the fayrer
will he promise to have it effected. Understand you mee?

SEMPR. Hush. No more. We are now at the gate,
and walls (they say) have eares.

CELEST. Knocke.

SEMPR. Tha, tha, tha.

CALISTO. Parmeno!

PARME. Sir.

CALISTO. What a pocks, art thou deafe? Canst thou
not heare?

PARMO. What would you, Sir?

CALISTO. Some body knocks at the gate. Runne.

PARME. Who's there?

SEMPR. Open the doore for this matronly Dame and
mee.

PARME. Sir, wot you who they are that knocke so loud?
It is Sempronio, and an old bawd hee hath brought along
with him. O how shee is bedawb'd with painting!

CALISTO. Peace, peace, you Villaine; she is my Aunt.
Run, run (you rascall) and open the doore. Well, it is an
old saying, and I perceive, as true, The fish leaps out of the
panne, and falls into the fire. And a man thinking to
shunne one danger, runnes into another, worse then the
former. For I thinking to keep close this matter from
Parmeno, (on whose neck, either out of love, faithfulnesse,
or feare, Reason hath laid her reynes) I have fallen into the
displeasure of this woman, who hath no lesse power over my
life, then Iove himselfe.

PAR. Sir, why doe you vexe your selfe? why grieve you?
Doe you thinke, that in the eares of this woman, the name,
by which I now call her, doth any way sound reproachfully?
Beleeve it not. Assure your selfe, she glories as much in
this name, as oft as shee heares it, as you do, when you
heare some voyce, Calisto to be a gallant Gentleman.
Besides, by this is she commonly called, and by this Title
is shee of all men generally knowne. If she passe along the
streetes among a hundred women, and some one perhaps blurts
out, See, where's the old Bawd; without any impatiency, or

38

CALISTO AND MELIBEA

any the least distemper, shee presently turnes her selfe about,
nods the head, and answers them with a smiling countenance
and cheereful looke. At your solemne banquets, your great
feasts, your weddings, your gossippings, your merry meet-
ings, your funeralls, and all other assemblies whatsoever,
where there is any resort of people, thither doth shee repaire,
and there they make pastime with her. And if shee passe
by where there be any dogs, they straightway barke out this
name; If shee come amongst birds, they have no other note
but this; If she light upon a flocke of sheepe, their bleatings
proclaime no lesse; If she meet with beasts, they bellow
forth the same: The frogges that lie in ditches, croake no
other tune; Come shee amongst your Smithes, your Car-
penters, your Armourers, your Ferriers, your Brasiers, your
Joyners: why, their hammers beate all upon this word. In
a word, all sorts of tooles and instruments returne no other
Eccho in the ayre; your Shoomakers sing this song; your
Combe-makers joyne with them, your Gardeners, your
Plough-men, your Reapers, your Vine-keepers passe away
the painefulnesse of their labours, in making her the subject of their discourse; your Table-players, and all other
Gamesters never lose, but they peale foorth her prayses: To
be short, be she wheresoever she be, all things whatsoever
are in this world, repeate no other name but this: O what
a devourer of rosted egges was her husband? What would
you more? Not one stone that strikes against another, but
presently noyseth out, Old whore.]

CALISTO. How canst thou tell? dost thou know her?

PARM. I shall tell you Sir, how I know her: It is a
great while ago, since my mother dwelt in her Parish, who
being intreated by this Celestina, gave me unto her to wait
upon her, though now she know me not, growne out perhaps
of her remembrance; as well by reason of the short time I
abode with her, as also through the alteration which age
hath wrought upon mee.

CALISTO. What service didst thou doe her?

PARME. I went into the market place, and fetch't her
vitailes; I waited on her in the streetes, and supplyed her
wants in other the like services, as farre as my poore suffi-

THE TRAGICK-COMEDY OF

ciency, and slender strength was able to performe.   So that
though I continued but a little while with her, yet I remember
every thing as fresh, as if it were but yesterday, in so much
that old age hath not been able to weare it out.   This good
honest whore, this grave matrone, forsooth, had at the very
end of the Citty, there where your Tanners dwell, close by
the waterside, a lone house, somewhat far from neighbours,
halfe of it fallen downe, ill contrived, and worse furnished.
Now, for to get her living, yee must understand, shee had
sixe severall Trades : shee was a Laundresse, a Perfumeresse,
a Former of faces, a Mender of crackt maiden-heads, a Bawd,
and had some smatch of a Witch : Her first Trade was a
cloak to all the rest; under color wherof, being withall a
piece of a Sempstresse, many young wenches that were of
your ordinary sorts of servants, came to her house to worke :
some on smockes, some on gorgets and many other things :
but not one of them that came thither, but brought with her
either bacon, wheate, flower, or a Jar of wine, or some other
the like provision, which they could conveniently steale from
their Mistresses, and some other thefts of greater quality,
making her house (for shee was the receiver, and kept all
things close) the Rendevous of all their Roguery : she was a
great friend to your Students, Noble mens Caterers, and
Pages : To these shee sold that innocent blood of these
poore miserable soules, who did easily adventure their virginities, drawne on by faire promises, and the restitution
and reparation which she would make them of their lost
maiden-heads.   Nay, shee proceeded so far, that by cunning
meanes, she had accesse and communication with your very
Vestalls, and never left them, till shee had brought her purpose to passe.   And what time do you think she chose when
she would deale with any of these ?   At the time of their
chiefest ceremonies ; as when they kept their most mysterious celebration of the feasts of their Vesta, nay, and that
most strictly solemnized day of Bona Dea, where it is death
to admit men : even then by unheard of disguises, she had
her plots and projects effectually working upon them, to the
utter abolition of their vowes and virginity.   Now, what
thinke you, were the trades and marchandise wherein she

40

CALISTO AND MELIBEA

dealt ? She professed her selfe a kinde of Phisician, and fained that shee had good skill in curing of little children : Shee would goe and fetch flaxe from one house, and put it forth to spinning to another, that she might thereby have pretence for the freer accesse unto all : One would cry, Here mother ; and another, There mother : Look, saies the third, where the old woman comes : Yonder comes that Bel-dame so well knowne to all. Yet notwithstanding all these her cares, troubles, and trottings to and fro, being never out of action, she would never misse any great meeting, any religious processions, any Nuptials, Love-ties, Balls, maskes or games whatsoever ; They were the onely markets, where she made all her bargaines. And at home in her owne house shee made perfumes, false and counterfait Storax, Benjamin, Gumme, Anime, Amber, Civit, Powders, Muske and Mosqueta : Shee had a chamber full of Limbecks, little vialls, pots, some of earth, some of glasse, some brasse, and some tinne, formed in a thousand fashions. Shee made sublimated Mercury, boyled confections for to clarifie the skinne, waters to make the face glister, paintings, some white, some vermillion, lip-salves, scarlet-dy'd cloathes, fitted purposely for women to rub their faces therewith, oyntments for to make the face smooth, lustrifications, clarifications, pargetings, fardings, waters for the morphewes, and a thousand other slibber slabbers : Some made of the lees of wine, some of daffadills, some of the barkes and rindes of trees, some of Scar-wolfe, otherwise called Cittibush, or Trifolium, some of Taragon, some of Centory, some of sowre grapes, some of Must, or new wine taken from the presse, first distilled, and afterwards sweetned with sugar. Shee had a tricke to supple and refine the skin with the juice of Lemmons, with Turpentine, with the marrow of Deere, and of Heron-shawes, and a thousand the like confections : shee distilled sweet-waters, of Roses, of Flowers, of Oranges, of Jesmine, of three-leafed Grasse, of Woodbine, of Gilly-flowers, incorporated with Muske and Civit, and sprinkled with wine : shee made likewise Lees, for to make the hayre turne yellow, or of the colour of Gold ; and this shee composed of the sprigs of the Vine, of Holme, of Rye, of Horehound intermixt with Salt-

F

THE TRAGICK-COMEDY OF

peter, with Allum, Mill-foyle, which some call Yarrow, or Nose-bleed, together with divers other things. The oyles, the butters, and the greases which shee used, it is lothsome to tell you, and would turne your stomacke: as of Kine, Beares, Horses, Camels, Snakes, Conyes, Whales, Herons, Bittours, Bucks, Cats of the mountaines, Badgers, Squirrells, Hedge-hogges and others. For her preparatives for bathings, it is a wonderfull thing to acquaint you with all the hearbes and rootes which were ready gathered and hung up a-high in the roofe of her house: as Camomill, Rose-mary, Marsh-mallowes, Maiden-haire, Blue-bottle, Flowers of Elder, and of Mustard, Spike and white Laurell, buds of Roses, Rosecakes, Gra-monilla, Wild-Savory, Green figs, Picodoræ, and Folia-tinct. The oyles which she extracted for the face, it is incredible to recount, of Storax and of Jesmine, of Lemmons, of Apple-kernels, of Violets, of Benivy, of Fistick-nuts, of Pine-apple kernels, of Grape-stones, of Jujuba, of Axenuz or Melan-thion, of Lupines, of Pease, of Carilla, and Paxarera; and a small quantity of Balsamum she had in a little viall, wher-with she cured that scotch given her overthwart her nose. For the mending of lost maiden-heads, some shee holpe with little bladders, and other some she stitch't up with the needle: shee had in a little Cabbinet, or painted worke-boxe, certain fine small needles, such as your Glovers sowe withall, and threds of the slenderest and smallest silke, rubb'd over with wax: she had also roots hanging there of Folia-Plasme, Fuste-sanguinio, Squill or Sea-Onion, and ground Thistle. With these she did work wonders; and when the French Embassadour came thither, shee made sale of one of her wenches, three severall times for a virgin.

CALISTO. So shee might a hundred as well.

PARME. Beleeve mee (Sir) it is true as I tell you. Be-sides, out of charity forsooth, she relieved many Orphanes, and many straggling wenches, which recommended them-selves unto her. In another partition, she had her knacks for to help those that were love-sicke, and to make them to be beloved againe, and obtaine their desires. And for this purpose, shee had the bones that are bred in a Stagges heart, the tongue of a Viper, the heads of Quailes, the braines of

42

CALISTO AND MELIBEA

an Asse, the kalls of young Coltes, when they are new foaled, the bearing cloth of a new-borne babe, Barbary beanes, a Sey-Compasse, a Horne-fish, the halter of a man that hath beene hang'd, Ivie berries, the prickles of a Hedge-hogge, the foote of a Badger, Fearne-seed, the stone of an Eagles nest, and a thousand other things. Many both men and women came unto her : of some she would demand a piece of that bread where they had bit it : of others, some part of their apparell : of some, shee would crave to have of their hayre : others, she would draw characters in the palmes of their hands with Saffrom ; with othersome she would doe the same with a kinde of colour, which you call Vermilion : to others she would give hearts made of waxe, and stucke full of broken needles ; and many other the like things, made in clay, and some in lead, very fearefull, and ghastly to behold : she would draw circles, portraite foorth figures, and mumble many strange words to her selfe, having her eyes still fixed on the ground. But who is able to deliver unto you those things that she hath done ? And all these were meere mockeries and lyes.

CALISTO. Parmeno, hold thy hand ; thou hast said inough ; what remaineth, leave it till some fitter opportunity. I am sufficiently instructed by thee, and I thanke thee for it ; Let us now delay them no longer, for necessity cuts off slackenesse. Know thou, that shee comes hither requested, and wee make her stay longer then stands with good manners. Come, let us goe, lest she be offended, and take it ill. I feare, and feare makes me more and more thinke upon her, quickens my memorie, and awakens in me a more provident carefulnesse how I communicate my selfe unto her. Well, let us goe, and arme our selves as well as we can against all inconveniences. But I pray thee Parmeno, let me intreat thee, that the envy thou bearest unto Sempronio, who is to serve and pleasure me in this businesse, be not an impediment to that remedy, wheron no lesse then the safety of my life relyeth. And if I had a doublet for him, thou shalt not want a Mandillion. Neither thinke thou, but that I esteeme as much of thy counsell and advice, as of his labour and paines ; and as bruite beasts (we see) doe labour more bodily then

43

THE TRAGICK-COMEDY OF

men, for which they are well respected of us, and carefully lookt unto; but yet for all this, we hold them not in the nature of friends, nor affect them with the like love: the like difference doe I make betweene thee and Sempronio. And laying aside all power and dominion in my selfe, under the privie-Scale of my secret love, signe my selfe unto thee for such a friend.

PARME. Sir, it grieves mee not a little, that you should seeme doubtfull of my fidelity, and faithfull service, which these your faire promises and demonstrations of your good affection, cannot but call into question and jealousie. When (Sir) did you ever see my envy proove hurtfull unto you? Or when for any interest of mine own, or dislike, did I ever shew my selfe crosse, to crosse your good, or to hinder what might make for your profit?

CALISTO. Take it not offensively, nor mis-conster my meaning: for assure thy selfe, thy good behaviour towards mee, and thy faire carriage, and gentle disposition, makes thee more gracious in mine eies, then any, nay, then all the rest of my servants. But because in a case so difficult and hard as this, not only all my good, but even my life also wholly dependeth; it is needfull that I should in all that I am able, provide for my selfe; and therefore seeke to arme my selfe in this sort as thou see'st, against all such casualties, as may indanger my desire; howsoever, perswade thy selfe, that thy good qualities, as farre excell every naturall good, as every naturall good excelleth the artificiall, from whom it hath it's beginning. But of this, for this time no more; but let us now goe and see her, who must work our well-fare.

CELEST. Soft: me thinkes I heare some body on the stayres; they are now comming downe: Sempronio, make as though you did not heare them: stand close, and listen what they say; and let me alone to speake for us both. And thou shalt see how handsomely I will handle the matter, both for thee and mee.

SEMPR. Doe so then. Speake thou.

CELEST. Trouble mee no more, I say, leave importuning me; for to overcharge one, who is heavy enough already laden with paine, and anguish, were to spurre a sicke beast. Alas,

44

CALISTO AND MELIBEA

poore soule, mee thinkes thou art so possessed with thy Masters paine, and so affected with his affliction, that Sempronio seemes to be Calisto; and Calisto to be Sempronio; and that both your torments are both but in one and the same subject. Besides, I would have you thinke, that I came not hither to leave this controversie undecided, but will dye rather in the demand and pursuite of this my purpose, then not see his desire accomplished.

CALISTO. Parmeno, stay, stay awhile, make no noyse; stand still I pray thee, and listen a little what they say. So, hush, that we may see in what state wee live; what wee are like to trust to, and how the world is like to goe with us. O notable woman! O worldly goods, unworthy to be possessed by so high a spirit! O faithfull, and trusty Sempronio! Hast thou well observ'd him (my Parmeno?) Hast thou heard him? Hast thou noted his earnestnesse? Tell me, have I not reason to respect him? What saist thou, man? Thou that art the Clozet of my secrets, the Cabinet of my Counsell, and Councell of my soule?

PARME. Protesting first my innocency for your former suspition, and cumplying with my fidelity, since you have given me such free liberty of speech, I will truly deliver unto you what I thinke. Heare mee therefore, and let not your affection make you deafe, nor hope of your pleasure blinde you; have a little patience, and be not too hasty; for many through too much eagernesse to hit the pinne, have shot farre beside the white. And albeit I am but young, yet have I seene somewhat in my dayes: besides, the observation and sight of many things, doe teach a man much experience. Wherefore, assure your selfe, and thereon I durst pawne my life, that they overheard what wee said, as also our comming downe the stayres, and have of set purpose fallen into this false and feyned expression of their great love and care, wherein you now place the end of your desire.

SEMPR. Beleeve mee (Celestina) Parmeno aimes unhappily.

CELEST. Be silent: For I sweare by my haly-doome, that whither comes the Asse, thither also shall come the saddle. Let mee alone to deale with Parmeno, and you shall

THE TRAGICK-COMEDY OF

ACTUS
I

see, I will so temper him e'r I have done with him, that I will make him wholly ours. And see what wee gaine, hee shall share with us : for goods that are not common are not goods; It is communication that makes combination in love : and therefore let us all gaine, let us all devide the spoile, and let us laugh and be merry all alike. I will make the slave so tame, and so gentle, that I will bring him like a bird to picke bread from my fist. And so we will be two to two, and all three joyne to coozen the fourth. Thou and I will joyne together, Parmeno shall make a third, and all of us cheate Calisto.

CALISTO. Sempronio.

SEMPR. Sir.

CAL. What art thou doing, thou that art the key of my life? Open the doore. O Parmeno ! now that I see her, I feele my selfe well, me thinks, I am now alive againe: See what a reverend Matrone it is : What a presence she beares, worthy respect ! A man may now see, how for the most part, the face is the Index of the mind. O vertuous old age! O inaged vertue ! O glorious hope of my desired end ! O head, the allayer of my passion ! O reliever of my torment and vivification of my life, resurrection from my death ! I desire to draw neer unto thee, my lips long to kisse those hands, wherein consists the fulnesse of my recovery; but the unworthinesse of my person debars mee of so great a favour. Wherefore I heere adore the ground whereon thou treadest, and in reverence of thee, bow downe my body to kisse it.

CELEST. Sempronio ; Can faire words make me the fatter? Can I live by this? Those bones which I have already gnawne, does this foole thy Master thinke to feede mee therewith ? Sure the man dreames ; when he comes to frye his egges, he will then finde what is wanting. Bid him shut his mouth, and open his purse : I missedoubt his words, much more his works. Holla, I say ; are you so ticklish ? I will curry you for this geare, you lame Asse : you must rise a little more early, if you meane to goe beyond me.

PARME. Woe to these eares of mine, that ever they should heare such words as these. I now see, that hee is a lost man, who goes after one that is lost. O unhappy Calisto,

46

deject wretch, blind in thy folly, and kneeling on the ground, to adore the oldest, and the rottennest piece of whorish earth, that ever rub'd her shoulders in the Stewes! He is undone, he is overthrowne horse and foote, hee is fallen into a trap, whence he will never get out; hee is not capable of any redemption, counsell, or courage.

CALISTO. Wat said my mother? It seemeth unto mee, that shee thinkes I offer words for to excuse my reward.

SEMPR. You have hit the nayle on the head, Sir.

CALISTO. Come then with mee, bring the keyes with you, and thou shalt see, I will quickely put her out of that doubt.

SEMPR. In so doing, you shall doe well, Sir. Let us goe presently: for it is not good to suffer weeds to grow amongst corne, nor suspition in the hearts of our friends, but to root it out streight with the weed-hooke of good workes.

CALISTO. Wittily spoken; come, let us goe, let us slacke no time.

CELEST. Beleeve me (Parmeno) I am very glad, that we have lighted on so fit an opportunity, wherein I may manifest and make knowne unto thee the singular love, wherewithall I affect thee; and what great interest (though undeservedly) thou hast in me, I say undeservedly, in regard of that, which I have heard thee speake against me: whereof I make no more reckoning, but am content to let it passe. For, vertue teacheth us to suffer temptations, and not to render evill for evill; and especially when wee are tempted by young men, such as want experience, and are not acquainted with the courses of the world, who out of an ignorant and foolish kinde of loyalty, undoe both themselves and their Masters, as thou thy selfe dost Calisto. I heard you well inough, not a word you said, that escaped mine eare. Nor do you think, that with these my other outward senses, old age hath made me lose my hearing; for not onely that which I see, heare, and know, but even the very inward secrets of thy heart and thoughts, I search into, and pierce to the full with these my intellectuall eyes, these eies of my understanding. I would have thee to know (Parmeno) that Calisto is love-sicke, sicke even to the death. Nor art thou

THE TRAGICK-COMEDY OF

for this, to censure him to be a weak and foolish man : for unresistable love subdueth all things. Besides, I would have thee to know, if thou knowst it not already, that there are these two conclusions, that are evermore infallibly true. The first is, that every man must of force love a woman, and every woman love a man. The second is, that he who truely loves, must of necessity be much troubled and mov'd with the sweetnes of that superexcellent delight, which was ordain'd by him that made all things, for the perpetuating of mankind, without which, it must needs perish : and not only in humane kind, but also in fishes, birds, beasts, and all creatures that creepe and crawle upon the earth ; Likewise in your soules vegetative, some plants have the same inclination and disposition, that without the interposition of any other thing, they be planted in some little distance one of another, and it is determined and agreed upon by the generall consent of your Gardeners, and husband-men, to be Male and Female. How can you answer this, Parmeno ? Now my pretty little foole, you mad wagge, my soules sweet Genius, my Pearle, my Jewell, my honest poore silly Lad, my pretty little Monky-face, come hither you little whoreson ; Alack, how I pitty thy simplicity ! thou knowst nothing of the world, nor of it's delights. Let me run mad, and dye in that fit, If I suffer thee to come neere me, as old as I am. Thou hast a harsh and ill-favour'd hoarse voyce, by thy brizzled beard, it is easily guest what manner of man you are. Tell mee, is all quiet beneath ? No motions at all to make in Venus Court ?

PARME. O ! As quiet as the taile of a Scorpion.

CELEST. It were well, and it were no worse.

PARME. Ha, ha, he.

CELEST. Laugh'st thou, thou pocky rogue ?

PARME. Nay, mother, be quiet : hold your peace, I pray. Doe not blame me ; and doe not hold mee, though I am but young, for a foole. I love Calisto, tyed thereunto out of that true and honest fidelity, which every servant owes unto his Master ; for the breeding that he hath given me, for the benefit which I receive from him, as also because I am well respected, and kindely intreated by him, which

48

CALISTO AND MELIBEA

is the strongest chaine, that linkes the love of the servant to the service of his Master: As the contrary is the breaking of it. I see hee is out of the right way, and hath wholly lost himselfe; and nothing can befall a man worse in this world, then to hunt after his desire, without hope of a good and happy end; especially, he thinking to recover his game (which himselfe holdeth so hard and difficult a pursuite) by the vaine advice, and foolish reasons of that beast Sempronio, which is all one, as if he should goe about with the broade end of a Spade, to dig little wormes out of a mans hand. I hate it. I abhorre it. It is abominable: and with griefe I speake it, I doe much lament it.

CELESTINA. Knowst thou not, Parmeno, that it is an absolute folly, or meere simplicity to bewaile that, which by wayling cannot bee holpen?

PARME. And therefore doe I wayle, because it cannot be holpen: For if by wayling and weeping, it were possible to worke some remedy for my Master, so great would the contentment of that hope be, that for very joy, I should not have the power to weepe. But because I see all hope thereof to be utterly lost, with it have I lost all my joy, and for this cause doe I weepe.

CELEST. Thou weepest in vaine for that, which cannot by weeping be avoyded; thou canst not turne the streame of his violent passion; and therefore maist truly presume that he is past all cure. Tell mee (Parmeno) hath not the like happened to others, as well as to him?

PARME. Yes. But I would not have my Master through mourning and grieving, languish, and grow sicke.

CELESTINA. Thy Master is well inough. He is not sicke: and were hee never so sicke, never so much payned and grieved, I my selfe am able to cure him. I have the power to doe it.

PARME. I regard not what thou saist. For in good things, better is the Act, then the Power: And in bad things, better the Power, then the Act. So that, it is beter to be well, then in the way to bee well. And better is the possibility of being sicke, then to be sicke indeed: and therefore, Power in ill, is better then the Act.

G   49

ACTUS
I

CELEST. O thou wicked villaine! How idly dost thou talke, as if thou didst not understand thy selfe? It seemes thou dost not know his disease; What hast thou hitherto said? What wouldst thou have? What is't that grieves you, Sir? Why lamentest thou? Be you dispos'd to jest, and make your selfe merry? or are you in good earnest, and would'st faine face out truth with falsehood? Beleeve you what you list; I am sure hee is sicke, and that in Act, and that the Power to make him whole, lyes wholly in the hands of this weake old woman.

PARME. Nay rather, of this weake old Whore.

CELEST. Now the Hang-man be thy ghostly father, my little rascall, my pretty villaine; how dar'st thou be so bold with me?

PARM. How, as though I did not know thee?

CELEST. And who art thou?

PARM. Who? marry, I am Parmeno, sonne to Alberto thy gossip, who liv'd some little while with thee; for my mother recommended mee unto thee, when thou dwelt'st close by the rivers side in Tanners row.

CELEST. Good Lord, and art thou Parmeno, Claudina's sonne?

PARME. The very same.

CELEST. Now the fire of the pockes consume thy bones; for thy mother was an old whore, as my selfe: Why dost thou persecute me, Parmeno? It is he in good truth, it is hee. Come hither unto mee; come I say; many a good jerke, and many a cuffe on the eare have I given thee in my daies, and as many kisses too. A you little rogue, dost thou remember, sirrha, when thou lay'st at my beds feet?

PARM. Passing well: and sometimes also, though I was then but a little Apish boy, how you would take me up to your pillow, and there lye hugging of me in your armes; and because you savour'd somewhat of old age, I remember how I would fling and flye from you.

CELEST. A pocks on you for a rogue. Out (impudent!) art thou not ashamed to talke thus? But to leave off all jesting, and to come to plaine earnest; Heare me now (my childe) and hearken what I shall say unto thee. For, though

50

CALISTO AND MELIBEA

I am called hither for one end, I am come for another. And albeit I have made my selfe a stranger unto thee, and as though I knew thee not, yet thou wast the onely cause that drew mee hither. My sonne, I am sure thou art not ignorant, how that your mother gave you unto me, your father being then alive; who, after thou wentst from me, dyed of no other griefe, save onely what she suffered for the uncertainty of thy life and person. For whose absence in those latter yeeres of her elder age, she led a most painefull, pensive and carefull life. And when the time came, that she was to leave this world, shee sent for mee, and in secret recommended thee unto me, and told me, (no other witnesse being by, but heaven the witnesse to all our workes, our thoughts, our hearts, whom she alone interposed betweene her and mee) that of all loves I should doe so much for her, as to make inquirie after thee, and when I had found thee, to bring thee up, and foster thee as mine own : and that as soon as thou shouldst come to mans estate, and wert able to know how to govern thy selfe, and to live in some good manner and fashion; that then I should discover unto thee a certain place, where, under many a lock and key, she hath left thee more store of Gold and Silver, then all the revenewes come to, that thy Master Calisto hath in his possession. And because I solemnly vow'd, and bound my selfe by promise unto her, that I would see her desire, as far foorth as lay in me, to be well and truely performed, she peacefully departed this mortall life; and though a mans faith ought to be inviolably observed both to the living and the dead, yet more especially to the dead; for they are not able to doe any thing of themselves, they cannot come to me, and prosecute their right here upon earth. I have spent much time and mony in inquiring and searching after thee, and could never till now heare what was become of thee : and it is not above three daies since, that I first heard of your being, and where you abode. Verily, it hath much grieved me, that thou hast gon travelling, and wandring throughout the world, as thou hast done from place to place, losing thy time, without either gaine of profit, or of friends. For, (as Seneca saith) Travellers have many ends, and few

THE TRAGICK-COMEDY OF

friends. For, in so short a time they can never fasten friendship with any: and hee that is every where, is said to be no where. Againe, that meat cannot benefit the body, which is no sooner eaten, then ejected. Neither doth any thing more hinder it's health, then your diversities, and changes of meates. Nor doth that wound come to be healed, which hath daily change of tents, and new plasters. Nor doth that Tree never prove, which is often transplanted and removed from one ground to another. Nor is there any thing so profitable, which at the first sight bringeth profit with it. Therefore (my good sonne) leave off these violencies of youth, and following the doctrine, and rule of thy Ancestors, returne unto reason, settle thy selfe in some one place or other. And where better, then where I shal advise thee, taking mee, and my counsell along with thee, to whom thou art recommended both by thy father and mother? And I, as if I were thine owne true mother, say unto thee, upon those curses and maledictions, which thy parents have laid upon thee, if thou should'st be disobedient unto me, that yet a while thou continue heere, and serve this thy Master which thou hast gotten thee, till thou hearest further from mee, but not with that foolish loyalty, and ignorant honesty, as hitherto thou hast done; thinking to finde firmenesse upon a false foundation, as most of these Masters now a daies are. But doe thou gaine friends, which is a durable and lasting commodity; sticke closely and constantly unto them; doe not thou live upon hopes, relying on the vaine promises of Masters, who sucke away the substance of their servants, with hollow-hearted, and idle promises, as the horse-leaches suck bloud; and in the end fall off from them, wrong them, grow forgetfull of their good services, and deny them any recompence or reward at all. Wo be unto him that growes old in Court. The Masters of these times love more themselves then their servants; neither in so doing doe they doe amisse. The like love ought servants to beare unto themselves. Liberality was lost long agoe; rewards are growne out of date; magnificence is fled the countrie; and with her, all noblenesse. Every one of them is wholly now for himselfe, and makes the best hee can of his servants

52

CALISTO AND MELIBEA

service, serving his turne, as hee findes it may stand with his private interest and profit. And therefore they ought to doe no lesse, sithens that they are lesse then they in substance, but to live after their law, and to doe as they doe. My sonne Parmeno, I the rather tell thee this, because thy Master (as I am informed) is (as it seemeth likewise unto mee) a Rompenecios, one that befooles his servants, and weares them out to the very stumps, lookes for much service at their hands, and makes them small, or no recompence : He will looke to be served of all, but will part with nothing at all. Weigh well my words, and perswade thy selfe, that what I have said is true : Get thee some friends in his house, which is the greatest, and preciousest Jewell in the world. For, with him thou must not thinke to fasten friendship. A thing seldome scene, where there is such difference of estate and condition, as is betweene you two. Opportunity, thou seest, now offers her selfe unto us, on whose foretop, if wee will but take hold, wee shall all of us be great gainers, and thou shalt presently have something, wherewithall to help thy selfe. As for that which I told you of, it shall bee well and safely kept, when time shall serve ; in the meane while, it shall be much for thy profit, that thou make Sempronio thy friend.

PARME. Celestina, my hayre stands an end to heare thee, I tremble at thy words ; I know not what I should doe, I am in a great perplexity. One while I hold thee for my mother, another while Calisto for my Master, I desire riches, but would not get them wrongfully ; for, hee that rises by unlawfull meanes, falls with greater speed, then he got up. I would not for all the world thrive by ill gotten gaine.

CELEST. Marry, Sir, but so would I : right, or wrong, so as my house may be raised high inough, I care not.

PARME. Well, wee two are of contrary minds. For, I should never live contented with ill gotten goods ; for I hold cheerefull poverty, to be an honest thing. Besides, I must tell you, that they are not poore, that have little, but they that desire much ; And therefore say all you can, though never so much, you shall never perswade me in this, to be of your beliefe. I would faine passe

53

over this life of mine without envy: I would passe thorow solitary woods and wildernesses without feare: I would take my sleep without startings: I would avoyd injuries, with gentle answers: indure violence without reviling: and brooke oppression by a resolute resistance.

CELEST. O my sonne! it is a true saying; that Wisdome cannot be but onely in aged persons. And thou art but young.

PARM. True, but contented poverty is safe and secure.

CELEST. But tell mee, I pray thee, whom doth fortune more advance, then those that be bold and venturous? Besides, who is hee, that comes to any thing in a Common-wealth, who hath resolved with himselfe to live without friends? But (heaven be thanked) thou hast wealth inough of thine owne, yet thou knowest not what neede thou maist have of friends for the better keeping of them. Nor do thou think, that this thy inwardnesse with thy Master can any way secure thee. For the greater a mans fortune is, the lesse secure it is; and then most ticklish, when most prosper-ous. And therefore, to be armed against misfortunes, we must arme our selves with friends. And where canst thou get a fitter, neerer, and better companion in this kinde, then where those three kinde of friendships doe concurre in one? To wit, goodnesse, profit, and pleasure. For goodnesse; behold the good will of Sempronio, how agreeable, and con-formable it is to thine: and with it, the great similiancy, and suteableness, which both of you have in vertue. For profit; That lyes in this hand of mine, if you two can but agree together: For pleasure, That likewise is very likely. For now you are both in the prime of your yeeres, young and lusty, and fit for all kinde of sports and pleasures whatso-ever; wherein young men, more then old folks, do joyne and linke together: as in gaming, in wearing good clothes, in jesting, in eating, in drinking and wenching together. O Parmeno! if thou thy selfe wouldst, what a life might wee leade? Even as merry as the day is long. Sempronio, hee loves Elicia, Kinsewoman to Areusa.

PARM. To Areusa?

CELEST. I, to Areusa.

54

CALISTO AND MELIBEA

PARM. To Areusa, the daughter of Eliso?

CELEST. To Areusa, the daughter of Eliso.

PARM. Is this certaine?

CELEST. Most certaine.

PARM. It is marvellous strange.

CELEST. But tell me man; Dost thou like her?

PARM. Nothing in the world more.

CELEST. Well, now I know thy minde, let me alone. Heer's my hand; I will give her thee. Thou shalt have her; Man, she is thine owne, as sure as a Club.

PARMENO. Nay soft mother, you shall give mee leave not to beleeve you; I trust no body with my faith.

CELEST. He is unwise, that will beleeve all men; And hee is in an errour, that will beleeve no man.

PARME. I said, that I beleeve thee, but I dare not be so bold. And therefore let me alone.

CELEST. Alas, poore silly wretch; faint-hearted is hee that dares not venture for his good. Iove gives nuts to them, that have no teeth to cracke them: And beanes to those, that have no jawes to chew them. Simple as thou art, thou maist truely say, Fooles have fortune: for it is commonly seene, that they who have least wisedome, have most wealth: and that they who have the most discretion, have the least meanes.

PARM. O Celestina; I have heard old men say, that one example of luxury or covetousnesse, does much hurt. And that a man should converse with those that may make him better; and to forsake the fellowship of those whom hee thinkes to make better. As for Sempronio, neyther by his example shall I be won to be vertuous; nor he by my company be with-drawne from being vicious. And suppose that I should incline to that which thou saist, I would faine know this one thing of thee, how by example faults may bee concealed. And though a man overcome by pleasure, may goe against vertue; yet notwithstanding, let him take heed how hee spot his honesty.

CELEST. There is no wisdome in thy words; For, without company, there is no pleasure in the possession of any thing. Doe not thou then draw backe, doe not thou

THE TRAGICK-COMEDY OF

torment and vexe thy selfe. For, Nature shunnes whatsoever savours of sadnesse; and desires that which is pleasant and delightsome. And delight is with friends, in things that are sensuall; but especially in recounting matters of love, and communicating them, the one to the other. This did I do my selfe; this such a one told me; such a jest did wee breake; in this sorte did I winne her; thus often did I kisse her: thus often did shee bite me; thus I imbraced her; thus came wee neerer and neerer. O what speech, what grace, what sport, what kisses! Let us goe thither, Let us returne hither, Let us have musick, Let us paint Motto's, Let us sing songs, Let us invent some pretty devices; Let us tilt it; What shall be the Impresse? What the letter to it? To morrow shee will walke abroad; Let us round her streete; Read this her Letter; Let us goe by night; Hold thou the ladder; Guard well the gate; How did shee escape thee? Looke, where the Cuckold her husband goes; he left her all alone; Let us give another turne; Let us goe backe againe thither. And is there any delight (Parmeno) in all this, without company? By my fay, by my fay, they that have tryall can tell you, that this is the delight, this is the only pleasure; As for that other thing you wot of, your Asses have a better, and can doe better then you, or the best of you all.

PARMENO. I would not, mother, that you should draw mee on by your pleasing perswasions to follow your advice, as those have done, who wanting a good foundation to build their opinion on, have invited and drawne men to drinke of their heresies, sugring their cup with some sweet kinde of poyson, for to catch and captivate the wills of weake-minded men, and to blinde the eyes of their reason, with the powder of some sweet-pleasing affection.

CELEST. What is reason, you foole? What is affection, you Asse? Discretion (which thou hast not) must determine that; And discretion gives the upper hand to prudence; and prudence cannot be had without experience; and experience cannot bee found but in old folks, and such as are well strucken in yeeres. And therefore we are called fathers, and mothers; and good parents doe alwayes give their children good councell: as I more especially now doe thee; whose life

56

CALISTO AND MELIBEA

and credit, I preferre before mine owne. And when, or how, canst thou be able to requite this my kindenesse? For, Parents and Tutors can never receive any recompence, that may equall their desert.

PARME. I am very jealous and suspicious of receiving this doubtfull councell. I am afrade to venture upon it.

CELEST. Wilt thou not entertaine it? Well, I will then tell thee, Hee that wilfully refuseth councell, shall suddenly come to destruction. And so (Parmeno) I rid my selfe of thee, as also of this businesse.

PARM. My mother (I see) is angry; and what I were best to do, I know not. I am doubtfull of following her councell: it is as great an errour to beleeve nothing, as it is to beleeve every thing. The more humane and civill course, is, to have affiance and confidence in her. Especially in that, where besides the present benefit, both profit and pleasure is proposed. I have heard tell; that a man should beleeve his betters, and those whose yeers carry authority with them. Now; What is it she adviseth me unto? To be at peace with Sempronio: and to peace, no man ought to be opposite. For blessed are the peacefull. Love and charity towards our brethren, that is not to be shunned and avoided by us; and few are they, that will forgoe their profit. I will therefore seeke to please her, and hearken unto her. Mother, a master ought not be offended with his Schollers ignorance; at least, very seldome in matters of depth and knowledge. For though knowledge in its owne nature, be communicable unto all, yet is it infused but into few. And therefore I pray pardon me, and speake a new unto me; For, I will not only heare and beleeve thee, but receive thy councell as a singular kindnesse, and a token of thy great favour, and especiall love towards mee. Nor yet would I, that you should thanke mee for this; Because the praise and thankes of every action, ought rather to be attributed to the giver then to the receiver. Command mee therefore; for to your commandements shall I ever be willing, that my consent submit it selfe.

CELEST. It is proper to a man to erre; but to a beast, to persevere in an errour. It doth much glad me, Parmeno, that thou hast clear'd those thicke clouds, which darkened

H   57

THE TRAGICK-COMEDY OF

thy eye-sight, and hast answered mee according to the wise-dome, discretion, and sharpe wit of thy father, whose person, now representing it selfe fresh to my remembrance, doth make my tender eyes to melt into teares, which thou seest in such abundance to trickle downe my cheeks. He some-times would maintaine hard and strange propositions, but would presently (such was the goodnesse of his nature) see his errour, and imbrace the truth. I sweare unto thee; that in thus seeing thee to thwart the truth, and then suddenly upon it, laying down all contradiction, and to be conformable to that which was reason; me thinks, I doe as lively now behold thy father : as if he now were living, and present heere before mee. O what a man he was, how proper in his person, how able in his actions, what a port did he beare, and what a venerable and reverend countenance did hee carry! But hush, I heare Calisto comming, and thy new friend, Sempronio, whose reconcilement with him, I referre to some fitter oppor-tunity. For, two living in one heart, are more powerfull both for action, and understanding.

CALISTO. Deare mother, I did much doubt, considering my misfortunes, to finde you alive : but marvaile more, con-sidering my desire, that my selfe come alive unto you. Receive this poore gift of him, who with it offers thee his life.

CELEST. As in your finest gold, that is wrought by the hand of your cunningest, and curiosest Artificer, the worke-manship oftentimes doth farre surpasse the matter : So the fashion of your faire liberality doth much exceed the great-nesse of your gift. And questionlesse, a kindnesse that is quickely conferr'd, redoubles it's effect ; for hee that slacketh that, which he promiseth, seemeth in a manner to deny it, and to repent himselfe of his promised favour.

PARME. Sempronio, what hath hee given her ?

SEMPR. A hundred crownes in good gold.

PARME. Ha, ha, ha.

SEMPR. Hath my mother talk't with thee ?

PARME. Peace, shee hath.

SEMPR. How is it then with us ?

PARME. As thou wilt thy selfe. Yet for all this, mee thinkes I am still afraid.

58

CALISTO AND MELIBEA

SEMPR. No more. Be silent. I feare mee, I shall make thee twice as much afraide, e'r I have done with thee.

PARM. Now fie upon it. I perceive there can be no greater plague, nor no greater enemy to a man, then those of his owne house.

CALISTO. Now mother, goe your wayes, get you home and cheere up your owne house; and when you have done that, I pray hasten hither, and cheere up ours.

CELESTINA. Good chance attend you.

CALISTO. And you too : And so farewell.

THE END OF THE FIRST ACT.

ACTUS II

THE ARGUMENT

ELESTINA, *being departed from* Calisto, *and gone home to her owne house;* Calisto *continues talking with* Sempronio, *his servant; who like one that is put in some good hope, thinking all speed too slow, sends away* Sempronio *to* Celestina, *to solicit her for the quicker dispatch of his conceived businesse;* Calisto *and* Parmeno *in the mean while reasoning together.*

INTERLOCUTORS

Calisto, Sempronio, Parmeno.

CALISTO. Tell me (my Masters) The hundred crownes which I gave yonder old Bel-dame, are they well bestowed, or no?

SEMPR. Yes Sir, exceeding well. For, besides the saving of your life, you have gained much honour by it. And for what end is fortune favourable and prosperous, but to be a handmaide to our honour, and to wayte thereon, which of all worldly goods is the greatest? For honor is the reward

59

and recompence of vertue; and for this cause wee give it unto the Divine Essence, because wee have not any thing greater to give him. The best part whereof consisteth in liberality and bounty: and this close-fistednes, and uncommunicated treasure, doth eclypse and darken, whereas magnificence and liberality doth gaine, and highly extoll it. What good is it for a man to keep that to himselfe, which in the keeping of it, does himselfe no good? I tell you, Sir, and what I speake is truth; Better is the use of riches, then the possessing of them. O, how glorious a thing is it to give? and how miserable to receive? See, how much better action is then passion: so much more noble is the giver, then the receiver. Amongst the Elements, the fire, because it is more active, is the more noble: and therefore placed in the Spheares, in the noblest place. And some say; that noblenesse is a praise proceeding from the merit, and antiquity of our Ancesters. But I am of opinion, that another mans light can never make you shine, unlesse you have some of your owne. And therefore doe not glory in the noblenesse of your father, who was so magnificent a Gentleman, but in your owne. Shine not out of his, but your owne light; and so shall you get your selfe honour, which is mans greatest outward good. Wherefore not the bad, but the good, (such as your selfe) are worthy to partake of so perfect a vertue. And besides, I must tell you, that perfect vertue doth not suppose that Honour hath it's fellow: and therefore rejoice with your selfe, that you have beene so magnificent, and so bountifull. And thus, Sir, having told you my minde, let mee now advise you that you would be pleased to returne backe to your chamber, and there take some rest, sithence, that your businesse is deposited in such hands; assuring your selfe, that the beginning being so good, the end will be much better: and so let us goe presently to your chamber; where I shall treate more at large with you concerning this businesse.

CALISTO. Me thinkes (Sempronio) it is no good counsell, that I should rest heere accompanied, and that shee should goe all alone, who seekes to cure my ill: it were better that thou shouldst goe along with her, and hasten her on, since

CALISTO AND MELIBEA

thou knowst, that on her diligence dependeth my well-fare; on her slownesse, my painfulnesse, on her neglect, my despaire. Thou art wise, I know thee to bee faithfull, I hold thee a good servant. And therefore so handle the matter, that she shall no sooner see thee, but that shee may judge of that paine which I feele, and of that fire which tormenteth mee; whose extreme heat will not give me leave to lay open unto her the third part of my secret sickenesse. So did it tye my tongue, and tooke such hold on my sences, that they were not onely busied, but in a manner wasted and consumed; which thou, as one that is free from the like passion, maist more largely deliver, letting thy words runne with a looser reyne.

SEMPR. Sir, I would faine goe to fulfill your command : And I would fayne stay, to ease you of your care; your feare puts spurs to my sides; and your solitarinesse, like a bridle, pulls mee backe. But I will obey and follow your councell; which is, to goe and labour the old woman. But how shall I goe? For, if I leave you thus all alone, you will talke idlely, like one that is distracted; doe nothing but sigh, weepe, and take on, shutting your selfe up in darknesse, desiring solitude, and seeking new meanes of thoughtfull torment; wherein if you still persevere, you cannot escape either death or madnesse. For the avoyding whereof, get some good company about you, that may minister unto you occasion of mirth, by recounting of witty conceits, by intertaining you with Musicke, and singing merry songs, by relating Stories, by devising Motto's, by telling tales, by playing at cards, jesting, sporting. In a word, by inventing any other kinde of sweet and delightfull recreation, for to passe away the time, that you may not suffer your thoughts to run still wandring on in that cruell errour, whereinto they were put by that your Lady and Mistresse, upon the first trance and encounter of your Love.

CALISTO. How like a silly foole thou talkest! Know'st thou not, that it easeth the paine, to bewaile it's cause? O how sweet is it to the sorrowfull, to unsheathe their griefes! What ease doe broken sighes bring with them! O what a diminishing and refreshing to tearefull complaints, is the

61

THE TRAGICK-COMEDY OF

unfolding of a mans woes, and bitter passions! As many as ever writ of comfort, and consolation, doe all of them jumpe in this.

SEMPR. Read a little farther, and but turne over the leafe, and you shall finde they say thus: That to trust in things temporall, and to seek after matter of sorrow, is a kinde of foolishnesse, if not madnesse. And that Macias, the Idoll of Lovers, forgetfull of himselfe, because his mistresse did forget him; and carelesse of his well-fare, because she cared not for him, complaines himselfe thus: That the punishment of love consists in the contemplation thereof: And that the best remedy against love, is, not to thinke on thy love. The ease lies in the forgetting it. Kick not therefore against the pricke; feyne thy selfe to be merry, pluck up your spirits and be of good cheere, and all, you shall see, shall be well: for oftentimes, opinion brings things whither it listeth: Not that it should cause us to swarve from the truth; but for to teach us to moderate our sence, and to governe our judgement.

CALISTO. Sempronio, my friend, (for so thy love makes me stile thee) since it so grieves thee that I should be alone, call Parmeno hither, and hee shall stay with me: and henceforth, be thou, (as thou hast ever beene) faithfull and loyall unto mee. For, in the service of the servant, consisteth the Masters remuneration. O Parmeno!

PARME. Heere, Sir.

CALISTO. O I thinke not, for I cannot see thee. Leave her not, Sempronio: Ply her hard, follow her at an inch. Forget mee not, I pray thee. Now Parmeno, what thinkest thou of that which hath past to-day? My paine is great; Melibea stately, Celestina wise, she is her crafts Master, and we cannot doe amisse. Thou hast maynly opposed thy selfe against her: and to draw me to a detestation of her, thou hast painted her forth to the purpose, and set her out in her colours: and I beleeve thee. For such and so great is the force of truth, that it commands even the tongues of our enemies. But be she such, as thou hast described her to be; yet had I rather give her an hundred Crownes, then give another five.

62

CALISTO AND MELIBEA

PARME. Is the winde in that doore? Doe you beginne
to complaine already? Have you now better bethought
your selfe? Wee shall shortly complaine too at home; for I
feare mee, we shall fast for this frankenesse.

CALISTO. It is thy opinion, Parmeno, that I aske;
Gratifie mee therein: Hold, dost thou looke? Why hang'st
thou downe thy head, when thou shouldest answer me? But
I perceive, that as envy is sad, and sadnesse without a tongue;
thine owne will can doe more with thee, then feare of my
displeasure. What is that thou grumblest at? What didst
thou mutter to thy selfe, as though thou wert angry?

PARM. I say, Sir, that it had been better you had
imployed your liberality on some present, or the like services
upon Melibea her selfe, then to cast away your money upon
this old Bawd: I know well enough what shee is; and which
is worse, on such a one, as mindes to make you her slave.

CALISTO. How (you foole) her slave?

PARME. I, her slave. For to whom thou tellest thy
secret, to him doest thou give thy liberty.

CALISTO. It is something that the foole hath said; but
I would faine know this of thee; whether or no, when as
there is a great distance betwixt the intreater, and the
intreated, the suitor, and the party sued unto, either out of
authority of obedience, or greatnesse of estate and dignity,
or noblenesse of descent of bloud, as there is betwixt my
Mistresse, and my selfe; Whether or no (I pray) it be not
necessary to have an intercessour, or mediatour for mee, who
may every foot go to and fro with my messages, untill they
arrive at her eares, of whom, to have a second Audience, I
hold it impossible. And if it be thus with me, tell mee,
whether thou approvest of what I have done, or no?

PARM. The divell approve it for mee.

CALISTO. What saist thou?

PARME. Marry, I say, Sir, that never any errour came
yet unaccompanied; and that one inconvenience is the cause
of another, and the doore that opens unto many.

CALISTO. Thy saying I approve, but understand not
thy purpose.

PARME. Then thus, Sir, your losing of your Hawke the

63

other day, was the cause of your entring into the Garden, where Melibea was, to looke if she were there; your entring, the cause that you both saw her, and talked with her; your talke ingendred love; your love brought forth your paine; and your paine, will be the cause of your growing carelesse and wretchlesse both of your body, soule, and goods. And that which grieves me most, is, that you must fall into the hands of that same Trot-up-and-down, that maiden-head-monger, that same gadding to and fro Bawd, who for her villanies, and rogueries in that kinde, hath beene three severall times implumed.

CALISTO. Is 't e'n so, Parmeno? Is this all the comfort thou canst give me? Tell me rather something that may please me, and give mee better content then this can. And know withall, that the more thou dost dispraise, the better doe I like her. Let her cumply with mee, and effect my businesse, and let them implume her the fourth time too, if they will, I care not. Thou hast thy wits about thee; thou speak'st not having any sense of paine; thou art not heart-sicke, as I am, Parmeno, nor is thy minde touched with that sense of sorrow, as mine is.

PARME. I had rather, Sir, that you should be angry with me, and reprehend me out of your choller, for crossing your opinion, then out of your after-repentance, to condemne mee for not counselling you to the contrary. For I should but dissemble with you, if I should not tell you, That then you lost your liberty, when you did first captivate, and imprison your will.

CALISTO. This Villaine would be well cudgelled; Tell mee (thou unmanerly Rascall) Why dost thou blaspheme that which I adore? And you, Sir, who would seeme to be so wise, what wot'st thou of honour? Tell me, what is Love? shew me wherein Civility consisteth; Or what belongs to good maners? Thou wouldst faine be accounted discreet, and wouldst that I should thinke so, and yet dost not consider with thy selfe, that the first round in follies ladder, is for a man to thinke himselfe wise. If thou didst but feele the paine that I do: with other water wouldst thou bathe that burning, and wash that raging wound, which the cruell shaft

CALISTO AND MELIBEA

of Cupid hath made in my heart. See, what remedy Sempronio brings unto mee with his feete, the same dost thou put away with thy tongue, with thy vaine and uncomfortable words. And feyning thy selfe (forsooth) to be faithfull, thou art in realty of truth, nothing else but a meere Clot, and Lump of earth; a boxe fill'd with nothing but the very dregs and ground of malice: the very Inne and House, that gives open intertainement to Envy; not caring so as thou maist defame, and discredit this old woman, be it by right or by wrong, how thou puttest a disaffiance in my affection; thou knowing that this my paine, and overflowing griefe, is not ruled by reason, nor will admit advice, but is uncapable of counsell, which is as if one should tell mee; that That which is bred in the bone, may be fetcht out of the flesh: or that which is glewed to the very heart and intralls of a man, may be unloosed without renting the soule from the body. Sempronio did feare his going, and thy staying: it was mine owne seeking; I would needs have it so; And therefore worthily suffer the trouble of his absence and thy presence: and better is it, for a man to be alone, then ill accompanied.

PARME. Sir, it is a weake fidelity, which feare of punishment can turne to flattery; more especially, with such a Master, whom sorrow and affliction deprive of reason, and make him a stranger to his naturall judgement. Take but away this same vaile of blindenesse, and these momentary fires will quickly vanish; and then shall you know, that these my sharpe words are better to kill this strong Canker, and to stifle these violent flames, then the soft smoothings of soothing Sempronio, which feede your humor, quicken up your love, kindle afresh your flames, and joyne brands to brands, which shall never leave burning, till they have quite consumed you, and brought you to your grave.

CALISTO. Peace, peace, you Varlet; I am in paine and anguish, and thou readest phylosophy unto me. But I expect no better at thy hands; I have not the patience to heare thee any longer. Goe, be gone; Get foorth my horse; See hee be well and cleane drest; Girt him well. For I must passe by the house of my Melibea, or rather of my Goddesse.

I

PARM. Holla, boyes, where be you? Not a boy about the house. I must be faine to doe it my selfe; and I am glad it is no worse: for I feare mee ere it be long, wee shall come to a worse office, then to be boyes of the spurre, and to lackey it at the stirrop. Well, let the world slide, and things be as they may be, when they cannot be as they should be. My Gossips (I see as it is in the proverbe) are angry with mee for speaking the truth. Why, how now you Jade? Are you neighing too? Is not one jealous Lover inough in a house? Or dost thou winde Melibea?

CALISTO. When comes this horse? Why, Parmeno, what dost thou meane? why bringst thou him not away?

PARM. Heere hee is: Sosia was not within.

CALISTO. Hold the stirrop. Open the gate a little wider. If Sempronio chance to come in the meane while, and the old woman with him, will them to stay; for I will returne presently.

PARME. Goe, never to returne, and the divell goe with thee. Let a man tell these fooles all that he can for their owne good, they will never see it; and I, for my part beleeve; that if I should now at this instant give him a blow on the heele, I should beat more braine out of his heele then his head. Goe whither thou wilt for me: For I dare pawne my life, that Celestina and Sempronio will fleece you ere they have done with you, and not leave you so much as one Master-feather to maintaine your flight. O unfortunate that I am, that I should suffer hatred for my truth, and receive harme for my faithfull service! Others thrive by their knavery, and I lose by my honesty. The world is now growne to that passe, that it is good to be bad, and bad to be good; and therefore I will follow the fashion of the times, and doe as other men doe; since that Traitours are accounted wise and discreet, and faithfull men are deemed silly honest fooles. Had I credited Celestina, with her sixe dozen of yeeres about her, and followed her counsell, I had not beene thus ill intreated by Calisto. But this shall bee a warning unto mee ever heereafter, to say as he saies. If he shall say, Come, let us eate, and be merrie, I will say so too. If, Let us throw downe the house, I also will approve it. If hee will

66

CALISTO AND MELIBEA

burne all his goods, I will helpe to fetch the fire. Let him
destroy, hang, drowne, burne himselfe, and give all that hee
hath (if hee will) to Bawds; I for my part will hold my
peace, and helpe to devide the spoyle. Besides, it is an
ancient, and true received Rule; That it is best fishing in
troubled waters. Wherefore I will never any more be a
dogge in a mill, to be beaten for my barking.

THE END OF THE SECOND ACT

ACTUS III

THE ARGUMENT

EMPRONIO *goes to* Celestina's *house;*
Hee reprehends her for her slacknesse.
They consult what course they shall take
in Calisto's *businesse concerning* Melibea.
At last comes Elicia; Celestina, *shee*
hyes her to the house of Pleberio. *In*
the meane while, Sempronio *remaines in*
the house with Elicia.

INTERLOCUTORS

Sempronio, Celestina, Elicia.

SEMPRONIO. Looke what leysure the old bearded Bawd
takes! How softly she goes! How one leg comes drawling
after another! Now she has her money, her armes are
broken. Well overtaken, Mother, I perceive, you will not
hurt your selfe by too much haste.

CELEST. How now, sonne? What newes with you?

SEMPR. Why, this our sicke patient knowes not well
himselfe what hee would have. Nothing will content him;
hee will have his cake bak'd before it be dough; and his
meat rosted, before it be spitted. He feares thy negligence;
and curseth his owne covetousnesse; hee is angry with his
close fistednesse, and offended that he gave thee no more.

67

THE TRAGICK-COMEDY OF

CELEST. There is nothing more proper to Lovers, then impatience. Every small tarriance, is to them a great torment; the least delay breedes dislike; In a moment what they imagine, must be fully effected; nay, concluded before begunne; especially these new Lovers, who against any luring whatsoever, flie out to checke, they care not whither, without any advisement in the world, or once thinking on the harme which the meate of their desire may (by over-gorging) occasion unto them, intermingled amidst the affayres and businesses, concerning their owne persons, and their servants.

SEMPR. What sayst thou of servants? Thinkest thou, that any danger is like to come unto us, by labouring in this businesse? Or, that wee shall be burned with those Sparkles which scatteringly flye foorth of Calisto's fire? I had rather see him, and all his love goe to the divell; upon the first discovery therefore of any danger, (if things chance to goe crosse) I will eate no more of his bread, I will not stay with him, no not an houre. For, it is better to lose his service, then my life in serving him. But Time will tell mee what I shall doe. For, before his finall downe-fall, he will (like a house, that is ready to fall) give some token himselfe of his owne ruine. And therefore, Mother, let us in any case keepe our persons from perill; let us doe what may be done; if it be possible, let us work her for him this yeer: if not this, the next; if not the next, when we may; if never, the worse lucke his: Though there is not any thing so hard to suffer in it's beginning, which time doth not soften and reduce to a gentle sufferance. And there is no wound so painefull, which in time doth not slacken much of it's torment. Nor was there ever any pleasure so delightfull, which hath not by long continuance beene much diminished and lessened. Ill and good, prosperity and adversity, glory and griefe; all these with time, lose the force and strength of their rash and hasty beginning; Whereas matters of admiration, and things earnestly desired, once obtained, have no sooner beene come, then forgotten, no sooner purchased, but relinquished. Every day we see new and strange accidents, wee heare as many, and wee passe them over; leave those, and hearken after others; them also doth time

68

CALISTO AND MELIBEA

lessen and make contingible, as things of common course. And I pray, what wonder would you thinke it, if some should come and tell you; There was such an earth quake in such a place, or some such other things; tell me, would you not streight forget it? As also, if one should say unto you, Such a River is frozen, such a blinde man hath recovered his sight; thy father is dead; such a thunder-bolt fell in such a place; Granada is taken; the King enters it this day; the Turke hath receiv'd an over-throw; to morrow you shall have a great Eclypse; such a bridge is carried away with the flood; such a one is now made a Noble man; Peter is rob'd; Innes hath hang'd her selfe. Now in such cases, what wilt thou say, save onely this? That some three daies past, or upon a second view thereof, there will be no wonder made of it. All things are thus; they all passe after this maner; all is forgotten and throwne behind us, as if they had never beene. Just so will it be with this my Masters Love; the farther it goes on, the more it will slacken: For long custome doth allay sorrow, weakeneth and subdueth our delights, and lesseneth wonders. Let us make our profit of him, whilest this plea is depending; and if wee may with a dry foote doe him good, the easier the better; if not, by little and little wee will solder up this flaw, and make all whole by Melibea's holding him in scorne and contempt. And if this will doe no good upon him, Better it is, that the Master be pained, then his man perilled.

CELESTINA. Well hast thou said; I hold with thee, and jumpe in thy opinion; thy words have well pleased me, wee cannot erre. Yet notwithstanding (my sonne) it is necessary, that a good Proctour should follow his Clyents cause diligently and painfully; that hee colour his plea with some feyned show of reason; that hee presse some quillet or quirke of Law; to goe and come into open Court, though hee be check't; and receive some harsh words from the Judges mouth, to the end that they who are present, may both see and say, that though hee did not prevaile, yet he both spake and laboured hard for his fee. So shall not hee want Clyents, nor Celestina suitors in cases of Love.

SEMPR. Doe as thou thinkst good. Frame it to thine own

69

liking; This is not the first businesse thou hast taken in hand.

CELEST. The first, (my sonne?) Few virgins (I thanke Fortune for it) hast thou seene in this Citty, which have opened their shops, and traded for themselves, to whom I have not beene a broaker to their first spunne thread, and holpe them to vent their wares; there was not that wench borne in the world, but I writ her downe in my Register, and kept a Catalogue of all their names, to the intent that I might know how many escap'd my net. Why, what didst thou thinke of mee, Sempronio. Can I live by the ayre? Can I feed my selfe with winde? Doe I inherit any other land? Have I any other house or Vineyard? Knowest thou of any other substance of mine, besides this office? By what doe I eate and drinke? By what doe I finde clothes to my backe, and shooes to my feete? In this City was I borne; in it was I bred; Living (though I say it) in good credit and estimation, as all the world knowes. And dost thou thinke then, that I can goe unknowne? Hee that knowes not both my name, and my house, thou maist hold him a meere stranger.

SEMPR. Tell me, (Mother) what past betwixt you and my fellow Parmeno, when I went up with Calisto for the Crownes?

CELEST. I told him his dreame, and the interpretation thereof; and how that hee should gaine more by our company, and joyning in friendship with us, then with all his gay glozings, and imbroydered words which he uttereth to his Master; How he would alwaies live poore and in want, and be made a scoffe and laughing-stocke, unlesse he would turne over a new leafe, and alter his opinion; that he should not make himselfe a Saint, and play the hypocrite before such an old beaten bitch as my selfe. I did put him in minde of his owne mother relating unto him what a one she was, to the end that hee might not set my office at nought, her selfe having beene of the same Trade: for should hee but offer to speake ill of mee, hee must needes stumble first on her.

SEMPR. Is it long (mother) since you first knew her?

CELEST. This Celestina, which is heere now with thee, was the woman that saw her borne, and holpe to breed her

70

CALISTO AND MELIBEA

up: why, I tell thee (man) his mother and I were nayle, and flesh, buckle and thong; Of her I learned the better part of my trade. Wee did both eate, both sleep, both injoy our pleasures, our counsels, and our bargaines, intermutably one with another; we lived together like two sisters both at home and abroad: there was not a farthing which eyther of us gained, but was faithfully and truly divided betweene us. Had shee lived, I should never have lived to be deceived. But it was not my fortune to be so happy, shee dy'd too soone for mee. O death, death, how many doest thou deprive of their sweete and pleasing society! How many doest thou discomfort with thy unwelcome and troublesome Visitation? For one that thou eatest being ripe, thou croppest a thousand that are greene; For were shee alive, these my steps should not have beene unaccompanied, nor driven (as now I am) to walke the streets alone. I have good cause to remember her; for to me shee was a faithfull friend, and a good companion. And whilest shee was with me; she would never suffer mee to trouble my body, or my braines about any thing: if I brought bread, shee would bring meate; if I did spread the cloth, she would lay the napkins: she was not foolish, nor fantasticall, nor proud, as most of your women now-adaies are. And by my fay, I sweare unto thee, shee would goe barefaced from one end of the City to the other, with her Fan in her hand, and not one, all the way that she went, would give her any worse word, then Mistresse Claudina. And I dare be bold to say it, that there was not a woman of a better palate for wine in the world, nor better skill'd in any kind of marchandize whatsoever. And when you have thought that she had been scarce out of doores, with a whip-Sir John, e'r you could scarce say this, shee was heere againe. Every one would invite and feast her, so great was the affection which they bare unto her; And she never came home, till she had taken a taste of some eight or ten sorts of wine, bearing one pottle in her Jar, and the other in her belly: and her credit was so good, that they would have trusted her for a Rundlet or two upon her bare word, as if shee had pawned unto them a piece of plate. Why, her word was as currant as gold, in all the

71

THE TRAGICK-COMEDY OF

ACTUS
III

Innes and Tavernes in the Towne. If wee walked the streetes, whensoever we found our selves thirsty, we entred streight the next Taverne that was at hand, and called presently for a quart of wine for to moysten our mouthes withall, though we had not a penny to pay for it. Nor would they (as from others) take our vailes and our coyfes from off our heads, till we had discharged the reckoning, but score it up, and so let us go on our way. O Sempronio; Were it but Cat after kind, and that such were the son, as was the mother, assure thy selfe that thy master should remaine without a feather, and we without any farther care. But if I live, I will bring this iron to my fashion; I will worke him like waxe, and reckon him in the number of mine owne.

SEMPR. How dost thou thinke to make him thine? Hee is a crafty subtill foxe; Hee will hardly be drawne in; Hee is a shrewd fellow to deale withall.

CELEST. For such a crafty Knave, wee must have a Knave and a halfe, and intertaine two traytours for the taking of one. I will bring him to have Areusa, so and make him Cock-sure ours; and he shall give us leave without any let, to pitch our nets, for the catching of Calisto's coyne.

SEMPR. But dost thou thinke thou canst doe any good upon Melibea? Hast thou any good bough to hang by?

CELEST. There is not that Surgeon, that can at the first dressing, give a true judgement of his Patients wound: but what I see, and thinke for the present, I will plainely deliver unto thee. Melibea is faire; Calisto fond and frank; he cares not to spare his purse, nor I my paines; hee is willing to spend, and I to speed him in his businesse; Let his money be stirring, and let the suite hang as long as it will. Money can doe any thing; it splitteth hard Rocks; it passeth over Rivers dry-foote; there is not any place so high, whereunto an Asse laden with gold will not get up; his unadvisednesse, and ferventnesse of affection, is sufficient to marre him, and to make us. This I have thought upon; this I have searcht into; this is all I know concerning him and her: and this is that which must make most for our profit. Well, now must I goe to Pleberio's house. Sempronio, fare-well. For though Melibea brave it, and stands so high upon her

72

pantofles; yet is not shee the first that I have made to stoope, and leave her cackling; they are all of them ticklish, and skittish; the whole generation of them is given to winching and flinging: but after they are well weyghed, they proove good high-way Jades, and travell quietly; you may kill them, but never tyre them. If they journey by night, they wish it may never be morning. They curse the Cockes, because they proclaime it is day: the Clockes, because they go too fast: they lye prostrate, as if they lookt after the Pleyades and the North star, making themselves Astronomers and starre-gazers; But when they see the morning starre arise, they sigh for sorrow, and are ready to forsake their bodies. And the clearing of the day, is the clouding of their joy. And above all, it is worth the while, to note how quickely they change copy, and turne the Cat in the pan; They intreat him, of whom they were intreated; they indure torment for him, whom before they had tormented; they are servants to those, whose Mistresses they were; they breake thorow stone walls, they open windowes, feyne sicknesse; if the hinges of their doores chance to creake, they anoynt and supple them with oyle, that they may performe their office without any noyse. I am not able to expresse unto thee the great impression of that sweetnesse, which the primary and first kisses of him they love, leaveth imprinted in their hearts. They are enemies of the meane, and wholly set upon extremes.

SEMPR. Mother, I understand not these termes.

CELEST. Marry, I say, that a woman either loveth, or hateth him much, of whom she is beloved, so that, if she entertaine not his love, she cannot dissemble her hate; there are no reynes strong inough to bridle their dislike. And because I know this to be true, it makes mee goe more merrily and cheerefully to Melibea's house, then if I had her fast in my fist already. For I know, that though at the first I must be forced to woo her, yet in the end, she will be glad to sue to me. And though at present perhaps she threaten me, and flatly fall out with mee; yet at last will shee be well pleased, and fall as much a flattering, as she did a reviling me. Here in this pocket of mine, I carry a little parcel of

ACTUS
III

yarne, and other such like trinkets, which I alwaies beare about mee; that I may have some pretence at first to make my easier entrance and free accesse, where I am not throughly knowne: As Gorgets, Coyfes, Fringes, Rowles, Fillets, Hayrelaces, Nippers, Antimony, Ceruse, and sublimated Mercury, Needles and Pinnes; they shall not aske that thing, which I shall not have for them. To the end, that looke whatsoever they shall call for, I may be ready provided for them. And this baite upon the first sight thereof shall worke my acceptance, and hold fast the fish which I minde to take.

SEMPR. Mother, looke well about you. Take heed what you doe. For a bad beginning can never make a good ending. Thinke on her father, who is noble and of great power and courage; her mother jealous and furious, and thou, suspition it selfe. No sooner seene, but mistrusted: Melibea is the only child to them both, and she miscarrying, miscarrieth with her all their happinesse; the very thought whereof, makes me quake and tremble. Goe not to fetch wooll, and come home shorne your selfe; seeke not to plucke her wings, and [come back] your selfe without your plumes.

CELESTINA. Without my plumes, my sonne?

SEMPRO. Or rather implumed, mother, which is worse.

CELESTINA. Now by my fay, in an ill houre had I need of thee to be my companion. As though thou couldst instruct Celestina in her own Trade? As if I knew not better what to doe, then thou canst teach me? Before ever thou wast borne, I did eate bread with crust. O! you are a proper man to make a Commander, and to marshall other mens affaires, when thy selfe art so dejected with sinister divinations, and feare of insuing harmes.

SEMPR. Marvell not, Mother, at my feare, since it is the common condition of all men; That what they most desire, they thinke shall never come to passe. And the rather, for that in this case now in hand, I dread both thine, and my punishment; I desire profit; I would that this businesse might have a good end; not because my Master thereby might be rid of his paine, but I of my penury. And therefore I cast more inconveniences with my small experience, then you with all your aged Arte and cunning.

74

CALISTO AND MELIBEA

ELICIA. I will blesse my selfe; Sempronio, come; I will make a streake in the water, I will score it up. This is newes indeed: I had thought to have strewed greene rushes against your comming. What? Come hither twice? Twice in one day?

CELEST. Peace, you foole. Let him alone. We have other thoughts (I wisse) to trouble our heads withall; matters of more importance, then to listen to your trumperies. Tell me; Is the house cleare? Is the young wench gone, that expected the young Novice?

ELICIA. Gone? yes; and another come, since shee went, and gone too.

CELEST. Sai'st thou me so, Girle? I hope then it was not in vaine.

ELICIA. How? in vaine? No by my fay was it not; it was not in vaine; for though he came late, yet better late then never. And little need hee to rise earely, whom his starres have a purpose to helpe.

CELEST. Goe, hye you up quickely to the top of all the house, as high as you can goe, and bring me downe hither the bottle of that oyle of Serpents, which you shall find fastned to that piece of rope, which I brought out of the fields with me that other night, when it rained so fast, and was so darke: then open my chest where the paintings be, and on your right hand you shall find a paper written with the bloud of a Bat, or Flitter-mouse; bring it downe also with you, together with that wing of the Dragon, whereof yesterday we did cut off the clawes. And take heed, you do not shead the May-deaw, which was brought me for to make my confection.

ELICIA. It is not here, mother; you never remember where you lay your things.

CELEST. Doe not reprove me, I pray thee, in mine old age; mis-use me not, Elicia. Doe not you feyne untruthes, though Sempronio be heere, be not you proud of it. For hee had rather have mee for his counsellour, then you for his play-fellow; for all you love him so well. Enter into the chamber where my oyntments be, and there in the skinne of a blacke Cat, where I will'd you to put the eyes of the shee-

75

Wolfe, you shall not faile to finde it : and bring down the bloud of the hee Goat, and that little piece of his beard which you your selfe did cut off.

ELICIA. Take it to you (mother.) Lo, heere it is; while you stay heere, I will goe up, and take my Sempronio with me.

CELEST. I conjure thee (thou sad god Pluto) Lord of the infernall deepe, Emperor of the damned court, Captaine generall and proud Commander of the wicked spirits, Grand signor of those sulphureous fires, which the flaming hills of Ætna flash forth in most fearefull, and most hideous manner; Governour, and Supervisor both of the torments, and tormenters of those sinfull soules, that lye howling in Phlegeton; Prince, and chiefe Ruler of those three hellish Furies, Tesiphone, Meghera, and Alecto; Administrator of all the blacke things belonging to the kingdomes of Stix and Dis, with all their pitchy Lakes, infernall shades, and litigious Chaos; Maintainer of the flying Harpies, with all the whole rabblement of frightfull Hydraes; I Celestine, thy best knowne, and most noted Clyent, conjure thee by the vertue and force of these red Letters, by the bloud of this bird of the night, wherewith they are charactred, by the power and weight of these names and signes, which are contained in this paper, by the fel and bitter poyson of those Vipers, whence this oyle was extracted, wherewith I anoynt this clew of yarne, thou come presently without delay to obey my will, to invelop, and wrap thy selfe therin, and there to abide, and never depart thence, no, not the least moment of time, untill that Melibea, with that prepared opportunity, which shall be offred unto her, shall buy it of mee, and with it, in such sort be intangled and taken, that the more she shall behold it, the more may her heart be molified, and the sooner wrought to yeeld to my request: That thou wilt open her heart to my desire, and wound her very soule with the love of Calisto; and in that extreme, and violent manner, that despising all honesty, and casting off all shame, shee may discover her selfe unto me, and reward both my message, and my paines; Doe this, and I am at thy command, to doe what thou wilt have me: But if thou doe not doe it, thou shalt forthwith have mee thy Capitall foe, and Profest enemy.

76

CALISTO AND MELIBEA

I shall strike with light, thy sad and darksome dungeons; I shall cruelly accuse thy continuall lyings, and dayly falsehoods. And lastly, with my charming words, and inchanting termes, I will chaine and constringe thy most horrible name. Wherefore, againe and againe; once, twice, and thrice, I conjure thee to fulfill my command. And so presuming on my great power, I depart hence, that I may goe to her with my clew of yarne; wherein I verily beleeve, I carry thy selfe inwrapped.

THE END OF THE THIRD ACT

ACTUS IIII

THE ARGUMENT

CELESTINA, *going on her way, talks to her selfe, till she comes to* Pleberio's *gate, where she meets with* Lucrecia *one of* Pleberio's *maid-servants; she boords her, and enters into discourse with her, who being over-heard by* Alisa, Melibea's *mother, and understanding it was* Celestina, *causes her to come neer the house.* A *messenger comes to call away* Alisa, *shee goes her waies;* Celestina *in the meane while being left alone with* Melibea, *discovers unto her the cause of her comming.*

INTERLOCUTORS

Celestina, Lucrecia, Alisa, Melibea.

CELESTINA. Now that I am all alone, I will, as I walke by my selfe, weigh and consider that which Sempronio feared, concerning my travell in this businesse. For, those things which are not well weighed, and considered, though sometimes they take good effect, yet commonly fall out ill. ·So that much speculation brings foorth much good fruit; for although I dissembled with him, and did set a good face on the matter, it may be, that if my drift and intent should

77

THE TRAGICK-COMEDY OF

ACTUS
IIII

chance to be found out by Melibea's father, it would cost me little lesse then my life : Or at least, if they should not kill me, I should rest much impaired in my credit, either by their tossing me in a blanket, or by causing me to be cruelly whipt ; so that my sweet meats shall have sowre sauce : and my hundred Crownes in Gold be purchast at too deare a rate ; Ay wretched me ! into what a Labyrinth have I put my selfe ? What a trap am I like to fall into, through mine owne folly ? For that I might shew my selfe solicitous and resolute, I have put my selfe upon the hazard of the dice. Wo is me ; what shall I doe ? To goe backe, is not for my profit, and to goe on, stands not with my safety. Shall I persist ? or shall I desist ? In what a straite am I ? In what a doubtfull and strange perplexity ? I know not which I were best to choose. On my daringnesse dependeth manifest danger ; on my cowardize shamefull damage. Which way shall the Oxe goe, but he must needs plough ? Every way, goe which way I will, discovers to my eyes deepe and dangerous furrowes ; desperate downefalls ; if I be taken in the manner ; if the theft be found about me, I shall be either kill'd, or carted, with a paper-crowne set upon my head, having my fault written in great Text-letters. But in case I should not goe, what will Sempronio then say ? Is this all thou canst doe ? Thy power, thy wisedome, thy stoutnesse, thy courage, thy large promises, thy faire offers, thy tricks, thy subtilties, and the great care (forsooth) thou wouldst take ; What ? are they all come to this ? And his Master Calisto, what will he say ? what will hee doe ? or what will hee thinke ? save onely this ; That there is much deceit in my steps ; and that I have discovered this blot to Pleberio, like a prevaricating Sophistresse, or cunning Ambi-dexter, playing the traitour on both sides, that I might gaine by both ? And if he doe not entertaine so hatefull a thought, he will raile upon me like a mad-man ; he will upbraid mee to my face, with most reproachful termes ; He will propose a thousand inconveniences, which my hasty deliberation was the cause of ; saying, Out you old whore : Why didst thou increase my passions with thy promises ? False Bawd as thou art ; For all the world

78

CALISTO AND MELIBEA

besides, thy feete can walke, for mee onely thy tongue; Others can have works; I only words. Others can have remedy at thy hands; I onely the man that must endure torment. To all others, thy force can extend it selfe; and to me is it only wanting. To all others thou art Light; to me Darkenesse. Out thou old tretcherous, disloyall wretch; Why didst thou offer thy selfe and service unto me? For, it was thy offer that did put mee in hope: and that hope did delay my death, prolonged my life, and did put upon mee the Title of a glad man. Now, for that thy promises have not prov'd effectuall, neither shalt thou want punishment, nor I wofull despaire: so that, looke I on which side I will (miserable woman that I am) it is ill here, and it is ill there; paine and griefe on either hand: But when extremes shall want their meane, and no meanes to avoide either the one or the other; of two evils, it is the wiser course to incline to the lesser. And therefore I had rather offend Pleberio, then displease Calisto. Well then, I will goe. For greater will my shame be, to be condemned for a Coward, then my punishment, in daring to accomplish what I promised. Besides, Fortune still friendeth those that are bold and valiant. Lo, yonder's the gate; I have seene my selfe in greater danger then this in my daies. Coraggio, Coraggio, Celestina; Be of good cheere; Be not dismay'd; For, there are never suitors wanting for the mitigating, and allaying of punishment. All Divinations are in my favour, and shew themselves prospicious in my proceedings; or else I am no body in this my Art, a meere bungler, an Idiot, an Asse. Of foure men that I meete by the way, three of them were John's; whereof two were Cuckolds. The first word that I heard, passing along the street, was a Love complaint. I have not stumbled since I came foorth, as at other times I used to doe. Me thinkes the very stones of the streete did sunder themselves one from another, to give me way as I past. Nor did the skirts of my clothes wrumple up in troublesome folds, to hinder my feet. Nor do I feele any faintnesse, or wearinesse in my legs. Every one saluteth mee. Not a dog that hath once barked at me; I have neither seene any bird of a black feather, neither Thrush, nor Crow; nor any other of the like unlucky nature:

79

and which is a better signe of good lucke then all these, yonder doe I see Lucrecia, standing at Melibea's gate, which is kinsewoman to Elicia: it cannot but goe well with us; it is impossible wee should misse of our purpose; All is Cock-sure.

LUCRECIA. What old witch is this, that comes thus trayling her taile on the ground? Looke how shee sweepes the streetes with her gowne! Fie, what a dust shee makes!

CELESTINA. By your leave, sweet Beauty.

LUCRECIA. Mother Celestina, you be welcome. What wind, I trow, drives you this way? I doe not remember, that I have seene you in these parts this many a day. What accident hath brought you hither?

CELEST. My love (daughter, my love) and the desire I have to see all my good friends; and to bring you commendations from your Cousin Elicia: as also to see my old and young Mistresse, whom I have not seene since I went from this end of the Towne.

LUCRECIA. Is this your onely errand from home? Is it possible, you should come so farre for this? I promise you, you make me much to marvell; For I am sure you were not wont to stirre your stumps, but you knew wherefore; nor to goe a foote forth of doores, unlesse it were for your profit.

CELEST. What greater profit (you foole) would you have, then a man to cumply with his desires? Besides, such old women as we never want businesse: especially my selfe, who having the breeding of so many mens daughters as I have, I goe to see if I can sell a little yarne.

LUCRECIA. Did not I tell you so before? I wote well what I said; you never put in a penny, but you take out a pound: Be your paines never so little, you will be sure you will be well paid for it. But to let that passe, my old mistresse hath begunne a web; shee hath need to buy it, and thou hast neede to sell it. Come in, and stay heere awhile, you and I will not fall out.

ALISA. Lucrecia, who is that you talke withall?

LUCRECIA. With that old woman forsooth, with the scotch on her nose, who sometimes dwelt hard by here in Tanners Row, close upon the River-side.

ALISA. Now I am further to seeke then I was before; if

CALISTO AND MELIBEA

thou wilt give mee to understand an unknowne thing, by a
thing that is lesse knowne, [it] is to take up water in a Sieve.

LUCRECIA. Madame! Why, this old woman is better
knowne then the hearbe Rew. Doe not you remember her
that stood on the Pillory for a Witch? That sold young
wenches by the great and by whole sale? and that hath
mard many thousands of marriages, by sundring man and
wife, and setting them at oddes?

ALISA. What Trade is she of? What is her Profession?
it may be, by that I shall know her better.

LUCRECIA. Forsooth, she perfumes Calls, Vailes, and
the like; she makes your sublimate Mercury, and hath some
thirty severall Trades besides; shee is very skilfull in hearbs;
shee can cure little children: And some call her, The old
woman, The Lapidary, for her great dealing in stones.

ALISA. All this makes me never a whit the wiser. Tell
mee her name, if thou knowst it.

LUCRECIA. If I knew it? Why, there is neither young
nor old in all this City, but knowes it. And should not I
then know it?

ALISA. If you know it so well, why then doe not you
tell it me?

LUCRECIA. I am ashamed, forsooth.

ALISA. Goe too, you foole; Tell mee her name; Doe not
anger mee by this your delay.

LUCRECIA. Her name (saving your Reverence) is
Celestina.

ALISA. Hi, hi, hi! Now beshrew your fingers; O my
heart! O my sides! I am not able to stand for laughing,
to see that the lothing which thou hast of this poore old
woman, should make thee ashamed to name her unto me.
Now I call her to minde; Goe too; you are a wagge; No
more of this. Shee (poore soule) is come to begge somewhat
of mee. Bid her come up.

LUCRECIA. Aunt, it is my Mistresse pleasure, you
come up.

CEL. My good Lady; All blessings abide with you, and
your noble daughter. My many griefes and infirmities have
hindred my visiting of this your house, as in duty I was

L   81

THE TRAGICK-COMEDY OF

bound to doe; But heaven knowes how faire are the intralls of my inward affection, how free from any spot of foulnesse. It knowes the sincerity of my heart, and truenesse of my love. For, distance of place displaceth not that love, which is lodged in the heart: So that what heeretofore in my selfe I did much desire, now my necessity hath made mee to performe. And amongst other my many Crosses and miseries in this life, my Crosses in my purse grow dayly lesse and lesse; so that I have no better remedy to helpe my selfe withall, and to relieve this my poore estate, then to sell this little parcell of yarne of mine owne spinning to make Coyfes, and Kerchiefes; and understanding by your maid, that you had need thereof (howbeit I am poore in every thing, I praise my fate, save the richnesse of this grace) it is wholy at your command, if either it or I may doe you any service.

ALISA. Honest neighbour, thy discourse and kinde offer move me to compassion: and so move me, that I had rather light upon some fit occasion, whereby I might supply thy wants, then diminish thy web, still thanking thee for thy kinde offer: and if it be such as will serve my turne, I shall pay you well for it.

CELEST. Madame, by my life, as I am true old woman, or by any other oath you shall put me to, it is such, as all the whole Towne is not able to match it. Looke well upon it; it is as fine as the haire of your head, even and equall, as nothing more strong, as the strings of a Viall; white as a flake of Snow, spun all with mine owne fingers; recled and wound up with mine owne hands. Looke you (Lady) on some of the same in skaines; Did you ever see better? Three Royals, as I am true woman, I received no longer agoe then yesterday for an ounce.

ALISA. Daughter Melibea, I will leave this honest woman with you; For mee thinks it is now high time, if I have not stayed too long, to goe visit my sister, Wife unto Chremes: for I have not scene her since yesterday; and besides, her Page is now come to call mee, and tels me that her old fit hath already beene on her this pretty while.

CELEST. Now does the Divell goe preparing opportunity

82

CALISTO AND MELIBEA

for my Stratagem, by re-inforcing this sickenesse upon the other. Goe on, my good friend, stand stifly to your tackling; be strong and shrinke not. For now is the time or never; see you leave her not: and remoove away this woman from mee. But soft; I feare shee heares mee.

ALISA. Say, (friend) what is that thou sai'st?

CELEST. I say (Madame) Curst be the divell and my evill Fortune, that your sisters sickenesse is growne now upon her in such an unlucky houre, that we shall have no fit time to dispatch our businesse: But I pray, what is her sicknesse?

ALISA. A paine in her side, which takes her in such grievous manner, that if it be true which her Page tels me, I feare me it will cost her her life. Good neighbour, let mee intreate you for my sake to recommend her recovery unto your best devotions and prayers.

CELEST. Heere (Lady,) I give you my faithfull promise, that as soone as I goe hence, I will hye mee to my Vestalls, where I have many devout virgins, my friends, upon whom I will lay the same charge as you have laid upon mee.

ALISA. Doe you heare, Melibea? Content our neighbour, and give her that which is reason for her yarne. And you mother, I pray hold me excused, for I doubt not, but you and I shall have another day, when wee shall have more leysure to enjoy one another.

CELEST. Madame, there is no neede of pardon, where there is no fault committed. Iove pardon you, and I doe. For I thanke you, you have left mee heere with very good company. Iove grant shee may long enjoy her noble youth, and this her flourishing prime; a time wherein more pleasures and delights are found, then in this old decayed Carkasse of mine, which is nothing else but a very Spittle-house of diseases, an Inne full of infirmities, a Store-house, or Magazine of sad and melancholy thoughts, a friend to brangling and brawling, a continuall griefe, and incurable plague: pittying that which is past, punished in that which is present: and full of wretched care in that which is to come: A neere neighbour unto death; a poore Cabbin, without one bough of shelter, whereinto it raynes on all

83

THE TRAGICK-COMEDY OF

ACTUS
IIII

sides; a sticke of Willow; a staffe of weake Osiers, which is doubled with any the least stresse you put it to.

MELIB. Tell me (mother) why doe you speake so ill of that, which the whole world so earnestly desireth to enjoy and see?

CELEST. They desire so much their more hurt; they desire so much their more griefe; they desire to live to be old; because by living to be old, they live. And life (you know) is sweete; and living, they come to be old. Hence is it, that your children desire to be men; and your men to be old men; and your old men, to be more and more old; and though they live in never so much paine, yet doe they still desire to live. For, (as it is in the Proverbe) Faine would the Henne live, for all her pip; she would not be put out of her life, to be put out of her paine. But who is hee (Lady) that can recount unto you the inconveniences of old age? The discommodities it brings with it? it's torments, it's cares, its troubles, it's infirmities, it's colds, it's heates, it's discontentments, it's brawles, it's janglings, it's griefes, which like so many weights lye heavy upon it? Those deepe furrows and deepe wrinkles in the face? That change and alteration in the hayre? That fading of fresh and lively colour? That want of hearing? That weaknesse of sight? That hollownesse in the eyes? Seeing, as if they were shut up in a shade? That sinking and falling of the jawes? That toothlesnesse of the gummes? That failingnesse of force and of strength? That feeblenesse of legs? That slownesse in feeding? Besides, (Madame) which makes mee sigh to thinke upon it, when all these miseries I have told you of, come accompanied with poverty, all sorrowes to this must stoope and strike saile, when the appetite shall be great, and the provision small; The stomack good, and the dyet naught; For I never knew any worse habit, then that of hunger.

MELIBEA. I perceive, so goes the market, as it goes with you. And as you find your penniworths, so you speake of the Faire. And though you perhaps complaine, the rich will sing another song.

CELEST. Daughter, and Mistresse, there is no way so faire, but hath some foule; if you have one mile of good,

84

CALISTO AND MELIBEA

you have three of bad. At the foote of every hill, you have three Leagues of ill followes. And of a thousand that live contentedly, you have ten thousand doe the contrary: True contentednesse, rest, renowne, glory, and quietnesse, runne from the rich by other by-conduits, and gutters of subtilty and deceit; which pipes, whereby they are conveyed, are never perceived, because they are paved and brickt over with smooth and well wrought flatteries. He is rich that hath Gods blessing. I mary, that is wealth indeed. And shall I tell you, Lady? Safer it is with him that is despised, then with him that is feared. And a farre better sleepe doth the poore man take, then hee who is bound to keepe that with care which hee hath gotten with labour, and must leave with sorrow. My friend will not dissemble with me, but the rich mans will with him; I am loved for mine owne sake; the rich man for his wealths sake. A rich man shall never heare the truth; every one will flatter him, and seeke to please his humour in whatsoever he shall say. Besides, he lies open to every mans envy; and you shall scarce finde one rich man amongst a thousand, but will ingeniously confesse, that it had beene better for him to have bin in a middling estate, or in good honest poverty. For riches make not a man rich, but busied; not a Master, but a Steward. More are they that are possessed by their riches, then they that possesse their riches. To many they have beene a meanes of their death; and most men they have rob'd of their pleasure, and their good and commendable qualities; and to say the truth, they are enemies to all goodnesse. Have you not heard say, Men have lien downe, and dream'd of their riches, and behold, they have waked, and found nothing in their hands? Every rich man hath a dozen of sonnes, or Nephewes, which repeate no other prayer, nor tender any other Orison to God, but that he would be pleased to take him out of this world; and desire nothing more, then to see the houre that they may come to enjoy his estate; to see him under ground, and what was his, in their hands; and with a small charge, to lay him up in his last and everlasting mansion heere on earth.

MELIBEA. Me thinks, mother, it should be a great

85

THE TRAGICK-COMEDY OF

griefe unto you, to thinke upon those good daies of yours, which are past and gone. Would you not be willing to runne them over againe?

CELEST. That Travellour (Lady) were a foole, who having tyred out himselfe with a hard dayes travell, would, to begin his journey againe, desire to returne to the same place, from whence hee came. For all those things, whose possession is no whit pleasing, it is better to injoy them as they are, then to desire their longer stay. For then are they so much the neerer to their end, by how much the farther they are from their beginning. Nor is there any thing in the world more sweet, or more pleasing to him that is truely weary, then his Inne, wherein hee may rest himselfe. So that though youth be a thing very jocund, yet hee that is truly old, doth not desire it. But he indeed that wants reason and true understanding, that man in a manner loves nothing else, but the daies that are past and gone.

MELIBEA. Were it but onely to live, it is good to desire that which I say.

CELEST. As soone (Lady) dies the young Lambe as the old Sheep; they goe both to the shambles together; there is no man so old, but hee may live one yeere more; nor no man so young, but hee may dye to day: so that in this you have little, or no advantage of us.

MELIBEA. Thou hast scar'd mee with thy words; thy reasons put mee in remembrance that I have seene thee heeretofore. Tell me (mother) art not thou Celestina, that dwelt in Tanners Row, neere the River?

CELEST. Even the very same.

MELIBEA. By my fay you are an old woman. Well, I see it is a true saying; That daies goe not away in vaine. Now (never trust mee) I did not know you; neither should I, had it not been for that slash over your face; then were you fayre, now wonderfully altered.

LUCRECIA. She changed? Hi, hi, hi! the divell she is: shee was faire when she met with him (saving your reverence) that scotcht her over the nose.

MELIBEA. What saist thou foole? Speake, what is 't thou saist? What laugh'st thou at?

86

CALISTO AND MELIBEA

LUCRECIA. As though I did not know Mother Celestina?

CELEST. Madame, Take you hold on time, that it slip not from you. As for my complexion, that will never change: have you not read what they say, The day will come, when thou shalt not know thy selfe in a glasse? Though I am now growne gray before my time, and seeme double the yeeres I am of; of foure daughters which my mother had, my selfe was the youngest. And therefore, I am sure, I am not so old as you take me to be.

MELIBEA. Friend Celestina, I am very glad both to see and know thee; and I have taken great pleasure in thy discourse. Heere, take your money and fare-well; for thou lookest (poore soule) as if thou hadst eaten nothing all this day.

CELEST. O more then mortall image! O precious pearle! How truely have you guest! O! with what a grace doe thy words come from thee! I am ravisht hearing thee speake. But yet it is not only eating, that maintaineth a man or woman; especially me, who use to be fasting a whole, nay, two dayes together, in soliciting other folkes businesses. For, I intend no other thing, my whole life is nothing else; but to doe good offices for the good, and (if occasion serve) to dye for them. And it was evermore my fashion, rather to seeke trouble to my selfe by serving of others, then to please and content my selfe. Wherefore, if you will give me leave, I will tell you the necessitated cause of my comming, which is another manner of matter then any you have yet heard; and such as we were all undone, if I should returne in vaine, and you not know it.

MELIBEA. Acquaint mee (mother) with all your necessities and wants, and if I can helpe you in them, or doe you any good, I shall willingly doe it, as well out of our old acquaintance, as out of neighbour-hood, which in good and honest mindes, is a sufficient bond to tye them thereunto.

CELESTINA. My wants, Madame? My necessities doe you meane? Nay, others (as I told you) not mine. For mine owne, I passe at home with my selfe in mine owne house, without letting the whole Country to know them:

87

Eating when I may, and drinking when I can get it. For, for all my poverty, I never wanted a penny to buy me bread, nor a Quarte, that is, the eighth parte of sixe pence to send for wine, no, not in all this time of my widdow-hood. For before, I never tooke thought for any, but had alwaies a good Vessell still in my house. And when one was empty, another was full. I never went to bed, but I did first eat a toast well steept in wine, and two dozen of draughts, sipping still the wine after every sop, for feare of the Mother, wherwith I was then wont to be troubled. But now, that I husband all things my self, and am at mine own finding, I am faine to fetch my wine in a little poore Jarre, which will scarce hold a pottle. And sometimes in punishment of my sinnes (which Crosse I am willing to beare) I am forced to goe sixe times a day with these my silver hayres about my shoulders, to fill and fetch my wine my selfe at the Taverne. Nor would I by my good will dye, till I see my selfe have a good Rundlet or Terse of mine owne within mine owne doores. For (on my life) there is no provision in the world like unto it. For as the saying is; It is bread and wine, not the young man that is spruce and fine, that makes us rid the way, and travell with mettle; yet let me tell you, that where the good man is missing, all other good is wanting. For ill does the spindle moove, when the beard does not wagge above. And this I thought good to tell you by the way, upon those speeches which I used concerning others, and not mine owne necessities.

MELIBEA. Aske what thou wilt, be it either for thy selfe, or any body else, whom it pleaseth thee.

CELEST. My most gracious and courteous Lady, descended of high and noble parentage; your sweet words, and cheerefull gesture, accompanyed with that kinde and free proffer, which you are pleased to make to this poore old woman, gives boldnesse to my tongue, to speak what my heart even longeth to utter. I come lately from one, whom I left sicke to the death, who onely with one word, which should come from your noble mouth, and intrusted in this my bosome to carry it hence with me, I verily assure my selfe, it will save his life, so great is the devotion which he

CALISTO AND MELIBEA

beares to your gentle disposition, and the comfort he would
receive by this so great a kindenesse.

MELIBEA. Good woman ; I understand thee not, unlesse
thou deliver thy mind unto me in plaine termes. On the
one side thou dost anger me, and provoke mee to displeasure;
on the other thou doest move and stirre me to compassion.
Neither know I how to returne thee a convenient answer,
because I have not fully comprehended thy meaning; I
should thinke my selfe happy, if my words might carry that
force, as to save the life of any man, though never so meane.
For to doe good, is to bee like unto the Deity. Besides, he
that doth a benefit, receives it when it is done to a person
that desires it. And he that can cure one that is sicke, not
doing it, is guilty of his death ; and therefore give not over
thy petition, but proceed and feare nothing.

CELEST. All feare fled (faire Lady) in beholding your
beauty. For, I cannot be perswaded, that Nature did paint
in vaine one face fairer then another, more inrich't with
grace and favour, more fashionable, and more beautifull
then another ; were it not to make them Magazines of vertue,
mansions of mercy, houses of compassion and pitie, Ministers
of her blessings, and dispensers of those good gifts and graces,
which in her bounty shee hath bestowed upon them, and
upon your selfe in a more plentifull manner. Besides,
sithence wee are all mortall, and borne to dye ; as also, that
it is most certaine, that hee cannot bee said truely to be
borne, who is onely borne for himselfe ; for then should men
be like unto bruite beasts, (if not worse ;) Amongst which,
there are some, that are very pitifull : as your Unicorne, of
whom it is reported, that hee will humble and prostrate
himselfe at the feet of a Virgin. And your dogge, for all
his fiercenesse, and cruelnesse of nature, when hee comes to
bite another, if hee throw himselfe downe at his feet, hee
will let him alone, and doe him no harme ; and this is all
out of pitie. Againe, to come to your birds, and fowles of
the ayre ; your Cocke eateth not any thing, but hee first
calleth his Hens about him, and gives them part of his
feeding. The Pellicane, with her beake breaketh up her
owne brest, that she may give her very bowels and intrals to

M   89 her young ones to eat. The Storkes maintaine their aged parents as long in the nest, as they did give them food, when they were young and unable to helpe themselves. Now, if God and Nature gave such knowledge unto beasts and birds; why should wee that are men, be more cruell one to another? Why give we not part of our graces, and of our persons, to our neighbors? Especially when they are involved and afflicted with secret infirmities, and those such, that where the Medicine is, thence was the cause of the maladie?

MELIBEA. For Gods love, without any more dilating, tell me who is this sicke man, who feeling such great perplexity, hath both his sicknes and his cure, flowing from one, and the selfe-same Fountaine?

CELEST. You can not choose (Lady) but know a young Gentleman in this City, nobly descended, whose name is Calisto.

MELIBEA. Inough, inough; No more (good old woman;) Not a word, not a word more, I would advise you. Is this the sicke patient, for whom thou hast made so many prefaces to come to thy purpose? For what, or whom cam'st thou hither? Cam'st thou to seeke thy death? Know'st thou for whom (thou bearded Impudent) thou hast troden these dangerous steps? What ayles this wicked one, that thou pleadest for him with such passion? He is foole-sicke, is hee not? Is hee in his wits, I trow? What would'st thou have thought, if thou should'st have found me without some suspicion and jealousie of this foole? What a wind-lace hast thou fetcht, with what words hast thou come upon me? I see it is not said in vaine; That the most hurtfull member in a man, or woman, is the tongue. I will have thee burned, thou false Witch, thou enemy to honesty, thou Causeresse of secret errors; Fie upon thee Filth; Lucrecia, out of my sight with her, send her packing; away with her I pray, she makes me ready to swound: ay me, I faint, I dye; she hath not left me one drop of bloud in my body. But I well deserve this, and more, for giving eare to such a paltry huswife as shee is. Beleeve me, were it not, that I regarded mine honour, and that I am unwilling to publish to the world his presumptuous audaciousnesse and boldnesse, I

90

CALISTO AND MELIBEA

would so handle thee (thou accursed Hagge) that thy discourse, and thy life, should have ended both together.

CELEST. In an ill houre came I hither. If my spels
and conjuration faile mee. Goe to, goe to; I wot well
inough to whom I speake. This poore Gentleman, this your
brother, is at the poynt of death, and ready to dye.

MELIBEA. Darest thou yet speake before mee? and
mutter words between thy teeth, for to augment my anger,
and double thy punishment? Wouldst thou have me soyle
mine honour, for to give life to a foole, to a mad man?
Shall I make my selfe sad, to make him merry? Wouldst
thou thrive by my losse? And reape profit by my perdition?
And receive remuneration by my error? Wouldst thou have
me overthrow, and ruine my fathers house and honour, for
to raise that of such an old rotten Bawd as thou art? Dost
thou thinke, I doe not perceive thy drift? That I doe not
track thee step by step? Or that I understand not thy
damnable errand? But I assure thee, the reward that thou
shalt get thereby, shall be no other, save (that I may take
from thee all occasion of farther offending heaven) to give
an end to thy evill dayes. Tell me (Traitor as thou art)
how didst thou dare to proceed so farre with mee?

CELEST. My feare of you (Madame) doth interrupt my
excuse; but my innocency puts new courage into me: your
presence againe disheartens me, in seeing you so angry. But
that which grieves and troubles me most, is, that I receive
displeasure without any reason, and am hardly thought on
without a cause. Give mee leave (good Lady) to make an
end of my speach, and then will you neither blame it, nor
condemne me; then will you see, that I rather seek to doe
good service, then indeavour any dishonest course; and that
I do it more to adde health to the Patient, then to detract
any thing from the fame and worth of the Physician. And
had I thought that your Ladiship would so easily have made
this bad construction out of your late noxious suspicion, your
licence should not have beene sufficient warrant to have
imboldened me to speake any thing, that might concerne
Calisto, or any other man living.

MELIBEA. Let mee heare no more of this mad man,

91

ACTUS
IIII

name not this foole unto mee; this leaper over walls; this Hob-goblin; this night-walker; this phantasticall spirit; long-shanked, like a Stork; in shape and proportion, like a picture in Arras, that is ill-wrought; or an ill-favour'd fellow in an old sute of hangings; Say no more of him, unlesse you would have mee to fall downe dead where I stand. This is hee who saw mee the other day, and beganne to court mee with I know not what extravagant phrases, as if hee had not beene well in his wits, professing himselfe to be a great Gallant. Tell him (good old woman) if hee thinke that I was wholy his, and that he had wonne the field, because it pleased me rather to consent to his folly, then correct his fault, and yeeld to his errand, then chastise his errour; that I was willing rather to let him goe like a foole as hee came, then to publish this his presumptuous enterprize. Moreover, advise him, that the next way to have his sicknesse leave him, is to leave off his loving, and wholy to relinquish his purpose, if he purpose to impart health to himselfe; which if he refuse to doe, tell him from mee, that he never bought words all the daies of his life at a dearer rate. Besides, I would have him know, that no man is overcome, but he that thinks himselfe so to be. So shall I live secure, and he contented. But it is evermore the nature of fooles, to thinke other like themselves. Returne thou with this very answer unto him; for other answer of me shall he none, nor never hope for any: for it is but in vaine to intreat mercy of him, of whom thou canst not have mercy. And for thine owne part, thou maist thanke God, that thou scapest hence scot-free; I have heard inough of you heeretofore, and of all your good qualities, though it was not my hap to know you.

CELESTINA. Troy stood out more stoutly, and held out longer. And many fiercer Dames have I tamed in my dayes; Tush! No storme lasteth long.

MELIBEA. You mine enemy, what say you? Speake out, I pray, that I may heare you. Hast thou any thing to say in thy excuse, whereby thou maist satisfie my anger, and cleare thy selfe of this thy errour and bold attempt?

CELESTINA. Whilest your choler lives, my cause must

92

CALISTO AND MELIBEA

needes dye. And the longer your anger lasteth, the lesse shall my excuse be heard. But wonder not that you should be thus rigorous with mee: For a little heate will serve to set young bloud a boyling.

MELIBEA. Little heate, say you? Indeed thou maist well say little; because thy selfe yet lives, whilst I with griefe indure thy great presumption. What words canst thou demand of me for such a one as he is, that may stand with my good? Answer to my demand, because thou sayst thou hast not yet concluded. And perhaps thou maist pacifie me for that which is past.

CELESTINA. Mary, a certaine Charme, Madame, which (as hee is informed by many of his good friends) your Ladiship hath, which cureth the tooth-ache; as also that same admirable Girdle of yours, which is reported to have beene found and brought from Cumæ the Cave there, and was worne, 'tis thought, by the Sibilla, or Prophetesse of that place; which Girdle they say, hath such a singular and peculiar property and power, with the very tutch to abate and ease any ache or anguish whatsoever. Now this Gentleman I told you of, is exceedingly pained with the tooth-ache, and even at deaths doore with it. And this was the true cause of my comming: But since it was my ill hap to receive so harsh and unpleasing an answer, let him still for me continue in his paine, as a punishment due unto him, for sending so unfortunate a messenger. For since in that muchnesse of your vertue I have found much of your pity wanting; I feare mee, hee would also want water, should he send mee to the Sea to fetch it. And you know (sweet Lady) that the delight of vengeance, and pleasure of revenge endureth but a moment, but that of pity and compassion continueth for ever and ever.

MELIBEA. If this be that thou would'st have, why did'st thou not tell me of it sooner? Why went'st thou about the bush with mee? What needed all those circumstances? Or why did'st thou not deliver it in other words?

CELEST. Because my plaine and simple meaning made me beleeve, that though I should have propos'd it in any other words whatsoever, had they beene worse then they were,

93

yet would you not have suspected any evill in them. For, if I were failing in the fitnesse of my preface, and did not use so due and convenient a preamble as I should have done, it was, because truth needeth no colours. The very compassion that I had of his paine, and the confidence of your magnificency, did choake in my mouth, when I first beganne to speake the expression of the cause. And for that you know (Lady) that sorrow workes turbation, and turbation doth disorder and alter the tongue, which ought alwaies to be ty'de to the braine; for heavens love, lay not the fault on me; and if he hath committed an errour, let not that redound to my hurt; for I am no farther blameable of any fault, then as I am the messenger of the faulty. Breake not the rope where it is weakest. Be not like the Cobweb, which never shewes it's force, but on poore little Flyes. No humane Law condemnes the father for the sonnes offence, nor the sonne for the fathers: nor indeed (Lady) is it any reason, that his presumption should occasion my perdition; though considering his desert, I should not greatly care, that hee should be the delinquent, and my selfe be condemned, since that I have no other Trade to live by, save to serve such as hee is; This is my occupation, this I make my happinesse. Yet withall (Madame) I would have you to conceive, that it was never in my desire to hurt one, to helpe another, though behind my backe, your Ladiship hath perhaps been otherwise informed of mee. But the best is, it is not the vaine breath of the vulgar, that can blast the truth; assuredly I meane nothing in this, but onely plaine and honest dealing. I doe little harme to any; I have as few enemies in this City, as a woman can have; I keepe my word with all men; and what I undertake, I performe as faithfully, as if I had twenty feete, and so many hands.

MELIBEA. I now wonder not, that your Ancients were wont to say; That one onely teacher of Vice, was sufficient to marre a great City. For I have heard such and so many tales of thy false and cunning tricks, that I know not whether I may beleeve, thy errand was for this charme.

CELESTINA. Never let me pray: or if I pray, let me

CALISTO AND MELIBEA

never be heard, if you can draw any other thing from me, though I were to be put to a thousand torments.

MELIBEA. My former late anger will not give mee leave to laugh at thy excuse. For I wot very well, that neither oath nor torment shall make thee to speake the truth. For it is not in thy power to doe it.

CELESTINA. You are my good Lady and Mistresse, you may say what you list, and it is my duty to hold my peace; you must command, and I must obey, but your rough language (I hope) will cost your Ladiship an old petticoate.

MELIBEA. And well hast thou deserv'd it.

CELEST. If I have not gain'd it with my tongue, I hope I have not lost it with my intention.

MELIBEA. Thou dost so confidently plead thy ignorance, that thou makest me almost ready to beleeve thee; yet will I in this thy so doubtfull an excuse, hold my sentence in suspence, and will not dispose of thy demand upon the relish of so light an interpretation. Neither for all this would I have thee to thinke much of it, nor make it any such wonder, that I was so exceedingly moved; For two things did concurre in thy discourse, the least of which was sufficient to make me runne out of my wits. First, in naming this Gentleman unto me, who thus presumed to talke with me: then, that thou shouldst intreat me for him, without any further cause given; which could not but ingender a strong suspition of intention of hurt to my honor. But since all is well meant, and no harme intended, I pardon all that is past; for my heart is now somewhat lightned, sithence it is a pious, and a holy worke, to cure the sick, and helpe the distressed.

CELEST. I, and so sicke (Madame) and so distressed, that did you know it as well as I, you would not judge him the man, which in your anger you have censured him to be. By my fay, the poore Gentleman hath no gall at all, no ill meaning in his heart. Hee is indewed with thousands of graces; for bounty, he is an Alexander; for strength, an Hector; he has the presence of a Prince; hee is faire in his carriage, sweet in his behaviour, and pleasant in his conversation; there is no melancholy, or other bad humour, that

95

raigneth in him ; Nobly descended, as your selfe well knowes ; a great Tilter ; and to see him in his armour, it becomes him so well, that you would take him to be another Saint George. Hercules had not that force and courage as he hath ; His diportment, his person, his feature, his disposition, his agility, and activenesse of body, had neede of another manner of tongue to expresse it, then mine. Take him all together, and for all in all, you shall not finde such another ; and for admired forme, a miracle : and I am verily perswaded, that that faire and gentle Narcissus, who was inamored with his owne proper beauty, when as in a glasse he view'd himselfe, in the water was nothing so faire as he, whom now one poore tooth, with the extremity of its paine, doth so torment, that hee doth nothing but complaine.

MELIBEA. The Age, I pray ; How long hath hee had it ?

CELEST. His age (Madame ?) Mary, I thinke hee is about some three and twenty. For heere stands shee, who saw him borne, and tooke him up from his mothers feet.

MELIBEA. This is not that which I aske thee ; Nor doe I care to know his age. I aske thee how long he hath beene troubled with his tooth-ache ?

CELEST. Some eight daies (Madame) but you would thinke he had had it a yeere, hee is growne so weake with it, and the greatest ease, and best remedy he hath, is, to take his Viall, whereto hee sings so many songs, and in such dolefull notes, that I verily beleeve, they did farre exceed those, which that great Emperor and Musician Hadrian composed concerning the soules departure from the body ; the better to endure without dismayment, his approaching death. For though I have but little skill in musicke, me thinks he makes the Viall, when he plaies thereon, to speake ; and when hee sings thereunto, the birds with a better will listen unto him, then to that Musician of old, which made the trees and stones to move. Had he been borne then, Orpheus had lost his prey. Weigh then with your selfe (Sweet Lady) if such a poore old woman as I am, have not cause to count my selfe happy, if I may give life unto him, to whom the heavens have given so many graces ? Not a woman that sees him, but praiseth Natures workemanship, whose hand did draw so perfect a piece ; and if it bee their hap to talke with him, they are no more mistresses of themselves, but are wholy at his disposing ; and of Commanders, desire to be commanded by him. Wherfore, seeing I have so great reason to doe for him, conceive (good Lady) my purpose to be faire and honest, my courses commendable, and free from suspicion and jealousie.

MELIBEA. O how I am falne out with mine owne impatience ! How angry with my selfe, that hee being ignorant, and thou innocent of any intended ill ; thou hast endured the distemperature of my inraged tongue ! But the great reason I had for it, frees mee from any fault of offence, urged thereunto by thy suspicious speaches : but in requitall of thy sufferance, I will forthwith fulfill thy request, and likewise give thee my Girdle. And because I have not leysure to write the charme, till my mother comes home, if this will not serve the turne, come secretly for it to morrow morning.

LUCRECIA. Now, now, is my Mistresse quite undone. All the world cannot save her ; she will have Celestina come secretly to morrow. I smell a Rat ; there is a Padde in the straw ; I like not this, Come secretly to morrow ; I feare mee, shee will part with something more then words.

MELIBEA. What sai'st thou, Lucrecia ?

LUCRECIA. Mary, I say, Madame, you have worded well. For it is now somewhat late.

MELIBEA. I pray (mother) say nothing to this Gentleman of what hath passed betwixt you and mee, lest he should hold me either cruell, sudden, or dishonest.

LUCRECIA. I did not lye even now ; I see well inough how ill the world goes.

CELEST. Madame, I much marvell you should entertaine any the least doubt of my service. Feare you not ; for I can suffer, and cover any thing : and I well perceive, that your great jealousie and suspicion of mee, made you (as commonly it doth) to interpret my speeches to the worst sense. Well, I will take my leave, and goe hence with this Girdle so merrily, as if I did presently see his heart leaping for joy,

N

that you have graced him with so great a kindnesse; and
I doubt not, but I shall finde him much eased of his
paine.

MELIBEA. I will doe more for your sicke Patient then
this, if need require, in requitall of your great patience.

CELEST. Wee shall need more, and you must doe more
then this, though perhaps you will not so well like of it,
and scarce thanke us for it.

MELIBEA. Mother, what's that thou talkest of thankes?

CELESTINA. Mary I say (Madame) That we both give
you thanks, that wee are both at your service; and rest both
deepely indebted to your Ladiship; and that the paiment
is there most certaine, where the party is most bound to
satisfie.

LUCRECIA. Heere's Cat in the Panne. What Chop-
Logicke have we heere?

CELESTINA. Daughter Lucrecia; Hold thy peace;
Come hither to me. If to morrow I may see thee at my
house, I will give thee such a Lye, as shall make thy haire
as yellow as gold; but tell not your Mistresse of it. Thou
shalt also have a powder of mee to sweeten thy breath,
which is a little of the strongest. There is not any in this
kingdome, that can make it but my selfe. And there is not
any thing in a woman that can be worse then a stinking
breath.

LUCRECIA. A blessing on your aged heart; for I have
more need of this, then of my meate.

CELESTINA. And yet (you foole) you will be talking
and prating against mee. Hold thy peace; for thou know'st
not what need thou maist have of mee. Doe not exasperate
your Mistresse, and make her more angry now, then shee was
before. But let mee goe hence in peace.

MELIBEA. What sai'st thou to her, mother?

CELEST. Nothing (Madame) wee have done already.

MELIBEA. Nay, you must tell me what you said to her;
for I cannot abide, that any body should speake any thing
in my presence, and I not have a part therein. And therefore, without any more adoe, let mee know it.

CELEST. I intreated her to put your Ladiship in minde

98

CALISTO AND MELIBEA

of the Charme, that it might be writ out ready for mee: and that shee should learne of mee to temper her selfe in the time of your anger, putting her in mind of that ancient Adage ; From an angry man, get thee gone but for a while ; but from an enemy, for ever. But you (Madame) had onely a quarell to those words of mine which you suspected, and not any enmity to my person. And say, they had bin such as you conceited them ; yet were they not so bad, as you would have made them to be. For it is every daies experience, to see men pain'd and tormented for women ; and women as much for men. And this, Nature worketh ; and Nature (you know) is crafts master, and works nothing that is ill : So that my demand (you see) was (as my desire was it should be) in it selfe commendable, as having its growth from so good a root. Many the like reasons could I render you, were not prolixity tedious to the hearer, and hurtfull to the speaker.

MELIBEA. Thou hast showne a great deale of temper, as well in saying little, when thou saw'st mee angry, as also in thy great and singular sufferance.

CELESTINA. Madame, I indured your chiding with feare, because I knew you were angry with reason. Besides, a fit of anger is but like a flash of lightning ; which made me the more willing to give way, till your heate were overpast.

MELIBEA. This Gentleman is beholding unto you, whom I recommend to your care.

CELEST. Not so, Madame ; His deserts challenge more at my hands. And if by my intreaties, I have done him any good, I feare me, by my over long-stay, I have done him as much harme. And therefore if your Ladiship will license me, I will haste to see how he does.

MELIBEA. Had'st thou spoke for it sooner, sooner hadst thou beene sped. Goe thy wayes, and a good lucke with thee : for neither thy comming hither hath done mee any good ; nor thy going hence can doe mee any harme ; Thy message being as bootlesse, as thy departure shall be harmelesse.

THE END OF THE FOURTH ACT

99

THE TRAGICK-COMEDY OF

ACTUS V

THE ARGUMENT

ELESTINA *having taken her leave of* Melibea, *trudges along the street mumbling and muttring to her selfe. Being come home, there shee found* Sempronio, *who stai'd expecting her returne. They goe both talking together, till they come to* Calisto's *house. And being espied by* Parmeno, *he tels it his Master, who wills him to open the doore.*

INTERLOCUTORS

Celestina, Sempronio, Parmeno, Calisto.

CELESTINA. O cruell incounter! O daring and discreet attempt! O great and singular sufferance! O how neere had I beene to my death, if my much subtilty and cunning craft had not shifted in time the sailes of my suite! O braving menaces of a gallant Lady! O angry and inraged Damsell! O thou Divell whom I conjured! O how well hast thou kept thy word with me in all that I desired! I am much bound unto thee; so handsomely hast thou appeased this cruell Dame by thy mighty power, and afforded mee so fit a place and opportunity, by reason of her mothers absence, to utter my minde unto her. O thou old Celestina; cheere up thy heart, and thinke with thy selfe; that things are halfe ended, when they are well begunne! O thou oyle of Serpents! O thou delicate white thread; how have you bestirred your selves in my businesse! whose favourable furtherance if I had not found, I would utterly have broken and destroyed all the inchantments which either I have already, or heereafter are to be made; nor would I ever any more have had any beliefe in hearbes, stones, or words. Be merry then (old Stinkard) Frollicke with thy selfe (old wench) for, thou shalt get more by this one suite, then by soldring

100

of fifteene crackt Maidenheads. A pocks upon these long and large playtings in my Petticoates; Fie how they rumple and fold themselves about my legges, hindring my feete from hasting thither, whither I desire my good newes should come. O good fortune, what a friend art thou to the valiant! what a foe to those that are fearefull! Nor by flying doth the Coward flye death. O how many failed of that which I have effected! How many have strucke at, but mist that naile, which my selfe onely have hit on the head! What in so strong and dangerous a straite as this, would these young Graduates in my Art have done? Perhaps have bolted out some foolish word or other to Melibea, whereby they would have lost as much by their prattling, as I have gained by my silence. And therefore it is an old saying; Let him play that hath skill: and that the better Physician is hee that hath experience, then hee that hath learning; For experience, and frequent warnings, make men Artists in their professions; and it must be such an old woman as I am who at every little Channell holds up her coates, and treades the streetes with leysurely steps, that shall prove a Proficient in her trade. O girdle, my pretty girdle, let mee hugge thee a little! O how my heart leaps in looking upon thee! If I live, I will make thee bring her to mee by force, who is so unwilling to come to mee of her owne accord, that I had much adoe to get a good word from her.

SEMP. Either mine eyes are not matches, or that is Celestina. Now the Divell goe with her; how her gowne comes dragging on the ground! how the skirts of her coate trouble her! how her mouth goes! Sure, she is muttring something to her selfe.

CELEST. Why dost thou keepe such a crossing of thy selfe? I beleeve, thou blessest thy selfe to see mee.

SEMP. I will tell thee: why? Rarity (you know) is the mother of admiration; and admiration being conceived in the eyes, entreth straight into the minde: and the minde is inforced againe by the eyes, to discover it selfe by these outward signes. Who did ever see thee walke the streetes before with thy head hanging in thy bosome; with thy eyes

101

ACTUS
V

cast downe to the ground? Who did ever see thee goe thus mumbling of thy words to thy selfe? and to come in such post-haste, as if thou wert going to get a Benefice? so that the rarity and strangenesse thereof, makes those who know thee, to wonder what it should meane? But to let this passe; Tell me of all loves, what good newes thou bringst. Say: Is it a Son, or a Daughter? That is, whether we have sped well or ill? For ever since one of the Clocke I have waited here for you; all which while, I have had no greater or better token of comfort, then that of your long staying.

CELEST. This foolish Rule (my Sonne) is not alwaies true; for had I stayd but one houre longer, I might perhaps have left my nose behind me, and two other noses, had I had them, and my tongue to boot: so that the longer I had stayed, the dearer it would have cost me.

SEMPR. Good mother, as you love mee, goe not hence, till you have told mee all.

CELEST. Sempronio, my friend, neither have I time to stay heere, nor is this a fit place to tell it thee. Come, goe along with mee to Calisto, and thou shalt heare wonders (my Bully.) For by communicating my selfe to many, I should as it were deflowre my Embassage, whose maidenhead I meane to bestow on your Master; for, I will that from mine owne mouth, hee heare what I have done; for though thou shalt have parcell of the profit, I minde to have all the thankes for my labour.

SEMPR. What? Are you at your parcels now? Doe you thinke, Celestina, to put me to my parcels? Tho you shall have your parcell; mary, come up: I tell you plainly, I doe not like this word, that I doe not. And therefore parcell me no more of your parcels.

CELEST. Goe to, you foole; Hold your peace, be it part or parcell, man, thou shalt have what thou wilt thy selfe. Doe but aske, and have; what is mine, is thine: Let us laugh and be merry, and benefit our selves the best that we can: Hang all this trash, this putrified durt, rather then thou and I should fall out about deviding the spoyle; yet must I tell you, (which is no more then your selfe

102

CALISTO AND MELIBEA

knowes) that old folkes have more need then young; Especially you, who live at full table, upon free cost.

SEMPR. There goes more (I wisse) to a mans life, then eating and drinking.

CEL. What, Sonne? A dozen of poynts, a hat, or a stone-bow, to go from house to house shooting at birds, ayming at other birds with your eye, that take their standing in windowes. I meane pretty wenches (you foole) such birds (you mad-cap) as have no wings to flye from you: you know my meaning, Sir; for there is no better Bawd, for them, then a bow: under colour whereof, thou maist enter any house whatsoever, making it thy excuse to seeke after some bird thou shootst at, etc. It is your only delicate tricke you can use. But wo (Sempronio) unto her, who is to uphold and maintaine her credit, and beginnes to grow old, as I now doe.

SEMPR. O cogging old Hagge; O old Bawd, full fill'd with mischiefe; O covetous and greedy Cormorant; O ravenous glutton! I perceive she would as willingly coozen me, as I would my Master; and all to inrich her selfe. But seeing she is so wickedly minded, and cares not who perish, so as shee may thrive, I will marre her market; I will looke to her water heereafter; I will keepe her from fingring any more Crownes; nor will I any longer rent out the gaines unto her, which I make of my Master, but reserve the profits for my selfe: or rather (which is the surer and honester course) seek to save his purse, and play the good husband for him. For he that riseth by lewd and unlawfull meanes, comes tumbling downe faster then hee clambred up. O! how hard a thing is it to know man! True is that vulgar saying, No manner of marchandize, or beast, is halfe so hard to be knowne. Cursed old witch, shee is as false as truth is truth; I thinke the Divell brought mee acquainted with her: it had beene better for mee, to have fled from this venemous Viper, then to put her, as I have done, in my bosome; but it was mine owne fault, I can blame no body but my selfe: and therefore let her gaine what she can gaine, be it by right or wrong, I will keepe my word with her.

CELESTINA. What say'st thou Sempronio? Whom dost

ACTUS
V

thou talke to? Goest thou gnawing of my skirts? What is that thou grumblest at? Why commest thou not forward?

SEMPR. That which I say (mother Celestina) is this; that I doe not marvaile that you are mutable: for therein you doe, but as others have done before you, following that common tracke that many more have trod in: you told mee, you would deferre this businesse, leading my Master along in a fooles paradise; and now thou runn'st head-long without either sence or wit, to tell Calisto of all that hath passed. Know'st thou not, that men esteeme those things most, which are most difficult to be atchieved? And prize them the more, the more hardly they come by them? Besides, Is not every day of his paine, unto us a double gaine?

CELEST. A wise man altreth his purpose, but a foole persevereth in his folly: a new busines requires new counsell; and various accidents, various advice. Nor did I thinke (Son Sempronio) that fortune would have befriended mee, so soone. Besides, it is the part of a discreete messenger to doe that which the time requires; especially, when as the quality of the businesse cannot conceale or admit of dissembled time. And moreover, I know that thy Master (as I have heard) is liberall, and somewhat of a womanish longing; and therefore will give more for one day of good newes, then for a hundred, wherein he is pained. And with his paine, mine will be increased: his in loving, mine in trudging to and fro. For your quicke and speedie pleasures beget alteration; and great alteration doth hinder deliberation. Againe, where will you finde goodnesse, but in that which is good? And noblenesse of blood, but in large and long continued rewards? Peace, you foole, let me alone with him, and you shall see how your old woman will handle him.

SEMPR. Then tell mee what passed concerning that noble Lady. Acquaint mee but with one word of her mouth; for trust mee, I long as much to know her answer, as my Master doth.

CELEST. Peace, you foole; What? Does your complexion change? Does your colour alter? I know by your nose, what porridge you love. You had rather have the

104

CALISTO AND MELIBEA

taste, then sent of this businesse. Come I prythee, let us ACTUS
hye us, for thy Master will be ready to runne mad, if we V
stay over-long

SEM. And I am little better, because you will not stay and tell me.

PARME. Master, Master?

CALISTO. What's the matter, you foole?

PARM. I see Sempronio and Celestina comming towards the house. And at every step they make a stop; and looke where they stand still, there Sempronio, with the point of his sword, makes streakes and lines in the ground. It is some earnest matter sure that they are debating, but what it should be, I cannot devise.

CALISTO. O thou carelesse absurd Asse; Canst thou discry land, and not make to the shoare? See them comming, and not hye thee to open the doore? O thou Supreme Deity: with what come they? What newes doe they bring? whose stay hath beene so long, that I have longed more for their comming, then the end of my remedy. O my sad cares, prepare your selves for that which you are now to heare: for in Celestina's mouth rests either my present ease, or eternall heart-griefe. O that I could fall into a slumber, and passe away this short, this little, little space of time, in a dreame wherein I might see the beginning, and ending of her speech. Now I verily beleeve, that more painefull to a Fellon, is the expecting of that his cruell and capitall sentence, then the Act it selfe, of his certaine and fore-knowne death. O leaden-heeled Parmeno; slower then the Snayle, dead-handed as thou art, dispatch, I say, and unbolt this troublesome doore, that this honourable woman may enter in, in whose tongue lies my life.

CELEST. Dost thou heare him, Sempronio? Your Master is now of another temper; these words are of another tune, then those wee lately heard both of Parmeno, and him, at our first comming hither. The matter I see is well amended; there is never a word I shall tell him, but shall be better to old Celestina, then a new petticoate.

SEMPR. Make at your comming in, as though you did not see Calisto, using some good words as you goe.

O 105

THE TRAGICK-COMEDY OF

CELEST. Peace, Sempronio; Though I have hazarded my life for him, yet Calisto's owne worth, and his, and your joynt intreaties, merit much more then this. And I hope, he will well reward me for my paines, being so franke and Noble a Gentleman as hee is.

THE END OF THE FIFTH ACT

ACTUS VI

THE ARGUMENT

ELESTINA *being entred* Calisto's *house,* Calisto *with great affection and earnestnesse, demandeth of her, what had hapned betwixt her and* Melibea? *While they continue talking together,* Parmeno *hearing* Celestina *speake wholy for her selfe, and her owne private profit, turning himselfe toward* Sempronio, *at every word he gives her a nip, for the which he is reprehended by* Sempronio. *In the end, old* Celestina *discovers to* Calisto *all the whole businesse, and shewes him the Girdle she brought from* Melibea. *And so taking her leave of* Calisto, *shee gets her home to her owne house, taking* Parmeno *along with her.*

INTERLOCUTORS

Calisto, Celestina, Parmeno, Sempronio.

CALISTO. What good newes (mother?) speak (deare mother.)

CELEST. O my good Lord and Master Calisto, How is it? how is it with you? O my new Lover (and not without just cause) of fairest Melibea! How canst thou make this old woman amends, who hath hazarded her life in thy service? What woman was ever driven to such narrow shifts? The very thought whereof, makes my heart to faint, emptying my vitall veynes of all their bloud. I would have given my

106

CALISTO AND MELIBEA

life for lesse then the price of this old tottred Mantle, which you see heere on my backe.

PARME. Thou art all (I see) for thy selfe. That is it thou shoot'st at. Thou art like a Lettice, that growes betwixt two Cole-worts; If thou be let alone, thou wilt over-top them. The next word I look for, is, that she begge a Kirtle for her Mantle : thou art all (I perceive) for thy selfe ; and wilt not aske any thing, whereof others may have part. The old woman will implume him, not leaving him so much as one feather ; how cunningly does shee worke him ! how craftly pitch her nets to catch me and my Master, seeking to make me faithlesse, and him foolish ! Doe but marke her (Sempronio) be still, and give her but the hearing, and you shall see, shee will not demand any money of my Master, because it is divisible.

SEMPRO. Peace, (thou despairefull fellow) lest Calisto kill thee, if he chance to heare thee.

CALISTO. Good mother, either cut off thy discourse, or take thou this sword and kill mee.

PARM. Now, what a Divell ailes he? He shakes and quivers like a fellow that hath had his senses over-toucht with quicke-silver. Looke, hee cannot stand on his legges ; would I could helpe him to his tongue, that I might heare him speake againe: sure, he cannot live long, if this fit continue. Wee shall get well by this his love, shall wee not? Every man his mourning weed, and there's an end.

CELEST. Your sword, Sir. Now I hope not: What? Take your sword and kill you? There's a word indeed to kill my heart. No; let your sword serve to kill your enemies, and such as wish you harme. As for mee, I will give thee life, man, by that good hope, which I have in her, whom thou lovest best.

CALISTO. Good hope, mother?

CELESTINA. I, good hope ; and well may it be called so, since that the gates are set open for my second returne. And shall I tell you? she will sooner receive me in this poore tottred Gowne and Kirtle, then others in their silks, and cloth of gold.

107

THE TRAGICK-COMEDY OF

PARME. Sempronio, sow mee up this mouth; for I can no longer hold. A pocks on her, she hath hedg'd in the Kirtle to her Gowne. Could not one alone have contented her?

SEMPR. You will hold your peace, will you not? By Iove you were best be quiet, or I shall set you hence in a divels name. What? Is there no ho with you? Say she begge her apparell of him, what's that to thee? she does well in it; and I commend her for it, having such need thereof as she has. And thou know'st, Where the Flamin sings, there hath he his offrings; he must have food and rayment.

PAR. True, he hath so; but as his service is, so is his allowance; he sings all the yeere long for it: and this old Jade would in one day, for treading some three steps, cast off all her rugged hayres, and get her a new coate; which is more then she could well doe these fifty yeeres.

SEM. Is this all the good she taught thee? Is all your old acquaintance come to this? Is this all the obligation you owe her for her paines in breeding you up? Sure, she has brought her Hogges to a good market, in bestowing so great kindenesse on so very a Pigge.

PAR. I could be well content, that she should pill and pole, aske and have, shave and cut, but not cut out all the cloth for her own coat.

SEMPR. It is her fault, I must confesse, but other Vice hath shee none, save onely that shee is a little too covetous. But let her alone, and give her leave to provide straw, first, for to thatch her owne walls, and to lay the joyses first of her owne house, then afterwards shall she boord ours; else had it beene better for her shee had never knowne us.

CALISTO. Mother, as you love goodnesse, if you be a good woman, tell mee what was shee doing? How got you into the house? How was she apparelled? On which side of the house did you find her? What countenance did shee shew thee at thy first entrance? How did shee looke on thee?

CELEST. With such a looke and countenance, as your brave fierce buls use towards those that cast sharp darts
108

CALISTO AND MELIBEA

against them, when they come for to be baited : or like your
wilde bores, when they make towards those Mastives which
set upon them.

CALISTO. Be these thy good hopes? These signes of
health? What then are those that are mortall? Why,
death it selfe could not be halfe so deadly. For that would
ease and rid me of this my torment, then which none is
greater, none more grievous.

SEMP. These are my Masters former fires; he renewes
afresh his wonted flames: What a strange kind of man is he?
He hath not the patience to stay to heare that which so
earnestly hee hath desired.

PARMENO. Now Sir; Who talkes now? I must not
speake a word; but did my Master heare you, he would
cudgell your coat, as well as mine.

SEMPR. Some evill fire consume thee : for thou speakest
predjudicially of all; but I offend no man. Let some intolerable mortall disease, or some pestilent plague seaze upon
thee, and consume thee; Thou quarrelsome, contentious,
envious, and accursed Caytiffe; Is this thy friendship, this
the amity thou hast contracted with Celestina and me? Goe
with the Divels name, if this be thy love.

CALISTO. If thou wilt not (thou that art sole Queene,
and soveraigne of my life) that I dye desperate, and that my
soule goe condemned from hence to perpetuall paine (so im-
patient am I of hearing these things) delay mee no longer, but
certifie mee briefely, whether thy glorious demand had a
happy end, or no? As also whether that cruell and sterne
looke of that impious face, whose frownes murder as many as
they are bent against, sorted to a gentle intertaining of thy
suite? For all that I have heard hitherto, are rather tokens
of hate, then of love.

CELESTINA. The greatest glory, which is given to that
secret office of the Bee, which little creature of nature, the
discreeter sort ought to imitate, is, that whatsoever he
toucheth, he converteth it into a better substance, then in it
selfe it was. In like manner hath it so befalne mee, with
those coy and squeamish speeches of Melibea, and all other
her scornefull and disdainefull behaviours; all her sowre

109

looks and words I turned into honey; her anger into milde-
nesse; her fury into gentlenesse; and her running from me,
into running to mee. Tell me, man, What didst thou thinke
Celestina went thither for? What would she make there,
whom you have already rewarded beyond her desert, unlesse
it were to pacifie her fury, to oppose my selfe to all accidents,
to be your shield and buckler in your absence, to receive
upon my mantle all the blowes that were strucke at you, to
endure those revilings, bitter tauntings, and those disdain-
full termes, which, such as she is, usually make show of, when
they are first sued unto for their love. And why forsooth
doe they this? Onely to the end, That what they give, may
the better be estemed; and therefore, they still speake
worst of him, whom they love best; and make a show of
most dislike, where they like most. Which if it should not
be so, there would be no difference between the love of a
common whore, and an honest Damsell that stands upon her
honour; if every one should say yea, as soone as she is asked.
And therefore, when they see a man loves them (though
themselves burne, and fry in the liveliest flames of love) yet
for modesties sake, they will outwardly show a coldnesse of
affection, a sober countenance, a pleasing kinde of strangenesse, a constant minde, a chaste intent, and powre forth
words as sharpe as Vineger, that their owne tongues wonder
at this their great sufferance, making them forcibly to confesse that with their mouthes, whose contrary is contained in
their hearts. But because I would have thee have some ease
of thy sorrowes, and take some repose, whilst I relate at large
unto thee all the words that passed betweene her and mee,
and by what meanes I made my first entrance into Melibea's
house; Know for thy comfort, that the end of her discourse
was very good.

CALISTO. Now (deare mother) that you have given mee
assurance, that I may boldly with comfort expect the
extremest vigour of her answer; say what thou wilt, and I
shall be attentive thereunto. Now my heart is at rest; now
my thoughts are quiet; now my veynes receive and recover
their lost bloud; now have I lost my feare; now doe I finde
some joy; now am I cheerefull. Let us (if it please you) goe

CALISTO AND MELIBEA

up; where, in my chamber you shall report that at full, which I have heard in briefe.

CELESTINA. With all my heart, Sir. Come, let us goe.

PARME. O what starting holes does this foole seeke for to flye from us, that he may, at his pleasure, weepe for joy with Celestina, and discover unto her a thousand secrets of his light, and doting appetite! First, to aske her, I know not how oft of every particular: and then have her answer him to the same, sixe severall times one after another, and never to make an end, but over, and over, and over with it againe, having no body by to tell him how tedious he is; Fie upon him, I am sick to think upon it. Go your wayes (you foole). Get you up with a murraine; but we will not stay long after you.

CALISTO. Marke (mother) how Parmeno goes mumbling to himselfe; see how the slave crosses himselfe, to heare what thou hast brought to passe by thy great diligence! Observe in what a maze he stands! Looke, looke, Celestina; dost thou see what hee is doing? See, and the villaine does not crosse himselfe againe? Come up, up, up; and sit you downe (I pray) whilest I on my knees give eare to thy sweete answer. Say on; And tell mee quickely, by what meanes thou gotst into the house?

CELEST. By selling a parcell of thread which I had; by which trick, I have taken in my daies, more then thirty of as good worth and quality as her selfe, (So it pleased fortune to favour mee in this world) and some better women, I wisse, and of greater rancke, were shee more honorable then shee is.

CALISTO. Greater (mother) perhaps in body, but not in noblenesse of birth, not in state, not in beauty, not in discretion, not in statelinesse, linked with gracefulnesse and merit, not in vertue, nor in speach.

PARME. Now the fooles steele beginnes to strike fire; now his bels beginne to jangle; marke how his clocke goes; it never strikes under twelve; the finger of his dyall point is still upon high noone; all upon the most. Sempronio, tell the clocke, keepe true reckoning, how standst thou gazing

111

like a wide-mouthed driveling foole, hearing his fooleries, and her lies?

SEMPR. O thou venomous-tongued Villaine; thou rayling Rascall; Why shouldst thou alone stop thy eares at that, to which all the world besides is willing to harken? And say they are but tales and fables which shee tels him; yet were it onely but for this, that their discourses are of love, thou oughtst to lend them a willing attention.

CELEST. Noble Calisto, Let thy cares be open to that which I shall tell thee, and thou shalt see what thy good fortune, and my great care have effected for thee. For, when I was about to pitch a price of my thread, and to sell it, Melibea's mother was called away to goe visit a sister of hers, that lay exceeding sicke: and because she could not stay with me her selfe (so necessary was her absence) she left Melibea to conclude the bargaine, and to drive such a price with mee, as shee should thinke fit.

CALISTO. O joy beyond compare! O singular opportunity! O seasonable time! O that I had layne hid underneath thy mantle, that I might have heard her but speake, on whom heaven hath so plentifully powred forth the fulnesse of his graces!

CELESTINA. Under my mantle (noble Sir?) Alacke, poore soule as I am, what would you have done there? Why shee must needes have scene you at least thorow thirty holes, should not fortune give mee a better.

PARM. Well, I will get me gon; I say nothing, Sempronio; heare you all for mee: I will be hang'd, if the foole my Master doe not measure with his thoughts, how many steps there be betweene this and Melibea's house. And if hee not contemplate every kinde of action and gesture shee might use; as how she lookt, how she stood, when shee was bargaining for the thread: All his senses, all the powers and faculties of his soule are wholy taken up, and possest with her: but he will finde in the end, that my counsell would have done him more good, then all the cunning tricks, and coozenages of Celestina.

CALISTO. Whats the matter with you there? I am hearing of a cause, that concernes no lesse then my life; and
112

CALISTO AND MELIBEA

you keepe a tattling and a prattling there (as you still use to doe) to trouble and molest me in my businesse, and provoke me to anger: as you love me, hold your tongues, and you will dye with delight; such pleasure will you take in the repetition of her singular diligence; Goe on (deare mother) what didst thou doe, when thou saw'st thou wast left all alone?

CELEST. O Sir, I was so overjoyed, that whosoever had seene me, might have read in my face the merriment of my heart.

CALISTO. It is so now with mee; But how much more had a man beforehand conceived some such image in his minde? But tell me, wast thou not strucken dumbe with this so sudden and unexpected an accident?

CELEST. No. But rather grew thereby the bolder to utter my minde unto her; it was the thing that I desired; it was even as I would have wisht it: There was nothing could have fell out so pat for me, as to see my selfe all alone with her: then beganne I to open the very bowels and intralls of my heart; then did I deliver my embassage, and told her in what extreme paine you lived, and how that one word of her mouth, proceeding favourably from her, would ease you of your mighty torment. And as one standing in suspence, looking wisely and steadily upon me, somewhat amazed at the strangenesse of my message, hearkning very attentively, till shee might come to know who this should be, that for want of a word of her mouth, liv'd in such great paine, and what manner of man he might be, whom her tongue was able to cure? In naming you unto her, she did cut off my words, and with her hand strooke her selfe a blow on the brest, as one that had heard some strange and fearefull newes; charging mee to cease my prattle, and to get mee out of her sight, unlesse I would her servants should become my Executioners, and make short worke with me in these my old and latter dayes; aggravating my audacious boldnesse; calling mee Witch, Sorceresse, Bawd, old Whore, false Baggage, bearded Miscreant, the Mother of mischiefe; and many other more ignominious names, wherewithall they feare children. And when she had ended with her Buggebeares, shee beganne to fall into often swownings and trances,

P

113

ACTUS
VI

making many strange gestures, full of feare and amazement, all her senses being troubled, her bloud boyling within her, throwing her selfe this way and that way, bearing in a strange kind of manner the members of her body one against another ; and then in a strong and violent fashion, being wounded with that golden shaft, which at the very voycing of your name, had struck her to the heart, writhing and winding her body, her hands and fingers being clinched one within another, like one struggling and striving for life, that you would have thought, shee would have rent them asunder, hurling and rowling her eyes on every side, striking the hard ground with her tender feete. Now, I all this while, stood me still in a corner, like a cloth that is shrunke in the wetting, as close as I could for my life, not saying so much as any one word unto her ; yet glad with all my heart, to see her in this cruell and pittifull taking. And the more her throwes and pangs were, the more did I laugh in my sleeve at it ; because I thereby knew, her yeelding would be the sooner, and her fall the neerer : yet must I tell you, that whil'st her anger did foame out it's froth, I did not suffer my thoughts to be idle, nor give them leave to runne a wooll-gathering, but recollecting my selfe, and calling my wits about mee, I tooke hold on Times fore-top, and found a salve to heale that hurt, which my selfe had made.

CALISTO. Deare mother, thou hast told me that, which whil'st I was hearing thee, I had fore-casted in mine owne judgement, I did still dreame it would come to this ; but I doe not see how thou couldst light upon a fit excuse, that might serve the turne, and prove good inough to cover and colour the suspition of thy demand ; though I know, that art exceeding wise, and in all that thou dost (to my seeming) more then a woman. Sithence, that as thou didst prognosticate her answer, so didst thou in time provide thee of thy reply. What could that Tuscane Champion (so much famoused thorowout all Italy) have done more ? Whose renowne (hadst thou then beene living) had beene quite lost ; who three daies before shee dyed, divined of the death of her old husband, and her two sonnes. Now doe I beleeve that, which is so commonly spoken ; that a woman is

114

CALISTO AND MELIBEA

never to seeke for an answer; and though it be the weaker
Sexe, yet is their wit more quicke and nimble then that of
men.

CELEST. Say you me so, Sir? Well, let it be so then;
I told her, your torment was the tooth-ache; and that the
word which I craved of her, was a kinde of Prayer, or
Charme, which she knew to be very good, and of great power
against that paine.

CALISTO. O admirable craft! O rare woman in thy
arte! O cunning creature! O speedy remedy! O discreet
deliverer of a message! What humane understanding is
able to reach unto so high a meanes of helpe? And I verily
perswade my selfe, that if our age might purchase those
yeeres past, wherein Æneas and Dido liv'd, Venus would not
have taken so much paines, for to attract the love of Elisa
to his sonne, causing Cupid to assume the forme of Ascanius,
the better to deceive her: but would (to make short worke
of the businesse) have made choyce of thee to mediate the
matter: and therefore doe I hold my death happily imployed,
since that I have put it into such hands, and I shall evermore
be of this minde, that if my desire obtaine not it's wished
effect, yet know I not what could be done more, according
to nature, for my good and welfare. What thinke you now
my Masters? What can yee imagine more? Was there
ever the like woman borne in this world? Had shee ever
her fellow?

CELESTINA. Sir, doe not stop me in the course of my
speach. Give me leave to goe on, for night drawes on. And
you know, Hee that does ill, hateth the light.

CALISTO. How? What's that? No, by no meanes;
For heavens sake, doe not offer it, you shall have Torches,
you shall have Pages, any of my servants, make choyce of
whom you will to accompany you home.

PARME. O yes, in any case! I pray take care of her;
because she is young and handsome, and may chance to bee
ravisht by the way. Sempronio, thou shalt goe with her,
because shee is afraide of the Crickets, which chirpe in the
darke, as shee goes home to her house.

CALISTO. Sonne Parmeno, what's that thou said'st?

115

THE TRAGICK-COMEDY OF

PARME. I said, Sir, it were meete, that I and Sempronio should accompany her home; For it is very darke.

CALISTO. It is well said, Parmeno: you shall by and by; proceed, I pray, in your discourse; and tell mee what farther past betweene you. What answer made she for the Charme?

CELEST. Mary, that with all her heart I should have it.

CALISTO. With all her heart? O Ioue! How gracious and how great a gift!

CELEST. Nay, this is not all; I craved more then this.

CALISTO. What, my honest old woman?

CELEST. Her Girdle, which continually she wore about her, affirming that it was very good for the allaying of your paine; because of some Supereminent Influence from the Sibilla Cumana.

CALISTO. But what said shee?

CELESTINA. Give mee *Albricias*; reward me for my good newes, and I will tell you all.

CALISTO. Take my whole house, and all that is in it, on condition you tell me; or else besides what thou wilt.

CELESTINA. Give but this poore old woman a Mantle, and I will give that into thy hand, which she weares about her.

CALISTO. What dost thou talke of a Mantle? Tut, a Kirtle, a Petticoate, any thing, all that I have.

CELEST. It is a Mantle that I need; that alone shall content me; Inlarge not therefore your liberality; Let not any suspectfull doubt interpose it selfe in my demand; My request is reasonable, and you know, it is a common saying; To offer much to him, that asketh but a little, is a kinde of deniall.

CALISTO. Runne, Parmeno, call hither my Taylour, and let him presently cut her out a Mantle and a Kirtle of that fine pure cloth, which hee tooke to cottening.

PARM. So, so; all for the old woman; because like the Bee, she comes home laden with lyes, as hee does with hony; as for mee, I may goe worke out my heart, and goe hang my selfe when I have done; whilest shee with a pockes must have every day change of rayment.

CALISTO. Now the Divell goe with him, with what an

116

CALISTO AND MELIBEA

ill will does he goe? I thinke there is not any man living so ill serv'd as I am; maintaining men that devise nothing but mischiefe, murmurers, grudgers of my good, repiners of my prosperity, and enemies to my happinesse. Thou Villaine, what goest thou mumbling to thy selfe? Thou envious wretch, what is that thou sayst? for I understand thee not. Doe as I command you, you were best, and that quickely too. Get you gone with a murraine, and vexe mee no more, for I have griefe inough already to bring me to my grave. There will as much of the piece be left (which remnant you may take for your selfe) as will serve to make you a Jerkin.

PARM. I say nothing, Sir, but that it is too late to have the Taylour for to come to night.

CAL. And have not I told you, that I would have you not divine of things aforehand, but to doe as I bid you? Let it alone then till to morrow; and for you (mother) let me intreat you out of your love to me, to have patience untill then; for that is not auferred, which is but deferred. Now I pray let me see that glorious girdle, which was held so worthy to ingirt so goodly a body, that these my eyes, together with the rest of my senses, may enjoy so great a happinesse, since that together, they have all of them beene a little affected with passion. My afflicted heart shall also rejoyce therein, which hath not had one minute of delight, since it first knew that Lady. All my senses have beene wounded by her, all of them have brought whole basket-fulls of trouble to my heart. Every one of them hath vexed and tormented it all they could; the eyes, in seeing her; the eares, in hearing her; and the hands in touching her.

CELEST. Ha; What's that? Have you toucht her with your hands? you make me startle.

CALISTO. Dreaming of her, I say in my sleepe.

CELESTINA. O! in your dreames; that's another matter.

CALISTO. In my dreames have I seene her so oft, night, by night, that I feare mee, that will happen unto mee, which befell Alcibiades, who dream'd that he saw himselfe in-wrapped in his mistresses mantle, and was the next day murdred, and found none to remove him from forth the

117

common street, no, nor any to cover him, save onely shee who did spread her Mantle over him. Though I, for my part, be it alive, or dead, would any way bee glad to see my selfe clothed with any thing that is hers.

CELESTINA. You have punishment, Sir, inough already; for when others take their rest in their beds, thou preparest thy selfe to suffer thy next daies torment. Be of good courage, Sir. Plucke up your heart: after a Tempest, followes a Calme ; affoord thy desire some time ; take unto thee this Girdle : for if death prevent mee not, I will deliver the Owner thereof into thy hands.

CALISTO. O new guest ! O happy girdle ! which hast had such power and worth in thee, as to hedge in that body, and be its inclosure, which my selfe am not worthy to serve. O yee knots of my passion, it is you that have intangled my desires ; Tell me, if thou wert present at that uncomfortable answer of fairest she, whom thou servest, and I adore. And yet the more I torment my selfe for her sake, mourning and lamenting night and day, the lesse it availes mee, and the lesse it profits me.

CELEST. It is an old Proverbe ; He that labours least, often-times gets most. But I will make thee by thy labouring, to obtaine that which by being negligent, thou shouldst never atchieve. For Zamora was not wonne in an houre ; yet did not her besiegers for all this despaire. No more was Rome built in one day : nor Troy ruined in a yeere.

CALISTO. O unfortunate that I am ! For Citties are incircled, and walled in with stones ; and stones by stones are easily over-throwne. But this my deare Lady hath her heart invironed with steele ; there is no mettle that can prevaile against her ; no shot of that force, as to make a breach : and should Ladders bee reared to scale the walls, shee hath eyes which let flye darts of repulsion, and a tongue which dischargeth whole volleis of reproches, if you once approach, forcing you to stand farther off, and so inaccessible is her Castle, that you cannot come neere it by halfe a league.

CELEST. No more, good Sir, no more ; bridle your passion ; for the stout courage, and hardy boldnesse of one

118

CALISTO AND MELIBEA

man, did get Troy. Doubt not then, but one woman may
worke upon another, and at last win her unto thee; thou
hast little frequented my house, thou art ignorant of my
courses, thou know'st not what I can doe.

CALISTO. Say, Mother, what thou wilt, and I will
beleeve thee, since thou hast brought me so great a Jewell,
as is this. O thou glorie of my soule, and incircler of so
incomparable a creature; I behold thee, and yet beleeve it
not. O girdle, girdle, thou lovely lace! Wast thou mine
enemy too? Tell me the truth; if thou wert, I forgive thee:
For it is proper unto good men, to forgive; but I doe not
beleeve it. For hadst thou likewise beene my foe, thou
wouldst not have come so soone to my hands, unlesse thou
hadst come to disblame and excuse thy doings. I conjure
thee, that thou answer mee truely, by the vertue of that
great power, which thy Lady hath over mee.

CELESTINA. Cease (good Sir) this vaine and idle humour;
for my eares are tyred with attention, and the Girdle almost
worne out with your often handling.

CALISTO. O wretch that I am! farre better had it beene
for mee, had the heavens made me so happy, that thou hadst
beene made and woven of these mine owne armes, and not of
silke, as now thou art, that they might have daily rejoyced
in clasping and inclosing with due reverence those members,
which thou without sense or feeling, not knowing what it is
to injoy so great a glory, holdest still in strict imbracements.
O what secrets shouldst thou then have scene of that so
excellent an image!

CELEST. Thou shalt see more, and injoy more, in a
more ample and better manner, if thou lose it not by talking
as thou dost.

CALISTO. Peace (good mother,) give mee leave a little;
for this, and I, well understand one another. O my eyes
call to your remembrance, how that yee were the cause of my
ill; and the very doore, thorow which my heart was wounded;
and that he is seene to doe the hurt, who doth give the cause
of the harme. Call to your remembrance, I say, that yee
are debtours to my well-fare. Looke here upon your medicine,
which is come home to your owne house to cure you.

119

THE TRAGICK-COMEDY OF

SEMPR. Sir, it is not your rejoycing in this girdle, that can make you to enjoy Melibea.

CALISTO. How like a foole thou pratest, without cyther wit or reason? Thou disturber of my delight, what meanest thou by this?

SEMPR. Mary, that by talking, and babbling so much as you doe, you kill both your selfe, and those which heare you; and so by consequence, overthrow both thy life and understanding; either of which to want, is sufficient to leave you darkling, and say good night to the world. Cut off your discourse therefore, and listen unto Celestina, and heare what she will say unto thee.

CALISTO. Mother, are my words troublesome unto you? or is this fellow drunke?

CELEST. Howbeit they be not, yet should you not talke thus as you doe; but rather give an end to these your long complaints. Use a girdle like a girdle, that you may know to make a difference of your words, when you come to Melibea's presence; let not your tongue equall the apparell, with the person; making no distinction betwixt her, and her garments.

CALISTO. O my much honoured Matrone, my mother, my comfortresse! Let mee glad my selfe a little with this messenger of my glory. O my tongue! Why doest thou hinder thy selfe in entertaining any other discourse? leaving off to adore that present Excellency, which, peradventure, thou shalt never see in thy power? O yee my hands! With what presumption, with what slender reverence doe you touch that Treacle, which must cure my wound? Now that poyson cannot hurt mee, wherewith that cruell shot of Cupid hath it's sharpe point deepely indipped. For now I am safe, since that shee who gave mee my wound, gives mee also my medicine. O deare Celestina! Thou that art the delight of all old Dames, the joy of young wenches, the case of the afflicted, and comfort of such comfortlesse wretches as my selfe; do not punish me more with feare of thee, then I am already punished with shame of my selfe; suffer me to let loose the reines of my contemplation; give me leave to goe foorth into the streets with this jewell, that they who

120

CALISTO AND MELIBEA

see mee, may know, that there is not any man more happy then my selfe.

SEMPR. Doe not infistulate your wound, by clapping on it still more and more desire. Sir, it is not this string, nor this girdle alone, wherein your remedy must depend.

CALISTO. I know it well, yet have I not the power to abstaine from adoring so great a relique! so rich a gift!

CELEST. That's a gift, which is given gratis; but you know that shee did this for to ease your tooth-ache; and to cloze up your wounds; and not for any respect or love, which shee beares to you: But if I live, shee shall turne the leafe, ere I leave her.

CALISTO. But the Charme you talkt of?

CELESTINA. Shee hath not given it mee yet.

CALISTO. And what was the cause why shee did not?

CELESTINA. The shortnesse of time; and therefore will'd mee that if your paine did not decrease, I should returne to her againe to morrow.

CALISTO. Decrease? Then shall my paine decrease, when I see a decrease of her cruelty.

CELEST. Sir, content your selfe with that, which hath hitherto bin said and done; shee is already bound, I have shew'd you, how (as farreforth as shee is able) shee will be ready to yeeld you any helpe for this infirmitie of yours, which I shall crave at her hands. And tell me, I pray, if this bee not well for the first bowt. Well, I will now get me home; and in any case, have a care, that if you chance to morrow to walke abroad, that you goe muzzled about the cheeks with a cloth, that she seeing you so bound about the chaps, may not accuse mee of petitioning a false-hood.

CALISTO. Nay, to doe you service, I will not sticke to clap on foure double clothes: but of all loves tell me, past there any thing more betweene you? For I dye out of longing, for to heare the words which flow from so sweet a mouth. How didst thou dare, not knowing her, be so bold, to shew thy selfe so familiar, both in thy entrance, and thy demand?

CELEST. Not knowing her? They were my neighbours for foure yeeres together; I dealt with them; I conversed

Q   121 with them; I talked with them; and laught together with them day and night. O! how merry wee have beene! Her mother, why she knowes me better then her owne hands: and Melibea too, though now shee bee growne so tall, so great, so courteous, and discreete a Lady.

PARMENO. Sempronio, a word with you in your eare.

SEMPRONIO. Say on: What's the matter?

PARMENO. Mary this: Celestina's attention gives matter to our Master to inlarge his discourse; give her a touch on the toe; or make some signe to her that shee may be gone, and not waite thus, as shee doth upon his answers. For, there is no man, bee hee never so much a foole, that speakes much, when hee is all alone.

CALISTO. Didst thou say Melibea was courteous? I thinke it was but in a mocke. Was her like ever borne into the world? Did God ever create a better, or more perfect body? Can the like proportion be painted by any pensill? Is she not that Paragon of beautie, from whence all eyes may copy forth a true patterne of unimitable excellence? If Hellen were now alive, for whom so great a slaughter was made of Greekes and Trojanes, or faire Polixena, both of them would have done their reverence to this Lady, for whom I languish. If she had been present in that contention for the Apple with the three Goddesses, the name of contention had never been questioned: For without any contradiction, they would all of them have yeelded, and joyntly have given their consent, that Melibea should have borne it from them: so that it should rather have been called the Apple of concord, then of discord. Besides, as many women as are now borne, and doe know her, curse themselves and their fortune; complaining of heaven, because it did not remember them, when it made her, consuming as well their bodies as their lives with envy, being ready to eat their owne flesh for very anger, still augmenting martyrdomes to themselves, thinking to equall that perfection by arte, which Nature had bestowed upon her without any labour. They pill, and dis-haire their eye-browes with nippers, with playsters of Pitch or Barme, and other the like instruments: They seeke after Wall-wort, and the like hearbs, roots, sprigs, and flowres to make Lyes,

122

CALISTO AND MELIBEA

wherewithall to bring their haire to the colour of hers, spoyl-
ing and martyring their faces, clothing them with divers
colourings, glissenings, paintings, unctions, oyntments, strong
waters, white and red pargetings, which, to avoide prolixity,
I repeate not. Now judge then, whether shee whom Nature
hath so richly beautified, be worthy the love and service of
so meane a man as my selfe?

CELEST. Sempronio, I understand your meaning; but
give him leave to runne on; for he will fall anon from
his Asse, and then his journey will be at an end: you
shall see, he will come by and by to a full poynt, and so
conclude.

CALISTO. In her, Nature, as in a glasse did wholy behold
her selfe; that she might make her most absolutely perfect;
for those graces, which she had diffused unto divers, she had
joyntly united them in her, and over-viewed this her worke
with so curious an eye, that nothing might be added to make
it fairer. To the end that they might know, who had the
happinesse to see her, the worthinesse and excellency of her
Painter : only a little faire Fountaine-water with a combe
of yvorie, is sufficient (without any other slibber-slabbers)
to make her surpasse all other of her Sexe, in beauty and
courtesie. These are her weapons; with these she kils and
over-comes; and with these hath she bound mee in so hard
and strong a chaine, that I must for ever remaine her
prisoner.

CELESTINA. Sir, put a period to your words, trouble
your selfe no more; for this chaine which shackles thee, is
not so strong, but my file is as sharpe to cut it in sunder,
which I will doe for thee, that thou mayst be at liberty.
And therfore give me now licence to take my leave of you;
For it growes very late; and let me have the girdle along
with me. For you know, I must needs use it.

CALISTO. O disconsolate that I am! my misfortunes
still pursue me; for with thee, or with this girdle, or with
both, I would willingly have beene accompanied all this darke
and tedious night. But because there is no perfect happinesse
in this our painefull and unhappy life; let solitarinesse
wholy possesse my soule, and cares be my continuall com-

123

panions. What ho? Where be these men? Why Parmeno, I say!

PARMENO. Heere, Sir.

CALISTO. Accompany this Matrone home to her house; and as much pleasure and joy goe with her, as sorrow and woe doth stay with me.

CELEST. Sir, fare you well. To morrow I shall make my returne, and visit you againe; not doubting but my gowne and her answer shall meete heere together; for now time doth not serve. And in the interim, let me intreate you to be patient. Settle your thoughts upon some other things, and doe not so much as once thinke upon her.

CALISTO. Not thinke upon her? It is impossible. Nay, it were prophane to forget her, for whom my life onely pleaseth mee.

THE END OF THE SIXTH ACT

ACTUS VII

THE ARGUMENT

ELESTINA *talkes with* Parmeno, *inducing him to concord, and amitie with* Sempronio; Parmeno *puts her in mind of the promise she made him, for the having of* Arcusa, *whom he exceedingly loved. They goe to* Arcusa's *house, where that night* Parmeno *remained.* Celestina *hies her home, to her owne house; and knocking at the doore,* Elicia *opens it unto her, blaming her for her tarrying so long.*

INTERLOCUTORS

Celestina, Parmeno, Arcusa, Elicia.

CELESTINA. Parmeno, my sonne; since we last talkt together, I have not had any fit opportunitie to expresse unto thee the infinitenesse of that love which I beare unto

124

CALISTO AND MELIBEA

thee, and as all the world can well witnesse for mee, how well I have spoken of thee in thy absence. Every mans eare hath beene filled with the good reports I have made of thee. The reason thereof I need not to repeate; for I ever held thee to be my sonne, at least, by adoption; and therefore thought thou wouldst have shew'd thy selfe more naturall and loving towards me. But in stead thereof, thou gav'st me bad payment, even to my face; crossing, whatsoever I said; thinking ill of all that I spake; whispering and murmuring against me in the presence of Calisto. I was well perswaded, that after thou hadst once yeelded to my good counsell, that you would not have turned your heele, and kickt against me as you did, nor have falne off from your promise. But notwithstanding all this, I perceive some old relique yet still remaining of thy former folly. And so speaking rather to satisfie thine owne humor, then that thou canst render any reason for it; thou dost hinder thy selfe of profit, to give thy tongue contentment. Heare me (my sonne) if thou hast not heard me already. Looke, I say, and consider with thy selfe, that I am old, and well strucken in yeeres; and good counsell only lodgeth with the elder sort, it being proper to youth, to follow pleasure and delight. But my hope is, that of this thy errour, thy youth onely is in fault: and I trust that you will beare your selfe better towards mee heereafter, and that you will alter your ill purpose, together with your tender yeeres; For as it is in the Proverbe: Our customes suffer change, together with our hayres; and wee vary our disposition, as we vary our yeeres. I speake this (my sonne) because as we grow in age, so grow we in experience; new things daily offring themselves to our view: for youth lookes no farther then to things present, occupying his eie only in that he sees set before him; but riper yeeres omit neither things present, things past, nor things to come. And sonne Parmeno, if you would but bethink your selfe of the love I have heeretofore borne you, I know it cannot escape your knowledge, that the first nights lodging that you tooke, when you were a stranger, and came newly to this City, was in my house. But you young men care not for us that are old; but governe your

125

selves according to the savour and relish of your owne
palates; you never think that you have, or shall have need
of us: you never thinke upon sicknesse; you never think,
that this flowre of your youth shall fade. But doe you
heare me, (my friend) and marke what I say unto you;
That in such cases of necessitie, as these, an old woman,
(bee shee well experienced) is a good helpe, a comforter, a
friend, a mother; nay, more then a mother: A good Inne,
to give ease and rest to a sound man; and a good Hospitall
for to cure a sicke man; a good Purse in time of need; a
good Chest, to keepe money in prosperitie; a good Fire in
winter, invironed with spits of good rost-meat; a good
Shade in summer, and a good Taverne to eate and drinke
in. Now my pretty little foole, what sai'st thou to all this?
What dost thou thinke of it? I know, thou art by this
time ashamed of that which thou hast spoken to day; thou
can'st not say B to a Battle-doore; thou art strucke so
dumbe, and so dead: and therefore I will presse thee no
further, nor crave any more at thy hands, then that which
friendship craves of thee, which is, Looke upon Sempronio;
next under heaven, my selfe have made him a man; I could
wish you would live and love together as brothers and
friends: for being in league with him, thou shalt live in
the favor and love of thy Master, and in good repute with
all the world: for Sempronio, I tell thee, is well belov'd, hee
is diligent, a good Courtier, a proper servant, a fellow of a
good fashion, and one that is willing to imbrace thy friendship, which will turne to both your profits, if you will but
hand-fast your affections each to other. Besides, you
know, that you must love, if you will be beloved. Trowtes
cannot bee taken with drie breeches. And if the Cat will
have fish, she must wet her foote. Nor does Sempronio owe
this of right unto thee; nor is hee bound to love thee, unlesse thou exchange love for love: it is meere simplicitie, not
to be willing to love, and yet looke to be beloved of others.
And as great folly, to repay friendship with hatred.

PARM. Mother, I confesse my second fault; and craving
pardon for what is past, I offer my selfe to be ordred by
you in all my future proceedings. But yet me thinkes

126

:CALISTO AND MELIBEA

it is impossible, that I should hold friendship with Sempronio; hee is frappish, and I cannot beare; he is chollericke, and I can carrie no coles. How then is it possible to make a true contract betwixt two such contrary natures?

CELEST. But you were not wont to be thus froward.

PARM. In good fay (mother) you say true. But the more I grow in yeeres, the lesse I grow in patience; Tush, I have forgotten that lesson, as if I had never knowne what it meant; I am (I confesse) [not] the man I was, nor is Sempronio himselfe; neyther can hee, nor will hee stead mee in any thing. I never yet tasted any the least kindnesse from him.

CELEST. A sure friend is knowne in a doubtfull matter; and in adversity is his faith proved. Then comes he neerest unto him, when hee is farthest from comfort; and with greater desire doth hee then visit his house, when as prosperous fortune hath forsaken it. What shall I say unto thee, Sonne, of the vertues of a good and fast friend? There is nothing more to bee beloved; nothing more rare: he refuseth no burden. You two are equalls, and paritie of persons, similitude of manners, and simpathy of hearts are the maine props that up-hold friendship. Take heed (my sonne;) for if thou hast any thing, it is safely kept for thee. Be thou wise to gaine more; for this is gain'd already to your hands. Your father, O what paines tooke hee for it! But I may not put it into your hands, till you lead a more reposed life, and come to a more compleate and full age.

PARM. Mother, what do you call a reposed life?

CELEST. Mary sonne, to live of your selfe. Not to goe thorow other mens houses, nor to set thy foote under another mans table: which thou shalt still bee inforced to doe, unlesse thou learne to make profit of thy service; for out of very pitty to see thee goe thus totred and torne, not having a ragge almost to hang on thy breeche, did I beg that mantle which thou saw'st, of Calisto, not so much for the mantles sake, as for that there being a Taylor belonging to the house, and thou before being without a Jerkin, hee might bestow it upon thee. So that I speake not for mine

THE TRAGICK-COMEDY OF

owne profit, (as I heard you say) but for thy good. For, if you rely onely upon the ordinary wages of these Gallants, it is such, that what you get by it after tenne yeeres service, you may put it in your eye and never see the worse. Injoy thy youth, good daies, good nights, good meate, and good drinke; when thou mai'st have these things, lose them not; Let that be lost that will be lost. Doe not thou mourne for the wealth which was left thy Master (for that will but shorten thy daies) sithence wee can injoy it no longer then wee live. O Sonne Parmeno, (and well may I call thee sonne, since I had the breeding of thee so long a time) follow my counsell, seeing it proceeds out of pure love, and an earnest desire, to see thee grow up in honour. O! how happy should I be, might I but see thee and Sempronio agree; see you two friends, and sworne brothers in every thing, that yee may come to my poore house to be merrie, and to see mee now and then, and to take your pleasure each of you with his Wench!

PARME. His Wench, mother?

CELEST. I, his Wench; and a young one too: As for old flesh, my selfe am old enough, and such a wench as Sempronio would be glad of with all his heart, with t'one halfe of that regard and affection which I shew to thee. What I speake, comes from my intralls, and the verie bowels of mee.

PARMENO. Mother, you shall not be deceived in mee.

CELEST. And if I should, the matter is not great; For what I doe, I do for charitie, and for that I see thee here alone in a strange Land, and for the respect which I beare unto those bones of her, who recommended thee unto me. When you are more man, you will thinke of all this, and come to a truer knowledge of things, and then thou wilt say, that old Celestina gave me good counsell.

PARME. I know that as well now, though I am but young, as if I were elder: and howbeit I spake against you to day, it was not because I thought that to be ill spoken which you said; but because I saw, when I told my Master the truth, and advised him for the best, he ill intreated mee, and therefore henceforth let us shake hands, and use him

128

CALISTO AND MELIBEA

accordingly; doe what thou wilt unto him, I will hold my peace; for I have already too much offended, in not crediting thee in this businesse concerning him.

CELEST. In this and all other, thou shalt not onely trip, but fall, as long as thou shalt not take my counsell with thee, which comes from thy true and faithfull friend.

PARMENO. Now, I blesse the time wherein I served thee: counting those daies happy, under which thou bredst mee up of a childe, since old age brings with it such store of fruite.

CELESTINA. Sonne, no more. For mine eyes already runne over, and my teares beginne to breake over those bankes, which should bound them in. O! had I in all this world, but such another friend? Such another companion? Such a comfortresse in my troubles? Such an easer, and lightner of my hearts heavinesse? Who did supply my wants? Who knew my secrets? To whom did I discover my heart? Who was all my happinesse, and quietnesse, but thy mother? She was neerer and dearer unto me, then my gossip, or mine owne sister. O! how well-favored was she, and cheerefull of countenance? How lustie? How quicke? How neate? How portly and majesticall in her gate? How stout and manly? Why, shee would goe you at midnight without or paine, or feare, from Church-yard, to Church-yard, seeking for implements appertaining to our Trade, as if it had been day. Nor did she omit either Christians, Moores, or Jewes, whose Graves and Sepulchres she did not visit. By day she would watch them, and by night shee would dig them out; taking such things as should serve her turne. So that she tooke as great pleasure in darknesse of the night, as thou dost comfort in the brightnesse of the day. She would usually say; that the night was the sinfull mans cloak, that did hide and cover all his rogueries, that they might not be scene, though perhaps she had not the like [in] dexteritie and skill in all the rest of those tricks that appertained to her Trade: yet one thing shall I tell thee, because thou shall see what a mother thou hast lost, though I was about to keepe it in; but it makes no matter, it shall out to thee. She did pull out seven teeth out of a fellowes head that was hang'd, with a

R   129 paire of Pincers, such as you pull out stubbed haires withall; whil'st I did pull off his shooes. She was excellent at a Circle, and would enter it farre better then my selfe, and with greater boldnes, though I also was very famous for it in those dayes, more I wisse, then I am now; who have together with her, lost almost my cunning. What shall I say more unto thee, but that the very Divels themselves did live in feare of her? Shee did hold them in horrour, and dread, making them to tremble and quake, when shee beganne to exercise her exorcismes, her spels, her incantations, her charmes, her conjurations, and other words of most horrisonous roaring, and most hideous noyse. Shee was as well knowne to them all, as the begger knowes his dish; or as thy selfe in thine owne house. One Divell comming tumbling in upon the necke of another, as fast, as it pleased her to call them up, and not one of them durst tell her a lye; such power had shee to binde them: so that ever since shee dy'd, I could never attaine to the truth of any thing.

PARMENO. May this woman no better thrive, then shee pleaseth mee with those her wordy prayses.

CELEST. What sai'st thou, my honest Parmeno? My sonne, nay, more then my sonne.

PARM. I say, How should it come to passe, that my mother should have this advantage of you, being the words which shee and you spake, were both one?

CELEST. How? Make you this so great a wonder? Know you not, the Proverbe tels us: That there is a great deale of difference betwixt Peter and Peter? Trust mee truely, wee cannot all be alike in all. Wee cannot all of us attaine to those good gifts and graces of my deceased Gossip. And have not you your selfe seene amongst your Artizans some good, and some others better then they? So likewise was it betwixt mee and your mother. Shee was the onely woman in our Arte, she had not her fellow: and for such a one was she of all the world both knowne and sought after, as well of Cavalleroes, as marryed men, old men, young men, and children, besides, Maides and Damsels, who did as earnestly pray for her life, as for that of their owne fathers and mothers. Shee had to doe with all manner of persons;

130

CALISTO AND MELIBEA

shee talked with all sorts of people. If wee walked the
streetes, as many as we met, they were all of them her God-
sonnes. For her chiefest profession for some sixteene yeares
together, was to play the Mid-wife : so that albeit thou
knew'st not these secrets, because thou wast then but young,
now it is fit that thou should'st know them, sithence that
she is dead, and thou growne up to be a man.

PARM. Tell mee, mother : When the Justice sent
Officers to apprehend you, at which time I was then in
your house, was there any great acquaintance betweene
you ?

CELEST. Any great acquaintance ? You are disposed to
jest. Our cases were both alike ; they tooke us both alike ;
they accused us both alike ; and they did punish us both
alike, which (if I be not deceived) was the first punishment
that ever we had. But thou wast a little one then. I
wonder how thou shouldst remember it ; For, it is a thing of
all other, the most forgotten, that hath hapned in this Citie ;
so many, and so dayly in this world are those new occurrents,
which obliterate the old. If you goe but out into the market-
place, you shall every day see, *Peque y Pague* ; the Peccant
and his punishment.

PARMENO. It is true, but the worser part of wickednesse, is the perseverance therein.

CELEST. How deadly the foole bites ! Hee hath hit mee
home, and prickt me to the quick ; I will therefore be now
Tom-tell-troth. And assure thy selfe, sithence thou hast
galled me, I will wring thee till I make thee winch and fling ;
I will tickle thee on the right veyne.

PARME. What say you mother ?

CELEST. Mary I say, sonne, that besides this, your
mother was taken foure severall times, shee her selfe alone :
and once shee was accused for a Witch ; For shee was found
one night by the watch, with certaine little candles in her
hand, gathering I know not what earth in a crosse way ; for
which shee stood halfe a day in the open market-place upon
a Scaffold, with a high paper Hat, like the coffin of a Suger-
loafe, painted full of Divels, whereon her fault was written
(being brought thither, riding thorow the streetes upon an

131

THE TRAGICK-COMEDY OF

Asse, as the fashion is in the punishment of Bawds and Witches.) Yet all this was nothing; for men must suffer something in this wicked world, for to up-hold their lives, and their honours. And marke, I pray, what small reckoning they made of it, because of her great wisdome and discretion. For shee would not for all this, give over her old occupation; and from that day forward followed it more earnestly, then shee did before, and with happier proofe. This I thought good to tell you, to crosse that opinion of yours, touching perseverance in that, wherein we have once already erred; for all that shee did, did so well become her, and such a grace had she with her, that upon my conscience, howbeit she stood thus disgracefully upon the Scaffold, every one might perceive, that shee cared not a button for those that stood beneath, staring and gazing upon her; such was her behaviour and carriage at that instant: looke they might their fill, but I warrant you, she was not a farthing in debt, no not to the proudest of them all; wherein, I thought fit to instance, to shew thereby unto you; that they, who have any thing in them as shee had, and are wise, and of worth, fall farre more easily and sooner into errour, then any other. Doe but weigh and consider with your selfe, what a manner of man Virgil was; how wise in all kinde of knowledge; and yet I am sure you have heard, how in a wicker basket hee was hung out from a Towre, all Rome looking upon him; yet for all this, was hee neither the lesse honoured, neyther lost he the name of Virgil.

PARM. That is true which you say; but it was not injoyned by the Justice.

CELEST. Peace, you foole, thou art ignorant what a sinister and course kinde of Justice was used, and rigorously executed upon thy mother, to the most extremity, which, as all men confesse, is a meere injury. And the rather, because it was commonly spoken of all men, that wrongfully, and against all right and reason, by suborning of false witnesses, and cruell torments, they inforced her to confesse that, which in realitie of truth was not. But because shee was a woman of a great spirit, and good courage, and her heart had beene accustomed to endure, shee made matters lighter then they

132

CALISTO AND MELIBEA

were; And of all this, shee reckoned not a Pinne: for a thousand times have I heard her say; If I broke my legge, it was all for my good; for this made mee better knowne then I was before. And certainely so shee was, and the more noted and respected, nay, and thrived the better by it, both she and I, and the more plentifull our harvest and incomes of customers of the best, and wee loved and lived merrily together to her last. And be but thou unto me, as she was; that is to say, a true and faithfull friend; and withall, indeavour thy selfe to be good, since thou hast so good a patterne to follow. And for that which thy father left thee, thou hast it safely kept for thee.

PARM. Let us now leave talking of the dead, and of patrimonies, and let us parley of our present businesses, which concernes us more then to draw things past unto our remembrance. If you be well remembred, it is not long since that you promised me, I should have Areusa, when as I told you at my Masters house, that I was ready to dye for love; so fervent is my affection towards her.

CELEST. If I did promise thee, I have not forgot it; nor would I you should thinke, that I have lost my memory with my yeeres. For I have thrice already, and better, given her the checke, concerning this businesse, in thy absence; but now I thinke the matter is growne to some ripenesse. Let us walke towards her house; for now, doe what shee can, shee shall not avoyde the Mate. For this is the least thing of a thousand, that I will undertake to doe for thee.

PARM. I was quite out of hope ever to have her; for I could never come to any conclusion with her, no, not to finde so much favour, as but to speake with her, or to have but a word with her. And as it is in the proverbe: In love it is an ill signe, to see his Mistresse flye, and turne the face. And this did much dis-hearten mee in my suite.

CELEST. I marvaile not much at thy discouragement, considering I was then a stranger unto thee; at least, not so well acquainted with thee as now I am: and that thy selfe did not then know, (as now thou dost), that thou mai'st command her, who is the Doctresse of this Arte; but now thou shalt see, what favour thou shalt finde for my sake;

what power I have over these wenches; how much I can prevaile with them; and what wonders I can worke in matters
of love: but hush, tread softly; Loe, heeres the doore, let
us enter in with still and quiet steps, that the neighbours
may not heare us. Stay, and attend mee heere at the staires
foote, whil'st I goe up and see what I shall be able to doe
with her, concerning the businesse wee talkt of; and it may
be, wee shall worke more with her, then either thou or I did
ever dreame of.

AREUSA. Who's there? Who is that, that at this time
of night comes up into my chamber?

CELESTINA. One, I assure you, that meanes you no ill;
one that never treads step, but shee thinkes on thy profit;
one that is more mindfull of thee, then of her selfe; one
that loves thee as her life, though I am now growne old.

AREUSA. Now the Divell take this old Trot! what
newes with you, that you come thus stealing like a Ghost,
and at so late an houre? How thinke you (Gentlewoman)
is this a faire houre to come to ones chamber? I was even
putting off my clothes to goe to bed.

CELESTINA. What? To bed with the Hen, daughter?
So soone to roost? Fye for shame; Is this the way to thrive?
Thinke you ever to be rich, if you goe to bed so timely?
Come, walke a turne or two, and talke with mee a little; let
others bewaile their wants, not thou. Herbs feed them that
gather them. Who but would, if hee could, leade such a
life?

AREUSA. How cold it is! I will go put on my clothes
againe: beshrew me if I am not cold at my very heart.

CELESTINA. Nay, by my fay shall you not; but if you
will goe into your bed, doe; and so shall wee talke more conveniently together.

AREUSA. Yes indeed, I have neede so to doe; for I have
felt my selfe very ill all this day; so that necessity, rather
then lazinesse, hath made me thus early to take my sheetes,
in stead of my petticoat, to wrap about me.

CELEST. Sit not up, I pray any longer, but get you to
bed, and cover your selfe well with clothes, and sinke lower
in, so shall you be the sooner warme. O! how like a Syren

134

CALISTO AND MELIBEA

doest thou looke! How faire, how beautifull! O! how sweetely every thing smells about thee, when thou heavest and turnest thy selfe in thy bed! I assure you, every thing is in very good order : how well have I alwaies beene pleased with all thy things, and thy doings! You will not thinke, how this neatnesse, this handsomenesse of yours in your lodging doth delight me ; to see every thing so trimme and tricksie about you ; I promise you, I am even proud of it. O! how fresh dost thou looke! What sheets! What quilts be here! What pillowes! O! how white they be! Let me not live, if every thing heere doth not like me wonderfull well : My Pearle, my Jewell of gold, see whether I love you or no, that I come to visit you at this time of night! Let my eye take its fill in beholding of thee; it does me much good to touch thee, and to looke upon thee.

AREUSA. Nay (good mother) leave, doe not touch me; pray you doe not, it doth but increase my paine.

CELEST. What paine (Sweet heart?) Tell me (pretty Ducke.) Come, come, you doe but jest, I am sure.

AREUSA. Jest? Let mee never taste of joy, if I jest with you ; it is scarce foure houres since, that every minute I was ready to dye with paine of the Mother, which rising in my brest, swell'd up to my throate, and was ready to stifle me; that I still lookt when I should leave the world ; and therefore am not so gamesome and wanton as you thinke I am : now I have little mind of that.

CELEST. Goe to, give mee leave a little to touch you ; and I will try what I can doe. For I know something of this evill, which every one calls the Mother, and the passion thereunto belonging.

AREUSA. Lay your hand higher up towards my stomacke.

CELEST. Alack (poore heart) how I pitty thee : that one so plump, so faire, so cleare, so fresh, so fragrant, so delicate, so dainty a creature, that art indeede the very abstract of beauty, the most admired modell for complexion, feature, comelinesse, and rarest composure ; every Limme, every Lineament carrying such an extraordinary lustre and ornament by reflection from thee. I say, How doe I pitty thee, that any ache, sicknesse, or infirmity should dare to

135

scaze, or presume to usurp over such a Peerelesse Potent, a commanding Power, as thy imperious unparaleld beauty! But I dare say, it is not so, nor so; No no, your disease is selfe-conceited, and the pride of your good parts, this puffs you and makes you slight and contemne all. Goe to, goe to, (daughter) you are to blame if it be so, and I tell you, it is a shame for you, that it is, not to impart these good graces and blessings, which heaven hath bestowed upon you, to as many as wish you well; For they were not given you in vaine, that you should let them wither, and lose the flowre of your youth under sixe linings of Woollen, and Linnen; have a care, that you be not covetous of that, which cost you but little; doe not, like a Miser, hoord up your beauty; make not a hidden treasure of it, sithence in it's owne nature it is as communicable, and as commonly currant as money from man to man. Be not the Mastive in the garden, nor the Dog in the manger: and since thou canst not take any pleasure in thy selfe, let others take their pleasure; and do not think thou wast borne for nothing: for when thou wast borne, man was borne: and when man was borne, woman was borne; nothing in all this wide world was created superfluous, nor which Nature did not provide for with very good consonancy, and well suiting with reason. But thinke on the contrary, That it is a fault to vexe and torment men, when it is in thy power to give them remedy.

AREUSA. Tush, mother, these are but words, and profit mee nothing; give me something for my evill, and leave your jesting.

CELEST. In this so common a griefe, all of us, (the more misfortune ours) are in a manner Physicians to our selves; that which I have seene practised on others, and that which I found good in my selfe, I shall plainely deliver unto you: but as the states of our bodies are divers, and the qualities differing; so are the medicines also divers, and the operations different. Every strong sent is good: as Penny-royall, Rue, Wormewood, smoake of Partridge feathers, of Rosemary, and of the Soles of old shooes, and of Muske-roses, of Incense, of strong perfumes, received kindly, fully, and greedily, doth worke much good; much slaketh and

136

easeth the paine, and by little and little returnes the Mother to it's proper place. But there is another thing that passeth all these, and that I ever found to be better then any one, or all of them put together; but what it is, I will not tell you, because you make your selfe such a piece of nicenesse.

AREUSA. As you love me, (good mother) tell me : see'st thou mee thus payned, and concealest thou thy selfe ?

CELEST. Goe to, goe to, you understand me well enough ; doe not make your selfe more foole then you are.

AREUSA. Well, well, well; now trust mee no more, if I understood thee. But what is it thou wouldst have mee to doe ? you know that my friend went yesterday with his Captaine to the wars ; would you have me to wrong him ?

CELESTINA. O! take heed, great wrong, I promise you.

AREUSA. Yes indeed, for hee supplies all my wants ; hee will see I shall lacke nothing ; hee holds mee honest ; hee does love mee, and uses mee with that respect, as if I were his Lady and Mistresse.

CELEST. Suppose all this to be true, be it in the best sort it may be, yet what of all this? This retirednesse is no cure for your disease ; you must be free and communicable, for I must tell you, there are griefes and pangs cannot easily be posted off, and dispossessed, and some not to be removed but by being a mother, (you know my meaning ;) and such is your disease, and you can never recover it, but by living sole and simple (as you now doe) without company.

AREUSA. It is but my ill hap, and a curse laid upon mee by my parents, else had I not beene put to prove all this misery and paine, which now I feele. But to let this passe, because it is late, tell mee I pray, what winde drove you hither ?

CELEST. You know already what I have said unto you concerning Parmeno ; who complaines himselfe unto me, that you refuse to see him ; that you will not vouchsafe him so much as a looke : what should be the reason, I know not, unlesse because you know, that I wish him well, and make account of him, as of my sonne. I have a better care of your matters, and regard your friends in a kinder fashion. Not a neighbour that dwels neere you, but she is welcome

S

137

unto me, and my heart rejoyceth as often as I see them, and all because they converse with thee, and keepe thee company.

AREUSA. It is true (Aunt) that you say; and I acknowledge my beholdingnesse.

CELEST. I know not whether you doe or no: Dost thou heare me (girle?) I must beleeve workes; for words are winde, and are sold every where for nothing; but love is never pay'd, but with pure love: and works with works. Thou know'st the alliance betweene thee and Elicia, whom Sempronio keepes in my house. Parmeno and hee are fellowes and companions, they both serve the Gentleman you wot of; and by whom you may gaine great good, and grace unto your selfe. Doe not therefore deny him that, the granting whereof will cost thee so little; you are kinsewomen, and they companions: see, how pat all things fall! farre better then we our selves could have wished; and to tell you truly, I have brought him along with mee: how say you? Shall I call him up?

AREUSA. Now, heavens forbid. Fye; What did you meane? Ay me; I feare mee, hee hath heard every word.

CELEST. No: for hee stayes beneath; I will call to him to come up; for my sake shew him good countenance; take notice of him; speake kindly unto him; entertaine him friendly; and if you thinke fit, let him injoy you, and you him; and both one another; for though he gayne much, I am sure, you shall lose nothing by the bargaine.

AREUSA. Mother, I am not ignorant, that as well these, as all other your former speeches unto me, have ever beene directed to my good and benefit: but how is it possible, that I should doe this, that you would now have mee? For you know to whom I am bound to give an account, as already you have heard; and if hee know I play false, he will kill me. My neighbours, they are envious and malicious, and they will straight-way acquaint him therewith. And say, that no great ill should befall me, save only the losing of his love; it will be more then I shall gaine, by giving contentment to him, for whom you intreate, or rather command mee.

CELEST. For this feare of yours, my selfe have already provided: for wee entred in very softly.

138

CALISTO AND MELIBEA

AREUSA. Nay, I doe not speake for this night, but for many other that are to come. Tush, were it but for one night, I would not care.

CELESTINA. What? Is this your fashion? Is this the manner of your carriage? And you use these niceties, you shall never have a house with a double roome, but live like a begger all the daies of your life. What? are you afraide of our Sweet-heart now he is absent? What would you then doe, were he now in Towne? It hath ever beene my ill fortune, to give counsell unto fooles, such as cannot see their owne good ; say what I will, they will erre ; still stand in their owne light. But I doe not much wonder at it ; For though the world be wide, yet there are but few wise in it. Great is the largenesse of the earth, but small the number of those that have experience. Ha, daughter! Did you but see your cousins wisedome, or but know what benefit my breeding, and counsell hath brought her, how cunning, how witty, and what a Mistresse in her arte ; you would be of another minde ; say what I will unto her, shee patiently indures my reprehensions, shee hearkens to my advice, and does all what I will have her doe ; shee will sometimes boast, that shee hath at one time had one in bed with her ; another wayting at the doore ; and a third sighing for her within the house ; and yet hath given good satisfaction to them all. And art thou afraide, who hast but two to deale withall ; Can one cock fill all thy Cisternes? One conduit-pipe water all thy Court? If this be your diet, you may chance to rise a hungred, you shall have no meate left against another time ; I will not rent your fragments ; I cannot live upon scraps ; One could never please mee ; I could never place all my affection upon one ; two can doe more then one ; they give more, and they have more to give. It goes hard (Daughter) with that Mouse, that hath but one hole to trust to ; for if that be stopt, shee hath no meanes to hide her selfe from the Cat : he that hath but one eye, you see in what danger he goes? One sole Act maketh not a Habit. It is a rare, and strange thing to see a Partridge flye single ; to feed alwaies upon one dish, brings a loathing to the stomacke ; one Swallow makes not a Summer ; one witnesse alone is of no

139

validitie in Law. Hee that hath but one suite of clothes, and shee that hath but one gowne to her backe, quickly weares them out. What would you doe (daughter) with this number of one? Many more inconveniences can I tell thee of this single soale number (if one may be a number.) If you be wise, be never without two; for it is a laudable and commendable company, as you may see it in your selfe; who hath two eares, two feet, and two hands; two sheets upon one bed; and two smockes wherewith to shift you; and the more you have, the better it is for you; for still, (as it is in the Proverbe) The more Moores, the better market; and honour without profit, is no other but as a Ring upon the finger. And because one Sacke cannot hold them both, apply your selfe to your profit. Sonne Parmeno, come up.

AREUSA. O let him not come up if you love mee: the pockes be my death, if I am not ready to swound, to thinke on't; I know not what to doe for very shame. Nay fie, mother, what meane you to call him up? you know that I have no acquaintance with him; I never exchang'd a word with him, in all my life; Fye, how I am ashamed!

CELEST. I am here with thee (wench;) I, who will stand betwixt him and thee; I will quit thee of this shame, and will cover thee close, and speake for you both: For hee is as bashfull as you for your life.

PARME. Gentlewoman, heavens preserve this gracious presence of yours.

AREUSA. You are welcome, gentle Sir.

CELEST. Come hither you Asse, whither goe you now, to sit moping downe in a corner? Come, come, be not so shamefast, for it was the bashfull man whom the Divell brought to Court; for hee was sure, he should get nothing there; hearken both of you, what I shall now say unto you: You, my friend Parmeno, know already what I promist you: and you (daughter) what I intreated at your hands. Laying aside therefore the difficultie, in drawing thee to grant that which I desired, few words I conceive to be best, because the time will not permit mee to be long. He for his part hath hitherto liv'd in great paine and griefe for your sake: and therefore you seeing his torment, I know you will not kill

CALISTO AND MELIBEA

him: and I likewise know, that your selfe liketh so well of
him, that it shall not be amisse, that he stay with you heere
this night in the house.

AREUSA. For my mayden-heads sake (mother) let it
not be so, pray doe not command it me.

PARME. Mother, as you love my life, as you love goodnesse, let me not goe hence, untill we be well agreed: for
shee hath wounded me with her eyes, to death, and I must
dye through love, unlesse you helpe me; offer her all that
which my father left with you for me; tell her, I will give her
all that I have besides, doe you heare? Tell her, that me
thinks, she will not vouchsafe to looke upon me.

AREUSA. What doth this Gentleman whisper in your
eare? Thinks he that I will not performe ought of your
request?

CELEST. No, daughter, no such matter; he saies that he
is very glad of your good love and friendship, because you
are so honest, and so worthy; and that any benefit shall
light well, that shall fall upon you. Come hither (Modesty)
Come hither you bashfull foole.

AREUSA. He will not be so uncivill, as to enter into
another bodies ground without leave, especially, when it lies
in severall.

CELEST. So uncivill? Doe you stand upon leave?
Would you have him stand with cap in hand, and say, I
pray shall I? Will you give me leave forsooth? And I
know not what fiddle-come-faddles? Well, I will stay no
longer with you: and I will passe my word, that you shall
rise to morrow painelesse.

AREUSA. Nay fye, good Sir, for modesties sake, I
beseech you let me alone: content yourself, I pray. I pray
let be. If not for my sake, yet looke backe upon those gray
haires of that reverend old Dame, which stands by you, and
forbeare for her sake. Get you gone, I say, for I am none
of those you take mee to be, I am none of your common
hackneyes, that hire out their bodies for money. Would I
might never stirre, if I doe not get mee out of the house, if
you doe but touch so much as a cloth about me.

CELEST. Why, how now Areusa, what's the matter with

141

ACTUS
VII

you? Whence comes this strangenesse? Whence this coy-nesse of yours? This nicenesse? Why (Daughter) doe you thinke that I know not what this meanes? Did I never see a man and woman together before? And that I know not all their tricks and devices? What they say, and what they doe? I am sorry to heare that I doe. Besides, I must tell you, I was once as wanton as you are now, and thought my penny as good silver as yours: and many a friend I had that came unto mee: yet did I never in all my life exclude either old man, or old woman out of my company, or that ever I refused their counsell, were it publike or private. By my little honesty, I had rather thou hadst given mee a boxe on the eare, then to heare what I heare. You make of me, as if I had been borne but yesterday. O! how cunning for-sooth, how close you be? for to make your selfe seeme honest, you would make mee a foole. I must be a kinde of Ignoramus, without shame, secrecie, and experience. Yee would discredit mee in my Trade, for to winne your selfe credit in your owne. But the best is, betwixt Pirate and Pirate, there is nothing to be got but blowes and empty barrels. And well I wot, that I speake farre better of thee, behinde thy backe, then thou canst thinke of thy selfe before me.

AREUSA. Mother, if I have offended, pardon me, for I had rather give contentment to you, then to my selfe. I would not anger you for a world.

CELESTINA. No, I am not angry, I doe but tell you this against another time, that you may beware you doe so no more. And so good night, for I will be gone, I will get mee away alone by my selfe.

AREUSA. Good night, Aunt.

PARM. Mother, will you that I waite upon you? Shall I accompany you home?

CELEST. No mary shall you not; that were but to strip one, and cloath another; or againe, it needs not, for I am old, and therefore feare not to be forced in the streets. I am past all danger of ravishing.

ELICIA. The dogge barkes. The old Witch comes hobbling home.

CALISTO AND MELIBEA

CELEST. Tha, tha, tha.

ELICIA. Who is there? who knockes at doore?

CELEST. Daughter, Come downe, and open the doore.

ELICIA. Is this a time to come in? You are disposed still to be out thus a nights. To what end (I trow) walke you thus late? What a long time (mother) have you beene away? What doe you meane by it? You can never finde the way home, when you are once abroad: but it is your old wont, you cannot leave it; and so as you may pleasure one, you care not and you leave a hundred discontented: you have been sought after to day, by the father of her that was betrothed, which you brought from the Prebendary upon Easter day, whom he is purposed to marry within these three dayes, and you must needs helpe her, according as you promised, that her husband may not finde her virginity crackt.

CELEST. Daughter, I remember no such matter. For whom is it that you speake?

ELICIA. Remember no such matter? Sure, you have forgot your selfe. O! what a weake memory have you? Why, your selfe told mee of it, when you tooke her hence; and that you had renewed her maidenhead seven times at the least.

CELEST. Daughter, make it not so strange, that I should forget. For hee that scattereth his memory into many parts, can keepe it stedfast in no part. But tell me, Will he not returne againe?

ELICIA. See whether hee will returne or no? He hath given you a bracelet of Gold, as a pledge for your paines: and will hee not then returne againe?

CELEST. O! was't hee that brought the bracelet? Now I know whome you meane. Why did you not prepare things in a readinesse, and beganne to doe something against I came home? For in such things you should practise your selfe when I am absent, and trye whether you can doe that by your selfe, which you so often have seene mee doe; otherwise, you are like to live all your lifetime like a beast, without either arte, or in-come: and then when you grow to

143

my yeeres, you will too late lament your present lazinesse; for an idle, and lazy youth brings with it a repentfull, and a painfull old age. I tooke a better course I wisse, when your Grandmother shew'd mee her cunning: for, in the compasse of one yeere, I grew more skilfull then her selfe.

ELICIA. No marvell; for many times, (as it is in the Proverbe) a good Scholler goes beyond his Master; and it is all in the will and desire of him that is to learne; for no Science can be well imployed on him, who hath not a good minde and affection thereunto. But I had as liefe dye, as goe about it. I am sicke (mee thinkes) when I set my selfe to it; and you are never well, but when you are at it.

CELEST. You may say what you like. But beleeve me, you will dye a begger for this. What? doe you thinke to live alwaies under my wing? Thinke you never to goe from my elbow?

ELICIA. Pray let us leave off this melancholy talke; now is now; and then is then. When time serves, we will follow your counsell; but now let us take our pleasure, while we may. As long as we have meat for to day, let us not thinke on to morrow: Let to morrow care for it selfe; as well dies he that gathers much, as hee that lives but poorely; the Master, as the servant; he that is of a Noble Linage, as he that is of a meaner stocke: and thou with thy arte, as well as I without it; we are not to live for ever: and therefore let us laugh and be merry, for few are they that come to see old age; and they who doe see it, seldome dye of hunger. I desire nothing in this world, but meate, drinke, and clothing, and a part in pleasure. And though rich men have better meanes to attaine to this glory, then he that hath but little; yet there is not one of them that is contented, not one that saies to himselfe, I have enough. There is not one of them, with whom I would exchange my pleasures for their riches. But let us leave other mens thoughts and cares to themselves; and let us go sleepe, for it is time; and a good sound sleepe without feare, wil fat me more, and doe me more good, then all the Treasure and wealth of Venice.

THE END OF THE SEVENTH ACT

CALISTO AND MELIBEA

ACTUS VIII

THE ARGUMENT

HE *day appeares;* Parmeno *departs, and takes his leave of* Areusa, *and goes to his Master* Calisto. *He findes* Sempronio *at the doore; they enter into amitie; goe joyntly to* Calisto's *chamber; they finde him talking with himselfe; being risen, hee goes to Church.*

INTERLOCUTORS

Parmeno, Areusa, Calisto, Sempronio.

PARMENO. It is day. O what a spight is this? Whence is it, that it is so light in the chamber?

AREUSA. What doe you talke of day? Sleepe, Sir, and take your rest; for it is but even now, since we lay down. I have scarce shut mine eyes yet, and would you have it to be day? I pray you open the window by you, the window there by your beds head, and you shall then see whether it be so or no?

PARM. Gentlewoman, I am in the right; it is day: I see it is day: I am not deceived. No, no; I knew it was broad day, when I saw the light come thorow the chinks of the doore. O what a Villaine am I! Into how great a fault am I falne with my Master! I am worthy of much punishment. O how farre daies is it!

AREUSA. Farre daies?

PARME. I, farre daies; very farre daies.

AREUSA. Never trust mee; Alas, I am not eased of my Mother yet. It paines me still; I know not what should be the reason of it.

PARMENO. Deare love, what wouldst thou have mee to doe?

AREUSA. That wee talke a little on the matter concerning my indisposition.

PARME. What should we talke (Love) any more? if

that which hath been said already be not sufficient, excuse that in me, which is more necessary; for it is now almost high noone: and if I stay any longer, I shall not be welcome to my Master. To morrow is a new day, and then I will come to see you againe; and as often afterwards as you please: and therefore was one day made after another, because that which could not be performed in one day, might bee done in another: as also, because wee should see one another the oftener. In the meane while, let me intreate you to doe mee the favour, that you will come and dine with us to day at Celestina's house.

AREUSA. With all my heart; and I thanke you too. Fare-well, good lucke be with you. I pray pull the doore after you.

PAR. And fare you well too. O singular pleasure! O singular joy! What man lives there this day, that can say he is more fortunate then I am? Can any man be more happy? any more successefull then my selfe, that I should enjoy so excellent a gift? so curious a creature? and no sooner aske then have? Beleeve me, if my heart could brooke this old womans treasons, I could creepe upon my knees to doe her a kindnesse. How shall I bee able to requite her? O heavens! To whom shall I impart this my joy? To whom shall I discover so great a secret? To whom shall I discover some part of my glorie? It is true that the old woman told mee; That of no prosperitie, the possession can be good without company; and that pleasure not communicated, is no pleasure. O! who can have so true a feeling of this my happinesse, as my selfe? But lo, yonder is Sempronio, standing at our doore; hee hath beene stirring betimes; I shall have a pittious life with my Master, if he be gone abroad; but I hope hee is not; if hee be, hee hath left his old wont. But being he is not now himselfe, no marvell if he breake custome.

SEMPR. Brother Parmeno, if I knew that countrey, where a man might get wages by sleeping, it should goe hard, but I would make a shift to get thither. For, I would not then come short of any man; I would scorne to be put downe; but would gaine as much as another man, be hee who hee

146

CALISTO AND MELIBEA

will be that beares a head. But what is the matter, that thou, like a carelesse and retchles fellow, loytring, I know not where, hast been so negligent, and slow in thy returne? I cannot devise, what should be the cause of this thy so long stay, unlesse it were to give old Celestina a warming to night; or to rub her feete, as you were wont to doe, when you were a Little-one.

PARME. O Sempronio, my good friend, I pray thee doe not interrupt, or rather corrupt my pleasure; Doe not intermix thy anger with my patience; doe not involve thy discontentment with my quiet; Doe not soyle with such troubled water, the cleare liquor of those gladsome thoughts, which I harbour in my heart; Doe not sowre with thy malicious taunts and hatefull reprehensions, the sweetnesse of my delight. Receive me cheerefully, imbrace me with joy, and I shall tell thee wonders of my late happy proceedings.

SEMPR. Come, out with it, out with it. Is it any thing touching Melibea? Say, Lad, hast thou seene her?

PARM. What talk'st thou to me of Melibea? It is touching another, that I wish better unto then Melibea. And such a one (if I be not deceived) as may compare with her both in handsomnes, and beauty. Melibea? Why, she is not worthy to carry her shooes after her: as though forsooth, the world and all that therein is, be it beauty, or otherwise, were onely inclosed in Melibea?

SEMPR. What meanes this fellow? Is hee mad? I would fayne laugh, but I cannot. Now I see, wee are all in love: the world is at an end. Calisto loves Melibea; I, Elicia: and thou out of meere envy, hast found out some one, with whom thou might'st lose that little wit thou hast.

PARM. Is it folly (say you) to love? Then am I a foole. But if foolishnesse were a paine, some in every house would complaine.

SEMPR. I appeale to thy selfe; by thine owne judgement thou art no better: For my selfe have heard thee give vaine and foolish counsell to Calisto, and to crosse Celestina in every word shee spake, to the hinderance of both our profits. O Sir, you were glad of this; it was meate alone to you. Who, you? No, not for a world, would you beare a part

147

with us. But since I have caught you in my clutches, I will
hamper you yfaith. Now, that thou art in those hands, that
may hurt thee, they shall doe it; assure thy selfe they shall.

PARM. It is not, Sempronio, true courage, nor manly
valour, to hurt or hinder any man, but to doe good, to heale,
and helpe him : and farre greater is it to be_willing so to doe.
I have evermore made reckoning of thee, as of mine owne
brother. Let not that be verified of thee, which is commonly
spoken amongst us ; that a slight cause should part true
friends ; I tell you, you doe not use me well. Nay, you
deale very ill with mee ; I know not whence this rancor
should arise. Doe not vexe me (Sempronio ;) Torment me
not with these thy wounding words. And shall I tell you?
It is a very strange and strong kinde of patience, which
sharpe taunts and scoffs, which like so many needles
and bodkins set to the heart, cannot pierce and pricke
thorow.

SEMPR. I say nothing, but that now you have your
wench, you will allow one pilchard more to the poore boy
in the Stable.

PARME. You cannot hold, your heart would burst, if you
should not vent your choler. Well, I will give way, and
should you use me worse, I will pocket up all your wrongs :
and the rather, because it is an old saying, No humane
passion is perpetuall.

SEMP. But you can use Calisto worse ; advising him to
that, which thou thy selfe seek'st to shunne : never letting
him alone, but still urging him to leave loving of Melibea :
wherein, thou art just like unto a signe in an Inne, which
gives shelter to others, and none to it selfe. O Parmeno,
now mai'st thou see, how easie a thing it is to finde fault
with another mans life, and how hard to amend his owne.
I say no more, your selfe shall be your own Judge : and from
this day forward, we shall see how you behave your selfe,
sithence you have now your porrenger, as well as other folkes.
If thou hadst beene my friend (as thou professest) when I
stood in need of thee, thou should'st then have favoured
mee, and made shew of thy love, and assisted Celestina in
all that had beene for my profit, and not to drive in at every

CALISTO AND MELIBEA

word a nayle of malice. Know moreover, that as wine in the Lees, when it is drawne to the very dregges, driveth drunkards from the Taverne : the like effect hath necessity, or adversity with a fained friend : and false mettle, that is gilded but slightly over, quickly discovers it selfe to be but counterfeit.

PARMENO. I have often-times heard it spoken, and now by experience I see it is true ; that in this wretched life of ours, there is no pleasure without sorrow ; no contentment without some crosse, or counterbuffe of fortune. We see our fairest daies, our clearest Sunne-shines are over-cast with clouds, darkenesse and raine : our solaces and delights are swallowed up by dolours and by death : laughter, mirth, and merriment are waited on by teares, lamentations, and other the like mortall passions. In a word ; Sweet meate will have sowre sauce : and much ease and much quietnesse, much paine and much heavinesse. Who could come more friendly, or more merrily to a man, then I did now to thee ? And who could receive a more unkind wellcome, or unfriendly salutation ? Who lives there, that sees himselfe, as I have scene my selfe, raised with such glory to the height of my deare Areusa's love ? And who, that sees himselfe more likely to fall from thence, then I, being so ill intreated, as I am of thee ? Nay, thou wilt not give mee leave to tell thee, how much I am thine, how much I will further thee in all I am able, how much I repent me of that which is past, and what good counsell and reprehensions I have received of Celestina, and all in favour of thee, and thy good, and the good of us all. And now, that we have our Masters and Melibea's game in our owne hands ; now is the time that wee must thrive or never.

SEMPRONIO. I like your words well, but should like them better, were your workes like unto them : which as I see the performance, so shall I give them credence ; but tell me, I pray thee, what's that, me thought, I heard you talke even now of Areusa ? Doe you know Areusa, that is Cousin to Elicia ?

PARME. Why, what were all the joy I now injoy, did I not injoy her ?

149

THE TRAGICK-COMEDY OF

SEMPRONIO. What does the foole meane? He cannot speake for laughing. What doest thou call this thy injoying her? Did shee shew her selfe unto thee out at a window?

PARM. No great matter. Onely I have left her in doubt, whether shee be with childe or no.

SEMPR. Thou hast strucke mee into a maze; continuall travell may doe much; often dropping makes stones hollow.

PARME. How? Continuall travell? Why, I never thought of having her till yesterday; then did I worke her; and now shee is mine owne.

SEMPR. The old woman had a finger in this businesse, had shee not?

PARMENO. Why should you thinke so?

SEMPR. Because shee told mee how much shee loved you, how well she wisht you, and that she would worke her for you; you were a happy man, Sir, you had no more to doe, but to come and take up. And therefore they say, It is better with him whom fortune helpeth, then with him that riseth early. But was shee the godfather to this businesse?

PARM. No, but shee was the godmother, which is the truer of the two. And you know, when a man comes once to a good tree, he will stay a while by it, and take the benefit of the shade. I was long a comming, but when I came, I went quickly to worke: I dispatcht it in an instant. O brother, what shall I say unto thee of the graces that are dwelling in that wench, of her language, and beauty of body? But I will deferre the repetition thereof to a fitter opportunitie.

SEMPR. Shee can be no other but cousin to Elicia; thou canst not say so much of her, but that this other hath as much, and somewhat more. But what did shee cost thee? Hast thou given her any thing?

PARME. No, not any thing, but whatsoever I had given her, it had beene well bestowed: for shee is capable of every good thing; and such as shee, are by so much the better esteemed, by how much the dearer they are bought: and like Jewels, are the higher prized, the more they cost us. But, save in this my Mistresse, so rich a thing was never purchast at so low a rate. I have invited her to day to

150

dinner to Celestina's house; and if you like of it, let us all
meet there.

SEMP. Who, brother?

PARME. Thou and she, and the old woman and Elicia; and there wee will laugh and be merry.

SEMPR. O good heavens, how glad a man hast thou made mee! Thou art franke, and of a free and liberall disposition, I will never faile thee: now I hold thee to be a man; now my minde gives me, that Fate hath some good in store for thee: all the hatred and malice which I bare thee for thy former speeches, is now turned into love; I now doubt not, but that the league which thou hast made with us, shall be such as it ought to be. Now I long to imbrace thee; Come, let us now live like brothers; and let the divell go hang himselfe. All those contentious words notwithstanding, whatsoever have passed between us, let there be now no falling out, and so have peace all the yeere long; for, the falling out of friends, is evermore the renewing of love; let us feast and be merry, for our Master will fast for us all.

PARME. What does that man in desperation doe?

SEMPR. Hee lyes where you left him last night, stretching himselfe all along upon his pallate, by his bed-side; but the Divell a winke that hee sleepes; and the Divell a whit that hee wakes, but lies like a man in a trance, betweene them both, resting, and yet taking no rest. If I goe in unto him, hee falls a rowting, and a snorting; If I goe from him, hee either sings or raves: nor can I for my life comprehend (so strange is his carriage heerein) whether the man bee in paine or ease; whether hee take griefe or pleasure in it.

PARME. What a strange humour is this? But tell me (Sempronio) Did hee never call for mee? Did hee not remember mee when I was gone?

SEMPR. Hee remembred not himselfe; Why should hee then remember you?

PARME. Even in this also fortune hath beene favourable unto me. And since all things goe so well, whilest I thinke on it, I will send thither our meate, that they may the sooner make ready our dinner.

SEMPRO. What hast thou thought upon to send thither,

that those pretty fooles may hold thee a compleat Courtier, well bred and bountifull?

PAR. In a plentifull house a supper is soone provided : that, which I have heere at home in the Larder, is sufficient to save our credit. Wee have good white bread, wine of Monviedro, a good gammon of Bacon, and some halfe doozen couple of dainty Chickens, which my Masters Tenants brought him in the other day, when they came to pay their rent; which if hee chance to aske for, I will make him beleeve, that he hath eaten them himselfe : and those Turtle-doves, which hee will'd mee to keepe against to day; I will tell him, that they were a little to blame, and none of the sweetest, and that they did so stinke, that I was faine to throw them away; and you shall justifie it, and beare me witnesse. We will take order, that all that hee shall eate thereof, shall doe him no harme; and that our owne Table (as good reason it is it should) be well furnished; and there with the old woman, as oft as we meet, wee will talke more largely concerning this his love, to his losse, and our profit.

SEMP. Calst thou it love? Thou mai'st call it sorrow with a vengeance. And by my fay, I sweare unto thee, that I verily thinke, that he will hardly now escape eyther death or madnesse : but since it is, as it is, dispatch your businesse, that we may goe up, and see what hee does.

CALISTO. { In perill great I live,
And strait of force must dye :
Since what desire doth give,
That, hope doth mee deny.

PARME. Harke, harke, Sempronio! Our Master is a riming : Hee is turn'd Poet, I perceive.

SEMPR. O whore-sonne Sot! What Poet, I pray? The great Antipater Sidonius, or the great Poet Ovid, who never spake but in Verse? I, it is he; the very same : we shall have the Divell turne Poet too shortly, he does but talke idlely in his sleepe; and thou think'st the poore man is turn'd Poet.

CALISTO. { This paine, this martyrdome,
O heart, well dost thou prove,
Since thou so soone wast wonne
To Melibea's love.

152

CALISTO AND MELIBEA

PARM. Loe, did I not tell thee hee was turn'd true
Rimer?

CALISTO. Who is that, that talkes in the Hall? Why ho?

PARMENO. Anon, Sir.

CALISTO. How farre night is it? Is it time to goe to bed?

PARME. It is rather, Sir, too late to rise.

CALISTO. What sai'st thou foole? Is the night past
and gone then?

PARMENO. I, Sir, and a good part of the day too.

CALISTO. Tell mee (Sempronio) does not this idle-headed
Knave lye, in making mee beleeve it is day?

SEMPR. Put Melibea (Sir) a little out of your minde,
and you will then see, that it is broad day: for through that
great brightnesse and splendour, which you contemplate in
her cleare shining eyes, like a Partridge dazeled with a buffit,
you cannot see, being blinded with so sodaine a flash.

CALISTO. Now I beleeve it, and 'tis farre day too. Give
mee my clothes; I must goe to my wonted retirement to the
Mirtle-grove, and there begge of Cupid, that hee will direct
Celestina, and put my remedy into Melibea's heart, or else
that hee will shorten my sorrowfull dayes.

SEMPR. Sir, doe not vexe your selfe so much: you cannot doe all that you would in an houre: nor is it discretion
for a man to desire that earnestly, that may unfortunately
fall upon him. If you will have that concluded in a day,
which is well, if it be effected in a yeere, your life cannot be
long.

CALISTO. I conceive your meaning; you would inferre
that I am like Squire Gallego's boy, who went a yeere without breeches, and when his Master commanded a paire to be
cut out for him, he would have them made in a quarter of
an houre.

SEMPRONIO. Heaven forbid (Sir) I should say so: for
you are my Master, and I know besides, that as you will recompence me for my good counsell, so you will punish mee,
if I speake amisse; though it be a common saying, that the
commendation of a mans good service, or good speech, is not
equall to the reprehension and punishment of that which is
eyther ill done or spoken.

U

153

THE TRAGICK-COMEDY OF

CALISTO. I wonder (Sempronio) where thou got'st so much philosophie ?

SEMPR. Sir, all that is not white, which differs from blacke; nor is all that gold which glisters. Your accelerated, and hasty desires, not being measured by reason, make my counsels to seeme better then they be. Would you, that they should yesterday, at the first word, have brought Melibea manacled, and tyed to her girdle, as you would have sent into the market for any other marchandize ? Wherein there is no more to doe, then to goe into the market, and take the paines to buy it. Sir, bee of good cheere; give some ease and rest to your heart; for no great happinesse can happen in an instant. It is not one stroke that can fell an Oake; prepare your selfe for sufferance, for wisdome is a laudable blessing; and he that is prepared, may withstand a strong incounter.

CALISTO. Thou hast spoken well, if the quality of my evill would consent to take it so.

SEMPR. To what end serves understanding, if the will shall rob reason of her right.

CALISTO. O thou foole, thou foole ! The sound man sayes to the sicke, Heaven send thee thy health. I will no more counsell, no more hearken to thy reasons : for, they doe but revive, and kindle those flames afresh, which burne and consume mee. I will goe and invocate Cupid; and will not come home, till you call me, and crave a reward of mee for the good newes you shall bring mee, upon the happy comming of Celestina: nor will I eate any thing, till Phœbus his horses shall feed, and graze their fill in those greene meddowes where they use to baite, when they come to their journeys end.

SEMP. Good Sir, leave off these circumlocutions; leave off these poeticall fictions; for that speech is not comely, which is not common unto all: which all men partake not of, as well as your selfe : or which few doe but understand. Say, till the Sunne set, and every one will know what you meane. Come, eate in the meane while, some Conserves, or the like confection, that you may keepe some life in you, till I returne.

CALISTO. Sempronio, my faithfull servant, my good

154

CALISTO AND MELIBEA

counsellour, my loyall follower ; Be it as thou wilt have it : for I assure my selfe (out of the unspottednesse of thy pure service) that my life is as deare unto thee as thine owne.

SEM. Dost thou beleeve it, Parmeno ? I wot well that thou wilt not sweare it. Remember, if you goe for the Conserves, that you nimme a barrell for those you wot of ; you know who I meane. And to a good understanding every thing will light in his lap : or (as the phrase is) fall into his Cod-pisse.

CALISTO. What say'st thou, Sempronio ?

SEMPR. I speake, Sir, to Parmeno, that hee should runne quickly and fetch you a slice of Conserves, of Citron, or of Limons.

PARM. Loe (Sir) heere it is.

CALISTO. Give it me hither.

SEMPR. See, how fast it goes downe ! I thinke the Divell makes him make such quicke worke. Looke, if hee does not swallow it whole, that hee may the sooner have done !

CALISTO. My spirits are returned unto me againe ; I promise you it hath done me much good. My Sonnes both, farewell. Goe looke after the old woman, and waite for good newes, that I may reward you for your labour.

PARME. So, now hee is gone. The divell and ill fortune follow thee ; for in the very same houre hast thou eaten this Citron, as Apuleius did that poyson which turned him into an Asse.

THE END OF THE EIGHTH ACT

THE TRAGICK-COMEDY OF

ACTUS IX
THE ARGUMENT

EMPRONIO *and* Parmeno *goe talking each with other to* Celestina's *house; being come thither, they finde there* Elicia *and* Areusa. *They sit downe to dinner; being at dinner,* Elicia *and* Sempronio *fall out; being risen from Table, they grow friends againe. In the meane while comes* Lucrecia, *servant to* Melibea, *to call* Celestina *to come and speake with* Melibea.

INTERLOCUTORS

Sempronio, Parmeno, Celestina, Elicia, Areusa, Lucrecia.

SEMPRONIO. Parmeno, I pray thee bring downe our Cloakes, and our Rapiers; for I thinke it be time for us to goe to dinner.

PARME. Come, let us goe presently; for I thinke they will finde fault with us, for staying so long. Let us not goe thorow this, but that other streete, that wee may goe in by the Vestals, so shall we see, whether Celestina have ended her devotions, and take her along with us.

SEMPR. What? Doe you thinke to finde her at her Theme now? Is this a fit houre? This a time for her to be at her Orizons?

PARME. That can never be said out of time, which ought to be done at all times.

SEMPR. It is true, but I see, you know not Celestina; when she has any thing to do, she never thinks upon heaven, the divell a whit that she cares then for devotion; when she hath any thing in the house to gnaw upon, farewell all holinesse, farewell all prayers: and indeed, her going to any of these Ceremonies, is but to spy and pry only upon advantages for such persons as she may prevaricate and make for her profit. And though shee bred thee up, I am better

156

CALISTO AND MELIBEA

acquainted with her qualitics, then you are. That which shee doth ruminate: how many crack't maiden-heads shee hath then in cure; how many Lovers in this City; how many young wenches are recommended unto her; what Stewards afford her provision; which is the more bountifull: and how she may call every man by his name; that when shee chanceth to meet them, shee may not salute them as strangers. When you see her lips goe, then is she inventing of lies, and devising sleights, and tricks for to get money; then doth she thus dispute with her selfe; In this maner will I make my speech; In this fashion will I cloze with him. Thus then will he answer mee; And to this I must thus reply. Thus lives this creature, whom we so highly honour.

PARM. Tush, this is nothing; I know more then this. But because you were angry the t'other day, when I told Calisto so much, I will forbeare to speake of it.

SEMPR. Though wee may know so much for our owne good, yet let us not publish it to our owne hurt; For, to have our Master to know it, were but to make him discard her for such a one as she is, and not to care for her; and so leaving her, hee must needs have another, of whose paines wee shall reape no profit, as we shall be sure to doe by her, who by faire meanes, or by foule, shall give us part of her gaines.

PARME. Well, and wisely hast thou spoken; but hush: the doore is open, and shee in the house. Call before you goe in; peradventure, they are not yet fully ready; or things are not in that order as they would have it; and then will they be loth to be seene.

SEMP. Goe in, man, never stand upon those niceties; for we are all of a house. Now, just now, they are covering the Table.

CELEST. O my young amorous youths, my Pearles of gold! Let the yeere goe about as well with me, as you are both welcome unto mee.

PARMENO. What complements has the old Bawd? Brother, I make no question, but you well enough perceive her foystings, and her flatteries.

157

THE TRAGICK-COMEDY OF

ACTUS
IX

SEMPRONIO. O! you must give her leave, it is her living. But I wonder what divell taught her all her knacks, and her knaveries.

PARME. What? Mary, I will tell you. Necessity, Poverty, and Hunger; then which there are no better Tutours in the world: No better quickeners, and revivers of the wit. Who taught your Pyes, and your Parrats to imitate our proper Language, and tone, with their slit tongues, save onely necessitie?

CELEST. Hola: wenches, girles: where be you, you fooles? Come downe; Come hither quickly, I say; for there are a couple of yong Gallants that would ravish mee.

ELICIA. Would they would never have come hither for me. O! it is a fine time of day! is this a fit houre, when you have invited your friends, to a feast? You have made my cousin to waite heere these three long houres: but this same lazy-gut (Sempronio) was the cause, I warrant you, of all this stay; for hee has no eyes to looke upon mee.

SEMPR. Sweet-Heart; I pray thee be quiet. My Life, my Love! you know full well, that he that serves another, is not his own man. He that is bound, must obey. So that my subjection frees me from blame. I pray thee be not angry. Come, let us sit downe, and fall to our meate.

ELICIA. I, it is well, you are ready at all times to sit downe, and eate, as soone as the cloth is laid, with a cleane payre of hands, but a shamelesse face.

SEMPRO. Come, we will chide and brawle after dinner: Now let us fall to our vitailes. Mother Celestina, will it please you to sit downe first?

CELEST. No, first sit you downe (my sonne) for heere is roome enough for us all; let every one take their place, as they like, and sit next her whom he loves best: as for me, who am a sole woman, I will sit me down heere by this Jar of wine, and this good goblet. For I can live no longer, then while I talke with one of these two. Ever since that I was growne in yeeres, I know no better office at boord, then to fall a skinking, and to furnish the Table with pots and flagons: For he that handles hony, shall feele it still clinging to his fingers. Besides, in a cold winters night, you cannot

158

CALISTO AND MELIBEA

have a better warming-panne. For, when I tosse off two of
these little pots, when I am e'en ready to goe into my bed,
why, I feele not a jot of cold all the night long. With this,
I furre all my clothes at Christmas: This warmes my blood;
This keepes me still in one estate; This makes mee merry,
where-e're I goe; This makes me looke fresh, and ruddy, as
a Rose. Let me still have store of this in my house, and a
figge for a deare yeere, it shall never hurt mee: for one crust
of Mouse-eaten bread will serve me three whole dayes; This
drives away all care and sorrow from the heart, better then
either Gold or Corall; This gives force to a young man, and
vigour to an old man; It addes colour to the discoloured;
courage to the coward; diligence to the slothfull; it com-
forteth the braine; it expels cold from the stomacke; it
takes away the stinkingnesse of the breath; it makes cold
constitutions, to be potent and active: it makes husband-
men endure the toyle of tillage; it makes your painefull
and weary mowers to sweat out all their watrish ill humours;
it remedies Rheumes; and cures the tooth-ache. This may
you keepe long at Sea without stinking; so can you not
water: I could tell you more properties of this wholsome
liquor, than all of you have hayres on your head. So that
I know not the man, whom it doth not delight to heare it
but mentioned, the very name of it is so pleasing: onely, it
has but this one fault: That that which is good, costs us
deare; and that which is bad, does us hurt. So that what
maketh the Liver sound, the same maketh the purse light;
but for all this, I will be sure to seeke after the best; for
that little which I drinke, which is onely some dozen times a
meale. Which number, I never passe, unlesse now, when I
am feasted, or so.

PARME. It is the common opinion of all: That thrice
in a dinner, is good, honest, competent, and sufficient for any
man. And all that doe write thereof, doe allow you no
more.

CELEST. Sonne, the phrase is corrupted; they have put
three time, in stead of thirteene.

SEMPR. Aunt, wee all like well of your glosse. Let us
eate, and talke, and talke and eate: For else wee shall not

159

THE TRAGICK-COMEDY OF

afterwards have time to discourse of the love of our lost Master, and of that faire, handsome, and courteous Melibea, lovely gentle Melibea.

ELICIA. Get thee out of my sight, thou distastefull companion, thou disturber of my mirth; the Divell choake thee with that thou hast eaten. Thou hast given me my dinner for to day; now as I live, I am ready to rid my stomack, and to cast up all that I have in my body, to heare that thou shouldst call her faire and courteous, lovely, and gentle. I pray thee how faire, how lovely, how courteous, how gentle is she? It angers mee to the heart-bloud, to see you have so little shame with you. How gentle, how faire is she, more then other women? Beleeve me, if she be as thou reportest her; nay, if she have any jot in her of beauty, or any the least gracefulnesse. But I see there are some eyes, that make no difference betwixt Ione, and my Lady, and that it is with every one as hee likes, as the good man said, when he kist his Cow. Draffe I perceive is good enough for Swine. I will crosse my selfe in pitty of thy great ignorance, and want of judgement; Who I pray, had any minde to dispute with you, touching her beauty, and her gentlenesse? Gentle Melibea? Faire Melibea? And is Melibea so gentle, is shee so faire as you make her to be? Then it must be so; and then shall both these hit right in her, when two Sundaies come together. All the beauty shee hath, may be bought at every Pedlers, or Painters shop for a penny matter, or the like trifle: and beleeve me, I my selfe, upon mine owne knowledge, know, that in that very streete where shee dwels, there are foure maydens at the least, if not more, to whom Nature hath imparted a greater part of beauty, and other good graces in greater abundance, then she hath on Melibea; and if shee have any jot of handsomenesse in her, shee may thanke her good clothes, her neate dressings, and costly Jewels, which if they were hung upon a post, thou wouldst as well say by that too, that it were faire and gentle; and by my fay (be it spoken without ostentation) I thinke my penny to be as good silver as hers, and that I am every way as faire as your Melibea.

AREUSA. O sister! hadst thou seene her as I have seene

CALISTO AND MELIBEA

her (I tell thee no lye) if thou shouldst have met her fasting, thy stomacke would have taken such a loathing, that all that day thou would'st not have been able to have eaten any meat. All the yeere long she is mewed up at home, where she is dawbed over with a thousand sluttish slibber-slabbers; all which (forsooth) she must indure, for once perhaps going abroad in a twelve-month to be seene : shee anoynts her face with gall and honey, with parched grapes and figges crushed and pressed together, with many other things, which for manners sake, and reverence of the Table, I omit to mention. It is their riches, that make such creatures as shee to be accounted faire; it is their wealth, that causeth them to be thus commended, and not the graces, and goodly features of their bodies : For, shee has such brests, being a maid, as if shee had been the mother of three children ; and are for all the world, like nothing more, then two great Pompeans, or bigge bottled-Goords. Her belly I have not seene, but judging it by the rest, I verily beleeve it, to be as slacke, and as flaggy, as a woman of fifty yeere old. I know not what Calisto should see in her, that for her sake, hee should forsake the love of others, whom hee may with great ease obtaine, and farre more pleasure injoy : Unlesse it be, that like the Pallate that is distasted, hee thinketh sowre things the sweetest.

SEMPR. Sister, it seemeth here unto me, that every Pedler prayseth his owne needles; but I assure you, the quite contrary is spoken of her throughout the whole Citie.

AREUSA. There is nothing farther from truth, then the opinion of the vulgar, and nothing more false, then the reports of the multitude, nor shalt thou ever live a merry life, if thou governe thy selfe by the will of the common people : and these conclusions, are uncontrollable, and infallibly true ; that whatsoever thing the vulgar thinks, is vanity : whatsoever they speake, is false-hood : what they reprove, that is good : what they approve, that is bad. And since this is a true rule, and common custome amongst them, doe not judge of Melibea's either goodnesse or beauty, by that which they affirme.

SEMPR. Gentlewomen ; let mee answer you in a word.

X   161

Your ill tongued multitude, and pratling vulgar, never pardon the faults of great persons, no, not of their Soveraigne himselfe, which makes me to thinke, that if Melibea had so many defects, as you taxe her withall, they would e're this have beene discovered by those who know her better then wee doe. And howbeit I should admit all you have spoken to be true, yet pardon me, if I presse you with this particular. Calisto is a Noble Gentleman; Melibea the Daughter of Honourable parents; So that, it is usuall with those, that are descended of such high Linage, to seeke and inquire each after other; and therefore it is no marvell, if he rather love her, then another.

AREUSA. Let him be base, that holds himselfe base; they are the Noble Actions of men, that make men Noble. For in conclusion, we are all of one making, flesh and bloud all. Let every man strive to be good of himselfe, and not goe searching for his vertue in the Noblenesse of his Ancestors.

CELEST. My good children; as you love mee, cease this contentious kinde of talke: and you Elicia; I pray you come to the Table againe; sit you downe, I say, and doe not vexe, and grieve your selfe, as you doe.

ELICIA. With this condition, that my meate may be my poyson; and that my belly may burst with that I eate. Shall I sit downe and eate with this wicked Villaine, that hath stoutly maintained it to my face, and no body must say him nay, That Melibea: That Dish-clout of his, is fairer then I?

SEMPR. I prythee (Sweet-heart) be quiet, it was you that made the comparison; and comparisons (you know) are odious: and therefore it is you that are in the fault, and not I.

AREUSA. Come, sister, come, and sit with us; I pray, come eate with us. Have you no more wit, then to be angry with such a crosse foole as hee? I would not doe him so much pleasure, as to forbeare my meate for him; let him goe hang, if hee be peevish, will you be peevish too? I pray you sit downe, unlesse you will have me likewise to rise from the Table.

ELICIA. The necessity which I have imposed upon my

162

selfe, to please thee in all things, and in all thy requests, makes mee against my will, to give contentment to this enemy of mine ; and to carry my selfe out of my respect to this good company more fairely towards him, then otherwise I would.

SEMPRONIO. Ha, ha, he.

ELICIA. What dost thou laugh at ? Now the evill Canker eate and consume that unpleasing and offensive mouth of thine.

CELEST. Sonne, I pray thee no more. Do not answer her ; for then we shall never make an end : This is nothing to the present purpose ; Let us follow our businesse, and attend that which may tend to our good. Tell me, How does Calisto? How hap't it you left him thus all alone ? How fell it out, that both of you could slip away from him ?

PARME. He flung from us with a vengeance, fretting and fuming like a mad-man, his eyes sparkeling foorth fire, his mouth venting forth curses, despairefull, discontented in minde, and like one that is halfe besides himselfe : and is now gone to Saint Mary Magdalens, to desire of God, that thou maist well and truely gnaw the bones of these Chickens ; vowing never to come home, till hee heare that thou art come with Melibea in thy lap. Thy gowne and kirtle, and my cassocke are cock-sure. For the rest let the world slide ; but when we shall have it, that I know not, all the craft is in the catching.

CELEST. Let it come when it will come, it shall be welcome, when e're it comes. A cassocke is good weare after winter. And sleeves are good after Easter : Every thing makes the heart merry that is gotten with ease, and without any labour, especially comming from thence, where it leaves so small a gap, and from a man of that wealth and substance, who with the very branne and scraps of his house, would make me of a begger, to become rich : such is the surplus and store of his goods ; and such as hee, it never grieves them what they spend, considering the cause wherefore they give : For they feele it not ; when they are in the heat and passion of their love, it paines them not ; they neither see, nor heare ; which I judge to be true by others, that I have knowne to be lesse passionate, and lesse scorched in the fiery flames of love, then Calisto is ; in so much, that I have seen them neither eat nor drink ; neither laugh nor weep ; neither sleep nor wake ; neither speake nor hold their peace ; neither live in paine, nor yet finde ease ; neither be contented, nor yet complaine of discontentment, answerable to the perplexity of that sweet and cruell wound of their hearts. And if naturall necessity forceth them to any one of these, they are so wholly forgetfull of themselves, and strucke into such sudden senslesnesse of their present being and condition, that eating, their hands forget to carry their meat to their mouthes. Besides, if you talke with them, they never answer you directly. Their bodies are there with you, but where they love, there are their hearts, and their senses. Great is the force of love. His power doth not only reach over the earth, but passeth also over the seas. He holds an equall command over all mankinde. He breaks thorow all kinde of difficulties, and dangers whatsoever. It is a tormentfull thing, full of feare, and of care. His eye roles every way ; nothing can escape him. And if any of you that be heere, were ever true lovers, and did love faithfully indeede, hee will say I speake the truth.

SEMPR. Mother, you and I are both of a minde. For heere is she present who caus'd me once to become another Calisto, desperate, and senslesse in my doings ; weary in my body, idle in my braine, sleeping ill a daies, and watching too well a nights, up by breake of day, playing the foole with thousands of gesticulations, and odde Anticktricks, leaping over walls, putting my life every day in hap-hazard and manifold dangers, standing in harms way before Bulls, Running-horses, throwing the Bar, tossing the Pike, tyring out my friends, cracking of blades, making ladders of ropes, putting on armor, and a thousand other idle acts of a Lover, making Ballads, penning of Sonnets, painting Mottos, making purposes, and other the like devices. All which I hold well spent, and thinke my selfe happy in them, sithence they gained mee so great and faire a Jewell.

ELICIA. You doe well to perswade your selfe so : But howsoever you conceit you have gained mee, I assure thee,

CALISTO AND MELIBEA

thy backe is no sooner turn'd, but another is presently with me, whom I love better then thee, and is a properer man then thou art, and one that will not goe vexing and angring mee, as thou dost. It is a yeere ere your worship forsooth, can find in your heart to come and see me ; And then as good have your roome, as your company, unlesse it were better.

CELEST. Sonne, give her leave to ease her stomake, let her speake her minde ; for the wench (I thinke) is mad. And the more shee talkes thus lavishly and wildly ; assure thy selfe, she is the more confirmed in thy love. All this stirre is, because you commended Melibea so highly ; and shee (poore soule) knowes not how to be even with you, but to pay you home in this coorse kinde of coyne, and hard language. And I beleeve, I shall not see her cate yet a while, for a thing that I know ; and this other her Cousin heere, I know her meaning well enough. Goe too (my masters,) take the benefit of your youth, injoy the flowre of this your fresh and lively age. For he that will not when he may, when hee would, hee shall have nay. And repentance shall be the recompence of his tarriance, who hath time, and will not take it, as I my selfe doe now repent me of those houres, which I sometimes lost, when I was young, when men did esteeme of me, and when they loved me ; for now (the worse lucke mine) I am a decayed creature, I waxe old, withered, and full of wrinkles ; no body will now looke after mee, yet my minde is still the same ; and want rather ability, then desire. Fall to your flap (my masters) kisse and clip, as for mee, I have nothing else to doe, but to looke on and please mine eye. It is some comfort to me yet, to be a spectator of your sports. Never stand upon nice tearmes, for whil'st you sit at boord, it is lawfull to doe any thing from the girdle upwards. All play above boord is faire and pardonable ; when you are alone by your selves, close together at it in a corner, I will not clap a fine on your heads, because the King doth not impose any such taxation. And as for these young wenches, I know, they will never accuse you of ravishment. And as for old Celestina, because her teeth will be on edge, shee will mumble with her dull and empty gums the crums off the Napkins.

ELICIA. Mother, some body knocks at the doore.

CELEST. Daughter, looke who it is.

ELICIA. Either the voyce deceives mee, or else it is my cousin Lucrecia.

CELEST. Open the doore and let her come in, for shee also understands somewhat touching that poynt, whereof wee discoursed last; though being shut up so close at home, as shee is: shee is mightily hindered in the fruition of her friculation, and cannot injoy her youth with the like liberty as others doe.

AREUSA. Now, I see it is most true, that these same Chamber-maides, these forsooth that wait upon Ladies, injoy not a jot of delight, nor are acquainted with the sweet rewards of love. They never converse with their kindred, nor with their equalls, with whom they may say, Thou for thou; or, so haile fellow, well met, as to aske in familiar language; Wench, what hast thou to supper? Art thou with childe yet? How many Hens dost thou keepe at home? Shall wee goe make our bever at thy house? Come, let us goe laugh and be merry there. Sirrah, shew mee thy Sweet-heart, which is hee? Oh wonderfull! How long is it since I saw thee last? How is it with thee, wench? How hast thou done this great while? Tell me I pray thee, who are thy neighbours now? and a thousand other the like unto these. O Aunt! how hard a name it is, how troublesome, and how proud a thing to carry the name of a Lady up and downe continually in ones mouth! And this makes mee to live of my selfe ever since I came to yeeres of understanding and discretion. For I could never endure to be called by any other name, then mine owne; especially by these Ladies wee have now adaies. A wench may wait upon them, and spend in their service the better part of their time, and with an old cast-gowne, which hath scarce e're a whole piece in it, they make payment of tenne yeeres service. They will revile their mayds, and call them all to naught; they will use them extreme hardly, and keepe them in such awe, and continuall slavery, that they dare as well be hang'd, as to speake but one word before them. And when they see the time draw on, that they be ready and ripe for marriage, and that they

166

CALISTO AND MELIBEA

should both in reason and conscience doe them some good that waies, they take occasion to wrangle, and fall out with them, and falsely to object unto them, that they have trod their shoo awry, eyther with some one of her Ladiships servants, or with her sonne, or put jealousies betwixt her and her husband; or that they bring men privily into her house; or that they have stolne such a gobblet, or lost such a Ring: for which they will not sticke to strip them, and lamme them soundly, bestowing perhaps 100. stripes upon them, and afterwards thrust them out of dores, with their haire about their eares, and their fardles at their backs, rating them in most vile manner, crying, Out of my doors, you thiefe, you whore, you strumpet: this is no place for such paltry baggages. Thou shalt not spoyle my house, I will not be thus dishonoured by thee. So that in stead of expected recompence, they receive nothing but bitter revilements. Where they expect to goe preferred out of the house, they goe prejudiced out of the house. And where they expect to be well married, they are quite mar'd in their reputation. And where they expect jewels and wedding apparell, there are they sent out naked, and disgraced: these are their rewards, these their benefits, and these the payments they receive for their service. They are bound to give them husbands, and in liew thereof, they strip them of their clothes. The greatest grace and honour which they have in their Ladies house, is to be imployed in walking the streetes from one Ladie to another, and to deliver their Ladies message: (As, My Lady hath sent to know how you doe? how you did rest to night? how your physicke wrought with you; and how many occasions it gave your Ladiship, etc.?) They never heare their owne name out of their Ladies mouth. But the best they can call them by, is, Come hither, you whore, Get you gone, you drabbe, or I'll set you going: Whither gadde you now, you mangy harlotry; you pockey slut? what have you done to day, you loytring Queane? why did you eate this, you ravening thing, you gor-belly, you greedy cormorant? A you filthy Sow, how cleane this frying panne is kept? This pispot (Minion) it is well scowr'd, is it not? why you lazy bones, did you not brush my clothes,

167

when I left them off, and make cleane my Mantle? Why said you thus and thus, you Sot, you foolish Asse? Who lost the piece of plate, you scatter-good, you draggle-tayle? Whats become of my handkercher, you purloyning thiefe? you have given it to one of your copes-mates, some sweet-heart of yours, that must helpe to make you a whore: Come hither, you foule flappes, say, Where is my Henne, my cramm'd Henne, that I cannot finde her? you were best looke her mee out, and that quickly too, unlesse you meane I shall make you pay for her, when I come to pay you your wages. And besides all this, her pantofles shall walke about her eares a thousand times a day; pinchings, cudgellings, and scourgings shall be as common to her as her meat and drinke. There is not any that knowes how to please and content them; not any that can indure their tartnesse and curstnesse: their delight is to speake loud; their glory to chide and to brawle, and the better one does, and the more one seeks to please them, the lesse are they contented. And this (mother) is the reason, why I have rather desired to live free from controlement, and to be mistresse in a poore little house of mine owne, then to live a slave, and at command in the richest palace of the proudest Lady of them all.

CELESTINA. Thou art in the right, my girle; I will take no care for you, you will shift for your selfe; I perceive you know what you doe, you need not to be told on which side your bread is buttred, you are no baby, I see: and wise men tell us, that better is a crust of bread, and a cup of cold water with peace and quietnesse, then a house full of dainties, with brabbling and wrangling. But now let us leave this argument, for heere comes Lucrecia.

LUCRECIA. Much good to you (good Aunt) and to all this faire company and great meeting.

CELESTI. So great, daughter? hold you this so great a meeting? It appeares that you have not knowne me in my prosperity, which is now some twenty yeeres since. There be those that have seene mee in better case then I am now; and hee that now sees mee, I wonder his heart doth not burst with sorrow. I tell thee, (wench) I have seene at this table, where your kinswomen now sit, nine gallant young wenches,

168

much about your age; for the eldest was not above eighteene, and not one of them under foureteene. But such is this world, it comes and goes upon wheeles. We are like pots in a water-wheele, or like buckets in a Well: one up, and another downe, one full, and another empty; it is fortunes Law, that nothing can continue any long time in one, and the selfe-same state of being. Her order is alteration; Her custome, change. I cannot without teares deliver unto you the great honour I then liv'd in; though now, (such is my ill fortune) by little and little, it hath gone decaying: And as my daies declined; so diminished and decreased my profit. It is an old saying; That whatsoever is in this world, it doth either increase or decrease. Every thing hath it's limits; Every thing it's degrees of more or lesse: my honour did mount to that height, as was fitting for a woman of my quality to rise unto; and now of force, it must descend and fall as much: By this I know, that I am neere to my end, and that the Lease of my life is now expiring, and all my yeeres are almost spent and gone: and I also well know, that I did ascend, that I might descend; that I flourished, for to wither; that I had joy, that I might have sorrow; that I was borne to live; liv'd, to grow; grew, to grow old; and grow old to dye: and though it did alwaies appeare unto me, that I ought in this respect to suffer my misery the more patiently, yet as I am formed of flesh and bloud, and beare this heavy masse of sinne about me, I cannot but thinke on't now and then with griefe, nor can I wholy as I would, blot every thought thereof out of the wofull role of my wretched remembrance.

LUCRECIA. Me thinkes (mother) it could not choose but be wondrous troublesome unto you, to have the charge of so many young wenches. For they are very dangerous Cattell to keepe, and will aske a great deale of paines.

CELEST. Paines, Sweet-heart? Nay, they were an ease, and pleasure unto me; they did all of them obey me; they did all of them honour me; they did all of them reverence mee: not one of them that would swarve from my will: what I said, stood for a Law; it was good and currant amongst them; not any one of them, to whom I gave entertainement, ever made their owne choise any further then it stood with my liking; were he lame, crooked, squint-ey'd, or crippled: all was one, he was the welcom'st and the soundest, that brought me the soundest gaines; mine was the profit, and theirs the paines. Besides, I needed no servants; for in keeping them, I had servants enow. Why, your Noblemen, your Knights, your old men, your young men, your learned men, men of all sorts and dignities, from the highest to the lowest; why, they were all at my service: and when I came to a feast, my foote was no sooner in, but I had presently as many Bonnets vailed unto me, as if I had been a Dutchesse: he that had least acquaintance, least businesse with me, was held the most vile, and basest fellow. They spying me almost a League off; they would forsake their most earnest occasions, one by one, two by two, and come to me, to see if I would command them any service; and withall, aske me severally, how his love, how his mistresse did? When they saw me once passe by, you should have such a shuffling and scraping of feet, and all in such a generall gaze, and so out of order, that they did neither doe nor say any thing aright. One would call mee mistresse, another Aunt, others their love, others honest old woman. There, they would consent, when they should come to my house: there they would agree when I should goe unto theirs; there they would offer mee mony; there they would make me large promises; there likewise present me with gifts: some kissing the lappet of my Coat; and some other my cheeke, that by these kindnesses, they might give mee contentment, and worke me to their will. But now Fortune hath brought mee to so low a place in her wheele, that you may say unto me, Mich you good dich you with your old ware, your hindges are now growne rustie for want of oyling.

SEMPR. Mother, you make my haire stand on end, to heare these strange things, which you recount unto us; would your Nobles, your Knights, and Learned men fall so low? I am sure, they are not all of them so badde as you make them to be.

CELEST. No (my son) Iove forbid that I should raise any such report, or lay a generall scandall upon any of their

CALISTO AND MELIBEA

ranke. For, there were many old good men amongst them, with whom I had but small dealings, and could scarce endure to see me: But amongst the greatest, as they grew great in number, so had I a great number of them: some of one sort, and some of another; some I found very chaste, and some that took the charge upon them to maintaine such Traders as my selfe. And I am still of this beliefe, that of these there is no lack; and these, forsooth, would send their Squires and young men to waite upon me, whithersoever I went: and I should scarce have set my foote within mine owne doores, but straight at the heeles of me, you should have one come in with chickens, another with Hens, a third with Geese, a fourth with Ducks. This man sends me in Partriges, that Man Turtle Doves, he a gammon of Bacon, such a one a Tart, or a Custard; and some good fellow or other a good sucking Pigge, or two: for every one, as soone as he had a convenient present, so they came presently to register them in my house; that I, and those their pretty soules, might merrily eat them together: and as for wine, we wanted none; the best that a man could lay his lips to in the whole City, was sent unto me from divers parts and corners of the Towne: as that of Monviedro, of Luque, of Toro, of Madrigall, of San Martin, and many other Townes and Villages; And indeed so many, that albeit I still keepe the differences of their taste and relish in my mouth, yet doe I not retaine the diversity of their soyles in my remembrance. For it is enough for such an old woman as I, that when a good cuppe of wine comes neer my nose, I can be able to say, This is such a wine, or it comes from such a place, or person; why, your presents from all parts, from all sorts came upon me as thicke as hops, as flies to a pot of hony, or as stones that are throwne upon a stage: boyes came tumbling in at my doore, with as much provision, as they could carry on their backs. But now those good daies are past, I have eaten all my white bread in my youth, and know not how in the world to live, being fallen from so happy an estate.

AREUSA. Since we are come hither to be merry, (good mother) doe not weepe, I pray, doe not vexe your selfe: be

THE TRAGICK-COMEDY OF

of good cheere, plucke up your heart like a woman; the world while wee are in it, is bound to keepe us all, and no doubt but you shall have enough.

CELEST. O daughter! I have cause enough, I think, to weep, when I call to mind those pleasant daies that are past and gone, that merry life which then I led, and how I had the world at will, being served, honoured, and sought to of all. Why, then there was not any new fruit, or any the like dainty, which I had not in my hands, before others knew they were scarce blossom'd: in those daies, they were sure to be found in my house, if any one with child should long for such a Toy.

SEMPR. Mother, the remembrance of the good time we have had, doth profit us nothing, when it cannot be recovered againe, but rather brings griefe and sorrow to our selves, as this interrupting discourse hath done: but mother, we will goe off and solace our selves, whil'st you stay heere: and give this maid her answer.

CELEST. Daughter Lucrecia, passing over our former discourse, I pray you tell mee what is the cause of your happy comming hither?

LUCRECIA. Beleeve me, I had almost forgot my chiefe errand unto you, with thinking on that merry time which you talkt of. Me thinkes, I could continue fasting almost a whole yeere in harkening unto thee, and thinking on that pleasant life, which those young wenches led; me thinkes, that with the very talking therof, I have a conceit with my selfe, that at this present, I feele my selfe in the same happinesse with them. I shall now, mistresse, give you to understand the cause of my comming: I am sent unto you for my Ladies Girdle; and moreover, my Ladie intreats you, that you would come and visit her, and that out of hand, for shee feeles her selfe very ill, and much pained and troubled with griefes and pangs about the heart; I assure you, she is very heart-sicke.

CELESTINA. Of these petty griefes, the report is more then the paine. Is 't about the heart, say you? I marvell (I promise you) that so young a Gentlewoman as shee is, should be pained at the heart.

172

CALISTO AND MELIBEA

LUCRECIA. Would thou wert as well drag'd along the strectes (thou old traiterous Hagge) as thou know'st well inough what shee ayles. The subtill old Bawd comes, and does her witcheries, and her tricks, and then goes her waies, and afterwards when one comes unto her for helpe, she makes forsooth as if she knew no such matter, it is newes (forsooth) to her.

CELEST. What sai'st thou, Daughter?

LUCRECIA. Mary, I say (mother) would we were gone [at] once; and that you would give me the Girdle.

CELEST. Come, let us goe. I will carry it along with me.

THE END OF THE NINTH ACT

ACTUS X

THE ARGUMENT

 HILEST Celestina *and* Lucrecia *goe onward on their way,* Melibea *talkes, and discourses with her selfe. Being come to the doore, first enters* Lucrecia, *anon after, causes* Celestina *to come in.* Melibea, *after some exchange of words, opens her mind to* Celestina; *telling her how fervently she was falne in love with* Calisto. *They spy* Alisa, Melibea's *mother comming; they take their leave each of other.* Alisa *askes her daughter* Melibea, *what businesse she had with* Celestina? *and what she made there? disswading her from conversing with her, and forbidding her, her company.*

INTERLOCUTORS

Melibea, Celestina, Alisa, Lucrecia.

MELIBEA. O wretch that I am! O unfortunate Damsell! Had I not beene better yesterday, to have yeelded to Celestina's petition and request, when in the behalfe of that

173

Gentleman, whose sight hath made me his prisoner, I was so earnestly sued unto : and so have contented him, and cured my selfe, then to be thus forcibly driven to discover my heart, when haply he will not accept of it ; when as already disaffianced in his hope, for want of a good and faire answer, hee hath set both his eyes and his heart upon the love and person of another ? how much more advantageous unto me, would an intreated promise have beene, then a forced offerture ? to grant being requested, then to yeeld being constrained ? O my faithfull servant, Lucrecia, what wilt thou say of me, what wilt thou thinke of my judgement and understanding, when thou shalt see me to publish that, which I would never discover unto thee ? how wilt thou stand astonished to my honesty and modesty, which (like a Recluse, shut up from all company) I have ever hitherto kept inviolable ? I know not whether thou hast suspected, or no, whence this my sorrow proceedeth, or whether thou art now comming with that Solicitresse of my safety ? O thou high and supreme Power ! thou, unto whom, all that are in misery and affliction, call, and cry for helpe ; the appassionated begge remedy, the wounded crave healing ; thou, whome the heavens, seas, earth, and the Center of hell it selfe doth obey ; thou who submittedst all things unto men, I humbly beseech thee, that thou wilt give sufferance and patience to my wounded heart, whereby I may be able to dissemble my terrible passion. Let not this Leafe of my chastity lose it's guylding, which I have laid upon this amorous desire, publishing my paine to be otherwise then that, which indeed tormenteth me. But how shall I be able to doe it ; That poysoned morsell so cruelly tormenting mee, which the sight of that Gentlemans presence gave me ? O Sexe of womankind ! feeble and fraile in thy being ; why was it not granted as well unto women, to discover their tormentfull and fervent flames, as unto men ? For then neither should Calisto have cause to complaine, nor I to live in paine.

LUCRECIA. Aunt, stay heere a while behinde this doore, whilest I goe in, and see with whom my Mistresse is talking. Come in ; she is talking alone to her selfe.

MELIBEA. Lucrecia, make fast the doore there, and pull
174

downe the hanging over it. O wise and honest old Dame, you are exceeding welcome ; what thinke you, that chance should so dispose of things, and fortune so bring about her wheele, that I should stand in neede of this wisdome, and crave so suddenly of you, that you would pay me in the selfe-same coyne, the courtesie which was by you demanded of me for that Gentleman, whome you were to cure by the vertue of my Girdle ?

CELEST. Say, Lady, what is your disease, that you so lively expresse the tokens of your torment, in those your maiden blushes ?

MELIBEA. Truly, mother, I thinke there be some Serpents within my body, that are gnawing upon my heart.

CELEST. It is well, even as I would have it. I will be even with you (you foole) for your yesterdaies anger, I will make you pay for it with a witnesse.

MELIBEA. What's that you say ? Have you perceived by my lookes, any cause from whence my malady proceedeth ?

CELEST. You have not, Madame, told me the quality of your disease ; and would you have mee divine of the cause ? That which I say, is this, that I am heartily sorry to see your Ladiship so sad and so ill.

MELIBEA. Good old woman ; Doe thou make me merry then. For I have heard much of thy wisdome.

CELEST. Madame, as farre as humane knowledge can discerne of inward griefe, I dare presume. And for as much, as for the health and remedy of infirmities, and diseases, these graces were imparted unto men, for the finding out of fit and convenient medicines, whereof some were attained to by experience, some by Art, and some by a naturall instinct ; some small portion of these good gifts, this poore old creature my selfe have gotten, who is heere present to doe you the best service she can.

MELIBEA. O how acceptable and pleasing are thy words to mine eares ! it is a comfortable thing to the sicke patient, to see his physician to look cheerfully upon him. Me thinks I see my heart broken betweene thy hand in pieces, which with a little labour, and by power and vertue of thy tongue,

ACTUS
X

thou art able (if thou wilt) to joyne together, and make it whole againe : even as easily, as Alexander that great King of Macedon dream't of that wholesome roote in the mouth of a Dragon, wherewith he healed his servant Ptolomy, who had beene bitten by a Viper ; and therefore, for the love of Iove, disroabe your selfe, that you may more easily, and more diligently looke into the nature of my disease, and affoord me some remedy for it.

CELEST. A great part of health, is the desiring of health. And a good signe of mending, to be willing to mend. For which reason I reckon your griefe the lesse, and hold it the lesse dangerous ; But that I may minister a wholesome medi-cine unto you, and such a one as may be agreable to your disease ; it is requisite, that you first satisfie me in these three particulars. The first is, on which side of your body your paine doth lye most ? The second, how long you have had this paine ; whether it hath taken you but of late, or no ? For your newly growing infirmities are sooner cured in the tendernesse of their growth, then when they have taken deepe rooting by over-long persevering in their office : So beasts are sooner tamed when they are young, and more easily brought to the yoake, then when their hide is throughly hardned : So far better doe those plants grow up, and prosper, which are remooved when they are young and tender, then those that are transplanted, having long borne fruit. The third is, whether this your evill hath proceeded of any cruell thought, which hath taken hold on you ? This being made knowne, you shall see mee set my selfe roundly to worke about your cure ; for it is very fit and convenient, that you should open the whole truth, as well to your Phy-sician, as your Confessour.

MELIBEA. Friend, Celestina, Thou wise Matrone, and great Mistresse in thy Art, thou hast well opened unto me the way, by which I may manifest my maladie unto thee. Beleeve me, you have questioned me like a wise woman, and like one that is well experienced in these kind of sicknesses. My paine is about my heart, it's residence, neere unto my left Pappe ; but disperseth it selfe over every part of my body. Secondly, it hath beene so but of late ; nor did I

176

CALISTO AND MELIBEA

ever thinke, that any paine whatsoever could have so deprived me of my understanding, as this doth ; it troubles my sight, changes my countenance, takes away my stomacke, I cannot sleepe for it, nor will it suffer mee to injoy any kinde of pleasure : touching the thought, which was the last thing you demanded, concerning my disease, I am not able to deliver it unto you, and as little the cause thereof; For neither death of kinsfolke, nor losse of temporall goods, nor any sudden passion upon any vision, nor any doting dreame, nor any other thing can I conjecture to be the cause of it, save onely a kinde of alteration, caused by your selfe upon your request, which I suspected in the behalfe of that Gentleman Calisto, when you entreated me for my Charme.

CELEST. What, Madame? Is Calisto so bad a man? Is his name so bad ; that onely but to name him, should, upon the very sound thereof, send forth such poyson ? Deceive not your selfe ; Doe not beleeve that this is the cause of your griefe : I have another thing in the winde, there is more in't then so ; but since you make it so daintie, if your Ladiship will give mee leave, I will tell you the cause of it.

MELIBEA. Why, how now, Celestina, what a strange request is this that thou mak'st unto me ? Needest thou to crave leave of me, who am to receive helpe from thee? What Physician did ever demand such security, for to cure his patient ? Speake, speake what you please ; for you shall alwaies have leave of mee to say what you will ; alwaies excepted, that you wrong not my honour with your words.

CELESTINA. I see (Lady) that on the one side you complaine of your griefe, and on the other side, I perceive, that you feare your remedy, your feare strikes a feare into mee ; which feare causeth silence, and silence truce betwixt your malady and my medicine ; so that your selfe will be the cause that your paine shall not cease, nor my cunning cure you.

MELIBEA. By how much the longer you deferre my cure, by so much the more doe you increase my paine, and augment my passion. Either thy medicines are of the powder of infamy, and of the juyce of corruption, confectionated with some other cruell paine, then that which thy patient

Z   177 already feeles; or else thy skill is nothing worth; For if either the one, or the other did not hinder thee, thou wouldst tell mee of some other remedy boldly, and without feare, sithence I intreate thee to aquaint me therewith, my honour still preserved.

CELEST. Madame, thinke it not strange, that it is harder for him that is wounded, to indure the torment of hot-scalding Turpentine, and the sharpe incisions, which gall the heart, and double the paine; then the wound that is newly inflicted on him that is whole. And therefore, if you be willing to be cured, and that I should discover unto you the sharp point of my needle, without any feare at all, frame for your hands and feet a bond of patience and of quietnesse; for your eyes, a veile of pitty and compassion; for your tongue, a bridle of silence; for your eares, the bumbast, or stuffing of sufferance and bearing; and then shall you see, what effects this old Mistresse in her Art, will worke upon your wounds.

MELIBEA. O how thou killest me with delayes! For Gods love, speake what thou wilt, doe what thou wilt, exercice thy skill, put thy experience in practice. For, there is not any remedy so sharpe, as can equall the bitternes of my paine and torment. No, though it touch upon mine honour, though it wrong my reputation, though it afflict my body, though it rip and breake up my flesh, for to pull out my grieved heart. I give thee my faith, to do what thou wilt securely; and if I may find ease of my payne, I shall liberally reward thee.

LUCRECIA. My Mistresse hath lost her wits: she is exceeding ill: this same sorceresse hath captivated her will.

CELEST. One divell or other is still haunting me. One while here, another while there. I have escaped Parmeno, and have fallen upon Lucrecia.

MELIBEA. Mother, what is 't you say; what said the wench unto you?

CELESTINA. I cannot tell (Lady) I did not well heare her. But let her say what she wil; yet let me tell you: That there is not any thing more contrary in great Cures, before strong and stout-hearted Surgeons, then weake and

CALISTO AND MELIBEA

fainting hearts, who with their great lamentations, their pittyfull words, and their sorrowfull gestures strike a feare into the patient, make him despaire of his recovery, and anger and trouble the Surgeon, which trouble makes him to alter his hand, and direct his needle without any order. By which you may clearely knowe, that it is very necessary for your safetie, that there bee no body about you ; no, not so much as Lucrecia. And therefore, it is very meete, that you command her absence : daughter Lucrecia, you must pardon me.

MELIBEA. Get you out quickly, be gone.

LUCRECIA. Well, well, we are all undone. I goe, madame.

CELEST. Your great paine and torment doth likewise put boldnes into me, as also that I perceive by your suspition, you have already swallowed some part of my cure. But notwithstanding it is needful, that we bring a more manifest remedy, and more wholesome mitigation of your paine, from the house of that worthy one Calisto.

MELIBEA. Mother, I pray you, good now hold your peace; fetch not any thing from his house, that may worke my good. If you love me, doe not so much as once name him unto me.

CELEST. Madame, I pray be patient. That which is the chiefe and principall piller, must not be broken. For then all our labour is lost : your wound is great, and hath need of a sharpe cure. And hard with hard, doth smooth and mollifie more effectually and more delicately. And wise men say, That the cure of a launcing Surgeon, leaves behind it the greater skarre : And that without danger, no danger is overcome. Have patience then with your selfe. For seldome is that cured without paine, which in it selfe is painefull. One nayle drives out another. And one sorrow expels another. Doe not conceive hatred nor disaffection, nor give your tongue leave to speake ill of so vertuous a person, as Calisto, whom, if you did but knowe him.

MELIBEA. O you kill me! no more of him, for Gods sake no more. Did not I tell you, that you should not commend him unto me? and that you should not speake a word of him neither good nor bad?

179

CELEST. Madame, this is that other, and maine point in my cure; which if you, by your impatience will not consent unto, my comming can little profit you. But if you will (as you promist) be patient, you shall remaine sound, and out of doubt, and Calisto be well apaid, and have no cause to complaine. I did before acquaint you with my cures, and with this invisible needle, which before it come at you to stitch up your wound, you feele it, onely but having it in my mouth, and naming it unto you.

MELIBEA. So often wilt thou name this Gentleman unto mee, that neither my promise, nor the faith I plighted thee, will suffice to make me any longer to indure your words. Wherein should he be well apaid? What doe I owe unto him? Wherein am I bound unto him? What charge have I put him to? What hath he ever done for me? What necessity is there, that wee must be driven to use him, as the instrument of my recovery? More pleasing would it be unto me, that you would teare my flesh and sinewes asunder, and teare out my heart, then to utter such words as these.

CELESTINA. Without any rupture, or renting of your garments, love did lance your brest; and therefore will not sunder your flesh, to cure your sore.

MELIBEA. How call you this griefe, that hath seazed on the better part of my body?

CELESTINA. Sweet Love.

MELIBEA. Tell mee then, what thing this sweete Love may be? For onely in the very hearing of it nam'd, my heart leapes for joy.

CELEST. It is a concealed fire; a pleasing wound; a savoury poyson; a sweet bitternesse; a delightfull griefe; a cheerfull torment; a sweet, yet cruell hurt; and a gentle death.

MELIBEA. O wretched, that I am! for if thy relation be true, I rest doubtfull of my recovery: For, according to the contrariety which these names doe carry, that which shall be profitable for one, shall to another bring more passion.

CELEST. Let not your noble youth be diffident of recovery; be of good cheere; take a good heart to you; and

CALISTO AND MELIBEA

doubt not of your welfare: For where heaven gives a wound, there it gives a remedy; and as it hurts, so it heales; and so much the sooner, because I know where the flowre growes, that will free you from all this torment.

MELIBEA. How is it called?

CELEST. I dare not tell you.

MELIBEA. Speake and spare not.

CELESTIN. Calisto. O Madame; Melibea; ah woe is mee, why woman, what meane you? What a cowardly heart have you? What a fainting is heere? O miserable that I am, hold up your head, I pray lift it up; O accursed old woman! Must my steps end [in] this? If she goe thus away in a swound, they will kill me; if shee revive, shee will be much pained: For she will never indure to publish her paine, nor give mee leave to exercise my cure. Why, Melibea, my sweete Lady; my faire Angel; What's the matter, Sweet-heart? Where is your griefe? why speake you not unto me? What is become of your gracious and pleasing speach? Where is that cheerefull colour, that was wont to beautifie your cheekes? Open those brightest Lamps, that ever nature tinded: Open your eyes, I say, those cleare sunnes, that are able to give light to darknesse. Lucrecia, Lucrecia, Come hither quickly; come quickely, I say, you shall see your Lady lye heere in a swound in my armes; runne downe quickly for a Jarre of water.

MELIBEA. Softly, speake softly I pray; I 'le see if I can rise; In no case doe not trouble the house.

CELESTINA. Ay me! Sweet Lady, doe not sinke any more: speake, speake unto mee as you were wont.

MELIBEA. I will, and much more then I was wont. But peace, I pray a while, and doe not trouble mee.

CELESTIN. What will you have me to doe (my precious pearle?) Whence arose this sudden qualme? I beleeve, my points are broken.

MELIBEA. No; it is my honesty that is broken; it is my modesty that is broken; my too much bashfulnesse and shamefastnesse, occasioned my swowning, which being my naturall and familiar friends, and companions, could not sleightly absent themselves from my face, but they would

181

also carry away my colour with them for a while, my strength, my speach, and a great part of my understanding. But now (my good Mistresse, my faithfull Secretary) since that which thou so openly knowst, it is in vaine for mee to seeke to smother it; many, yea many daies, are now overpast, since that noble Gentleman motioned his love unto mee; whose speach and name was then as hatefull, as now the reviving thereof is pleasing unto me: with thy Needles thou hast stitcht up my wound; I am come to thy Bent; it is in thy power to do with me what thou wilt. In my girdle, thou carriedst away with thee the possession of my liberty: His anguish was my greater torment; his paine my greater punishment. I highly praise and commend your singular sufferance, your discreet boldnes, your liberall paines, your sollicitous and faithfull steps, your pleasing speach, your good wisedome, your excessive solicitude, and your profitable importunity: the Gentleman is much bound unto you, and my selfe more; for my reproaches and revilings could never make thee to slacke thy courage, thy strong continuance, and forcible perseverance in thy suite, relying still on thy great subtilty and strength of wit; or rather bearing thy selfe like a most faithfull and trusty servant, being then most diligent, when thou wast most reviled; the more I did disgrace thee, the more wast thou importunate; the harsher answer I gave thee, the better didst thou seeme to take it: when I was most angry, then wast thou most milde and humble: and now, by laying aside all feare, thou hast gotten that out of my bosome, which I never thought to have discovered unto thee, or to any other whosoever.

CELEST. My most deare both Lady and friend, wonder not so much at this; for those ends, that have their effect, give me daringnesse to indure those craggy and dangerous by-waies, by which I come to such Recluses as your selfe. True it is, that untill I had resolved with my selfe, as well on my way hitherwards, as also heere in your house, I stood in great doubt, whether were I best discover my petition unto you or no? When I did thinke on the great power of your father, then did I feare; but when withall, I weygh'd the noblenesse of Calisto, then I grew bold againe; when I

182

CALISTO AND MELIBEA

observed your discretion, I waxed timorous; but when I considered your vertue, and your courtesie, I recovered new courage : in the one, I found feare ; in the other, safety. And since, Madame, you have beene willing to grace me with the discovery of so great a favour, as now you have made knowne unto mee, declare your will unto mee, lay your secrets in my lappe ; put into my hands the managing of this matter, and I will give it such a forme, as both you and Calisto shall very shortly accomplish your desires.

MELIBEA. O my Calisto ! my deare Lord, my sweete and pleasing joy, if thy heart feele the like torment, as mine, I wonder how thy absence gives thee leave to live. O thou, both my mother, and mistresse, so handle the businesse, that I may presently see him, if you desire I should live.

CELEST. See him ? you shall both see him, and speake with him.

MELIBEA. Speake with him ? it is impossible.

CELEST. Nothing is impossible to a willing minde.

MELIBEA. Tell mee how ?

CELEST. I have it in my head : Mary thus, within the doores of thy house.

MELIBEA. When ?

CELEST. This night.

MELIBEA. Thou shalt be glorious in mine eyes, if thou compasse this. But soft, at what houre ?

CELEST. Just when the clocke strikes twelve.

MELIBEA. Goe, be gone, hye you, good Mistresse, my faithfull friend, and talke with that Gentleman, and will him that hee come very softly at his appointed houre, and then wee will conclude of things, as himselfe shall thinke fit to order them.

CELEST. Farewell. Loe, yonder is your mother making hitherward.

MELIBEA. Friend Lucrecia, my loyall servant, and faithfull secretary, you have heere seene, that I have no power over my selfe ; and what I have done, lies not in my hands to helpe it. Love hath made me prisoner to that Gentleman. I intreat thee (for pittie sake) that you will signe what you have seene, with the scale of secresy, whereby

183

I may come to the enjoying of so sweet a Love: In requitall whereof, thou shalt be held by me, in that high regard, as thy faithfull service deserveth.

LUCRECIA. Madame, long afore this, I perceived your wound, and sounded your desire: I did much pitty your torment; for, the more you sought to hide from me the fire which did burne you, the more did those flames manifest themselves in the colour of your face, in the little quietnesse of your heart, in the restlesnes of your members, in your tossing to and fro, in eating without any appetite, and in your unablenesse to sleepe: So that I did continually see from time to time, as plainely as if I had beene within you, most manifest, and apparant signes of your wretched estate; but because in that instant, when as will reigneth in those whom we serve, or a disordinate appetite, it is fitting for us that are servants, to obey them with bodily diligence, and not to checke and controle them with the Artificiall counsels of the tongue. And therefore did I suffer with paine, held my peace with feare, concealed with fidelity; though I alwaies held it better to use sharpe Counsell then smooth flattery. But since that your Ladiship hath no other remedy for your recoverie, but either to die or to live; it is very meete, that you should make choice of that for the best, which in it selfe is best.

ALISA. How now neighbour? What's the matter with you, that you are here thus day by day?

CELESTINA. I wanted yesterday a little of my weight in the threed I sold, and now I am come (according to my promise) for to make it up. And now that I have delivered it, I am going away. Iove have you in his good keeping.

ALISA. And you too. Daughter Melibea, what would this old woman have?

MELIBEA. She would have sold me a little sublimated Mercury.

ALISA. I mary, I rather beleeve this, then that, which the old lewd Hag told me. Shee was afrayd, I would have beene angry with her, and so she pop't me in the mouth with a Lye. Daughter, take heede of her. For shee is an old crafty Foxe; and as false as the divell. A whole Country

184

CALISTO AND MELIBEA

can not afford you such another treacherous huswife. Take you heed therefore (I say) of her. For, your cunning and crafty theeves goe alwayes a prolling about your richest houses. She knowes by her treasons and false merchandize, how to change chaste purposes. She causeth an ill report, bringeth a bad name and fame upon those that have any thing to do with her. If she be but seene to have entred one house thrice, it is inough to ingender suspition.

LUCRECIA. My old Ladies Counsell comes too late.

ALISA. I charge you (Daughter) upon my blessing, and by that love which I beare unto you, that if she come hither any more, when I am out of the way, that you do not give her any entertainement, no manner of welcome, no, not so much as to shew her any the least countenance of liking, lest it should incourage her to come againe. Let her finde, that you stand upon your honesty and reputation. And be you round and short with her in your answers, and she will never come at you againe. For true vertue is more feared then a sword.

MELIBEA. Is shee a blade of that making? is shee such a whipster? Is shee one of those, you know what? She shall never come at mee more. And beleeve me (Madame) I much joy in your good advice, and that you have so well instructed me, of whom I ought to beware.

THE END OF THE TENTH ACT

THE TRAGICK-COMEDY OF

ACTUS XI

THE ARGUMENT

ELESTINA *having taken her leave of* Melibea, *goes mumbling and talking along the streetes to her selfe. Shee espies* Sempronio *and* Parmeno, *who are going to Saint* Marie Magdalens *to looke out their Master.* Sempronio *talkes with* Calisto ; *In the meane while comes in* Celestina. *They go all to* Calisto's *house.* Celestina *delivereth her message ; and the meanes for their meeting appointed by* Melibea. *In the interim that* Celestina *and* Calisto *are discoursing together,* Sempronio *and* Parmeno *fall a talking betweene themselves ;* Celestina *takes her leave of* Calisto, *and gets her home to her owne house. She knocks at the doore ;* Elicia *opens it unto her. They sup, and then goe to take their rest.*

INTERLOCUTORS

Celestina, Sempronio, Calisto, Parmeno, Elicia.

CELESTINA. O thrice happy day! would I were at home with all my joy, wherewith I goe laden. But I see Parmeno and Sempronio going to the Mirtle-Grove : I will after them. And if I meete with Calisto there, we will all along together to his house, to demand a reward for the great good newes that I bring him.

SEMPRONIO. Take heede, Sir, lest by your long stay, you give occasion of talke to the world. For your honesty have a care, that you make not your selfe become a by-word to the people. For now-a-dayes, it is commonly spoken amongst them, He is an Hypocrite, that is too devout. For, what will they say of you, if they see you thus, but scoffe in dirision at you, and say, He is gone to the Mirtle-Grove to sacrifice some halfescore Hecatombes of sighs and ay-mees to Venus sonne, to prosper and preferre him to the favour and

186

CALISTO AND MELIBEA

fruition of some Mistresse? If you are opprest with passion, indure it at home in your owne house, that the world may not perceive it. Discover not your griefe unto strangers, since the drumme is in their hands, who know best how to beate it: and your businesse in her hands, who knowes best how to manage it.

CALISTO. In whose hands?

SEMPRONIO. In Celestina's.

CELESTINA. Who is that names Celestina? What saist thou of this slave of Calisto's? I have come trudging all along the Augurs street, to see if I could overtake you. I did put my best legge formost, but all would not doe: the skirts of my Petticoate were so long, and did so often interfold themselves betweene my feet.

CALISTO. O thou joy of the world! thou ease of my passions, thou relieveresse of my paine, my eyes looking-glasse, my heart doth even exult for joy, in beholding so honoured a presence, an age so innobled with yeeres; tell me, what is't thou com'st with, what good newes dost thou bring? For I see thou lookst cheerfully: And yet I know not of what tearmes my life doth stand; in what it consisteth.

CELEST. In my tongue.

CALIST. What saist thou then? Speake, thou that art my glory and comfort. Deliver it more at large unto mee.

CELESTINA. Sir, let us first goe more privately; and as wee goe home to your house, I will tell you that, which shall make you glad indeede.

PARME. Brother, the old woman lookes merrily; Sure, shee hath sped well to day.

SEMPR. Soft, listen what shee saies.

CELESTINA. All this day, Sir, have I beene labouring in your businesse, and have neglected other weighty and serious affaires, which did much concerne mee: many doe I suffer to live in paine, onely that I may yeeld you comfort. Besides, I have lost more by it, then you are aware of; but farewell it. All is well lost, sithence I have brought my businesse to so good an end: And heare you mee, for I will

187

THE TRAGICK-COMEDY OF

tell it you in few words (for I love to be short) Melibea is wholy at your service.

CALISTO. O what doe I heare?

CELEST. Nay, shee is more yours then her owne: more at your service and command, then of her father Pleberio.

CALISTO. Speake softly (good mother) take heede what you say; let not my men heare you, lest they should call thee foole. Melibea is my mistresse, Melibea is my desire, Melibea is my life, I am her servant, I am her slave.

SEMPR. Good Sir, with this distrustfulnesse of yours, with this undervalewing of your selfe, you intersert such doubts, as cut off Celestina, in the midst of her discourse; you would tire out a whole world with your disordered, and confused interruptions. Why doe you crosse and blesse your selfe? Why do you keep such a wondring? It were better you would give her some thing for her paines. For these words are worthy better payment, and expect no lesse at your hands.

CALISTO. Well hast thou spoken; deare mother, I wot full well, that my small reward can no waies reward your paines; but in stead of a gowne and a kirtle (because Tradesmen shall not share with you) take this little chaine, put it about your necke, and goe on with your discourse, and my joy.

PARM. Call you that a little chaine? Heard you him, Sempronio? This Spend-thrift makes no reckoning of it; but I assure you, I will not give my part thereof for halfe a Marke of gold, let her share it never so ill.

SEMPR. Peace, I say, for should my Master have overheard you, you should have had worke enough, to pacifie him, and to cure your selfe; So offended is he already with your continuall murmuring. As you love me (brother) heare, and hold your peace; for to this end, thou hast two eares, and but one tongue.

PARM. He hath hang'd himselfe so fast to that old womans mouth, that hee is both deafe, dumbe and blind, like a body without a soule, or a bell without a clapper; in-

CALISTO AND MELIBEA

somuch, that if wee should point at him scornefully with
our fingers, he would say, We lifted up our hands to heaven,
imploring his happy successe in his love.

SEMPR. Peace, hearken, listen well unto Celestina. On
my soule, shee deserves it all, and more too, had hee given it
her. She speakes wonders.

CELEST. Noble Calisto, to such a poore weake old
woman as my selfe, you have shewed your selfe exceeding
franke and liberall; but as every gift is esteemed great, or
little, in regard of him that gives it, I will not therefore
compare therewith my small desert, which it surpasseth both
in qualitie and quantitie; but rather measure it with your
magnificence, before which it is nothing. In requitall
whereof, I restore unto thee thy health, which was upon
losing; thy heart, which was upon fainting; and thy wits,
which were upon turning. Melibea is pained more for you,
then you for her: Melibea loves you, and desires to see you:
Melibea spends more houres in thinking upon you, then on
her selfe: Melibea calls her selfe thine; and this shee holds as
a Title of libertie, and with this, shee allayes that fire, which
burnes more in her, then thy selfe.

CALISTO. You my servants; Am I heere? Heare I
this? Looke whether I am awake or not. Is it day, or is
it night? O thou great God of heaven, I beseech thee, this
may not proove a dreame; Sure, I doe not sleepe; mee thinkes
I am fully awake. Tell mee, mother, dost thou make sport
with mee, in paying me with words? Feare nothing, but
tell mee the truth; for thy going to and fro deserveth a great
deale more then this.

CELEST. The heart, that is wounded with desire, never
entertaineth good newes for certaine; nor bad for doubtfull. But whether I jest, or no; your selfe shall see, by
going this night to her house (her selfe having agreed
with mee about the time) appointing you to be just
there as the clocke strikes twelve, that you may talke together thorow the chinks of the doore; from whose owne
mouth, you shall fully know my sollicitude, and her desire,
and the love which shee beares unto you, and who hath
caused it.

189

CALISTO. It is enough; Is it possible, I should hope for so great a happinesse? Can so great a blessing light upon Calisto? I dye till that houre come. I am not capable of so great a glory. I doe not deserve so great a favour, nor am I worthy to speake with so faire a Lady, who of her owne free-will, should affoord mee so great a grace.

CELEST. I have often heard, that it is harder to suffer prosperous, then adverse fortune; because the one hath never any quietude, and the other still taketh comfort. It is strange, Sir, that you will not consider who you are, nor the time that you have spent in her service; nor the person, whome you have made to be your meanes: And likewise, that hitherto, thou hast ever beene in doubt of having her, and yet didst still endure all with patience; and now, that I doe certifie unto thee the end of thy torment, wilt thou put an end to thy life? Consider, consider, I pray, with thy selfe, that Celestina is on thy side; and that although all should be wanting unto thee, which in a Lover were to be required, I would sell thee for the most complete gallant of the world; for I would make for thee mountaines of most craggy rocks, to grow plaine, and smooth. Nay, more, I would make thee to goe thorow the deepest channell, or the highest swelling sea, without wetting of thy foot: you know not on whom you have bestowed your Largesse.

CALISTO. Remember your selfe, mother, did you not tell me, that shee would come to mee of her owne accord?

CELESTINA. Yes, and that upon her very knees.

SEMPR. Pray heaven it be not a false alarme; one thing rumord, another purposed: It may be a false fire-worke, to blow us all up. I feare mee, it is a false traine, a made match, and a trappe purposely set to catch us all. Bethinke your selfe, mother, that so men use to give crooked pinnes wrapt up in bread; poysonsome pilles roll'd up in Suger, that they may not be seene and perceived.

PARMENO. I never heard thee speake better in my life: the sudden yeelding of this Lady, and her so speedy consenting to all that Celestina would have her, ingenders a strong suspition within mee; and makes me to feare, that deceiving
190

CALISTO AND MELIBEA

our will with her sweet and ready words, she will rob us on the wrong side, as your Gypsies use to doe, when they looke in our hands to tell us our fortunes. Besides, mother, it is an old saying: that with faire words, many wrongs are revenged: and the counterfet stalking horse, which is made but of Canvasse, with his dissembled gate, and the alluring sound of the tinckling of a bell, drives the Partridges into the net: the songs of the Syrens deceive the simple Mariner with the sweetenesse of their voices: Even so, shee with her exceeding kindnesse, and sudden concession of her love, will seaze hand-smooth on a whole drove of us at once, and purge her innocency with Calisto's honour, and our deaths: Being like heerein to the teatling Lambe, which suckes both her damm's teat, and that of another Ewe. Shee by securing us, will be revenged both of Calisto, and all of us; so that with the great number of people which they have in the house, they may catch both the old ones and the young one together in the nest, whilest shee shrugging and rubbing her selfe by the fire side, may safely say, Hee is out of gun-shot, that rings the bell to the battell.

CALISTO. Peace, you Knaves, you Villaines, you suspitious Rascalls, will you make mee beleeve that Angels can doe ought that is ill? I tell you, Melibea is but a dissembled Angell, that lives heere amongst us.

SEMPRO. What? will you still play the Hereticke? Harken to him, Parmeno; but take thou no care at all; let it not trouble thee. For, if there be any double dealing, or that the play prove foule, he shall pay for all; for our feete be good, and wee will betake us to our heeles.

CELESTINA. Sir, you are in the right, and these in the wrong; over-lading their thoughts with vaine suspitions and jealousies; I have done all that I was injoyned: and so I leave you to your joyes. Good Angels defend you and direct you: as for my selfe, I am very well satisfied. And if you shall have further occasion to use mee, eyther in this particular, or any thing else, you shall finde mee ever ready to doe you the best service I can.

PARMENO. Ha, ha, he.

SEMPRONIO. I pray thee, why dost thou laugh?

PARME. To see what haste the old Trot makes to be gone: shee thinkes every houre a yeere, till shee be gone cleare away with the chaine ; she cannot perswade her selfe, that it is as yet sure inough in her hands ; for shee knowes, that shee is as little worthy of that chaine, as Calisto is of his Melibea.

SEMPR. What would you have such an old whorish Bawd as she, to doe? who knowes and understands that which wee silence and keepe secret, and useth to patch up seven Virginities at a clap for two pieces of Silver: And now, that shee sees her selfe to be laden with gold, what, I say, would you have her to doe, but to make it safe and sure, by taking possession thereof, for feare lest hee should take it from her againe, after that hee hath had his desire? But let us beware of the Divell, and take heede that wee goe not together by the eares, when wee come to devide the spoyle.

CALISTO. Mother, fare you well, I will lay mee downe to sleepe, and rest my selfe a while, that I may redeeme the nights past, and satisfie the better for that, which is to come.

CELESTINA. Tha, ta, ta.

ELICIA. Who knockes?

CELESTINA. Daughter Elicia, open the doore.

ELICIA. How chance you come so late? It is not well done of you (being an old woman, as you are) for you may hap to stumble, where you may so fall, that it may be your death.

CELEST. I feare not that (wench:) For I consult with my selfe in the day, which way I shall goe in the night ; for I never goe neere any bridge, bench, pit or Causey: for (as it is in the Proverbe) He goes not safe, nor never shall, who goes too close unto the wall: And hee goes still most safe and sound, whose steps are plaste on plainest ground : and I had rather foule my shooes with durt, then be-bloody my Kerchiefe at every walls corner. But does it not grieve thee to be heere?

ELICIA. Why should it grieve mee?

192

CALISTO AND MELIBEA

CELEST. Because the company I left heere with you, is gone, and you are all alone.

ELICIA. It is some foure houres agoe, since they went hence; and would you have mee to thinke on that now?

CELEST. Indeed the sooner they left you, the more reason you had to thinke thereon; but let us leave to talke of their speedy going, and of my long staying, and let us first provide for our supper, and then for our sleepe.

THE END OF THE ELEVENTH ACT

ACTUS XII

THE ARGUMENT

IDNIGHT *being come*, Calisto, Sempronio, and Parmeno, *being well armed, goe towards the house of* Melibea. Lucrecia and Melibea *stand at the doore, watching for* Calisto. Calisto *comes;* Lucrecia *first speakes unto him; she calls* Melibea. Lucrecia *goes aside;* Melibea *and* Calisto *talke together, the doore being betwixt them;* Parmeno *and* Sempronio *withdraw themselves a little waies off. They heare some people comming along the street; they prepare themselves for flight.* Calisto *takes his leave of* Melibea, *leaving order for his returne the next night following;* Pleberio *awakened with the noise which he heard in the street, calls to his wife* Alisa; *they aske of* Melibea *who that was, that walk't up and downe in her chamber?* Melibea *answers her father, by faining she was athirst.* Calisto *with his servants, goe talking home to his house. Being come home, he laies him downe to sleepe;* Parmeno *and* Sempronio *goe to* Celestina's *house, they demand their share of her paines;* Celestina *dissembles the matter, they fall a wrangling; they lay hands on* Celestina, *they murther her.* Elicia *cryes out; the Justice comes, and apprehends them both.*

2 B   193

THE TRAGICK-COMEDY OF

INTERLOCUTORS

Calisto, Lucrecia, Melibea, Parmeno, Sempronio, Pleberio, Alisa, Celestina, Elicia.

CALISTO. Sirs, what's a clock?

SEMPR. It strooke now tenne.

CALISTO. O how it discontents me, to see servants so wretchlesse! Of my much mindfulnesse for this nights meeting, and your much unmindfulnesse, and extreme carelesnesse, there might have been had some indifferent both remembrance, and care; how inconsiderately (knowing how much it importeth mee, to be either tenne or eleven) dost thou answer mee at hap-hazard, with that which comes first to mouth! O unhappy I, if by chance I had overslept my selfe! and my demand had depended on the answer of Sempronio, to make of eleven, ten; and of twelve, but eleven! Melibea might have come forth; I had not gone out; and shee returned backe: so that, neither my misery should have had an end, nor my desire have taken effect. And therefore it is not said in vaine, That another mans harme hangs but by one haire, no man caring whether hee sinke or swimme.

SEMPR. Me thinks it is as great an errour in a man, to aske what hee knowes, as to answer to what hee knowes not. It were better (Sir) that we should spend this houre that remaineth, in preparing weapons, then in propounding questions.

CALISTO. The foole saies well, I would not at such a time receive a displeasure. I will not thinke on that which may be, but on that which hath beene; not on the harme which may arise by his negligence, but on the good which may come by my carefulnesse. I will give leasure to my anger, and will either quite dismisse it, or force it to be more remisse. Parmeno, Take down my Corslets, and arme your selves, so shall we goe the safer: For it is in the Proverbe, Halfe the battell is then waged, when a man is well prepared.

PARME. Lo, Sir, heere they bee.

CALISTO. Come helpe mee heere to put them on. Doe

194

CALISTO AND MELIBEA

you looke out, Sempronio, and see if any body be stirring in the street.

SEMPR. Sir, I see not any, and though there were, yet the darkenesse of the night is such, and so great, that it is impossible for any that shall meet us, either to see or know us.

CALISTO. Let us along then. Heere, my masters, this way; for though it be somewhat about, yet is it the more private way, and the lesser frequented. Now it strikes twelve, a good houre.

PARME. Wee are neere unto the place.

CALISTO. Wee are come in very good time. Goe thou, Parmeno, and peepe in at the dore, to see if that Lady be come or no.

PARMENO. Who, I, Sir? God forbid, that I should marre that which I never made. Much better were it (Sir) that your presence should be her first incounter, lest in seeing mee, shee should be moved to anger, in seeing so many acquainted with that, which she so secretly desires to be done, and undergoeth with so great feare: as also, because she may haply imagine that you mocke her.

CALISTO. O how well hast thou spoken! thou hast given mee my life, by giving mee this sound advice; for there needeth nothing more to beare me home dead to my house, then that she through my improvidence, should have gone her waies backe: I will goe thither my selfe, and doe you stay heere.

PARMENO. What dost thou thinke (Sempronio) of the foole our Master, who thought to have made me to be his Target, for to receive the incounter of this first danger? What doe I know, who stands betweene or behind the dores? What know I if there be any treason intended, or no? What can I tell, whether Melibea have plotted this, to cry quittance with our Master, for this his great presumption? Besides, wee are not sure, whether the old Trot told him truth or no. Thou knowst not, Parmeno, how to speake. Thy life shall be taken from thee, and thou ne'r the wiser for it: thy soule shall be let forth, and thou not know who was he that did it. Do not thou turne flatterer, nor sooth up thy Master in every thing, that he would have thee,

195

and then thou shalt never have cause to weepe for other mens woes, or to mourne for others miseries. Doe thou not follow Celestina's counsell in that which is fit and convenient for thee, and thou wert as good goe breake thy neck blind-fold. Goe on with thy good perswasions, and faithfull admonitions, and thou shalt bee well cudgell'd for thy labour. Turne the leafe now no more, lest thou be forced to bid the world good night, before thou be willing to leave it. I will solemnize this as my birth-day, since I have escaped so great a danger.

SEMPR. Hush, I say, softly (Parmeno) softly. Doe not you keepe such a leaping and skipping, nor for joy make such a noise, lest you may hap to be heard.

PARMENO. Content your selfe (brother) hold your peace, I pray, for I cannot containe my selfe for very joy, to thinke, that I should make him beleeve, that it was most fit for him to goe to the doore; when as indeed, I did onely put him on, because I held it fittest for mine owne safety. Who could ever have brought a businesse more handsomely about for his owne good then I my selfe have done? Thou shalt see mee doe many such things, if thou shalt heerafter but ob-serve mee, which every man shall not know of, as well towards Calisto himselfe, as all those who shall any way inter-meddle, or interpose themselves in this businesse. For, I am assured that this Damsell is but the baite to this hooke, whereat hee must hang himselfe: or that flesh which is throwne out to Vultures, whereof hee that eateth, is sure to pay soundly for it.

SEMP. Let this passe, ne'r trouble thy head with these jealousies, and suspitions of thine; no, though they should happen to be true. But prepare thy selfe, and like a tall souldier, be in readinesse upon the first Alarme, or word given, to betake thee to thy heeles. Do like the men of Villa-Diego, who being besieged, ranne away by night, with their Breeches in their hands.

PARMENO. Wee have read both in one booke, and are both of the same mind; I have not only their Breeches, but their light easie Buskins, that I may runne away the nimbler, and out-strip my fellowes. And I am glad (good brother)

196

that thou hast advised mee to that, which otherwise, even for very shame, and feare of thee, I should never have done: as for our Master, if he chance to be heard, or otherwise discovered, he will never escape, I feare mee, the hands of Pleberio's people; whereby hee may heereafter demand of us, how wee behav'd our selves in his defence, or that he shall ever be able to accuse us, that wee cowardly forsooke him.

SEMP. O my friend (Parmeno) how good and joyfull a thing is it, for fellowes and companions to live together in love and unity! And though Celestina should proove good to us in no other thing, save onely this; yet in this alone hath shee done us service enough, and deserved very well at our hands.

PARMENO. No man can deny that, which in it selfe is manifest. It is apparant, that we for modesties sake, and because wee would not be branded with the hatefull name of cowardize, wee stai'd heere, expecting together with our Master, no lesse then death, though we did not so much deserve it as he did.

SEMPR. Melibea should be come. Harke, mee thinkes I heare them whispering each to other.

PARM. I feare rather that it is not shee, but some one that counterfaytes her voyce.

SEMPR. Heavens defend us from the hands of Traytours; I pray God, they have not betaken themselves to that street thorow which we were resolved to flye. For I feare nothing else but that.

CALISTO. This stirring and murmur which I feare, is not of one single person alone. Yet will I speake, come, what will come, or be who as will be there. Madame; Mistresse, be you there?

LUCRECIA. If I be not deceived, this is Calisto's voyce. But for the more surety, I will goe a little neerer. Who is that that speakes? Who is there without?

CALISTO. He that is come addressed to your command.

LUCRECIA. Madame, why come you not? Come hither, I say, be not afraid, for heere is the Gentleman you wot of.

MELIBEA. Speake softly (you foole.) Marke him well, that you may be sure it is hee.

LUCRECIA. Come hither I tell you, it is hee, I know him by his voice.

CALISTO. I feare mee, I am deluded, it was not Melibea that spake unto me, I heare some whispering; I am undone. But live or dye, I have not the power to be gone.

MELIBEA. Lucrecia, goe a little aside; and give mee leave to call unto him. Sir, what is your name? Who willed you to come hither?

CALISTO. She that is worthy to command all the world, she whom I may not merit to serve. Let not your Ladiship feare to discover her selfe to this Captive of your gentle disposition; for the sweete sound of those your words, which shall never fall from my eares, give me assurance that you are that Lady Melibea, whom my heart adoreth; I am your servant Calisto.

MELIBEA. The strange and excessive boldnesse of thy messages, hath inforced me (Calisto) to speake with thee: who having already received my answer to your reasons, I know not what you may imagine to get more out of my love, then what I then made knowne unto you. Banish therefore from thee, those vaine and foolish thoughts, that both my honour and my person may be secured from any hurt they may receive by an ill suspition. For which purpose, I am come hither to take order for your dispatch, and my quietnesse. Doe not, I beseech you, put my good name and reputation upon the ballance of back-biting and detracting tongues.

CALISTO. To hearts prepared with a strong and dauntlesse resolution against all adversities whatsoever, nothing can happen unto them, that shall easily be able to shake the strength of their wall. But that unhappy man, who weaponlesse, and disarmed, not thinking upon any deceit or Ambuscado, puts himselfe within the dores of your safe-conduct and protection, whatsoever in such a case falls out contrary to my expectation, it cannot in all reason but torment me, and pierce thorow the very soule of me, breaking all those Magazines and storehouses, wherein this sweet newes was laid up. O miserable and unfortunate Calisto!

CALISTO AND MELIBEA

O, how hast thou beene mocked and deluded by thy servants!
O thou coozening and deceitfull Celestina; thou mightst at
least have let me alone, and given me leave to dye, and not
gone about to revive my hope, to adde thereto more fuell
to the fire, which already doth sufficiently waste and consume me. Why didst thou falsifie this my Ladies message?
Why hast thou thus with thy tongue given cause to my
despaire, and utter undoing? Why didst thou command
mee to come hither? Was it that I might receive disgrace,
interdiction, diffidence, and hatred, from no other mouth,
but that which keepes the keyes of my perdition, or happinesse? O thou enemy to my good! Didst not thou tell
mee, that this my Lady would be favourable, and gracious
unto mee; Didst not thou tell mee, that of her owne accord,
shee had commanded this her captive to come to this very
place, where now I am? Not to banish mee afresh from her
presence, but to repeale that banishment, whereunto shee
had sentenced mee by her former command? Miserable
that I am, whom shall I trust, or in whom may I hope to
find any faith? Where is truth to be had? Who is voyde
of deceit? Where doth not falsehood dwell? Who is he
that shewes himselfe an open enemy? or who is he that
shewes himselfe a faithfull friend? Where is that place,
wherein treason is not wrought? Who, I say, durst tres-
passe so much upon my patience, as to give me such cruell
hope of destruction?

MELIBEA. Cease (good Sir) your true and just complaints. For neither my heart is able to endure it, nor
mine eyes any longer to dissemble it; thou weepest out of
griefe, judging me cruell; and I weep out of joy, seeing thee
so faithfull. O my dearest Lord, and my lifes whole happinesse; how much more pleasing would it be unto me, to see
thy face, then to heare thy voyce! But sithence that at this
present we cannot injoy each other as wee would, take thou
the assignement, and seale of those words, which I sent unto
thee, written, and ingrossed in the tongue of that thy diligent and carefull messenger. All that which I then said, I
doe heere confirme. I acknowledge it as my Deede, and
hold the Assurance I have made thee, to be good and per-

fect. Good Sir, doe not you weepe; dry up your teares, and dispose of mee as you please.

CALISTO. O my deare Lady! Hope of my glory; Easeresse of my paine, and my hearts joy: What tongue can be sufficient to give thee thankes, that may equall this so extraordinary and incomparable a kindnesse; which in this instant of so great and extreme a sorrow, thou hast bin willing to conferre upon me; in being willing (I say) that one so meane, and unworthy as my selfe, should be by thee inabled to the injoying of thy sweetest love; whereof, although I was evermore most desirous, yet did I alwaies deeme my selfe unworthy thereof, weighing thy greatnesse, considering thy estate, beholding thy perfection, contemplating thy beauty, and looking into my small merit, and thy great worth; besides, other thy singular graces, thy commendable, and well-knowne vertues? Againe; O thou great God, how can I be ungratefull unto thee, who so miraculously hast wrought for mee so great and strange wonders? O, how long agoe did I entertaine this thought in my heart, and as a thing impossible, repeld it from my memory, untill now, that the bright beames of thy most cleare shining countenance, gave light unto my eyes, inflamed my heart, awakened my tongue, inlarged my desert, abridged my cowardize, unwreathed my shrunke-up spirits, reinforced my strength, put life and metall into my hands and feet; and in a word, infused such a spirit of boldnesse into me, that they have borne me up by their power, unto this high estate, wherin (with happinesse) I now behold my selfe, in hearing this thy sweet-pleasing voyce; which if I had not heertofore knowne, and sented out the sweet and wholsome savour of thy words, I should hardly have beleeved they would have been without deceit. But now, that I am well assured of thy pure and noble, both bloud and actions, I stand amazed at the gaze of my good, and with a stricter eye, beginne to view and looke upon my selfe, to see whether I am that same Calisto, whom so great a blessing hath befalne?

MELIBEA. Calisto; Thy great worth, thy singular graces, and thy noblenesse of birth, have (ever since I had true notice of thee) wrought so effectually with mee,

200

CALISTO AND MELIBEA

that my heart hath not so much as one moment bin absent from thee. And although (now these many dayes) I have strove, and strove againe to dissemble it, yet could I not so smother my thoughts, but that as soone as that Woman returned thy sweet name unto my remembrance, I discovered my desire, and appointed our meeting, at this very place and time : Where, I beseech thee to take order for the disposing of my person, according to thine owne good will and pleasure. These doores debarre us of our joy, whose strong locks and barres I curse, as also mine owne weake strength. For were I stronger, and they weaker, neither shouldst thou be displeased, nor I discontented.

CALISTO. What (Madame) is it your pleasure, that I should suffer a paltry piece of wood to hinder our joy? Never did I conceive, that any thing, save thine owne will, could possibly hinder us. O troublesome and sport-hindring doores, I earnestly desire, that you may be burned with as great a fire, as the torment is great, which you give me ; for then the third part thereof would be sufficient to consume you to ashes in a moment. Give me leave (sweet Lady) that I may call my servants, and command them to breake them open.

PARME. Harke, harke (Sempronio) Hearest thou not what he saies? He is comming to seeke after us ; wee shall make a badde yeere of it, we shall runne into a peeke of troubles. I tell you truely, I like not of his comming. This love of theirs, I verily perswade my selfe, was begunne in an unlucky houre ; if you will goe, goe ; for I 'll stay heere no longer.

SEMPR. Peace, harke ; shee will not consent wee come.

MELIBEA. What meanes my Love? Will you undoe me? Will you wound my reputation? Give not your will the reines : your hope is certaine, and the time short : even as soone as your selfe shall appoint it. Besides, your paine is single, mine double : yours for your selfe, mine for us both : you onely feele your owne griefe, I both your own and mine. Content your selfe therefore, and come you to morrow at this very houre, and let your way be by the wall of my garden ; for if you should now breake downe these

THE TRAGICK-COMEDY OF

ACTUS XII cruell doores, though haply wee should not be presently heard, yet to morrow morning there would arise in my fathers house a terrible suspition of my errour: and you know, besides, that by so much the greater is the errour, by how much the greater is the party that erreth: And in the turning of a hand, will be noysed thorow the whole City.

SEMPR. In an unfortunate houre came we hither this night; we shall stay heere, till the day hath overtaken us, if our master goe on thus leysurely, and make no more haste. And albeit fortune hath hitherto well befriended us in this businesse; yet I feare me, if we stay overlong, we shall be overheard, either by some of Pleberio's houshold, or of his neighbours.

PAR. I would have had thee bin gone 2. houres ago; for he wil never give over, but still find some occasion to continue his discourse.

CALISTO. My deare Lady, my joy and happinesse; why dost thou stile this an error, which was granted unto me by the Destinies; and seconded by Cupid himselfe, to my petitions in the Mirtle-Grove?

PARME. Calisto talkes idly, surely, he is not well in his wits. I am of the beliefe (brother) that he is not so devout. That which that old traiterous Trot, with her pestiferous Sorceries hath compassed and brought about, he sticks not to say, that the Destinies have granted, and wrought for him: and with this confidence, he would adventure to breake ope these doores; who shall no sooner have given the first stroke, but that presently he will be heard, and taken by her fathers servants, who lodge hard by.

SEMPR. Feare nothing (Parmeno) for we are farre inough off. And upon the very first noyse that we heare, we will betake us straight to our heeles, and make our flight our best defence. Let him alone, let him take his course, for if he doe ill, he shall pay for it.

PARM. Well hast thou spoken; thou knowst my mind, as well as if thou hadst bin within me. Be it as thou hast said; let us shun death; for we are both young; and not to desire to dye, nor to kill, is not cowardize, but a naturall goodnesse. Pleberio's followers, they are but fooles and mad-

202

CALISTO AND MELIBEA

men, they have not that minde to their meate and their sleep, as they have to be brabbling and quarrelling. What fooles then should we be, to fall together by the eares with such enemies, who doe not so much affect Victory and Conquest, as continuall Warre, and endlesse contention? O, if thou didst but see (brother) in what posture I stand, thou wouldst be ready to burst with laughing. I stand sideling, my legs abroad, my left foote formost, ready to take the start; the skirts of my Cassocke tuckt under my girdle, my Buckler clapt close to my arme, that it may not hinder me; and I verily beleeve, that I should out-runne the swiftest Buck; so monstrously am I afraid of staying heere.

SEMPRONIO. I stand better; for I have bound my Sword and Buckler both together, that they may not fall from me when I run; and have clapt my Caske in the cape of my cloake.

PARME. But the stones you had in it, What hast thou done with them?

SEMPRO. I have turn'd them all out, that I might goe the lighter; for I have inough to doe to carry this Corslet, which your importunity made me put on; for I could have been very well content to have left it off, because I thoght it would be too heavy for me, when I should runne away. Harke, harke, hearest thou Parmeno? the businesse goes ill with us; wee are but dead men. Put on, away, be gone, make towards Celestina's house, that we may not be cut off, by betaking us to our owne house.

PARMENO. Flye, flye, you runne too slowly. Passion of me, if they should chance to overtake us. Throw away thy Buckler and all.

SEMPR. Have they kild our Master? Can you tell?

PARMENO. I know not. Say nothing to mee, I pray; Runne, and hold your peace; as for him, he is the least of my care.

SEMPRONIO. Zit, zit, Parmeno, not a word; turne, and be still; for it is nothing, but the Alguazills men, who make a noyse as they passe thorow this other street.

PARME. Take your eyes in your hand, and see you be sure. Trust not I say, too much to those eyes of yours;

they may mistake, taking one thing for another; they have not left mee one drop of bloud in my body. Death had e'n almost swallowed me up; for me thought still as I ranne, they were cutting and carbonading my shoulders. I never in my life remember, that I was in the like feare, or ever saw my selfe in the like danger of an affront, though I have gone many a time thorow other mens houses, and thorow places of much perill, and hard to passe. Nine yeeres was I servant to Guadaluppe, and a thousand times my selfe and others were at buffets, cutting one another for life, yet was I never in that feare of death, as now.

SEMPRONIO. And did not [I] (I pray) serve at Saint Michaels? and mine Host in the Market-place? and Molleias the gardiner; I also (I tro) was at fisty-cuffes with those which threw stones at the Sparrowes, and other the like birds, which sate upon a green Popler that we had, because with their stones, they did spoile the hearbes in the garden; But God keepe thee, and every good man from the sight of such weapons as these: these are shrewd tooles; this is true feare indeede: and therefore it is not said in vaine; Laden with Iron, laden with feare. Turne, turne backe; for it is the Alguazill, that 's certaine.

MELIBEA. What noyse is that (Calisto) which I heare in the street? It seemes to be the noise of some that flye and are pursued; for your owne sake and mine, have a care of your selfe; I feare me, you stand in danger.

CALISTO. I warrant you, Madame, feare you nothing; for I stand on a safegard. They should be my men, who are madcaps, and disarme as many as passe by them; and belike, some one hath escapt them, after whom they hasten.

MELIBEA. Are they many, that you brought?

CALISTO. No (Madame) no more but two; but should halfe a dozen set upon them, they would not be long in disarming them, and make them flye; they are such a couple of tall lusty fellowes; they are men of true, and well approved metall; choyce lads for the nonste; for I come not hither with a fire of straw, which is no sooner in, but out. And were it not in regard of your honour, they should have broken these doores in pieces; and in case we had been heard, they should

CALISTO AND MELIBEA

have freed both your selfe and me from all your fathers servants.

MELIBEA. O! of all loves, let not any such thing be attempted; yet it glads me much that you are so faithfully attended; that bread is well bestowed which such valiant servants eat. For that love (Sir) which you beare unto me, since Nature hath inricht them with so good a gift, I pray make much of them, and reward them well; to the end that in all things, they may be trusty and secret, that concerne thy service; and when for their boldnesse and presumption, thou shalt either checke, or correct them; intermixe some favours with thy punishments, that their valour and courage may not be daunted, and abated, but be stirred and provoked to out-dare dangers, when thou shalt have occasion to use them.

PARME. Sist, Sist; Heare you Sir? make haste and be gone, for heere is a great company comming along with Torches; and unlesse you make haste, you will be seen, and knowne; for heere is not any place, where you may hide your selfe from their view.

CALISTO. O unfortunate that I am! How am I inforced (Lady) against my will to take my leave! Beleeve me, the feare of death would not worke so much upon me, as the feare of your honor doth; but since it is so, that we must part; Angels be the guardians of thy faire person. My comming (as you have ordred it) shall be by the garden.

MELIBEA. Be it so, and all happinesse be with you.

PLEBERIO. Wife, are you asleepe?

ALISA. No, Sir.

PLEBERIO. Doe not you heare some noyse, or stirring in your daughters withdrawing chamber?

ALISA. Yes mary doe I. Melibea, Melibea?

PLEBERIO. She does not heare you; I will call a little lowder. Daughter Melibea?

MELIBEA. Sir.

PLEBERIO. Who is that, that tramples up and downe there, and makes that stirring to and fro in your chamber?

MELIBEA. It is Lucrecia (Sir) who went forth to fetch some water for me to drinke, for I was very thirsty.

205

THE TRAGICK-COMEDY OF

PLEBERIO. Sleepe againe (daughter) I thought it had
beene something else.

LUCRE. A little noyse (I perceive) can wake them; me
thought they spoke somewhat fearefully, as if all had not
beene well.

MELIBEA. There is not any so gentle a creature, who
with the love or feare of it's young, is not somewhat moved.
What would they have done, had they had certaine, and
assured knowledge of my going downe?

CALISTO. My Sonne, shut the dore; and you Parmeno,
bring up a light.

PARM. You were better (Sir) to take your rest; and that
little that it is till day, to take it out in sleepe.

CALISTO. I will follow thy counsell; for it is no more
then needeth. I want sleepe exceedingly; but tell mee,
Parmeno, what dost thou thinke of that old woman, whom
thou didst dispraise so much unto me? what a piece of worke
hath she brought to passe? what could wee have done
without her?

PARME. Neither had I any feeling of your great paine;
nor knew I the gentlenesse, and well-deservingnesse of
Melibea; and therefore am not to be blamed. But well
did I know both Celestina, and all her cunning trickes
and devices; and did thereupon advise you, as became
a servant to advise his Master, and as I thought, for the
best; but now I see, shee is become another woman, she
is quite chang'd from what she was, when I first knew
her.

CALISTO. How? chang'd? How dost thou meane?

PARMENO. So much, that had I not seene it, I should
never have beleeved it: but now, heaven grant you may live
as happy, as this is true.

CALISTO. But tell me; didst thou heare what past
betwixt me and my Mistresse? what did you doe all the
while? were you not afraid?

SEMPR. Afraid, Sir? of what? all the world could not
make us afraid; did you ever finde us to be fearefull? did
you ever see any such thing in us? we stood waiting for you
well provided, and with our weapons in our hands.

206

CALISTO AND MELIBEA

CALISTO. Slept you not a whit? tooke you not a little nappe?

SEMPRONIO. Sleepe, Sir? It is for boyes and children to sleepe; I did not so much as once sit downe, nor put one legge over another, watching still as diligently as a Cat for a Mouse; that if I had heard but the least noyse in the world, I might presently have leapt forth, and have done as much as my strength should have beene able to performe. And Parmeno, though till now, he did not seeme to serve you in this businesse with any great willingnesse, hee was as glad, when he spy'd the Torches comming, as the Wolfe, when hee spies the dust of a drove of cattell, or flocke of sheepe; hoping still that he might make his prey, till he saw how many they were.

CALISTO. This is no such wonder (Sempronio) never marvaile at it; for it is naturall in him to be valiant; and though he would not have bestirred himselfe for my sake, yet would he have laid about him because such as he cannot goe against that which they be us'd unto; for though the Foxe change his haire, yet he never changeth his nature; hee will keepe himselfe to his custome, though hee cannot keep himselfe to his colour. I told my Mistresse Melibea, what was in you, and how safe I held my selfe, having you at my back for my gard. My sonnes; I am much bound unto you both, pray to heaven for our wellfare and good successe; and doubt not, but I will more fully guerdon your good service. Good night, and heaven send you good rest.

PARM. Whither shall wee goe (Sempronio?) To our chamber and goe sleepe, or to the Kitchin and breake our fast?

SEMPR. Goe thou whither thou wilt, as for me, e'r it be day, I will get me to Celestina's house, and see if I can recover my part in the chaine: she is a crafty Hileding, and I will not give her time to invent some one villainous tricke or other whereby to shift us off, and coozen us of our shares.

PARME. It is well remembred, I had quite forgot it; let us goe both together, and if she stand upon points with us, let us put her into such a feare, that she may be ready to bewray her selfe; for money goes beyond all friendship.

SEMPR. Cist, cist, not a word ; for her bed is hard by this little window heere ; let mee knocke her up : Tha, tha, tha ; Mistresse Celestina, Open the doore.

CELEST. Who calls ?

SEMPRONIO. Open doore, your Sonnes be heere.

CELEST. I have no sonnes that be abroad at this time of night.

SEMPRONIO. It is Parmeno, and Sempronio ; open the doore ; we are come hither to breake our fast with you.

CELEST. O ye mad lads, you wanton wags, Enter, enter, how chance you come so earely ? It is but now break of day, what have you done ? what hath past ? Tel me, how goes the world ? Calisto's hopes, are they alive or dead ? Has he her, or has he her not ? how stands it with him ?

SEMPRONIO. How, mother ? Had it not beene for us, his soule e'r this had gone seeking her eternall rest ; and if it were possible to prize the debt wherein hee stands bound unto us, all the wealth hee hath, were not sufficient to make us satisfaction. So true, is that triviall saying ; that the life of man, is of more worth, then all the gold in the world.

CELEST. Have you beene in such danger, since I saw you ? Tell mee, how was it ? How was it I pray ?

SEMPRONIO. Mary in such danger, that as I am an honest man, my blood still boyles in my body, to thinke upon it.

CELEST. Sit downe, I beseech you, and tell me how it was.

PARMENO. It will require a long discourse ; besides, we have fretted out our hearts, and are quite tired with the trouble and toile, we have had, you may doe better to provide something for his and my breakefast : it may be, when wee have eaten, our choller will be somewhat allayd ; for I sweare unto thee, I desire not now to meet that man that desires peace. I should now glory to light upon some one, on whom I might revenge my wrath, and stanch my anger ; for I could not doe it on those that caused it ; so fast did they flye from my fury.

CELESTINA. The pockes canker out my carkasse to death, if thou makest mee not afraide to looke on thee, thou lookest so fierce and so ghastly. But for all this, I doe be-

208

CALISTO AND MELIBEA

leeve you doe but jest. Tell me, I pray thee Sempronio, as thou lov'st me what hath befalne you?

SEMPRONIO. By heavens, I am not my selfe, I come hither I know not how, without wit, or reason. But as for you (fellow Parmeno) I cannot but finde fault with you, for not tempring of your choller, and using more moderation in your angry mood ; I would have thee looke otherwise now, and not carry that sowre countenance heer, as thou didst there, when we incountred so many ; for mine owne part, before those, that I knew could doe but little, I never made show that I could doe much. Mother, I have brought hither my armes all broken and battred in pieces, my Buckler without it's ring of Iron, the plates being cut asunder, my Sword like a Saw, all to behack't and hewd, my Caske strangely bruised, beaten as flat as a Cake, and dented in with the blowes that came hammering on my head : so that I have not any thing in the world to goe further with my Master, when hee shall have occasion to use mee. For it is agreed on, that my Master shall this night have accesse unto his Mistresse, by the way of her garden. Now for to furnish my selfe anew, if my life lay on it, I know not where to have one penny or farthing.

CELEST. Since it is spoiled and broken in your Masters service, goe to your Master for more, let him (a Gods name) pay for it. Besides, you know it is with him, but aske and have ; he will presently furnish you, I warrant you. For hee is none of those who say to their servants : Live with mee, and looke out some other to maintaine thee ; he is so franke, and of so liberall a disposition, that hee will not give thee money for this only, but much more, if neede be.

SEMPR. Tush, what's this to the purpose? Parmeno's be also spoyled and marr'd. After this reckoning, we may spend our Master all that he hath in armes. How can you in conscience thinke, or with what face imagine, that I should be so importunate, as to demand more of him, then what he hath already done of his owne accord? He for his part hath done inough, I would not it should be said of me, that hee hath given mee an inch, and that I should take an ell. There is a reason in all things ; he hath given us a

2 D 209

ACTUS
XII

hundred crownes in gold ; he hath given us, besides, a chaine; three such picks more, will picke out all the waxe in his eare ; hee hath, and will have a hard market of it. Let us content our selves with that which is reason ; Let us not lose all, by seeking to gaine more then is meet ; for he that imbraceth much, holdeth little.

CELEST. How wittily this Asse thinks he hath spoken ! I sweare to thee, by the reverence of this my old age, had these words beene spoken after dinner, I should have said, that wee had all of us taken a cuppe too much ; that we had beene all drunke. Art thou well in thy wits, Sempronio ? What has thy remuneration to doe with my reward ? Thy payment with my merit ? Am I bound to buy you weapons ? Must I repaire your losses, and supply your wants ? Now I thinke upon it ; let me be hang'd, or dye any other death, if thou hast not tooke hold of a little word, that carelesly slipt out of my mouth the other day, as we came along the street ; for as (I remember) I then told you, that what I had was yours ; and that I would never be wanting unto you in any thing, to the utmost of my poore ability ; and that if Fortune did prosper my businesse with your Master, that you should lose nothing by it ; But you know (Sempronio) that words of compliment and kindenesse, are not obligatory, nor binde me to doe, as you would have mee ; all is not gold that glisters, for then it would be a great deale cheaper then it is. Tell me (Sempronio) if I have not hit the right nayle on the head ? Thou maist see by this, that though I am old, that I can divine as much as thou canst imagine. In good faith (Sonne) I am as full of griefe, as ever my heart can hold, I am even ready to burst with sorrow and anguish. As soone as ever I came from your house, and was come home ; I gave the chaine I brought hither with me, to this foole Elicia, that she might looke upon it, and cheere her selfe with the sight thereof; and she, for her life, cannot as yet call to mind what shee hath done with it : and all this live-long night, neither shee nor I have slept one winke, for very thought and griefe thereof : Not so much for the valew of the chaine (for it was not much worth) but to see, that she should be so carelesse in the laying of it up ; and to see

CALISTO AND MELIBEA

the ill lucke of it; at the very same time that we mist it, came in some friends of mine, that had beene of my old and familiar acquaintance; and I am sorely afraide, lest they have lighted upon it, and taken it away with them; meaning to make use of that vulgar saying, *Si spie it, tum sporte fac; Si non spie it, packe and away Iacke.* But now (my Sonnes) that I may come a little neerer unto you both, and speake home to the point: If your Master gave mee any thing, what he gave me, that (you must thinke) is mine: As for your cloth of gold doublet, I never ask't you any share out of it, nor ever will. We all of us serve him, that he may give unto us all, as he sees wee shall deserve: And as for that which he hath given me, I have twice indangered my life for it; more blades have I blunted in his service then you both; more materiall and substantiall stuffe have I wasted, and have worne out more hose and shooes; And you must not thinke (my Sonnes) but all this costs mee good money. Besides, my skill, which I got not playing or sitting still, or warming my taile over the fire, as most of your idle huswives doe, but with hard labour and paines-taking: as Parmeno's mother could well witnesse for me, if she were living. This I have gained by mine owne industry and labour; as for you, what have you done? If you have done any thing for Calisto, Calisto is to requite you. I get my living by my Trade and my travell; you, yours, with recreation and delight; and therefore you are not to expect equall recompence, injoying your service with pleasure, as I, who goe performing it with paines: but whatsoever I have hitherto said unto you, because you shall see, I will deale kindly with you: if my chaine be found againe, I will give each of you a paire of Scarlet Breeches, which is the comeliest habit that young men can weare. But if it be not found, you must accept of my good will, and my selfe be content to sit downe with my losse; and all this I doe out of pure love, because you were willing that I should have the benefit of managing this businesse before another: and if this will not content you, I cannot doe withall. To your owne harme be it.

SEMPR. This is not the first time I have heard it spoken;

THE TRAGICK-COMEDY OF

how much in old folkes, the sinne of avarice reigneth: as
also that other, When I was poore, then was I liberall;
when I was rich, then was I covetous: So that covetousnesse
increaseth with getting, and poverty with coveting: and
nothing makes the covetous man poore but his riches. O
heavens! How doth penury increase with abundance, and
plenty? How often did this old woman say, that I should
have all the profit that should grow from this busines?
thinking then perhaps, that it would be but little: but now
she sees how great it growes, she will not part with any
thing, no, not so much as the parings of her nailes; that
she may comply with that common saying of your little
children: Of a little, a little; of much, nothing.

PARME. Let her give thee that which she promised; let
her make that good, or let us take it all from her. I told
you before (would you have beleeved mee) what an old
coozening companion you should finde her.

CELESTINA. If you are angry eyther with your selves,
your Master, or your armes, wreck not your wrath upon mee;
for I wot well inough whence all this growes, I winde you
where you are: I now perceive on which foot you halt, not
out of want of that which you demand; nor out of any
covetousnes that is in you: but because you thinke I will tye
you to Racke and Manger, and make you captives all your
life-time to Elicia, and Areusa, and provide you no other
fresh ware, you make all this adoe, quarrell thus with me
for money, and seeke by fearing me, to force mee to a parting
and sharing of stakes. But be still (my boyes) and content
your selves; for she who could helpe you with these, will not
sticke to furnish you with halfe a score of handsome wenches
apiece, fairer then these by farre, now that I see, that you
are growne to greater knowledge and more reason, and a
better deservingnesse in your selves. And whether or no,
in such a case as this, I am able to be as good as my word,
let Parmeno speake for me. Speake, speake, Parmeno, be
not ashamed, man, to tell what did betide us, with that
wench you wot of, that was sicke of the Mother?

SEMPR. I goe not for that which you thinke. You talke
of Chalke, and we of Cheese. Doe not thinke to put us off

212

CALISTO AND MELIBEA

with a jest; our demands desire a more serious answer. And assure your selfe (if I can helpe it) you shall take no more Hares with this Grayhound; and therefore lay aside these tricks, and do not stand arguing any longer on the matter; I know your fetches too well: To an old dogge, a man need not cry, Now, now. Come off therefore quickly, and give us two parts of that which you have received of Calisto. Dispatch, I say, and doe not drive us to discover what you are; come, come, exercise your wits upon some other. Flap those in the mouth, you old Filth, with your coggings and foistings, that know you not; for wee know you too well.

CELEST. Why, what am I, Sempronio? What do you know me to be? Didst thou take me out of the Puteria. Broughtst thou me, as a whore, out of the Stewes? Bridle your tongue for shame, and doe not dishonour my hoary hayres. I am an old woman of Gods making, no worse then all other women are: I live by my occupation as other women doe, very well, and handsomely; I seeke not after those who seeke not after me; they that will have me, come home to my house to fetch me; they come home, I say, and intreat mee to doe this or that for them. And for the life that I lead, whether it be good or bad, heaven knowes my heart: and doe not thinke out of your choller to mis-use mee, for there is Law and Justice for all, and equall to all; and my tale, I doubt not, shall be as soone heard (though I am an old woman) as yours, for all you be so smoothly kemb'd. Let me alone, I pray, in mine owne house, and with mine owne fortune. And you, Parmeno, doe not you thinke that I am thy slave, because thou knowst my secrets, and my life past, and all those matters that hapned betwixt mee, and that unfortunate mother of thine; for shee also was wont to use mee on this fashion, when she was disposed to play her prankes with mee.

PARM. Doe not hit mee in the teeth with these thy idle memorialls of my mother, unlesse thou meanst I should send thee with these thy tydings, unto her, where thou mayst better make thy complaint.

CELESTINA. Elicia, Elicia, arise and come downe

ACTUS XII

quickly, and bring me my mantle; for by heaven, I will hye mee to the Justice, and there cry out and raile at you, like a made woman. What is 't you would have? What do you meane, to menace me thus in mine owne house? Shall your valour and your bravings be exercised on a poore silly innocent sheepe? On a Hen, that is tyed by the leg, and cannot flye from you? On an old woman of sixty yeeres of age? Get you, get you, for shame, amongst men, such as your selves; goe and reake your anger upon such as are girt with the Sword, and not against me and my poore weake Distaffe: it is an infallible note of great cowardize, to assaile the weake and such as have but small, or very little power to resist: your filthy Flyes bite none but leane and feeble Oxen: and your barking Curres flye with greater eagernesse, and more open-mouth upon your poorest passengers. If shee that lies above there in the bed, would have hearkned unto me, this house should not have beene (as now it is) without a man in the night; nor wee have slept (as wee doe) by the naked shaddow of a candle. But to pleasure you, and to be faithfull unto you, wee suffer this solitude; and because you see wee are women, and have no body heere to oppose you, you prate, and talke, and aske, I know not what, without any reason in the world, which you would as soone have beene hang'd, as once dar'd to have proffer'd it, if you had heard but a man stirring in the house; for, as it is in the Proverbe, A hard adversary appeaseth anger.

SEMPR. O thou old covetous Cribbe, that art ready to dye with the thirst of gold! cannot a third part of the gaine content thee?

CELEST. What third part? A pocks on you both; out of my house in a divels name, you and your companion with you; doe not you make such a stirre heere as you doe. Cause not our neighbours to come about us, and make them thinke wee be madde. Put mee not out of my wits; make me not madde: you would not, I trow, would you, that Calisto's matters and yours should be proclaimed openly at the Crosse? Heere's a stirre indeed.

SEMPR. Cry, bawle, and make a noyse; all's one, we care not: eyther looke to performe your promise, or to end

214

CALISTO AND MELIBEA

your daies. Dye you must, or else doe as wee will have you.

ELICIA. Ah woe is mee! put up your Sword; hold him, hold him, Parmeno; for feare lest the foole should kill her in his madnesse.

CELESTINA. Justice, Justice; helpe neighbours, Justice, Justice; for heere be Ruffians, that will murder mee in my house. Murder, murder, murder.

SEMPR. Ruffians, you Whore? Ruffians, you old Bawd? have you no better tearmes? Thou old Sorceresse; thou witch, thou; looke for no other favour at my hands, but that I send thee poast unto hell; you shall have letters thither, you shall (you old Inchantresse) and that speedily too; you shall have a quicke dispatch.

CELEST. Ay me, I am slaine. Ay, ay. Confession, Confession.

PARMENO. So, so: kill her, kill her; make an end of her, since thou hast begunne; be briefe, be briefe with her; lest the neighbours may chance to heare us. Let her dye, let her dye; let us draw as few enemies upon us as wee can.

CELESTINA. Oh, oh, oh!

ELICIA. O cruell-hearted as you are! Enemies in the highest nature; shame and confusion light upon you; the extremity of Justice fall upon you, with it's greatest vigour, and all those that have had a hand in it. My mother is dead, and with her, all my happinesse.

SEMPRONIO. Flye, flye, Parmeno, the people beginne to flocke hitherward. See, see, yonder comes the Alguazil.

PARM. Ay me, wretch that I am! there is no meanes of escape for us in the world; for they have made good the doore, and are entring the house.

SEMPRONIO. Let us leape out at these windowes; And let us dye rather so, then fall into the hands of Justice.

PARM. Leape then, and I will follow thee.

THE END OF THE TWELFTH ACT

THE TRAGICK-COMEDY OF

ACTUS XIII

THE ARGUMENT

CALISTO *awakened from sleepe, talkes a while with himselfe; anon after hee calls unto* Tristan, *and some other of his servants. By and by* Calisto *falls asleepe againe;* Tristan *goes downe, and stands at the doore.* Sosia *comes weeping unto him;* Tristan, *demanding the cause,* Sosia *delivers unto him the death of* Sempronio *and* Parmeno; *they goe and acquaint* Calisto *with it, who knowing the truth thereof, maketh great lamentation.*

INTERLOCUTORS

Calisto, Tristan, Sosia.

CALISTO. O how daintily have I slept! Ever since that sweete short space of time, since that harmonious discourse I injoyed; I have had exceeding ease, taken very good rest; this contentment and quietude hath proceeded from my joy. Either the travaile of my body caused so sound a sleepe; or else the glory and pleasure of my minde: Nor doe I much wonder, that both the one and the other should linke hands, and joyne together to cloze the lids of mine eyes, since I travail'd the last night with my body and person, and tooke pleasure with my spirit and senses. True it is, that sorrow causeth much thought; and overmuch thought, much hindreth sleepe: as it was mine owne case within these few daies when I was much discomfited and quite out of heart, of ever hoping to injoy that surpassing happinesse, which I now possesse. O my sweete Lady, and dearest Love, Melibea, what dost thou thinke on now? Art thou asleepe, or awake? Thinkst thou on mee, or some body else? Art thou up and ready, or art thou not yet stirring? O most happy, and most fortunate Calisto, if it be true, and that it be no dreame, which hath already passed! Dream't I, or dream't I not?

216

CALISTO AND MELIBEA

was it a meere phantasie, or was it a reall truth? But now
I remember my selfe, I was not alone, my servants waited
on me, there were two of them with me; if they shall affirme
it to be no dreame, but that all that past was true, I am
bound to beleeve it: I will command them to be called, for
the further confirmation of my joy. Tristanico, Why ho?
Where are my men? Tristanico, Hye you and come up:
arise, I say, get you up quickly and come hither.

TRISTAN. Sir, I am up, and heere already.

CALISTO. Goe, runne, and call mee hither Sempronio
and Parmeno.

TRISTAN. I shall, Sir.

CALISTO. {
Now sleepe, and take thy rest,
   Once griev'd, and pained Wight;
Since shee now loves thee best,
   Who is thy hearts delight.
Let joy be thy soules guest;
   And care be banish't quite;
Since shee hath thee exprest
   To be her Favourite.

TRISTAN. There is not so much as a boy in the house.

CALISTO. Open the windowes, and see whether it be day
or no.

TRISTAN. Sir, it is broad day.

CALISTO. Goe againe, and see if you can finde them;
and see you wake me not, till it be almost dinner-time.

TRISTAN. I will goe downe and stand at the doore, that
my Master may take out his full sleepe; and to as many as
shall aske for him, I shall answer that hee is not within. O
what an out-cry doe I heare in the Market-place! whats the
matter a Gods name? There is some execution of Justice to
be done, or else they are up so earely to see some Bull-baiting.
I do not know what to make of this noyse, it is some great
matter, the noyse is so great; but lo, yonder comes Sosia,
my Masters foot-boy; hee will tell mee what the businesse is.
Looke how the Rogue comes pulling and tearing of his
hayre; he hath tumbled into one Taverne or other, where
he hath beene scuffling. But if my Master chance to sent
him, hee will cause his coat to be well cudgelled; for though

2 E

hee be somewhat foolish, punishment will make him wise; but mee thinkes hee comes weeping. What's the matter, Sosia? Why dost thou weepe? Whence com'st thou now? Why speak'st thou not?

SOSIA. O miserable that I am! what misfortune could be more? O what great dishonour to my Masters house! O what an unfortunate morning is this! O unhappy young men!

TRISTAN. What's the matter, man? Why dost thou keepe such adoe? Why griev'st thou thus? What mischiefe hath befalne us?

SOSIA. Sempronio, and Parmeno!

TRISTAN. What of Sempronio and Parmeno? What meanes this foole? Speake a little plainer, thou torment'st me with delayes.

SOSIA. Our old companions, our fellowes, our brethren.

TRISTAN. Thou art eyther drunke or mad; or thou bringest some ill newes along with thee. Why dost thou not tell mee what thou hast to say, concerning these young men?

SOSIA. That they lie slayne in the streete.

TRISTAN. O unfortunate mischance! Is it true? Didst thou see them? Did they speake unto thee?

SOSIA. No. They were e'n almost past all sense; but one of them with much adoe, when hee saw I beheld him with teares, beganne to looke a little towards me, fixing his eyes upon me, and lifting up his hands to heaven, as one that is making his prayers unto God; and looking on mee, as if hee had ask't mee, if I were not sorry for his death? And straight after, as one that perceiv'd whither he was presently to goe, he let fall his head, with teares in his eyes, giving thereby to understand, that hee should never see mee againe, till we did meete at that day of the great Judgement.

TRISTAN. You did not observe in him, that he would have askt you whether Calisto were there or no? But since thou hast such manifest proofes of this cruell sorrow, let us haste with these dolefull tidings to our Master.

SOSIA. Master, Master, doe you heare, Sir?

CALISTO AND MELIBEA

CALISTO. What, are you mad? Did not I tell you, I should not be wakened?

SOSIA. Rowze up your selfe, and rise : for if you doe not sticke unto us, we are all undone. Sempronio and Parmeno lie beheaded in the Market-place, as publike malefactors ; and their fault proclaimed by the common Cryer.

CALISTO. Now heaven helpe mee ! What is 't thou tell'st mee ? I know not whether I may beleeve thee, in this thy so sudden and sorrowfull newes. Didst thou see them ?

SOSIA. I saw them, Sir.

CALISTO. Take heede what thou say'st ; for this night they were with mee.

SOSIA. But rose too earely to their deaths.

CALISTO. O my loyall servants ! O my chiefest followers ! O my faithfull Secretaries and Counsellours in all my affaires ! Can it be, that this should be true ? O unfortunate Calisto ! thou art dishonoured as long as thou hast a day to live ; what shall become of thee, having lost such a paire of trusty servants ? Tell mee, for pitty's sake, Sosia, what was the cause of their deaths ? What spake the Proclamation ? Where were they slaine ? by what Justice were they beheaded ?

SOSIA. The cause, Sir, of their deaths, was published by the cruell executioner, or common hangman, who delivered with a loud voyce ; Justice hath commanded, that these violent murderers be put to death.

CALISTO. Who was it they so suddenly slew ? who might it be ? it is not foure houres agoe since they left me. How call you the party whom they murthered ? What was hee for a man ?

SOSIA. It was a woman, Sir, one whom they call Celestina.

CALISTO. What 's that thou sayest?

SOSIA. That which you heard me tell you, Sir.

CALISTO. If this be true, kill thou me too, and I will forgive thee. For sure, there is more ill behinde ; more then was either seene, or thought upon, if that Celestina be slaine, that hath the slash over her face.

SOSIA. It is the very same, Sir : for I saw her stretcht out in her owne house, and her maide weeping by her, having received in her body above thirty severall wounds.

CALISTO. O unfortunate young men! How went they? Did they see thee? Spake they unto thee?

SOSIA. O Sir, had you seen them, your heart would have burst with griefe : One of them had all his braines beaten out in most pittifull manner, and lay without any sense, or motion in the world : The other had both his armes broken, and his face so sorely bruised, that it was all blacke and blue, and all of a goare-bloud. For, that they might not fall into the Alguazils hands, they leapt downe out of a high window ; and so being in a manner quite dead, they chopt off their heads, when, I thinke, they scarce felt, what harme was done them.

CALISTO. Now I beginne to have a taste of shame ; and to feele how much I am toucht in mine honour : would I had excused them and had lost my life, so I had not lost my honour, and my hope of atchieving my commenced purpose, which is, the greatest griefe and distaste that in this case I feele. O my name and reputation, how unfortunately dost thou goe from Table to Table, from mouth to mouth ! O yee my secret, my secret actions, how openly will you now walke thorow every publike street, and open Market-place ? What shall become of me ? Whither shall I go ? If I goe forth to the dead, I am unable to recover them, and if I stay heere, it will be deemed cowardize. What counsell shall I take ? Tell me, Sosia, what was the cause they kild her ?

SOSIA. That maid (Sir) of hers, which sate weeping and crying over her, made knowne the cause of her death to as many as would heare it ; saying, that they slew her, because she would not let them share with her in that chaine of gold, which you had lately given her.

CAL. O wretched and unfortunate day ! O sorrow, able to breake even a heart of Adamant ! How goe my goods from hand to hand, and my name from tongue to tongue ? All will be published and come to light, whatsoever I have spoken, either to her, or them ; whatsoever they knew of my doings ; and whatsoever was done in this businesse. I dare not go forth of doores ; I am ashamed to looke any man in the face. O miserable young men ! that yee should suffer

220

CALISTO AND MELIBEA

death by so sudden a disaster. O my joyes, how doe you goe declining, and waining from me ! But it is an ancient Proverbe ; That the higher a man climbes, the greater is his fall. Last night I gained much ; to day I have lost much. Your Sea-calmes are rare, and seldome. I might have beene listed in the roll of the happy, if my fortune would but have allayd these tempestuous winds of my perdition. O Fortune ! how much, and thorow how many parts hast thou beaten mee ! But howsoever thou dost shake my house, and how opposite soever thou art unto my person, yet are adversities to be endured with an equall courage : and by them, the heart is prooved, whether it be of Oke, or Elder, strong, or weake ; there is no better Say, or Touchstone in the world, to know what finenesse, or what Characts of Vertue or of Fortitude remain in man. And therefore come what will come, fall backe, fall edge, I will not desist to accomplish her desire, for whose sake all this hath hapned. For it is better for mee to pursue the benefit of that glory, which I expect, then the losse of those that are dead. They were proud, and stout, and would have beene slaine at some other time, if not now. The old woman was wicked and false, as it seemes, in her dealings, not complying with that contract which shee had made with them : so that they fell out about the true mans cloake ; taking it from the true owner, to share it amongst themselves. But this was a just judgement of God upon her, that she should receive this payment, for the many adulteries, which by her intercession and meanes have beene committed. Sosia and Tristanico shall provide themselves ; they shall accompany me, in this my desired walke ; they shall carry the Scaling-ladders, for the walls are very high. To morrow I will abroad, and see if I can revenge their deaths ; if not, I will purge my innocency with a fained absence ; or else faine my selfe mad, that I may the better injoy this so tastefull a delight of my sweet Love ; as did that great Captaine Vlysses, to shunne the Trojane warre, that hee might lie dulcing at home with his wife Penelope.

THE END OF THE THIRTEENTH ACT

THE TRAGICK-COMEDY OF

ACTUS XIIII
THE ARGUMENT

ELIBEA *is much afflicted; she talkes with* Lucrecia, *concerning* Calisto's *slacknesse in comming, who had vowd that night to come and visit her. The which hee performed. And with him came* Sosia, *and* Tristan; *and after that he had accomplished his desire, they all of them betooke them to their rest.* Calisto *gets him home to his Palace; and there begins to complaine and lament, that he had staied so little a while with* Melibea; *and begs of* Phœbus, *that hee would shut his beames, that he might the sooner goe to renew his desire.*

INTERLOCUTORS

Melibea, Lucrecia, Sosia, Tristan, Calisto.

MELIBEA. Me thinks, the Gentleman, whome we looke for, stayes very long. Tel me (Lucrecia) what think'st thou? will he come, or no?

LUCRECIA. I conceive (Madame) he hath some just cause of stay, and it is not in his power to come so soone as you expect.

MELIBEA. Good spirits be his guard, and preserve his person from perill. For, his long stay doth not so much grieve mee: but I am afraid, lest some misfortune or other may befall him, as he is on his way unto us. For, who knowes, whether he comming so willingly to the place appointed, and in that kind of fashion, as such Gentlemen as hee, on the like occasion, and the like houre use to goe; whether, or no, I say, he may chance to light upon the night-watch, or be met by the Alguazils, and they not knowing him, have set upon him, and he to defend himselfe, hath either hurt them, or they him? Or whether some

222

CALISTO AND MELIBEA

roguish Curre or other with his cruell teeth (for such dogs as they make no difference of persons,) have perhaps unfortunately bit him? Or whether, he hath fallen upon the Causey, or into some dangerous pit, whereby he may receive some harme? But (Ay me) these are but inconveniences which my conceived love brings forth, and my troubled thoughts present unto me. Goodnes forbid, that any of these misfortunes should befall him! Rather let him stay as long as it shall please himselfe from comming to visit mee. But harke, harke, what steps are those that I heare in the street? And to my thinking likewise, I heare some body talking on this side of the garden.

SOSIA. Tristan, set the ladder here; for, though it be the higher, yet I take it to be the better place.

TRISTAN. Get up, Sir: And I will along with you. For, we know not who is there within, they are talking (I am sure) who-ere they be.

CALIST. Stay here (you foole) I will in alone, for I heare my Lady and Mistris.

MELIBEA. Your servant, your slave, Calisto, who prizes more yours then her owne life. O my deare Lord, take heed how you leape, leape not downe so high; you kill me, if you doe: I shall swound in seeing it. Come downe, come downe gently, I pray. Take more leasure in comming downe the ladder; as you love mee, come not so fast.

CALISTO. O divine Image; O precious pearle; before whom, the whole world appeareth foule! O my Lady and my glory; I imbrace and hug thee in mine armes, and yet I not beleeve it: such a turbation of pleasure seazeth on my person, that it makes me not feele the fulnes of that joy I possesse.

MELIBEA. My Lord, sithence I have intrusted my selfe in your hands, since I have beene willing to cumply with your will, let me not be worse thought of for being pittifull, then if I had bene coy and mercilesse. Nor doe not worke my undoing, for a delight so momentary and performed in so short a space. For, Actions that are ill, after they are committed, may easier be reprehended then amended. Rejoyce thou in that, wherein I rejoyce; which is, to see and draw

223

neere unto thy person, to view and touch thee. But do not offer either to aske or take that, which being taken away, is not in thy power to restore. Take heed (Sir) that you goe not about to overthrow that, which with all the wealth in the world, you are not able to repaire.

CALISTO. Deare Lady, since for to obtaine this favour, I have spent my whole life, what folly were it in me, to refuse that which you have so kindly conferr'd upon me? Nor (Madame) do I hope, that you will lay so hard a command upon me, or if you should, yet have I not power to containe my selfe within the limits of your command. Doe not impose such a point of cowardize upon me: For I tell you, it is not in any man that is a man, to forbeare in such a case, and to condition so hard with himselfe; much lesse in mee, loving as I do, and having swumme, as I have done all my life long, thorow this sea of thy desire and mine owne love. Will you then after my so many travels, deny me entrance into that sweet haven, where I may find some ease of all my former sorrowes?

MELIBEA. As you love me (Calisto) though my tongue take liberty to talke what it will: yet, I prythee, let not thy hands doe all what they can. Be quiet (good Sir) since I am yours, suffice it you content your selfe in the injoying of this outwardnes, which is the proper fruit of Lovers, and not to robbe me of the greatest Jewell, which Nature hath inrich't mee with: Consider besides. That it is the property of a good shepheard, to fleece, but not to slay his sheep; to sheare them, but not to uncase them.

CALISTO. Madame, What meane you by this? That my passions should not be at peace? That I shall runne over my torments anew? That I shall returne to my old voke againe? Pardon (Sweet Lady) these my impudent hands, if too presumptuously they presse upon you, which once did never thinke (so all together were they unworthy) not to touch, no not so much as any part of thy garments, that they now have leave to lay themselves with a gentle paine on this dainty body of thine, this most white, soft, and delicate flesh.

MELIBEA. Lucrecia, goe aside a little.

224

CALISTO AND MELIBEA

CALISTO. And why Madame? I should be proud to have such witnesses as she of my glory.

MELIBEA. So would not I, when I doe amisse. And had I but thought that you would have us'd mee thus, or beene but halfe so violent, as I now see you are, I would not have trusted my person with such a rough and cruell conversation.

SOSIA. Tristan, you heare what hath past, and how the geare goes.

TRISTAN. I heare so much, that I hold my Master the happiest man that lives. And I assure thee (though I am but a boy to speake of) me thinks, I could give as good account of such a businesse as my Master.

SOSIA. To such a jewell as this, who would not reach out his hand? But allow him this flesh to his bread, and much good may it doe him. For, he hath paid well for it : for a couple of his servants served to make sauce for this his Love.

TRISTAN. I had quite forgot that. But let them die, as instruments of their owne destruction. And let others as many as will, play the fools upon affiance to be defended. But for mine owne part, I well remember when I serv'd the Count, that my father gave mee this Councell : that I should take heed how I kill'd a man. Of all other things, that I should beware of that. For (quoth hee) you shall see the Master merry and kindly imbraced, when his man (poore soule) shall be hanged and disgraced.

MELIBEA. O my life and my deare Lord, how could you finde in your heart, that I should lose the name and crowne of a Virgin, for so momentary and so short a pleasure? O my poore Mother, if thou didst but know what wee have done, with what willingnes wouldst thou take thine owne death! and with what violence and inforcement give mee mine! How cruell a butcher wouldst thou become of thine owne blood! And how dolefull an end should I bee of thy dayes! O my most honoured father, how have I wrong'd thy reputation! And given both opportunitie and place to the utter overthrowing and undoing of thy house! O Traitour that I am! Why did I

2 F

not first looke into that great error, which would insue by thy entrance, as also that great danger; which I could not but expect?

SOSIA. You should have sung this song before. Now, it comes too late : you know, it is an old saying; when a thing is done, it cannot be undone. There is no fence for it, but what, if the foole Calisto should hap to heare me?

CALISTO. Is it possible? Looke and it be not day already: Me thinks, we have not been here above an houre, and the Clock now stricks three.

MELIBEA. My Lord, for Ioves love, now that all that I have, is yours; now, that I am your Mistris; now, that you cannot denie my love; deny mee not your sight. And on such nights as you shall resolve to come, let your comming bee by this secret place, and at the selfe same houre: for then, shall I still looke for you prepared with the same joy, wherewith I now comfort my selfe in the hopefull expectation of those sweete nights that are to come. And so for this present, I will take my leave. Farewell (my Lord) my hope is, that you will not be discovered, for it is very darke; Nor I heard in the house, for it is not yet day.

CALISTO. Doe you heare there? bring hither the ladder.

SOSIA. Sir, it is here ready for you to come downe.

MELIBEA. Lucrecia, come hither, I am now all alone. My Love is gone, who hath left his heart with me, and hath taken mine with him. Didst thou not heare us, Lucrecia?

LUCRECIA. No Madame, I was fast asleepe.

SOSIA. Tristan, wee must goe very softely, and not speake a word. For, just about this time, rise your rich men, your covetous money-mongers, your penny-fathers, your Venereans and Love-sicke soules, such as our Master; your day-labourers, your plough-men and your sheepheards; who about this time unpinne their sheepe, and bring them to their sheepcotts to be milk't. And it may be, they may heare some word escape us, which may wrong either Calisto's or Melibea's honour.

TRISTAN. Now you silly Asse, you whoresonne Horse-currier, you would have us make no noise, not a word, but

CALISTO AND MELIBEA

Mumme; and yet thy selfe doest name her. Thou art an excellent fellow to make a Guide or Leader to conduct an Army in the Moores Countrey: so that prohibiting, thou permittest; covering, thou discoverest; defending, offendest; bidding others hold their peace, thou thy selfe speak'st alowd, nay, proclaimes[t] it; and proclaiming, makes[t] answer thereunto. But though you are so subtill witted and of so discreet a temper, you shall not tell mee in what moneth our Lady day in harvest falls. For we know that we have more straw in the house this yeere, then thou art able to eat.

CALISTO. My Masters, what a noise make you there? My cares and yours are not alike. Enter softely, I pray, and leave your pratling, that they in the house may not heare us; Shut this doore, and let us go take our rest. For, I will up alone to my chamber, and there disarme mee. Goe get you to bed; O wretch that I am, how sutable and naturall unto mee is solitarinesse, silence, and darkenes. I know not whether the cause of it be, that there commeth now to minde, the treason that I have committed in taking my leave of that Lady, whom I so dearelie love, before it was further day? Or whether it be the griefe, which I conceive of my dishonour, by the death of my servants? I, I, I; this is it that greives mee, this is that wound whereof I bleed. Now, that I am growen a little cooler; now, that that bloud waxeth cold, which yesterday did boile in mee; now that I see the decaying of my house, my want of service, the wasting of my patrimony, and the infamie which lights upon mee by the death of my servants? what have I done? How can I possibly containe my selfe? How can I forbeare any longer, but that I should presently expresse my selfe, as a man much wronged? and shew my selfe a proud and speedy revenger of that open injurie which hath been offered mee? O the miserable sweetnes of this most short and transitorie life! who is he so covetous of thy countenance, who will not rather choose to die presently, then to injoy a whole yeere of a shamfull life? and to prorogue it with dishonour, loosing the good report and honourable memory of his noble Ancestours? Especially, sithence that in this world, wee have not any certaine or limited time: no not so much as a

227

ACTUS
XIIII

moment or a minute. We are debtours without time : wee
stand continually bound to present payment. Why have I
not gone abroad, and made all the inquiry I can, after the
secret cause of my open perdition ? O thou short delight of
the world, how little do thy pleasure[s] last ? and how much
doe they cost ? Repentance should not be bought so deare.
O miserable that I am, when shall I recover so great a losse ?
what shall I doe ? what counsell shall I take ? To whom
shall I discover my disgrace ? why do I conceale it from
the rest of my servants and kinsefolke ? They clip and note
my good name in their Councell-house and publike Assemblie,
and make mee infamous throughout the whole Kingdome :
and they of mine owne house and kindred must not know of
it ; I will out amongst them. But if I goe out and tell
them that I was present, it is too late ; if absent, it is too
soone. And to provide mee of friends, antient servants, and
neere allyes, it will aske some time, as likewise that we be
furnish'd with Armes, and other preparations of vengeance.
O thou cruell Judge, what ill payment hast thou made mee
of that my fathers bread, which so often thou hast eaten ?
I thought, that by thy favour I might have kill'd a thousand
men without controlment. O thou falsifier of faith, thou
persecutor of the truth, thou man moulded of the baser sort
of earth ! Truly is the proverbe verified in thee ; that for
want of good men thou wast made a Judge. Thou shouldst
have considered, that thy selfe, and those thou didst put to
death, were servants to my Ancestors and me, and thy
fellowes and companions. But when the base to riches doth
ascend, he regardeth neither kindred nor friend. Who
would have thought, that thou wouldst have wrought my
undoing ? But there is nothing more hurtfull, then an
unexpected enemy. Why wouldst thou that it should be
verified of thee, That that which came out of Ætna, should
consume Ætna ? And that I hatcht the Crow, which pick't
out mine eyes ? Thou thy selfe art a publike delinquent,
and yet punishest those that were private offendors. But I
would have thee to know ; that a private fault is lesse then
a publike, and lesse the inconvenience and danger : At least,
according to the Lawes of Athens, which were not written

CALISTO AND MELIBEA

in blood, but doe shew that it is a lesse error, not to condemne a delinquent, then to punish the innocent. O how
hard a matter is it, to follow a just cause before an unjust
Judge! How much more this excesse of my servants, which
was not free from offence! But consider with all spite of
all Stoicall Paradoxe, their guilt was not equall, though
their sufferings alike. What deserv'd the one, for that
which the other did? That onely because he was his companion, thou shouldst doome them both to death? But
why doe I talke thus? With whom doe I discourse? Am
I in my right wits? What's the matter with thee, Calisto?
Dream'st thou, sleep'st thou, or wak'st thou? Stand'st thou
on thy feete? Or liest thou all along? Consider with thy
selfe that thou art in thy chamber. Doest thou not see that
the offendor is not present? With whome doest thou contend? Come againe to thy self; weigh with thy selfe, that
the absent were never found just. But if thou wilt be up-
right in thy judgement, thou must keepe an eare for either
party. Doest thou not see, that the Law is supposed to be
equall unto all? Remember that Romulus, the first founder
of Rome, kill'd his owne brother, because he transgressed the
Law. Consider that Torquatus the Romane slew his owne
sonne, because he exceeded his Commission. And many
other like unto these did this man doe. Thinke likewise with
thy selfe, that if the Judge were here present, hee would
make thee this Answer; that the Principall and the Acces-
sary, the Actor and Consenter, doe merit equall punishment.
Howbeit, they were both notwithstanding executed, for that
which was committed but by one. And if that other had not
his pardon, but received a speedy judgement, it was, because
the fault was notorious, and needed no further proofes : as
also that they were taken in the very Act of murther, and
that one of them was found dead of his fall from the window.
And it is likewise to be imagined, That that weeping wench
which Celestina kept in her house, made them to hasten
the more by her wofull and lamentable noyse : And that the
Judge, that he might not defame mee, and that he might
not stay till the people should presse together, and heare
the proclaiming of that great infamy, which could not

ACTUS
XIIII

choose but follow mee, hee did sentence them so early as he did; and the common Hangman, which was the Cryer, could doe no otherwise, that he might cumply with their execution and his owne discharge. All which, if it were done as I conceive it to bee, I ought rather to rest his debtor, and thinke my selfe bound unto him the longest day of my life, not as to my fathers sometimes servant, but as to my true and naturall brother. But put case it were not so; or suppose I should not conster it in the better sence, yet call, Calisto, to mind the great joy and solace thou hast had, bethinke thy selfe of thy sweete Lady and Mistrisse, and thy whole and sole happines : and since for her sake thou esteemest thy life as nothing for to doe her service, thou art not to make any reckoning of the death of others : and the rather, because no sorrow can equall thy received pleasure. O my Lady and my life, that I should ever thinke to offend thee in thy absence ! And yet in doing as I doe, me thinks, it argues against mee, that I hold in small esteeme that great and singular favour, which I have received at thy hands. I will now no longer thinke on griefe ; I will no longer entertaine friendship with sorrow. O incomparable good ! O insatiable contentment ! And what could I have asked more of heaven, in requitall of all my merits in this life (if they be any) then that which I have already received ? Why should I not content my selfe with so great a blessing ? which being so, it stands not with reason that I should be ungratefull unto him, who hath conferr'd upon mee so great a good : I will therefore acknowledge it, I will not with care craze my understanding, lest that being lost, I should fall from so high and so glorious a possession. I desire no other honour, no other glory, no other riches, no other father nor mother, no other friends nor kinsfolkes. In the day, I will abide in my chamber : In the night, in that sweete Paradise, in that pleasant grove, that greene plot of ground amidst those sweete trees and fresh and delightsome walks. O night of sweet rest and quiet ! O that thou hadst made thy returne ! O bright shining Phœbus, drive on thy Charriot apace, make haste to thy journeys end ! O comfortable and delightfull starres, breake your wont, and appeare before

230

CALISTO AND MELIBEA

your time, and out of your wonted and continued course! O dull and slow clocke, I wish to see thee burned in the quickest and loveliest fire that Love can make. For didst thou but expect that which I doe, when thou strikest twelve, thou wouldst never indure to bee tyed to the will of the master that made thee! O yee hyematicall and winterly months, which now hide your heads, and live in darknes and obscurity! Why haste yee not to cut off these tedious daies with your longer nights? Me thinks, it is almost a yeere, since I saw that sweete comfort and most delightfull refreshing of my travels. But what doe I aske? Why like a foole doe I, out of impatiencie desire that which never either was or shall bee? For your naturall courses did never learne to wheele away. For to all of them there is an equall course, to all of them one and the selfesame space and time. Not so much as to life and death, but there is a settled and limited end. The secret motions of the high firmament of heaven, of the Planets and the North-starre, and of the increase and wane of the Moone, all of these are ruled with an equall reyne, all of these are moved with an equall spurre. Heaven, Earth, Sea, Fire, Wind, Heate and Cold. What will it benefit me, that this clocke of yron should strike twelve, if that of heaven doe not hammer with it? And therefore though I rise never so soone, it will never the sooner be day. But thou my sweete Imagination, thou, who canst onely helpe me in this case, bring thou unto my Phantasie the unparaleld presence of that glorious Image. Cause thou to come unto my eares that sweete Musicke of her words, those her unwilling hangings off without profit, that her prety, I prythee leave off; Forbeare, good Sir, if you love me; Touch me not; Doe not deale so discourteously with me. Out of whose ruddy lips, me thinks, I heare these words still sound, Doe not seek my undoing: which she would evermore be out withall. Besides, those her amorous imbracements betwixt every word; that her loosing of her selfe from me; and clypping mee againe; that her flying from mee and her comming to mee; those her sweete sugred Kisses; and that her last salutation where-with shee tooke her leave of mee. O with what paine did it

231

issue from her mouth! with what resuscitation of her spirits! with how many teares, which did seeme to be so many round pearles, which did fall without any noyse from her cleare and resplendent eyes!

SOSIA. What thinkst thou of Calisto? How hath he slept? It is now upon foure of the clocke in the after-noone, and he hath neyther as yet called us, nor eaten any thing.

TRISTAN. Hold your peace, for sleepe requires no haste. Besides, on the one side, he is oppressed with sadnes and melancholy for his servants: and on the other side transported with that gladsome delight and singular great pleasure, which he hath injoyed with his Melibea. And thou know'st, that where two such strong and contrary passions meete, in whomsoever they shall house themselves, with what forcible violence they will worke upon a weake and feeble subject.

SOSIA. Dost thou thinke that he takes any great griefe and care for those that are dead? If she did not grieve more, whom I see here out of the window goe along the street, she would not weare a vayle of that colour as she does.

TRISTAN. Who is that, brother?

SOSIA. Come hither and see her, before she be past. Seest thou that mournefull mayd, which wipes the teares from her eyes? That is Elicia, Celestina's servant, and Sempronio's friend: she is a good, pretty, handsome, welfavoured wench, though now (poore soule) shee be left to the wide world, and forsaken of all. For shee accounted Celestina her mother, and Sempronio her chiefest and best friend. And in that house, where you see her now enter, there dwels a very fayre woman, she is exceeding wel-favoured, very fresh and lovely, she is halfe Courtezane; yet happy is hee, and counts himselfe so to be, that can purchase her favour at an easie rate, and winne her to be his friend. Her name is Areusa, for whose sake, I know, that unfortunate and poore Parmeno indured many a miserable night. And I know, that shee (poore soule) is nothing pleased with his death.

THE END OF THE FOURTEENTH ACT

CALISTO AND MELIBEA

ACTUS XV

THE ARGUMENT

REUSA *utters injurious speaches to a Ruffian, called* Centurio, *who takes his leave of her, occasioned by the comming in of* Elicia, *which* Elicia *recounts unto* Areusa *the deaths, which had insued upon the love of* Calisto *and* Melibea. *And* Areusa *and* Elicia *agree, and conclude together, that* Centurio *should revenge the death of all those three, upon the two young Lovers. This done,* Elicia *takes her leave of* Areusa, *and would not be intreated to stay, because shee would not lose her market at home in her accustomed Lodging.*

INTERLOCUTORS

Elicia, Centurio, Areusa.

ELICIA. What ayles my Cousin, that shee cries, and takes on as shee does? It may be shee hath already heard of that ill newes, which I came to bring her: if she have, I shall have no reward of her for my heavy tydings. So, weepe, weepe on, weepe thy belly-full; let thine eyes breake their banks, and overflow thy bosome with an eternall deluge; for two such men were not every where to be had; it is some ease yet unto mee, that shee so risents the matter, and hath so true a feeling of their deaths. Doe, teare, and rent thy hayre, as I (poore soule) have done before thee: and thinke, and consider with thy selfe, that to fall from a happy life, is more miserable then death it selfe. O how I hugge her in my heart! How much more, then ever heeretofore, doe I now love her; that she can expresse her passion in such lively colours, and paint forth sorrow to it's perfect and true life!

AREUSA. Get thee out of my house, thou ruffianly Rascall; thou lying companion; thou cheating Scoundrell;

thou hast deluded mee, thou Villaine ; thou hast plai'd bob-foole with mee, by thy vaine and idle offers ; and with thy faire words and flattering speaches (A pocks on that smooth tongue of thine !) thou hast rob'd me of all that I have. I gave thee (you Rogue) a Jerkin and a Cloake, a Sword and a Buckler, and a couple of Shirts, wrought with a thousand devices, all of needle-worke ; I furnished thee with armes and a Horse, and placed thee with such a Master, as thou wast not worthy to wipe his shooes. And now that I intreat thee to do a businesse for mee, thou makest a thousand frivolous excuses.

CENTURIO. Command mee to kill tenne men, to doe you service, rather then to put me to walke a League on foot for you.

AREUSA. Why then did you play away your horse ? You must be a Dicer with a murraine ; had it not beene for mee, thou hadst beene hang'd long since. Thrice have I freed thee from the gallowes ; foure times have I disimpawnd thee, first from this, and then from that Ordinary, when as thou might'st have rotted in prison, had not I redeem'd thee, and paid thy debts. O that I should have any thing to doe with such a Villaine ! that I should be such a foole ! that I should have any affiance in such a false-hearted, white-liver'd slave ! that I should beleeve him and his lies ! that I should once suffer him to come within my doores ! What a divell is there good in him ? his hayre is curled, and shagg'd like a water Spaniell ; his face scotcht, and notcht ; he hath beene twice whipt up and downe the Towne ; hee is lame on his sword-arme, and hath some thirty whores in the common Stewes. Get thee out of my house, and that presently too ; looke mee no more in the face ; speake not to mee ; no not a word ; neyther say thou, that thou did'st ever know mee ; lest, by the bones of my father, who begot me, and of my mother, who brought me forth ; I cause 2000 Bastinadoes to be laid upon that Millers backe of thine. For, I would thou shouldst know, I have a friend in a corner, that will not sticke to doe a greater matter then that for mee, and come off handsomely with it, when he has done.

CENTURIO. The foole is mad, I thinke. But doe you

heare, Dame? if I be nettled, I shall sting some body; if my choller be moved, I shall drawe teares from some; I shall make some body put finger in the eye; I shall, yfaith. But for once, I will goe my wayes and say nothing; I will suffer all this at your hands, lest some body may come in, or the neighbours chance to heare us.

ELICIA. I will in, for that is no true sound of sorrow, which sends forth threatnings and revilings.

AREUSA. O wretch that I am; Is't you, my Elicia? I can hardly beleeve it. But what meanes this? Who hath cloath'd thee thus in sorrow? What mourning weede is this? Beleeve mee (Cousin) you much afright mee. Tell me quickly, what's the matter? For I long to know it. O, what a qualme comes over my stomack! Thou hast not left me one drop of bloud in my body.

ELICIA. Great sorrow, great losse; that which I shew, is but little to that which I feele and conceale. My heart is blacker then my mantle; my bowels, then my veyle. Ah, Cousin, Cousin; I am not able to speake through hoarsenesse; I cannot for sobbing, send my words from out my brest.

AREUSA. Ay miserable mee; why dost thou hold me in suspence? Tell mee, tell mee, I say, doe not you teare your hayre, doe not you scratch and martyre your face; deale not so ill with your selfe. Is this evill common to us both? Appertaines it also unto mee?

ELICIA. Ay, my Cousin! my deare Love, Sempronio and Parmeno are now no more; they live not; they are no longer of this world; dead, alasse they are dead.

AREUSA. What dost thou tell mee? No more I intreat thee; for pitty hold thy peace, lest I fall downe dead at thy feet.

ELICIA. There is yet more ill newes to come unto thine eares. Listen well to this wofull wight, and shee shall tell thee a longer Tale of woe; thy sorrowes have not yet their end; Celestina, shee whom thou knewst well; shee whom I esteemed as my Mother; shee who did cocker mee as her childe, shee who did cover all my infirmities; shee, who made me to be honoured amongst my equals; shee by whose meanes I was knowne thorow all the City and suburbs of the same, stands now rendring up an account of all her works. I saw her with these eyes stabb'd in a thousand places. They slew her in my lap, I folding her in mine armes.

AREUSA. O strong tribulation! O heavy newes worthy our bewayling! O swift-footed misfortunes! O incurable destruction! O irreparable losse! O how quickly hath fortune turned about her wheele! Who slew them? How did they dye? Thou hast made mee almost besides my selfe with this thy newes, and to stand amazed as one, who heares a thing that seemes to be impossible. It is not eight dayes agoe since I saw them all alive. Tell me (good friend) How did this cruell and unlucky chance happen?

ELICIA. You shall know. I am sure (Cousin) you have already heard tell of the love betwixt Calisto and that foole Melibea. And you likewise saw how Celestina, at the intercession of Sempronio, so as shee might be paid for her paines, undertooke the charge of that businesse, and to be the meanes to effect it for him; wherein shee used such diligence, and was so carefull in the following of it, that shee drew water at the second spitting. Now when Calisto saw so good and so quicke a dispatch, which he never hoped to have effected, amongst divers other things, hee gave this my unfortunate Aunt a chaine of gold. And as it is the nature of that metall, that the more we drinke thereof, the more wee thirst; shee, when she saw her selfe so rich, appropriated the whole gaine to her selfe, and would not let Sempronio and Parmeno have their parts, it being before agreed upon betweene them, that whatsoever Calisto gave her, they should share it alike. Now, they being come home weary one morning from accompaning their Master, with whom they had beene abroad all night, being in great choller and heate, upon I know not what quarrells and brawles, (as they themselves said) that had betyded them, they demanded part of the chayne of Celestina, for to relieve themselves therewith. Shee stood upon deniall of any such covenant or promise made betweene them; affirming the whole gaine to be due to her; and discovering withall other petty matters of some secrecie. For, (as it [is] in the Proverbe) when Gossips brawle, then out goes all.

CALISTO AND MELIBEA

So that they being mightily inraged, on the one side necessity did urge them, which rents and breaks all the love in
the world; on the other side, the great anger and wearinesse
they brought thither with them, which many times workes
an alteration in us. And besides, they saw that they were
forsaken in their fayrest hopes, shee breaking her faith and
promise with them : So that they knew not in the world
what to do ; and so continued a great while upon termes
with her, some hard words passing to and fro betweene them.
But in the end perceiving her covetous disposition, and finding that she still persevered in her denyall, they layd hands
upon their swords, and hackt and hew'd her in a thousand
pieces.

AREUSA. O unfortunate woman ! Wast thou ordained
to end thy dayes in so miserable a manner as this ?   But for
them, I pray what became of them ?   How came they to
their end ?

ELICIA. They, as soone as ever they had committed this
foule murder ; that they might avoyde the Justice, the
Alcalde passing by by chance at that very instant, made mee
no more adoe, but leapt presently out at the windowes ; and
being in a manner dead with the fall, they presently appre-
hended them, and without any further delay, chopt off their
heads.

AREUSA. O my Parmeno, my love ; what sorrow doe I
feele for thy sake ! How much doth thy death torment
mee ! It grieves me, for that my great love, which in so
short a space, I had settled upon him, sithence it was not
my fortune to injoy him longer.   But being that this ill
successe hath insued, being that this mischance hath hapned,
and being that their lives now lost, cannot be bought, or
restored by teares, doe not thou vexe thy selfe so much in
grieving and weeping out thine eyes : I grieve as much, and
beleeve, thou hast but little advantage of mee in thy sorrow-
ing ; and yet thou seest with what patience I beare it, and
passe it over.

ELICIA. O ! I grow mad. O wretch that I am, I am
ready to run out of my wits ! Ay me, there is not any
bodies griefe, that is like to mine ; there is not any body,

237

that hath lost that which I have lost! O how much better, and more honest had my teares beene in another persons passion, then mine owne! whither shall I goe? for I have lost both money, meate, drinke, and clothes; I have lost my friend, and such a one, that had hee beene my husband, hee could not have beene more kinde unto mee. O thou wise Celestina, thou much honoured Matrone, and of great authority; how often did'st thou cover my faults by thy singular wisdome! Thou took'st paines, whil'st I tooke pleasure; thou went'st abroad, whil'st I staid at home; thou went'st in tatters and ragges, whil'st I did ruffle in Silkes and Satens; thou still camest home like a Bee, continually laden, whil'st I did nothing but spend, and play the unthrift: for I knew not else what to doe. O thou worldly happinesse, and joy, which whilest thou art possessed, art the lesse esteemed! Nor dost thou ever let us know what thou art, till we know that thou art not; finding our losse, greater by wanting, then in injoying thee; never knowing what we have, till we have thee not. O Calisto and Melibea, occasioners of so many deaths! let some ill attend upon your love; let your sweete meate have some sowre sauce; your pleasure, paine; let your joy be turned into mourning, the pleasant flowres whereon you tooke your stolne solace, let them be turned into Serpents and Snakes; your songs, let them be turned into howlings; the shady trees of the garden, let them be blasted and withered with your looking on them; your sweet senting blossomes and buddes, let them be blacke and dismall to behold.

AREUSA. Good Cousin, content your selfe, I pray, be quiet; injoyne silence to your complaints; stop the Conduit-pipes to your teares; wipe your eyes; take heart againe unto you. For when fortune shuts one gate, she usually sets open another; and this estate of yours, though it be never so much broken, it will be soldred, and made whole againe: And many things may be revenged, which are impossible to be remedied; whereas this hath a doubtfull remedy, and a ready revenge.

ELICIA. But by whom shall we mend our selves? Of whom shall we be revenged, when as her death, and those

CALISTO AND MELIBEA

that slew her, have brought all this affliction and anguish
upon mee? Nor doth the punishment of the delinquent
lesse grieve me, then the errour they committed. What
would you have me to do, when as all the burden lies upon
my shoulders? I would with all my heart that I were now
with them, that I might not lie heere, to lament and bewaile
them all as I doe. And that which grieves mee most, is, to
see that for all this, that Villaine Calisto, who hath no sense,
╟nor feeling of his servants deaths, goes every night to see
and visit his filth Melibea, feasting and solacing himselfe in
her company, whilest she growes proud, glorying to see so
much bloud to be sacrificed to her service.

AREUSA. If this be true, of whom can wee revenge our
selves better? And therefore, hee that hath eaten the
meate, let him pay the shot; leave the matter to mee, let
me alone to deale with them: For, if I can but tracke them,
or but once find the sent of their footing, or but have the
least inkling in the world, when, how, where, and at what
houre they visit one another, never hold me true daughter to
that old pasty-wench whom you knew full well, if I doe not
give them sowre sauce to their sweete meate; and make that
their love distastefull, which now they swallow downe with
delight; and if I imploy in this businesse that Ruffian, whom
you found mee rayling against, when you came into the
house, if he prove not a worse Executioner for Calisto, then
Sempronio was for Celestina, never trust me more. O! how
quickely the Villaine would fat himselfe with joy, and how
happy would hee hold himselfe, if I would but impose any
service upon him! for he went away from me very sad and
heavy, to see how coursely I used him: and should I but now
send for him againe, and speake kindly unto him, he would
thinke himselfe taken up in some strange sweet rapture; so
much will he be ravished with joy. And therefore tell me
(Cousin) how I may learne, how this businesse goes, for I will
set such a trap for them, as, if they be taken in it, shall
make Melibea weepe as much, as now she laugheth.

ELICIA. Mary, I know (sweete Cousin) another companion of Parmeno's, Calisto's groome of the stable, whose
name is Sosia, who accompanies him every night that hee

ACTUS
XV

goes; I will see, what I can suck from him; and this (I suppose) will be a very good course for the matter you talke of.

AREUSA. But heare you me, Cousin, I pray doe me the kindnesse, to send Sosia hither unto me, I will take him in hand a little, I will entertaine talke with him; and one while I will so flatter him, another while make him such faire offers, that in the end, I will dive into him, and reach the very depth of his heart, and learne from him, as well what hath beene already, as what is to be done heereafter: At least learne so much as we desire to know, or may serve our turne; and when I shall have effected this, I will make him and his Master to vomit up all the pleasure they have eaten. And thou (Elicia) that art as deare to me, as mine owne soule, doe not you vexe your selfe any more, but bring your apparell, and such implements as you have, and come and live with mee; for there where you are, you shall remaine all alone: and sadnesse (you know) is a friend to solitarinesse. What wench! a new Love will make thee forget the old: one Sonne that is borne, will repaire the love of three that be dead. With a new successour, we receive anew the joyfull memory, and lost delights of fore-passed times. If I have a loafe of bread, or a penny in my purse, thou shalt have halfe of it. And I have more compassion of thy sorrow, then of those that did cause it. True it is, that the losse of that doth grieve a man more, which hee already possesseth, then the hope of the like good can glad him, be it never so certaine. You see, the matter is past all remedy; and dead men cannot be recald: you know the old saying: Fie upon this weeping, let them dye, and we live. As for the rest that remaine behinde, leave that to me; I will take order for Calisto and Melibea; and I shall give them as bitter a potion to drinke, as they have given thee. O Cousin, Cousin, how witty am I when I am angry, to turne all these their plots upside downe! and though I am but young, and a Girle to speake of, to breake the necke of these their devises, I shall overthrow them horse and foote.

ELICIA. Bethinke your selfe well, what you meane to

CALISTO AND MELIBEA

doe. For, I promise you, though I should doe as you would
have mee, and should send Sosia unto you, yet can I not be
perswaded that your desire will take effect. For the punishment of those who lately suffred for disclosing their secrets,
will make him scale up his lips, and looke a little better to
his life. Now for my comming to your house, and to dwell
with you; as the offer is very kinde, so I yeeld you the best
kinde of thankes I can render you; and Iove blesse you for
it, and helpe you in your necessity; for therein dost thou
well shew, that kindred and Alliance serve not for shadowes,
but ought rather to be profitable and helpfull in adversity;
and therefore, though I should be willing to doe, as you
would have mee, in regard of that desire, which I have to
injoy your sweet company; yet can it not conveniently be
done, in regard of that losse which would light upon me;
for I know, it cannot but be greatly to my hindrance; the
reason thereof I need not to tell you, because I speake to
one that is intelligent, and understands my meaning; for
there, Cousin, where I am, I am well knowne; there am I
well customed; that house will never lose the name of old
Celestina; thither continually resort your young wenches
bordring thereabouts, loving creatures, willing wormes, and
such as are best knowne abroad, being of halfe blood to
those, whom Celestina bred up; there they drive all their
bargaines, and there they make their matches, and doe many
other things besides, (as you know well enough) whereby
now and then I reape some profit. Besides, those few friends
that I have, know not elsewhere to seeke after mee. Moreover, you are not ignorant, how hard a matter it is, to forgoe
that which we have beene used unto; and to alter custome, is
as distastefull as death : A rolling stone never gathers mosse,
and therefore I will abide where I am : And if for no other
reason, yet will I stay there, because my house-rent is free,
having a full yeere yet to come, and will not let it be lost, by
lying idle and empty; so that though every particular reason
may not take place, yet when I weigh them altogether, I
hope I shall rest excused, and you contented. It is now
high time for mee to be gone ; what wee have talked of, I
will take that charge upon mee; and so farewell.

2 H   241

THE TRAGICK-COMEDY OF

ACTUS XVI

THE ARGUMENT

LEBERIO, and Alisa, *thinking that their daughter* Melibea *had kept her virginity unspotted and untoucht, which was (as it seemed) quite contrary; they fall in talke about marrying of* Melibea, *which discourse of theirs, she so impatiently endured, and was so grieved in hearing her father treate of it, that shee sent in* Lucrecia *to interrupt them, that by her comming in, she might occasion them to breake off both their discourse and purpose.*

INTERLOCUTORS

Melibea, Lucrecia, Pleberio, Alisa.

PLEBERIO. My wife, and friend Alisa; time (me thinks) slips (as they say) from betweene our hands; and our dayes doe glyde away like water downe a River. There is not any thing that flyes so swift, as the life of man: Death still followes us, and hedges us in on every side; whereunto we our selves now draw nigh. Wee are now (according to the course of nature) to be shortly under his banner; this wee may plainely perceive, if wee will but behold our equals, our brethren and our kinsfolke round about us; the grave hath devoured them all; they are all brought to their last home. And sithence we are uncertaine when we shall be called hence, seeing such certaine and infallible signes of our short abode, it behoveth us (as it is in the Proverbe) to lay our beard a soaking, when we see our neighbours shaving off, and to feare, lest that which befell them yesterday, may befall us to morrow. Let us therefore prepare our selves, and packe up our fardles, for to goe this inforced journey which cannot be avoyded. Let not that cruell and dolefull sounding trumpet of death, summon us away on the sudden and unprovided. Let us prepare our selves, and set things

242

CALISTO AND MELIBEA

in order whilest we have time, for it is better to prevent, then to be prevented ; let us conferre our substance on our sweet successour ; let us couple our onely daughter to a husband, such a one as may sute with our estate, that wee may goe quietly and contentedly out of this world.   The which with much diligence and carefulnesse, wee ought from henceforth to endevour and put in execution : and what we have at other times commenced in this matter, we ought now to consummate it.   I would not by our negligence have our daughter in Guardians hands ; I like not she should be a Ward ; she is now fit for marriage, and therefore much better for her to bee in a house of her owne, then in ours : by which meanes wee shall free her from the toungs of the vulgar ; for there is no vertue so absolute and so perfect, which hath not her detracting and foule-mouthed slanderers ; neyther is there any thing, whereby a Virgins good name is kept more pure and unspotted, then by a mature and timely marriage.   Who in all this City will refuse our Alliance ? who will not be glad to injoy such a Jewell, in whom those foure principall things concurre, which are demanded and desired in marriage ?   The first, Discretion, Honesty and Virginity. The second, Beauty.   The third, Noble birth and Parentage. The last, Riches.   With all these nature hath endowed her. Whatsoever they shall require of us, they shall find it to be full and perfect.

ALISA. My Lord Pleberio, heaven blesse her, and send her so to doe, that we may see our desires accomplished in our life time.   And I am rather of opinion that wee shall want one that is equall with our daughter, considering her vertue and noblenesse of blood, then that there are over-many that are worthy to weare her ; but because this office more properly appertaineth to the father then the mother, as you shall dispose of her, so shall I rest contented, and she remaine obedient, as shall best beseeme her chaste carriage, her honest life, and meeke disposition.

LUCRECIA. But if you knew as much as I doe, your hearts would burst in sunder.   I, I, you mistake your marke, shee is not the woman you wot of ; the best is lost ; an ill yeere is like to attend upon your old age.   Calisto hath

243

THE TRAGICK-COMEDY OF

pluckt that flowre wherein you so much glory. There is not
any that can now new filme her, or repaire her lost Virginity,
for Celestina is dead, the onely curer of a crackt maiden-head,
you have awaked somewhat of the latest; you should have
risen a little earelier. Harke, harke; good Mistresse Melibea,
harke, I say.

MELIBEA. What does the foole there sneaking in the
corner?

LUCRECIA. Come hither, Madame, and you shall heare
how forward your father and mother are to provide you a
husband, you shall be married out of hand, out of hand,
Madame.

MELIBEA.. For all loves sake speake softly; they will
heare you by and by} let them talke on, they beginne to
doat; for this month they have had no other talke; their
minde hath runne on nothing else; it may be their heart
tels them of the great love which I beare to Calisto, as also
of that which for this months space hath passed betweene us.
I know not whether they have had any inkling of our meeting? or whether they have over-heard us? nor can I devise
in the world, what should be the reason, why they should be
so hot upon the matter, and more eager for the marrying of
mee now, then ever heeretofore: but they shall misse of their
purpose; they shall labour it in vaine: for to what use serves
the clapper in the Mil, if the Miller be deafe? Who is he
that can remove me from my glory? Who can withdraw me
from my pleasure? Calisto is my Soule, my Life, my Lord;
on whom I have set up my rest, and in whom I have placed
all my hopes; I know that in him I cannot be deceived.
And since that hee loves me, with what other thing but love
can I requite him? All the debts in the world receive their
payment in a divers kind; but love admits no other payment, but love. I glad my selfe in thinking on him; I
delight my selfe in seeing him; and rejoyce my selfe in
hearing him. Let him doe with mee what he will, and dispose of me at his pleasure; if he will goe to Sea, I will goe
with him; if hee will round the world, I will along with
him; if he will sell mee for a slave in the enemies Countrey,
I will not resist his desire. Let my Parents let me injoy

244

CALISTO AND MELIBEA

him, if they meane to injoy me; let them not settle their
thoughts upon these vanities, nor thinke no more upon those
their marriages. For, it is better to be well belov'd, then ill
married; and a good friend is better then a bad husband.
Let them suffer mee to injoy the pleasure of my youth, if
they minde to injoy any quietnesse in their age; if not, they
will but prepare destruction for me, and for themselves a
Sepulchre. I grieve for nothing more, then for the time
that I have lost in not injoying him any sooner, and that
hee did not know me, as soone as he was knowne unto me.
I will no husband; I will not sully the knots of matrimony,
nor treade against the matrimoniall steppes of another man;
nor walke in the way of wedlocke with a stranger, as I finde
many have done, in those ancient bookes which I have read,
which were farre more discreete, and wiser then my selfe;
and more noble in their estate and Linage, whereof some
were held among the heathens for goddesses : as was Venus,
the mother of Æneas and of Cupid, the god of love, who being
married, broke her plighted troth of wedlocke : as likewise
divers others, who were inflamed with a greater fire, and did
commit most nefarious and incestuous errors : as Myrrha,
with her father; Semyramis with her sonne; Canace with
her brother; others also in a more cruell and beastly fashion,
did transgresse the Law of Nature : as Pasiphae, the wife of
King Minos, with a Bull : and these were Queenes and great
Ladies, under whose faults (considering the foulnesse of
them) mine may passe as reasonable, without note of shame,
or dishonesty. My love was grounded upon a good and just
cause, and a farre more lawfull ground. I was wooed and
sued unto, and captivated by Calisto's good deserts; being
thereunto solicited by that subtil and cunning Mistris in her
Art, Dame Celestina, who adventured her selfe in many a
dangerous Visit, before that ever I would yeeld my selfe true
prisoner to his love. And now for this month, and more (as
you your selfe have scene) hee hath not failed, no, not so
much as one night, but hath still scaled our garden walls, as
if hee had come to the scaling of a fort; and many times
hath beene repulsed, and assaulted it in vaine, being driven
to withdraw his siege. And yet for all this, hee continued

ACTUS XVI

more constant and resolute still, and never would give over, as one that thought his labour to be well bestowed. For my sake, his servants have beene slaine; for my sake, hee hath wasted and consumed his substance; for my sake, hee hath forued absence with all his friends in the City; and all day long hee hath had the patience to remaine close prisoner in his owne house, and onely upon hope (wherein bee counted himselfe happy) to see mee in the night. Farre, farre therefore from mee be all ingratitude: farre be all flattery and dissimulation towards so true and faithfull a Lover; for I regard (in my regard to him) neyther husband, father, nor kindred; for in losing my Calisto, I lose my life, which life of mine doth therefore please me, because it pleaseth him; which I desire no longer to injoy, then he shall joy in it.

LUCRECIA. Peace, Madame, harke, harke, they continue in their discourse.

PLEBERIO. Since (wife) mee thinkes you seeme to like well of this motion, it is not amisse, that wee make it knowne to our daughter; wee may doe well to tell her how many doe desire her, and what store of sutors would be willing to come unto her, to the end that she may the more willingly entertaine our desire, and make choyce of him whom she liketh best. For in this particular, the Lawes allow both men and women, though they be under paternall power, for to make their owne choyce.

ALISA. What doe you meane, husband? Why doe you talke, and spend time in this? Who shall be the messenger to acquaint our daughter Melibea with this strange newes, and shall not affright her therewith? Alasse, doe you thinke that she can tell what a man meanes, or what it is to marry, or be married? or whether by the conjunction of man and woman, children are begot or no? Doe you think, that her ample, and unspotted Virginity, can suggest unto her any futher desire, of that which as yet she neither knowes, nor understandeth; nor cannot so much as conceive what it meanes? It is the least part of her thought. Beleeve it, (my Lord Pleberio) she doth not so much as dreame on any such matter; and assure your selfe, be hee what hee will be, eyther noble or base, faire or foule, we will make her to

CALISTO AND MELIBEA

take whom it pleaseth us: whom we like, him shall shee like: shee shall confirme her will to ours, and shall thinke that fit, which wee thinke fit, and no further; for I know, I trow, how I have bred and brought up my daughter.

MELIBEA. Lucrecia, Lucrecia; runne, hye thee quickly, and goe in by the backe doore in the hall, and breake off their discourse with some fained errand or other, unlesse thou wouldst have me cry out, and take on like a Bedlam; so much am I out of patience with their misconceit of my ignorance.

LUCRECIA. I goe, Madame.

THE END OF THE SIXTEENTH ACT

ACTUS XVII

THE ARGUMENT

LICIA *wanting the chastity of* Penelope, *determines to cast off the care and sorrow which she had conceived upon the deaths of those for whom shee mourned, highly to this purpose commending* Areusa's *counsell; shee gets her to* Areusa's *house, whither likewise comes* Sosia, *out of whom,* Areusa, *by faire and flattring words, drew those matters of secrecy which past betwixt* Calisto *and* Melibea.

INTERLOCUTORS

Elicia, Areusa, Sosia.

ELICIA. I doe my selfe wrong, to mourne thus. Few doe visit my house; few doe passe this way. I can heare no musicke nor stirring betimes in the morning; I have no amorous ditties sung by my Lovers at my windowe; there are no frayes, nor quarrels before my doore; they do not cut and slash one another anights for my sake, as they were wont to doe: and that which most of all grieves me, is, that I see neither penny nor farthing, nor any other present to

247

come within my doores. But for this, can I blame no body but my selfe; my selfe only is in fault; for had I followed the counsell of her, who is my true and faithfull Sister, when as I brought her the other day the newes of this sad and heavy Accident, which hath brought all this penury upon mee, I had not liv'd alone mur'd up betweene two walls; nor others loathed to have come, and seene mee. The divell (I thinke) makes mee to mourne thus for him, who, had I beene dead, would scarce, perhaps, have shed one teare for mee. Now I dare boldly say, that Areusa told mee truth. Sister (quoth shee) never conceive, nor shew more sorrow for the misfortune, or death of another, then he would have done for thee. Sempronio, had I beene dead, would have beene ne'r a whit the lesse merry, he would not have wronged his delights, nor abridged his pleasures. And why then like a foole should I grieve and vexe my selfe, for one that is dead and gone, and hath lost his head by order of Law? And what can I tell, whether being a cholericke and hasty-hayre-braind fellow as he was, he might have killed mee too, as well as he did that old woman, whom I reckoned of as of mine owne mother? I will therefore by all meanes follow Areusa's counsell, who knowes more of the world then I doe; and goe now and then to visit her, that I may learne some-thing from her, how I may live another day. O what a sweet participation will this be! what a delightfull conver-sation! I see it is not said in vaine; That of more worth is one day of a wise man, then the whole life of a foole; I will therefore put off my mourning weedes, lay aside my sorrow, dismisse my teares, which have hitherto bin so ready to offer their service to my eyes. But sithence that it is the very first office that we doe, as soone as we are borne, to come crying into the world; I nothing wonder that it is so easie to beginne to cry; and so hard to leave off. But this may teach one wit, by seeing the hurt it does to the eyes; by seeing that good cloathes and neat dressings, make a woman seeme faire and handsome, though shee be nothing so, nor so; making her of old, young; and of young, younger. Your colour'd paintings, and your Cerusses which give woman such a pure white and red, what are they,

248

CALISTO AND MELIBEA

but a slimy clinging thing, a kind of bird-lime, wherewith men are taken and insnared ? Come then thou my glasse, come hither againe unto me ; and thou too my Antimonium ; for I have too much already wronged my eyes, and almost marr'd my face, with my blubbring and weeping. I will on with my white Vailes, my wrought Gorgets, my gay Garments, my more pleasing Attire, and such other apparell, as shall speake pleasure. I will presently provide some Lye for my hayre, which now through neglect, hath lost it's bright burnisht hiew. And this being done, I will count my Hens, I will make up my bed : for it glads a womans heart, to see things neat and handsome about her. I will have all well swept and made cleane before my doore, and the streete that buts upon it, sprinkled with water, as well to keepe it coole, as to lay the dust ; to the end, that they who passe by, may plainely thereby perceive, that I have banisht all griefe, and shaken hands with sorrow. But first of all, I will goe and visit my Cousin, to know whether Sosia have beene with her or no ? And what good shee hath done upon him ? For I have not seene him ; since I told him that Areusa would faine speake with him. I pray Iove, I may finde her all alone ; for shee is seldome any more without Gallants, then a good Taverne is without drunkards ; the doore is shut, there should be no body within ; I will knocke, and see. Tha, tha, tha.

AREUSA. Who's at doore ?

ELICIA. I pray open it ; it is Elicia.

AREUSA. Come in, good Cousin, heaven reward you for this kindnesse ; beleeve mee, I thinke my selfe much beholding unto you, that you would take the paines to come and visit me. I mary, wench, now it is as it should be ; now thou pleasest mee, thou canst not imagine what contentment my eye taketh, to see that habit of mourning and of sorrow, to be changed into garments of joy, and of gladnesse ; now wee will injoy one another ; wee will laugh and be merry ; now I shall have some heart to come and visit thee ; thou shalt come to my house, and I will come to thine ; it may be that Celestina's death will turne to both our goods ; for I finde, that it is better now with mee, then it was before ; and therefore it is said, that the dead doe open the eyes to

2 I

the living; to some by wealth; to other some by liberty, as it is with thee.

ELICIA. I heare some body at the doore; we are too soone cut off from our discourse, for I was about to aske you, whether Sosia had beene heere or no?

AREUSA. No, not yet; stay, wee will talke more anon. How loud hee knocks! I will goe downe and see who it is. Sure; either he is a mad-man, or our familiar friend. Who is 't that knocks there?

SOSIA. Open the doore, Mistresse: it 's Sosia, servant to Calisto.

AREUSA. Now in good time: The Wolfe is in the fable. Hide your selfe, sister, behinde these hangings, and you shall see how I will worke him; and how I will puffe him up with the wind of my faire and flattring words. And assure your selfe, that before we two part, I will make him wholy ours; he shall not goe hence the same Sosia that he came; but with my smooth and inticing termes, my soft and gentle handling of him, I will quite unmaw him, and draw from him all that hee either knowes concerning his Master or any body else, as hee drawes dust from his horses with his curry-combe. What? My Sosia? My inward friend? Him whom I wish so well unto, though perhaps he knowes not of it? Him, whom I have longed to know, led only by the fame and good report, which I heare of him? What? He that is so faithfull to his Master? So good a friend to his acquaintance? I will imbrace thee (my Love) I will hugge thee in mine armes; for now that I see thee, I see report comes short; and verily perswade my selfe, that there are more vertues in thee, then I have been told of. Fame hath been too sparing of thy praise; come (sweet heart) let us goe in, and sit downe in my chamber; for it does me good to looke upon thee. O! how thou dost resemble my unfortunate Parmeno! How lively doth thy person represent him unto mee! This is it that makes this day to shine so cleare, that thou art come to visit mee. Tell mee (gentle Sir) did you ever know mee before?

SOSIA. The fame (gentlewoman) of your gentle and sweete disposition of your good graces, discretion and wis-

CALISTO AND MELIBEA

dome, flies with so swift a wing, and in so high a pitch, through all this City, that you need not much to marvell, if you be of more knowne, then knowing. For there is not any man, that speakes any thing in praise of the fairest and beautifullest in this City, but that you are ranked in the first place, and remembred, as the prime and chiefest amongst them all.

ELICIA. This poore silly fellow, this wretched sonne of a whore, to see how hee exceedes himselfe, and speakes beyond the compasse of his common wit! hee doth not use to talke thus wisely. He that should see him goe to water his horses, riding on their bare ridge without a Saddle, and his naked legges hanging downe beneath his Canvasse frocke, cut out into foure quarters; and should now see him thus handsome, and well suited, both in his cloake, and other his cloathes, it would give a man wings, and tongue; and make him crow, as this Cockrell doth.

AREUSA. Your talke would make mee blush, and runne away for shame, were there any body heere, to heare how you play upon me. But (as it is the fashion of all you men) you never goe unprovided of such kinde of phrases as these: these false and deceitfull praises are too common amongst you; you have words moulded of purpose, to serve your turne withall, and to suite your selves as you see cause, to any woman whatsoever: yet for all this, am I not afraid of you, neyther will I start, or budge from you. But I must tell you (Sosia) by the way; this praising of me thus, is more then needs, for though thou shouldst not commend me, yet should I love thee. And that thereby thou shouldst thinke to gaine my love, is as needlesse; for thou hast gained it already. There are two things, which caused me (Sosia) for to send for thee, intreating thee to take the paines to come and see me; wherein if I finde you to double, or dissemble with mee, I have done with you. What they are, I will leave them to your selfe to relate, though I know it is for your owne good, which makes mee to doe as I doe.

SOSIA. Heaven forbid that I should use any cogging with you, or seeke by subtilty to deceive you. I came hither upon the assurance that I had of the great favors

251

which you intend, and now do me; holding my selfe not
worthy to pull off your shooes. Do thou therefore direct
my tongue; answer thou for mee to thine owne questions:
for I shall ratifie and confirme whatsoever thou shalt pro-
pound.

AREUSA. My Love, thou know'st how dearely I lov'd
Parmeno. And as it is in the Proverbe, Hee that loves
Beltram, loves any thing that is his; all his friends were
alwaies welcome unto mee; his good service to his Master
did as much please mee, as it pleased himselfe. When hee
saw any harme towards Calisto, hee did study to prevent it.
Now as all this is true, so thought I it good to acquaint
thee with it. First then did I send for thee, that I might
give thee to understand how much I love thee; and how
much I joy and ever shall, in this thy visiting mee; nor
shalt thou lose any thing by it, if I can helpe it, but rather
turne to thy profit and benefit. Secondly, since that I have
setled my eyes, my love and affection on thee, that I may
advise thee to take heede how thou commest in danger; and
besides, to admonish thee, that thou doe not discover thy
secrets to any: For you see what ill befell Parmeno and
Sempronio, by imparting things of secrecy unto Celestina;
for I would not willingly see thee dye in such an ill fashion,
as your fellow and companion did; it is enough for me that
I have bewayled one of you already, and therefore I would
have you to know, that there came one unto mee, and told
me that you had discovered unto him the love, that is betwixt
Calisto and Melibea; and how hee wanne her; and how you
your selfe night by night went along with him; and many
other things which now I cannot call to minde. Take heede
(friend) for not to keepe a secret, is proper onely unto women,
yet not unto all, but such as are fooles and children. Take
heede (I say) for heere-hence great hurt may come unto you:
and to this end did Nature give you two eares, and two eyes,
and but one tongue; to the end that what you see and heare,
should be double to that you speake. Take heede, and doe
not thinke your friend will keepe your secret, when you your
selfe cannot keepe it; when therefore thou art to goe with
thy Master, Calisto, to that Ladies house, make no noyse,

CALISTO AND MELIBEA

lest you be heard; for some have told me, that every night you keepe a coyle, and cannot containe your selves, as men transported and over-joyed.

SOSIA. O what busie-bodies, and what idle-headed persons be they who abuse your eares with such frivolous tales! whosoever told you that hee heard any such matter out of my mouth, hee told you an untruth; and some others, perhaps, because they see me goe anights when the Moone shines, to water my horses, whisling, and singing, and such like kinde of mirth, to drive away care, and to make me forget my toyling and my moyling, and all this before tenne a clocke at night, conceive an evill suspition; and of this suspition, make certaineties, and affirme that to be true, which themselves doe falsly surmize. And Calisto is not so madde, or foolish, that at such an houre as that, he should goe about a businesse of so great a consequence, but that he will first be sure that all abroad is quiet, and that every man reposes himselfe in the sweetenesse of his first sleepe: and lesse are you to suppose, that hee should goe every night unto her; for such a duty will not endure a daily visitation. And that you may (Mistresse) more manifestly see their falsehood; for (as the Proverbe is) A lyer is sooner ta'ne, then he that is lame; wee have not gone eight times a-month; and yet these lying babblers sticke not to avouch, we goe night after night.

AREUSA. If you love mee then (my deare Love) that I may accuse them to their faces, and take them in the nooze of their falsehood, acquaint mee with those dayes you determine to goe thither; and if then they shall erre in their report, I shall thereby be assured of your secrecy, and their roguery; for that being not true, which they tell mee, your person shall be secured from danger, and I freed from any sudden feare of your life, hoping long to enjoy you.

SOSIA. Mistresse, let us not stand any longer upon examination of witnesses. This very night, when the clocke shall strike twelve, they have appointed to meet by the way of the garden; to morrow, you may aske them what they know; whereof, if any man shall give you true notice, I will be content that hee shall scotch and notch me for a foole.

253

AREUSA. And on which side of the garden (my sweet-heart?) because I may contradict them the better, if I finde them varying.

SOSIA. By the streete where the fat Hostesse dwels, just on the backeside of her house.

ELICIA. No more (good man Ragge-tayle) it is enough, we need no more. Cursed is hee who makes such Muleters acquainted with his secrets. The Blockhead hath swallowed the bayte; hee hath let her unhinge him.

AREUSA. Brother Sosia; this that thou hast said, shall suffice to make knowne thy innocency, and their wickednesse; and so a good speed with thee: for I have some other businesse to dispatch, and I feare mee I have spent too much time with you.

ELICIA. O wise wench! O what a proper dismission, well befitting such an Asse, who hath so easily revealed his secrets!

SOSIA. Courteous sweet Mistresse, pardon mee, if my long stay hath beene troublesome unto you. And if it shall please you to accept of my service, you shall never light upon any that shall more willingly therein adventure his life. And so your owne best wishes attend you.

AREUSA. And you too. So: Are you gone, Muleter? How proudly the Villaine goes his way! I have put a tricke upon you (you Rogue) I have bored you, I wisse, thorow the nose; pardon me, if I turne my backe to thee, and with-draw my favour from thee. I will have your coat soundly cudgelled for this geare. But to whom doe I speake? Sister, come forth, tell me what dost thou thinke of him, whom I sent away? Have I not handsomely playd my part with him? Thus know I how to handle such fellowes; thus doe such Asses goe out of my hands, beaten and laden with blowes; thus your bashfull fooles, and no better do I use your discreeter men that are timorous; and your devout persons that are passionate; and your chaste men, when they are once set on fire. Learne of me therefore, Cousin: for this is another kinde of Art then that of Celestina; it is a tricke beyond any that she had in her budget; though she tooke mee for a foole, because I was content to be so

254

CALISTO AND MELIBEA

accounted at her hands. And sithence now that wee have squeez'd the Orange, and wrung out of this foole as much as wee desire to know; I thinke it not amisse, that we goe to seeke out that dogs-face, at his house, whom on Thursday last I rated so bitterly out of mine. You shall make show, as though you were desirous to make us friends, and that you had earnestly intreated me to come and see him.

THE END OF THE SEVENTEENTH ACT.

ACTUS XVIII

THE ARGUMENT

LICIA, *being resolved to make* Arcusa *and* Centurio *friends, as* Areusa *had before instructed her, they goe to* Centurio's *house; where they intreat him to revenge their friends deaths upon* Calisto *and* Melibea, *which he promiseth them to doe. And as it is the nature of such Ruffians as he, not to performe what they promise, he seekes to excuse himselfe, as you shall see in the sequell.*

INTERLOCUTORS

Elicia, Centurio, Areusa.

ELICIA. Who's at home heere?

CENTURIO. Boy, runne and see: Who dares presume to enter my house, and not first have the manners to knocke at the doore? Come, come backe againe, Sirrha; I now see who it is. Doe not cover your face (Mistresse) with your mantle, you cannot hide your selfe from me. For, when I saw Elicia come in before you, I knew shee could not bring with her any bad company, nor any newes that could offend mee, but rather that should please and delight mee.

AREUSA. If you love me (Sister) let us not in any further; for the Villaine stands upon his pantofles, and begins to looke big; thinking, perhaps, that I am come to cry him mercy. Hee had rather have such company as himselfe then ours; come, let us goe, for I am the worse to looke upon him; I am ready to swound with the very sight of such an ill-favour'd face. Think you (Sister) that you have us'd me well, to traine me thus along to such a walke as this? Is it a fit thing, that we should come from good company, and enter in heere to see this villainous fellow, that flayeth off the skinnes from dead mens faces, that hee may goe disguysed and unknowne?

ELICIA. If you love me, come backe againe; I pray you doe not you goe, unlesse you meane to leave halfe your mantle behinde you. I will hold you fast, indeede I will not let you goe.

CENTURIO. Hold her, as you love me, hold her. Do not let her goe.

ELICIA. I wonder, Cousin, what you meane by this? you seeme to be wiser then I am. Tell mee, what man is so foolish, or so voyd, of reason, that is not glad to be visited, especially by women? Come hither, Centurio; now trust mee, I sweare, shee shall imbrace thee, whether shee will or no; if shee will be angry, let her, I will beare the blame of it.

AREUSA. Imbrace him? Mary gup with a murraine! I had rather see him under the power and rigour of the Law; and had rather see him dye by the hands of his enemies, then that I should doe the slave such a kindnesse. No, no, I have done with him; I have nothing to say to him; as long as I live, he and I shall be two. And wherein (I pray) am I so beholding unto him, that I should imbrace him? nay, so much as once vouchsafe to looke upon such a professed enemy as hee? I did but intreat him the other day, to have gone but a little way for me about a businesse that did as much concerne mee as my life; and doe you thinke that I could get him to goe? Speake him faire, intreat him, doe what I could for my life, hee still answer'd mee, No. And shall I imbrace a Villaine, that regards me no more then so?

CENTURIO. Command mee, Mistresse, in such things a I know: exercise mee in my Art, and imploy mee in such

CALISTO AND MELIBEA

offices as appertaine to my profession: as, to fight for you
with three men at once; or say they should be more, for
your sake, I would not refuse them, but challenge them the
field. Command me to kill this or that man; to cut off a
leg or an arme; to slash any woman over the face, that shall
stand in competition with thee, and deface her beauty; such
trifles as these, shall be no sooner said, then done. But doe
not (I prythee) intreat me to walke afoote; nor to give thee
any money; for thou know'st I have it not. Gold and
Silver will not tarry with mee; they are flinchers, they will
not abide with mee. I may cut three Capers, and yet not
shake one poore blanke out of my breeches: no man gives
that which hee has not; you can have no more of a Cat, then
his skinne. Heart and good will, but not a ragge of money.
I live heere in a house as you see, wherein you may throw a
bowle and meet with never a rubbe; all the moveables that
I have, are not worth a button; my implements are such as
you see heere before mee; an old Jarre, with a broken
brimme; a rusty Spit without a point; the bed wherein I
lye, is bound about with hoopes of Bucklers, which I broke
in fight; my feather-bed, a bundle of broken pykes; my
sheetes, shirts of torne mayle; for my pillow, I have a pouch
fill'd with pibble stones. And should I bestow a collation on
you, I have nothing in the world that I can pawne, save this
poore ragged and thread-bare cloake, which I have on my
backe.

ELICIA. So let mee prosper, as his words doe exceedingly
please mee; why, hee is as obedient to you, as a servant; hee
speakes to you like a Suppliant, and hee hath said nothing,
but what is reason. What would you more of a man? I
prythee, as thou lov'st mee, speake unto him, and lay aside
your displeasure; suffer him not to live thus sad and
melancholy, but speake kindely unto him, and put him out
of his dumps, since hee offers his person so willingly to your
disposall.

CENTURIO. Offer my selfe, Elicia? I sweare unto thee,
by the Chriscrosse Row, by the whole Alphabet, and sillabi-
cation of the letters, that my arme trembles, to think what I
would execute for her sake; for it is, and ever shall be my

2 K   257

continuall meditation, to study how I may please her, but it is my unhappinesse, that it never hits right. The last night I was adream'd, that in her quarrell I challenged foure men into the field, all of them well knowne unto her, if I should name them; and mee thought I slew one of them; and for the rest which fled, he that scap't best, left his left arme at my foote. Much better should I have bestirr'd my selfe, had it beene day, and that I had beene awake, if the proudest of them should have once presumed but to have toucht her shoo.

AREUSA. I take thee at thy word; now wee be friends; and in good time have wee met. I heere pardon what is past, but upon condition that you revenge mee upon a Gentleman, called Calisto, who hath wronged both mee, and my Cousin.

CENTURIO. O! how I turne Renegado! How faine would I renew the condition! But tell mee; has hee made even with the world?

AREUSA. All's one for that, take you no care.

CENTURIO. Well, seeing you will have it so, let us send him to dine in hell, without company.

AREUSA. But doe you heare? Interrupt me not; Faile me not, I advise you; this night (if you will) you may take him napping.

CENTURIO. No more, I apprehend your meaning; I know the whole course of his love; how hee carries himselfe in it; how such and such suffred in the businesse: as also where you two are galled; I know whither hee goes, at what houre, and with whom. But tell mee, how many accompany him?

AREUSA. Onely two; and those young fellowes.

CENTURIO. This is too small a prey, too poore a pittance; my sword will have but a short supper; it would fare farre better at some other time, then that which now you have concluded on.

AREUSA. No, no; this is but to shift us off, and to excuse your not doing it. It will not serve your turne, you must give this bone to some other dogge to picke; I must not be fed with delaies: I will see whether sayings and

CALISTO AND MELIBEA

doings eate together at your Table; whether deedes and words sit both at one boord with you?

CENTURIO. If my sword should but tell you the deedes it hath done, it would want time to utter them. What does impeople Church-yards but it? Who makes Surgeons rich but it? Who sets Armourers aworke but it? Who hewes, and unriviteth the finest maile but it? Who drives before him, and shivers in pieces the bucklers of Barcelona, but it? Who slices the helmets of Calatayud, but it? Who shreds the casks of Almazan, as short as if they were made of Pumpions, but it? These twenty yeeres hath it found mee food; by meanes of it am I feared of men, and beloved of women, onely your selfe excepted; for it, the name of Centurio was given to my Grandfather; for it, my father likewise was called Centurio, and so am I.

ELICIA. But I pray, tell me, what did your sword, that your Grandfather should gaine his name by it? Was hee by it made Captaine of a hundred men?

CENTURIO. No, hee was made by it Champion to an hundred women.

AREUSA. Wee will have nothing to doe with your Pedigree, nor famous Acts of old; if you will doe that I spake to you of, resolve suddenly, for wee must be gone.

CENTURIO. I long more for this night, wherein I may give you content, then you long to be revenged. And that every thing may be done to your good liking; make your owne choyce, what death you will have him dye. For I can shew you a Bead-roll (if you will see it) wherein there are set downe some seven hundred and seventy severall sorts of deaths; which when you have scene, you may choose that which likes you best.

ELICIA. If you love mee (Areusa) let not this matter be put into such a mad-mans hands; hee is too bloudy for the businesse: and it were better to let all alone, then that the City should receive such a scandall; so that our second harme shall be worse then the first.

AREUSA. I pray content your selfe, Sister, hold your peace. Name that City unto us (if you can) which is not full of hurly-burlies, and where some scandals doe not arise.

259

THE TRAGICK-COMEDY OF

CENTURIO. The affronts and disgraces which are now in request, and wherin I am most conversant, are banging a man over the shoulders with a sword, having it's scabbard on; dry-beatings, without drawing of bloud; thumping him on the brest, or making his head ring noone with the pommell of my sword, or by falsifying of a thrust or blow, to give him his payment where hee least lookes for it. Others I use like Sives, pricking them full of holes with my ponyard; some I cut in a large size, giving them a fearefull stocada, or mortall wound: and now and then I use my cudgell, or bastonado, that my sword may keepe holy-day, and rest it selfe from it's labour.

ELICIA. For loves sake ha' done, tell us of no more. Bastonado him, I pray thee: for I would have him beaten, but not slaine.

CENTURIO. I sweare by the whole generation of Turke and Termagaunt, that it is as possible for this right arme of mine to bastonado a man, and not kill him, as it is for the Sunne to stand still in the Firmament, and never move.

AREUSA. Sister, let not you and I sorrow for the matter; why should wee seeme to pitty him? Let him doe with him what hee will; let him kill him, as hee findes himselfe humour'd, when hee comes to doe the businesse: let Melibea weepe as well as you have done before her: and so let us leave him. Centurio; see you give a good accompt of that which is committed to your charge. Take your owne course; any way, so as you revenge us on him, shall content us; but in any case take heed, that hee doe not escape without paying for his errour.

CENT. O Heavens! he is going to Pluto I warrant you already; I will give him his passe-port, I warrant you, unlesse hee betake him to his heeles, and runne away from me. Dearest in my affection, it glads mee to the heart, that I have this occasion offred unto mee (though it be but in a trifle) and a matter scarce worth thanks; that you may know by this, how farre I would (if occasion served) inforce my selfe for your sake.

AREUSA. Mars direct thy hand aright. And so farewell, for it is time for us to be gone.

CALISTO AND MELIBEA

CENTURIO. Well, adieu. Goe your waies, like a couple of headstrong and pertinacious whores as you be. Now will I bethinke my selfe, how I may excuse my selfe of my promise; and in such sort too, that they may be perswaded, that I used all possible diligence for to execute their desire, and that it was not of negligence, for the freeing of my selfe from danger. I will faine my selfe sicke: But what will that profit me? for then they will be at me againe when I am well. Againe, if I shall tell them that I have beene there, and that I forced them to flye, they will aske mee who they were? how many in number, and in what place I buckled with them? and what apparell they wore? and by what markes I knew them to be such and such? and the divell a whit shall I be able to tell them: And then all the fat is in the fire. What counsell then shall I take, that may cumply with mine own safety, and their desire? I will send for lame Thraso, and his companions, and tell them, that because this night I shall be otherwise imployed, they would goe and make a clattering with their Swords and Bucklers in manner of a fray, for to feare, and affright certaine young men, whom they shall finde in such a place, which service was faithfully recommended unto mee to execute. This I know is a sure course, and no other hurt can follow thereupon, save to make them fly, and so get them home to bed.

THE END OF THE EIGHTEENTH ACT

THE TRAGICK-COMEDY OF

ACTUS XIX

THE ARGUMENT

CALISTO, *going with* Sosia *and* Tristan *to* Pleberio's *garden to visit his* Melibea, *who staid looking for him, attended by* Lucrecia; Sosia *recounts unto* Tristan *all that which had passed betwixt him and* Areusa. Calisto *remaining in the garden with* Melibea : Thraso *and his companions come, sent thither by the appointment of* Centurio, *for the fulfilling of that which hee had promised to* Areusa, *and* Elicia. *Upon whom* Sosia *sallies forth. Now* Calisto *hearing from the garden where hee remained with* Melibea, *the clashing and clattering which they made, would needes goe forth amongst them. Which issuing forth was the cause that his daies were finished; for this is the recompence which such Lovers receive. Whence they may learne, that it is better for them not to love at all, then so to love.*

INTERLOCUTORS

Sosia, Tristan, Calisto, Melibea, Lucrecia.

SOSIA. Softly, that wee may not be heard. As wee goe from hence to Pleberio's garden, I will tell thee all (brother Tristan) that passed this day, betwixt Areusa, and my selfe, taking my selfe now to be the happiest man in the world. Thou shalt understand then, that upon the good report which shee heard of mee, shee fell extremely in love with mee, and sent me word by Elicia, that I would doe her the kindnesse, as to come and speake with her. But omitting many other speaches of good counsell, which then past betweene us, shee made present shew unto mee, that shee was now as much mine, as ever shee was Parmeno's. Shee requested mee, that I would continually come and visit her; and that she did not doubt, but that shee should long injoy my love. And I sweare to thee (brother) by that dangerous
262

CALISTO AND MELIBEA

way wherein wee walke, and as ever any good may heereafter befall mee, that twice or thrice it was as much as ever I could doe for my life, to forbeare from boording her; but that very shame did hinder mee, seeing her so faire, and so well clad, and my selfe in an old Mouse-eaten cloake: still as shee moved and advanced her selfe, shee did breathe forth a most sweet and redolent odour of Muske; and I never stirr'd, or heav'd my body, but I sent forth a most ranke sent of that horse-dung, which had got within my shooes: Shee had a hand as white as snow, and ever and anon, as she pull'd off her glove, thou wouldst have thought, that she had scattered flowres of Orenges about the roome; so that as well in regard of this, as also because at that time shee was somewhat busie, I was content to deferre my boldnesse till another day: as likewise because all things at the first sight are not so tractable; for the more they are communicated, the better are they understood in their participation.

TRISTAN. Friend Sosia, another more ripe and mature braine, and better experimented in matters of the world then mine is, were very necessary to be your adviser in this businesse; yet as farreforth as my tender age, and the meanes of my naturall parts and wit shall be able to reach unto; I will tell you what I thinke. This woman, (as you told me your selfe) is a known and noted whore; and therefore whatsoever hath past betweene you, flatter not your selfe, but rather beleeve, that her words doe not want deceit. Her offers, I perswade mee were false, though I know not to what end she made them. If shee love thee, because thou art a Gentleman; how many better then thy selfe hath she rejected? If because thou art rich; she knowes well enough that thou hast no other dust, then that which clings to the Curry-combe. If because thou art nobly descended, and of high Linage; she knowes thy name is Sosia, and so was thy fathers; and that he was borne and bred in a poore little Hamlet, getting his living by following the Plough-tayle, and breaking Clods of earth, for which thy selfe art more fit then to make a Lover. Be wise, Sosia, and consider with thy selfe, if she doe not goe a birding, to see if she could get out of thee, the secrecy of this walke, whereby to worke some heart-burning, and breed no good bloud betwixt Calisto and Pleberio, out of that envy which she beares to Melibea's pleasure. Beware (I say :) for Envy (I tell you) is an incurable infirmity, when it is once settled: shee is a guest that is alwaies more troublesome, then thankfull for her lodging, and is never merry, but at other folkes miseries ; nor ever laughes, but at a shrewd turne. Now then, if this be so: O! how this wicked woman will deceive thee with her smooth and subtill words, whereof, such as she are never to seeke, but have them still ready in the deck, and more perfect then their *Pater noster*! With this venemous vice, shee will not sticke to damne her soule, so as shee may please her appetite ; shee would faine turne all things topsiturvy, and set men together by the eares, and onely for to content her damnable desire. O Ruffianly Strumpet! O mankind Queane! With what white bread hath shee given thee crooked pinnes, to choake thee ? Shee cares not how shee sells and barters her body, so as shee may truck and exchange it for strife and contention. Heare mee, Sosia, and if thou doest as thou may'st presume upon it, that it is as I tell thee, deale (if thou wilt be advised by mee) as doubly with her ; for he that deceives the deceiver, you know what I meane : and if the Foxe be crafty, more crafty is hee that catches him. I would have thee make a counter-mine against these her wicked, and divellish imaginations. Set up scaling ladders to meete with her lewdnesse ; and then cry quittance with her, when shee thinkes her selfe most safe and secure ; and laugh at her afterwards, when thou art by thy selfe all alone in thy stable : the bay horse thinkes one thing, and hee that saddles him, another.

SOSIA. O Tristan! thou discreete young man ; more hast thou spoken then could be expected from one of thy yeeres. A shrewd suspition hast thou raised in mee, and I feare mee too true ; but because wee are hard by the garden, and our Master is close at our heeles, let us breake off this discourse, which is too large for the present, and deferre it to some fitter opportunity.

CALISTO. Do you heare there ? Set up the ladder, and see you make no noyse ; for mee thinkes I heare my Mistresse tongue. Sure it is shee, she is talking to some body, who-e'r

CALISTO AND MELIBEA

it be. I will get me up to the top of the wall, and there will
I stand harkning awhile, to see if I can heare from her any
good token of her love to mee, in this my absence.

MELIBEA. Sing on (Lucrecia) if thou lov'st mee; I
prythee sing on; for it does my heart good to heare thee;
sing on, I say, till my Lord come. Be not too loud, and let
us goe aside into this greene walke, that they that passe by
may not heare us.

LUCRECIA.
> O that I kept the Key,
> Which opes to these faire flowers,
>   To plucke them day by day,
> When you doe leave these bowers.
> The Lillies and the Roses,
> Put on their newest colours,
>   And when thy Love reposes,
> They breathe their freshest odours.

MELIBEA. O how sweet is thy musick to mine eares! it
makes my heart even to melt and dissolve for joy. I prythee
give not over.

LUCRECIA.
> Sweete is the fount, the place,
> I dranke at, being drie;
>   More sweete Calisto's face,
> In Melibea's eye.
>   And though that it be night,
> His sight my heart will cheere,
>   And when hee downe shall light,
> O how I'll clippe my Deare!
> The Wolfe for joy doth leape,
> To see the Lambkinnes moove,
>   The Kidde joyes in the teate,
> And thou joy'st in thy Love.
>   Never was loving wight,
> Of's friend desired so;
>   Ne'r Walkes of more delight,
> Nor nights more free from woe.

MELIBEA. Friend Lucrecia, me thinkes, I see that which
thou singest, represented most lively unto me; me thinks, I
see him as perfectly with these mine eyes, as if hee stood just
before mee. Goe on; for thou dost exceeding well, and with

2 L

THE TRAGICK-COMEDY OF

ACTUS
XIX

an excellent Ayre: I will beare a part with thee, and helpe thee as well as I can.

MELIBEA
and
LUCRECIA.

> Sweet trees who shade this mold
> Of earth, your heads downe bend,
> When you those eyes behold
> Of my best-loved friend.
> Faire starres whose bright appeare,
> Doth beautifie the skye,
> Why wake yee not my Deare,
> If he asleeping lie?

MELIBEA. Heare mee now, I prythee; I will sing alone.

MELIBEA.

> You birds, whose warblings proove
> Aurora draweth neere,
> Goe flye, and tell my Love,
> That I expect him heere.
> The night doth poasting moove,
> Yet comes hee not againe;
> God grant some other Love
> Doe not my Love detaine.

CALISTO. The sweetnesse of thy voyce hath ravish't mee; I cannot endure to let thee live any longer in a pained expectation. O my sweet Mistresse, and my lifes happinesse; what woman could ever be borne into the world, that should be able to deprive thee of thy great deservingnesse? O interrupted melody! O musick suddenly broke off! O short-timed pleasure! O my deare heart, why didst thou not continue thy harmony, without interrupting thy joy, and cumplying with both our desires?

MELIBEA. O pleasing treason; O sweete-sudden passion! What? my Lord? my soule; Is it hee? I cannot beleeve it; where hast thou beene, thou bright shining Sunne? In what place hast thou hid thy brightnesse from me? Is it not a pretty while since that thou heard'st mee? Why didst thou suffer me to send forth my words into the Ayre, senselesse and foolish as they were, and in this hoarse Swannish voyce of mine? looke on the Moone, and see how bright shee shines upon us: looke on the Cloudes, and see how speedily they racke away: harken to the gurgling waters of this

266

CALISTO AND MELIBEA

fountaine: how sweet a murmure, and what a pretty kind of purling they make, rushing along these fresh herbes, and pleasant flowres: harken to these high Cypresses, how one bough makes peace with another by the intercession of a milde, gentle, and temperate wind, which moves them to and fro. Behold these silent and quiet shades, how darke they are, and how excellently well prepar'd for the covering and concealing of our sports. Lucrecia? why, how now friend? what are you doing? art thou turn'd mad with pleasure? Let me alone with my Love; touch him not, I charge you; doe not you plucke and hale him from me; doe not burthen his body with your heavy armes. Let mee injoy what is mine, you shall not possesse any part of my pleasure.

CALISTO. Deare Lady, and glory of my life; if you love me, give not over your singing; let not my presence, which glads thee, be of a worse, and more unfortunate condition, then my absence which did grieve thee.

MELIBEA. Why (my Love) would you have mee sing? or how can I sing? for my desire of thee, was that which ruled my voyce, and made mee to ayre my notes. But now that thou art come, that desire disappeares, it is vanished, and the Tone of my voyce distempred, and out of tune. And because you, Sir, are the patterne of courtesie and good behaviour, how can you in reason require my tongue to speake, when as you cannot rule your owne hands, and keepe them quiet? Why doe not you forget these tricks, and learne to leave them? Lay your command upon them to be quiet, and will them to lay aside this offensive custome, and consider (my dearest) that as to see thee, whilest thou carriest thy selfe quietly and civilly, is the greatest happinesse that eyther my heart or my eye can injoy; so is it as displeasing unto me, to see thee handle me so roughly. Thy honest sporting pleaseth mee, but thy dishonest hands offend mee, especially when they are too farre out of reason. And, though love ofttimes forget reason, yet amongst your well-educated, and noble and generous spirits, kindnesse keepes a decorum, and revels not but with decency; let such (Sweet-heart) be our imbraces, such and so modest be our dalliance (my dearest Calisto, my Love, my Lord.) And

267

since I wholy subject my selfe to your pleasure; be it your pleasure, to take and make such worthy benefit of my affection, presence and service, as best beseemes true Lovers, and is agreeable to both our high births and breeding. But alas silly woman, why should I direct you? No, I will not. Doe, Calisto, doe what you will, and say what you will, I am yours to use; please your selfe, and you shall please mee.

CALISTO. Madame, fervency of love loves not to be idle; pardon then, I pray you, if I have beene too busie.

LUCRECIA. Now never trust mee againe, if I harken to them any longer. Heer's a life indeede! O how I feele my selfe melt within, like snow against the Sunne; and how squeamish my Mistresse seemes, because, forsooth, shee would faine be intreated! Assuredly, had I beene in her case, and have lost so much time, I should thinke the worse of my selfe the longest day of my life.

MELIBEA. Sir, shall I send Lucrecia to fetch you some sweet-meats?

CALISTO. No, Lady; no other sweet-meats for mee, save onely to imbrace this thy body, to fold it within mine armes, and to have the possession of thy beauty. Every where a man may eate and drinke for his money; that a man may have at any time; it is every where to be bought: but that which is not vendible, that which in all the world is not to be matched; and save onely in this garden, not to be found againe from one Pole to the other. Why wish you me not rather that I should not let slippe the least moment, in injoying so sweete a treasure?

LUCRECIA. My head akes with hearing; and yet their tongues ake not with talking, nor their armes with colling, nor their lips with kissing. Sure, they will make me gnaw the finger of my glove all to pieces.

CALISTO. O my deare Mistresse! I could wish it would never be day, that I might still injoy that sweet happinesse, and fulnesse of content, which my senses receive in the noble conversing with this thy delicate, and dainty sweete Selfe.

MELIBEA. Sir, it is I that injoy this happinesse, this fulnesse of content. If any body gaine by it, it is I; and I

268

CALISTO AND MELIBEA

must acknowledge my selfe most infinitly beholding unto you, that you would vouchsafe to visit mee in so kinde and loving a manner, as no thankes are able to requite so great a favour.

SOSIA. Out, you Ruffianly Rascals; come yee to fright those that feare you not? Had I bin ware of your comming, or had you staid any longer, I would have sent some of you packing, and have given you somewhat that should have stuck by you. Out, you Rogues.

CALISTO. Madame, this is Sosia's voyce; suffer mee to goe and see, that they doe not kill him, for there is no body with him but a little Page that came with me. Give me my cloake quickly, it lies under you.

MELIBEA. O unfortunate that I am! I pray do not go without your Curaces. If you love me, come back; I wil help to arme you my selfe.

CALISTO. That (Mistresse) which a sword, a cloak, and a good heart cannot doe, can never be effected by Curace, Caske or Cowardice.

SOSIA. Yea? are you come againe? I shall be with you to bring by and by; you come for wooll, doe you? But if you stay a little longer, I shall send you home without a fleece, I shall plume you, I shall, you Rascals.

CALISTO. Lady, if you love mee, let mee goe. The ladder stands ready for mee.

MELIBEA. O miserable mee! Why dost thou goe so furiously, and so fast? and all disarmed as thou art, to hazard thy life among'st thou know'st not whom? Lucrecia, come hither quickly; for Calisto is gone to thrust himselfe into a quarrell. Let us take his Curaces, and throw them over the wall; for he hath left them heere behinde him.

TRISTAN. Stay, Sir, doe not come downe. They are gone; it is no body but lame Thraso, and a company of other Rogues with him, that made a noyse as they past by: And Sosia is come backe againe. Take heed, Sir, hold fast by the ladder, for feare lest you fall.

CALISTO. Oh, oh. Looke upon me. Ay me! I am a dead man: oh.

TRISTAN. Come hither quickly, Sosia; for our unfortunate Master is falne from the ladder, and neither speakes nor wagges.

SOSIA. Master, Master, doe you heare, Sir? Let us call a little at this other doore. Hee heares on neyther eare; hee is as dead as a doore-nayle; there is no more life in him, then in my great grand-father, who dy'd some hundred yeeres since. O foule mishappe! What will become of us?

LUCRECIA. Harke, harke, Madame! what a great mischance is this?

MELIBEA. O wretch that I am! what doe I heare?

TRISTAN. O, my Master, my master is dead! and with him all my happinesse, all my good; hee is falne headlong downe; hee is dead; hee is dead: and (which is a fearefull thing) suddenly dead. O pittifull, O horrible sight. Helpe Sosia, helpe to gather up these braines, that lye scattered heere amongst the stones, and let us put them againe into his head. O unfortunate Master! O unlucky day! O sudden and unexpected end!

MELIBEA. O disconsolate woman that I am! What a thing is this? What vile mishap, that hath thus disturbed our quiet? What mischance can possibly prove so cruell, as that which I now heare? Help mee (Lucrecia) to get up this wall, that I may see my sorrow, unlesse you will have mee fill my fathers house with cries and skrikes? What? Is all my joy turned into smoake? Is all my pleasure lost? All my glory come to an end?

LUCRECIA. Tristan, what's the matter (my Love) why dost thou weepe so bitterly? why take you on so, beyond all measure and reason?

TRISTAN. I bewaile my great misery; I bewaile my many sorrowes. My Master Calisto hath falne from the ladder, and is dead; his head is in three pieces; hee dyed suddenly, and lamentably torne and dasht to pieces; beare this sad message to his new friend, that she must never more expect her pained Lover. Sosia, doe thou take up his feete, and let us carry his body hence, that hee may not in this place suffer dishonour, though hee have suffered death. Let mourning goe along with us; let solitarinesse accompany us; let discomfort waite upon us; let sorrow apparell us;

270

CALISTO AND MELIBEA

let mourning weedes cover us; and let us put on sad habits.

MELIBEA. Ay me, of all other the most miserable! So short a time, to possesse my pleasure? so soone, to see my sorrowes come upon me?

LUCRECIA. Madame, teare not your face; rent not your hayre: What? but even now all pleasure? and now all sorrow? Out alas! that one, and the self-same Planet should so suddenly affoord an effect so contrary? where is your courage? Fye, what a faint heart have you! pray you arise from the ground; let not your father find you in so suspitious a place: for if you continue thus, you cannot choose but be heard. Why, Madame, Madame, I say heare you me? Doe you heare, Lady? Of all loves, do not fall any more into these swounds. Be as valiant and couragious in induring your sorrow, as you were hot and hardy in committing your errour.

MELIBEA. Heare you what moane his poore servants make? heare you how wofully they lament his losse? wailing, and weeping, praying, and answering each to other, they carry away from mee all my good, all my happinesse; my dead joy, my dearest Love, they carry away from me; my time is come; I am but a dead woman; I can live no longer, since I may no more injoy the joy of my heart. O that I should let thee goe! that I should hold that Jewell no faster which I so lately held in my hands. O ungratefull mortals! O unthankefull as wee be, who never know our happinesse, untill wee want it!

LUCRECIA. Up, up, Madame; for it will be a greater dishonor unto you, to be found thus heere in the garden, then eyther the pleasure you received by his comming, or the sorrow which you take for his death. Come, let us into your chamber. And goe lay you downe on your bed; and I will call your father. Wee will faigne some other ill, since to hide this, it is impossible.

THE END OF THE NINETEENTH ACT

THE TRAGICK-COMEDY OF

ACTUS XX

THE ARGUMENT

UCRECIA *comes to* Pleberio's *chamber, and knockes at the doore.* Pleberio *askes her what's the matter?* Lucrecia *intreates him to come presently to see his daughter* Melibea. Pleberio *rises, and goes streight to* Melibea's *chamber. Hee comforts her; demanding what shee ayleth? and where was her griefe?* Melibea *faignes her paine to be about her heart.* Melibea *sends her father forth for some musicall Instruments. Shee and* Lucrecia *get them, when hee was gone, to the top of a tower. Shee sends away* Lucrecia, *and shuts the doore after her. Her father comes to the foote of the Tower,* Melibea *discovers unto him all the whole businesse of what had passed. That done, she throws her selfe downe from the top of the tower.*

INTERLOCUTORS

Pleberio, Lucrecia, Melibea.

PLEBERIO. What would you, Lucrecia? What meanes this exceeding haste, and with so great importunity, and troublednesse of mind? What ayles my daughter? What sudden sicknesse hath seazed on her, that I cannot have the leysure to put on my cloathes? nay, scarce so much time as to rise?

LUCRECIA. Sir, if you will see her alive, come quickely. What her griefe is, I know not; Nay, scarce know I her, so disfigured is her face.

PLEBERIO. Come, let us goe quickly; lead the way; in afore; lift up the hangings; open this same window; set it wide open, that I may have light enough to take a full view of her. Why, how now daughter? What's the matter? What is your paine? Where lies it? What a strange thing is this? What faintnesse doe I see? What weake-

272

CALISTO AND MELIBEA

nesse and feeblenesse? Looke upon me, daughter! I am thy father: Speake unto me, for pitties sake speake; and tell mee the cause of your griefe, that wee may the sooner provide a remedy. Send not my gray hayres with sorrow to the grave; thou knowest I have no other good but thee; no other worldly happinesse. Open thy gladsome eyes; looke cheerefully upon mee.

MELIBEA. Ay mee! What shall I doe?

PLEBERIO. What woe can equall mine, to see thee in such wofull plight? Your mother, as soone as ever shee but heard you were ill, fell presently into a swound, and lies in that extremity, and in a manner senslesse, that shee is not able to come and see thee. Be of good cheere, plucke up thy heart; and so raise up thy spirits, that thou may'st rise and goe along with mee to visit her. Tell mee (sweete soule) the cause of thy sorrow.

MELIBEA. My cure is remedilesse.

PLEBERIO. My deare daughter, the best beloved of thy aged father; for pitties sake, let not this thy cruell torment, cause thee to despaire of recovery, being carryed away with the violence and infirmity of thy passion: for sorrow still assaulteth the weakest hearts, and conquers them most, that are most cowardly: if thou wilt but tell me thy griefe, it shall presently be remedied ; for neither physick nor Physicians, nor servants shall be wanting, for the recovery of thy health, whether it consist in herbes, in stones, or in words, or remaine more secret in the bodies, and bowels of beasts. Doe not then vexe me any more; torment me no longer; force me not out of my wits; make me not madde, but tell me, good daughter, what, and where is your paine?

MEL. I feele a mortall wound, even in the very midst of my heart, the anguish whereof is so grievous unto mee, that it will scarce suffer mee to fetch my breath, much lesse to speake: there is no malady like unto mine; it is of a different nature from all other diseases. And before you can come to cure it in my heart, you must first take out my heart; for it lies even in the hidden and most secret place thereof.

PLEBERIO. Too too soone hast thou received this feeling and sense of elder yeeres; youth should be a friend to

2 M   273

pleasure and mirth, and an enemy unto care and sorrow. Rise then from hence, and let us goe and take some fresher ayre along by the River side; come, and make merry with your mother; you shall see, that will ease and rid away your paine. Take heed what you doe; doe not wilfully cast away your selfe; for if you flye and shunne mirth, there is not any thing in the world more contrary to your disease.

MELIBEA. Let us goe whither you please: and if it stand with your liking, Sir, let us goe up to the top of the Leades; for from thence I may injoy the pleasing sight of those Ships that passe to and fro, and perhaps it may give ease to my griefe.

PLEBERIO. Come, let us goe and take Lucrecia with us.

MELIBEA. With a very good will. I pray (father) will you cause some musicall instrument to be sent unto me, that by playing thereon, or singing thereunto, I may see if I can drive away this griefe; for though on the one side, the force and violence thereof doth much torment mee: yet on the other side, I doubt not but those sweet sounding Instruments and delightfull harmony, will much lessen and mitigate my sorrow.

PLEBERIO. This (daughter) shall presently be done: I will goe my selfe, and will it to be provided.

MELIBEA. Friend Lucrecia, this place (me thinkes) is too high; I am very loth to leave my fathers company. I prythee make a step down unto him, and intreat him to come to the foot of this Tower; for I have a word or two, which I forgot to tell him, that he should deliver from me to my mother.

LUCRECIA. I goe, Madame.

MELIBEA. They have all of them left me. I am now alone by my selfe, and no body with mee. The manner of my death falls fit and pat to my minde; it is some ease unto mee, that I and my beloved Calisto shall so soone meet againe. I will shut and make fast the dore, that no body may come up to hinder my death, nor disturbe my departure, nor to stop me in my journey, wherin I purpose to poast unto him; not doubting, but to visit him as well this very day, as he did mee this last night. All things fadge aright,

274

CALISTO AND MELIBEA

and have falne out as luckily, as I could wish it; I shall now
have time and leysure enough, to recount to my father
Pleberio, the cause of this my short and sudden end. I
confesse, I shall much wrong his silver hayres, and offer much
injury to his elder yeers; I shall work great wo unto him by
this my errour; I shall leave him in great heavinesse and
desolation all the daies of his life: But admit my death will
be the death of my dearest parents, and put case, that the
shortning of my daies, will be the shortning of theirs; who
doth not know, but that others have beene more cruell to
their parents then I am? Prusias, King of Bythinia, without
any cause, not induring that paine, which I doe, slew his
owne father Ptolomy, King of Egypt, slew both father and
mother, and brother and wife, and all for the love of his
Mistris. Orestes kil'd his mother, Clytemnestra, and that
cruell Emperour Nero, onely for the fulfilling of his pleasure,
murdred his owne mother. These, and such as they, are
worthe of blame. These are true Parricides; not I; who with
mine owne punishment, and with mine owne death, purge
away the guilt, which otherwise, they might moe justly lay
upon mee for their deaths. There have beene others, far
more cruell, who have slaine their own children, and their
owne brothers, in comparison of whose errours, mine is as
nothing; at least nothing so great. Philip, King of Macedon;
Herod, King of Iuryne; Constantine, Emperour of Rome:
Laodice, Queene of Cappadocca; and Medea the Sorceresse;
all these slew their owne sonnes and dearest children, and
that without any reason or just cause, preserving their owne
persons still in safety. To conclude, that great cruelty of
Phraates, King of the Parthians, occurres to my remembrance,
who, because hee would have no successour behinde him,
murdred Orodes, his aged father, as also his onely sonne,
besides some thirty more of his brethren. These were delicts
worthy blame indeed; because they keeping their owne
persons free from perill, butchered their Ancestours, their
successours, and their brethren. True it is, that though all
this be so, yet are we not to imitate them in those things
wherein they did amisse; but it is not in my power to doe
otherwise. And thou great Governour of the heavens, who

ACTUS
XX

art witnesse to my words, thou see'st the small power that I
have over my passion; thou seest how my liberty is captivated, and how my senses are taken with that powerfull
love of that late deceased Gentleman, who hath deprived
mee of that love, which I beare to my living parents.

PLEBERIO. Daughter Melibea, what make you there
alone? what is it you would have with mee? shall I come
up to you?

MELIBEA. No (good father) content you where you
are, trouble not your selfe, nor strive to come to me; you
shall but disturbe and interrupt that short speach which I
am now to make unto you. Now, by and by shalt thou be
suddenly wounded; thy heart shall presently be prickt with
griefe, and shall bleede abundantly, to see the death of thy
onely daughter. My end drawes neere; at hand is my rest,
and thy passion; my ease, and thy paine; my houre of
keeping company and thy time of solitarinesse. You shall
not need (my most honoured father) to seeke out any instruments of musick to asswage my sorrow; nor use any other
sound, save the sound of bels, for to ring my knell, and
bring my body to the grave. And, if thou canst harken
unto mee for teares, if thine eyes will give thine eares leave
to heare, thou shalt heare the desperate cause of this my
forced, yet joyfull departure; see thou neyther speake nor
weepe; interrupt me not, eyther with teares or words, unlesse
thou mean'st more heereafter to be tormented, in not knowing why I doe kill my selfe, then thou art now sorrowfull to
see my death. Neither aske, nor answer mee any thing; nor
question me any further, then what of mine owne accord I
shall willingly tell thee; for when the heart is surcharged
with sorrow, the eare is deafe to good counsell; and at such a
time, good and wholsome words rather incense, then allay
rage. Heare (my aged father) the last words that ever I
shall speake unto you. And if you entertaine them, as I
hope you will, you will rather excuse, then condemne my
errour. I am sure, you both well perceive and heare that
most sad and doleful lamentation, which is made thorowout
all this City; I am sure you heare this great noyse and ring-
ing of bells, the skriking and cryings out of all sorts of

CALISTO AND MELIBEA

people, this howling, and barking of dogges, this noyse and clattering of Armour. Of all this, have I beene the cause; I, even this very day, have clothed the greater part of the Knights, and Gentlemen of this City in mourning. I, even this very day, have left many servants orphaned, and quite destitute of a Master. I have beene the cause, that many a poore soule hath now lost it's almes and reliefe. I have beene the occasion, that the dead should have the company of the most complete Gentleman, for his good graces and qualities that ever was borne. I have beene the occasion, that the living have lost the onely Patterne and Paragon of courtesie, of gallant inventions, of witty devices, of neatnesse and decency in his cloathes, of speech, of gate, of kindnesse, and of vertue. I have beene the occasion, that the earth doth now injoy the most noble body, and the freshest flowre of youth, that ever was created in this age of ours. And because you may stand amazed and astonished at the sound of these my unusuall and unaccustomed crimes; I will open the businesse, and make this matter appeare more cleare unto you.

It is now (deare father) many dayes since that a Gentleman called Calisto, whom you well knew, as likewise his Ancestors, and noble Linage, did languish and pine away for my love. As for his vertues and goodnesse, they were generally knowne to the whole world. So great was his love-torment, and so little both place and opportunity to speake with me, that he was driven to discover his passion to a crafty and subtill woman, named Celestina, which Celestina, comming as a suiter unto mee in his behalfe, drew my secret love from forth my bosome, and made mee to manifest that unto her, which I concealed from mine own mother; she found the meanes to win me to her will; shee made the match betweene us; shee plotted how his desire and mine should take effect. And if hee dearely loved me, I was not therein deceived; shee made up that sad conclusion of that sweete and unfortunate execution of his will; and thus being over-come with the love of Calisto, I gave him entrance into your house; hee scaled your walls with ladders, and brake into your garden; brake my chaste purpose, by taking from mee the flowre of my Virginity. And thus almost this moneth have wee liv'd

277

in this delightfull errour of love. And as he came this last night unto mee, as hee was wont to doe, e'en just about the time that he should have returned home (as ill fortune would have it, who in the mutability of her nature, ordereth and disposeth all things, according to her disordered custome) the walls being high, the night darke, the ladder light and weake, his servants that brought it, unacquainted with that kinde of service, hee going downe somewhat hastily to see a fray, which he heard in the streete betweene his servants and some others that then passed by, being in choller, making more haste then good speed, thinking he should never come soone enough, not eying well his steps, he sets his foot quite besides the rounds, and so fell downe, and with that wofull and unfortunate fall, hee pitcht upon his head, and had his braines beaten out, and dasht in pieces against the stones and pavement of the streete. Thus did the destinies cut off his thred; thus cut off his life without confession; cut off my hope; cut off my glory; cut off my company. Things therefore being thus; tell me (father) What cruelty were it in me, he dying disbrained, that I should live pained all the daies of my life? His death inviteth mine; inviteth? nay, inforceth mee, that it be speedily effected, and without delay; it teacheth mee, that I should also fall headlong down, that I may imitate him in all things. It shall not be said of mee, that those that are dead and gone, are soone forgotten. And therefore I will seeke to content him in my death, since I had not time to give him content in my life. O my Love, and deare Lord, Calisto, expect mee, for now I come. But stay a little, though thou dost expect mee; and be not angry, I prythee, that I delay thee, being that I am now paying my last debt, and giving it my finall account to my aged father, to whom I owe much more. O my best beloved father, I beseech you, if ever you did love mee in this painefull forepassed life, that we may both be interred in one Tombe, and both our Obsequies be solemnized together. I would faine speake some words of comfort unto you, before this my gladsome and well-pleasing end, gathered and collected out of those ancient bookes, which for the bettering of my wit and under-

CALISTO AND MELIBEA

standing, you willed me to reade, were it not that my memory failes me, being troubled and disquieted with the losse and death of my Love: as also because I see your ill indured teares trickle so fast downe your wrinckled cheekes. Recommend mee to my most deare and best-beloved mother; and doe you informe her at large of the dolefull occasion of my death. I am glad with all my heart, that shee is not heere present with you; for her sight would but increase my sorrow. Take (aged father) the gifts of old age; for in large daies, large griefes are to be endured. Receive the pledge and earnest of thy reverend age; receive it at the hands of thy beloved daughter. I sorrow much for my selfe, more for you, but most for my aged mother: and so I recommend me to you both, and both of you unto your more happinesse, to whom I offer up my soule; leaving the care to you, to cover this body that is now comming downe unto you.

THE END OF THE TWENTIETH ACT

ACTUS XXI

THE ARGUMENT

PLEBERIO, *returning weeping to his chamber; his wife* Alisa *demands the cause of this so sudden an ill? Hee relates unto her the death of her daughter* Melibea; *shewing unto her, her bruised body, and so making lamentation for her, hee gives a conclusion to this Tragick Comedy.*

INTERLOCUTORS

Alisa, Pleberio.

ALISA. Why Pleberio? my Lord! what's the matter? why doe you weepe and sobbe? and take on in such extreme and violent manner? I have lyen ever since in a dead

ACTUS
XXI

swound, so was I overcome with griefe, when I heard that our daughter was so ill. And now hearing your pittifull lamentations, your loude cryings, your unaccustomed complaints, your mournings and great anguish, they have so pierced my very bowels, made so quicke a passage to my heart, and have so quickned and revived my troubled and benummed senses, that I have now put away the griefe, which I entertained : thus one griefe drives out another : and sorrow expelleth sorrow. Tell mee the cause of your complaint; Why doe you curse your honorable old age? Why do you desire death? Why doe you teare your milkwhite hayres up by the roates? Why doe you scratch, and rend your reverend face? Is any ill befalne Melibea? For I pray you tell mee; for if shee be not well, I cannot live.

PLEBERIO. Out alas! Ay mee; (my most noble wife.) Our solace is in the suds ; our joy is turn'd into annoy ; all our conceived hopes are utterly lost; all our happinesse is quite overthrowne ; let us now no longer desire to live. And because unexpected sorrowes leave a greater impression of griefe ; and because they may bring thee the sooner to thy grave ; as also, that I may not alone by my selfe bewayle that heavy losse which belongs to us both ; looke out and beholde her, whom thou broughtst forth, and I begot, dash't and broken all to pieces. The cause I understood from her selfe, but layd open more at large, by this her sadde and sorrowfull servant. Helpe to lament these our latter daies, which are now growing to an end. O yee good people, who come to behold my sorrowes, and you Gentlemen, my loving friends, doe you also assist to bewayle my misery! O my daughter! and my onely good! it were cruelty in mee, that I should out-live thee. My threescore yeeres were fitter for the grave, then thy twenty ; but the order of my dying was altred by that extremity of griefe, which did hasten thy end. O yee my hoary hayres, growne foorth to no other end, save sorrow ; it would better have suted with you, to have beene buryed in the earth, then with these golden tresses which lye heere before mee. Too too many are the dayes that I have yet to live ; I will complaine and cry out against death ; I will accuse him of

280

CALISTO AND MELIBEA

delay; how long will hee suffer mee to remaine heere after thee! Let my life now leave mee, since I must leave thy sweet company. O my deare wife, rise up from her, and if any life be left in thee, spend that little with mee in teares and lamentations, in sobbes, and in sighes; but in case thy soule resteth now with hers; if out of very griefe, thou hast left this life, why wouldst thou lay this heavy burthen on mee? why let mee remaine heere alone, and have no body to help me in the unsheathing of my sorrowes? In this, yee women have a great advantage of us that are men; for some violent griefe can make you goe out of the world without any paine; or at least cast you into a swound, which is some ease to your sorrowes. O the hard heart of a father, why dost thou not burst forth with griefe? why doe not your heart-strings crack in sunder, to see thy selfe bereav'd of thy beloved heyre? For whom didst thou build these Turrets? For whom got I honours? For whom planted trees? For whom built ships? O hard-hearted earth, why dost thou beare me any longer? Where shall my disconsolate old age finde any resting place? O variable fortune, and full of change, thou Ministresse, and high Stewardesse of all temporall happinesse; Why didst thou not execute thy cruell anger upon mee? Why didst thou not overwhelme him with thy mutable waves, who professes himselfe to be thy subject? Why didst thou not rob mee of my patrimony? Why didst thou not set fire on my house? Why didst thou not lay waste mine inheritance? Why didst thou not strip mee of my great revenewes? What is't I would not thou shouldst have done, so as thou hadst left mee that flourishing young plant, over which thou ought'st not to have had such power? Thou might'st, O fortune (fluctuant, and fluent as thou art) have given me a sorrowfull youth, and a mirthfull age; neyther have therein perverted order. Better could I have borne thy blowe, better indured thy persecutions, in that my more strong, and Oaky age, then in this my weake and feeble declining. O life fulfill'd with griefe, and accompanied with nought but misery! O world, world! much have men spoken of thee, much have men writ concerning thy deceits;

and much have I heard my selfe: And mine owne wofull experience is able to say something of thee, as one who have bin in the unfortunate fayre, and have often bought and sold with thee, but never had any thing that succeeded happily with mee. As one who many a time heeretofore, even to this present houre, have silenced thy false properties, and all because I would not purchase thy displeasure, and pull thy hatred upon mee: and that thou shouldst not untimely plucke this flowre from me, which this day thou hast cropt by the mightinesse of thy power. And therefore now will I goe without feare, like one that hath nothing to lose; or as one to whom thy company is now odious and troublesome; or like a poore traveller, who fearelesse of theeves, goes singing on his way. I thought in my more tender yeeres, that both thou and thy actions were governed by order, and ruled by reason: But now I see thou art *Pro* and *Con*; there is no certainty in thy calmes: thou seemest now unto me to be a Labyrinth of errours; a fearefull wildernesse; an habitation of wilde Beasts; a Dance full of changes; a Fen full of mire, and dirt; a Country full of thornes; a steepe and craggy mountaine, a field full of stones; a meddow full of Snakes and Serpents; a pleasant garden to looke to, but without any fruite; a fountaine of cares, a river of teares, a sea of miseries; trouble without profit; a sweet poyson, a vaine hope, a false joy, and a true sorrow. O thou false world! thou dost cast before us the baytes of thy best delights, and when we have swallowed them, they seeming savoury unto us, then doest thou shew us the hooke that must choake us. Nor can we avoyd it, because together with us, thou dost captivate our wills: Thou promisest mountaines, but performest Mole-hils: and then thou dost cast us off, that wee may not put thee in minde of making good thy vaine promises. We runne thorow the spacious fields of thy ranke vices, retchlesly, and with a loose reyne; and then doest thou discover thy ambushes unto us, when thou seest there is no way for us to retreat. Many have forsaken thee, fearing thy sudden forsaking of them. And well may they stile themselves happy, when they shall see, how well thou hast rewarded this poore heavy sorrowfull old

282

CALISTO AND MELIBEA

man, for his long service. Thou dost put out our eyes, and
then to make us amends, thou anointest the place with oyle:
thou breakest our head, and givest us a plaister; after thou
hast done us a great deale of harme, thou givest us a poore
cold comfort; thou dost hurt unto all, that no man may boast,
that others have not their crosses as well as wee; telling
them, that it is some ease to the miserable, to have companions in their misery. But I alas, disconsolate old man
stand all alone. I am singuler in my sorrowes; I am grieved,
and have no equall companion of my griefe. No mans misfortune is like unto mine; though I revolve in my troubled
memory, persons both present and past, I cannot instance in
the like. If I shall seeke to comfort my selfe with the
severity and patience of Paulus Æmilius, who having lost
two sonnes in seven daies, bore this brunt of fortune with so
undaunted a courage, that the people of Rome had rather
neede to be comforted by him, then he by them; yet cannot
this satisfie mee, for hee had two more remaining that were
his adopted sonnes. What companion then will they allot
me of my misery? Pericles, that brave Athenian Captaine?
or valiant Xenophon? Tush, they lost sonnes indeed, but
their sonnes dyed out of their sight, having lost their lives
abroad in forraine Countries, far from home; so that it was
not much for the one, not to change countenance, but to
take it cheerefully: nor for the other to answer the messenger, who brought him the ill tydings of his sonnes deaths,
that he should receive no punishment, because himselfe had
received no griefe; for all this is farre differing from mine;
lesse canst thou say (thou world replenished with evill) that
Anaxagoras, and I, were alike in our losse; that wee were
equall in our griefes: and that I should say of my dead
daughter, as he did of his onely sonne, when he said; Being
that I was mortall, I knew, that he whom I had begot was
to die. For my Melibea, willingly, and out of her owne
election, killed her selfe before mine eyes, inforced thereunto
through the extreme passion of her love, so great was her
torment; whereas his sonne was slaine in battell, in a just
and lawfull warre. O incomparable losse; O most wretched
and sorrowfull old man that I am! who the more I seeke

283

THE TRAGICK-COMEDY OF

ACTUS after comfort, the lesse reason doe I finde for my com-
XXI fort; for much more miserable doe I finde my misfortune,
and doe not so much grieve at her death, as I doe
lament the manner of her death. Now shall I lose
together with thee (most unhappy daughter) those feares,
which were daily wont to affright mee. Onely thy death
is that which makes mee secure of all suspitions and
jealousies. What shall I doe, when I shall come into
thy chamber, and thy withdrawing roome, and shall finde it
solitary and empty? What shall I doe, when as I shall call
thee, and thou shalt not answer me? Who is he that can
supply that want which thou hast caused? Who can stop
up that great breach in my heart which thou hast made?
Never any man did lose that which I have lost this day.
Thogh in some sort, that great fortitude of Lambas de
Auria, Duke of Genoa, seemeth to sute with my present
estate and condition, who seeing his sonne was wounded to
death, tooke him and threw him with his owne armes foorth
of the shippe into the sea. But such kinde of deaths as
these, though they take away life, yet they give reputation;
and many times, men are inforced to undergoe such actions,
for to cumply with their honour, and get themselves fame
and renowne. But what did inforce my daughter to dye,
but onely the strong force of love? What remedy now,
(thou flattering world) wilt thou affoord my wearisome age?
How wouldst thou have me to rely upon thee, I knowing thy
falsehoods, thy gins, thy snares, and thy nets, wherein thou
intrap'st and takest our weake and feeble wills? Tell me,
what hast thou done with my daughter? where hast thou
bestow'd her? who shall accompany my disaccompanied
habitation? who shall cherish me in mine old age? who
with gentle usage shall cocker my decaying yeeres? O Love,
Love, I did not thinke thou hadst had the power to kill thy
subjects! I was wounded by thee in my youth: I did passe
thorow the midst of thy flames. Why didst thou let me
scape? Was it that thou might'st pay me home (for my
flying from thee then) in mine old age? I had well thought,
that I had bin freed from thy snares, when I once began to
growe towards forty; and when I rested contented with my
284

CALISTO AND MELIBEA

wedded consort, and when I saw I had that fruit, which this
day thou hast cut down, I did not dreame that thou would'st
in the children have taken vengeance of the parents; and I
know not whether thou woundest with the sword, or burnest
with fire. Thou leavest our clothes whole, and yet most
cruelly woundest our hearts; thou makest that which is
foule, to seeme fayre and beautifull unto us. Who gave
thee so great a power? who gave thee that name which so
ill befitteth thee? If thou wert Love, thou wouldst love thy
servants; and if thou didst love them, thou wouldst not
punish them as thou dost. If to be thy fellow, were to live
merrily, so many would not kill themselves, as my daughter
now hath, and infinit of us. What end have thy servants and
their Ministers had? as also that false Bawd, Celestina, who
dy'd by the hands of the faithfullest companions, that ever
she lighted upon in her life, for their true performance in
this thy venomous and impoisoned service? They lost their
heads; Calisto, he brake his necke; and my daughter, to
imitate him, submitted her selfe to the selfe-same death.
And of all this thou wast the cause; they gave thee a
sweete name; but thy deedes are exceeding sowre: thou
dost not give equall rewards; and that Law is unjust, which
is not equall alike unto all. Thy voyce promiseth pleasure,
but thy actions proclaime paine; happy are they who have
not knowne thee, or knowing thee, have not cared for thee.
Some ledde with, I know not what error, have not stickt to
call thee a god; But I would have such fooles as these to
consider with themselves, it savors not of a Deity, to murder
or destroy those that serve and follow him. O thou enemy
to all reason! To those that serve thee least, thou givest
thy greatest rewards, untill thou hast brought them at last
into this thy troublesome dance. Thou art an enemy to thy
friends, and a friend to thy enemies; and all this is, because
thou dost not governe thy selfe according to order and reason.
They paint thee blind, poore, and young; they put a Bowe
into thy hand, wherein thou drawest, and shootest at ran-
dom; but more blind are they that serve thee. For they
never taste or see the unsavory and distastful recompence,
which they receive by thy service; thy fire is of hot burning

CALISTO AND MELIBEA

lightning, which scorches unto death, yet leaves no impression or print of any wound at all. The sticks which thy flames consume, are the soules and lives of humane creatures, which are so infinit, and so numberlesse, that it scarce accurreth unto me, with whom I should first begin ; not only of Christians, but of Gentiles and of Iewes ; and all forsooth in requitall of their good services. What shall I speak of that Macias of our times ; and how by loving, he came to his end ? Of whose sad and wofull death, thou wast the sole cause. What service did Paris do thee ? What Helena ? What Clytemnestra ? What Ægisthus ? All the world knowes how it went with them. How well likewise didst thou require Sapho, Ariadne, and Leander, and many other besides, whom I willingly silence, because I have enough to do in the repetition of mine own misery ? I complaine me of the world, because I was bred up in it ; for had not the world given me life, I had not therein begot Melibea ; not being begot, shee had not beene borne ; not being borne, I had not lov'd her ; and not loving her, I should not have mourned, as now I do, in this my latter and uncomfortable old age ! O my good companion ! O my bruised daughter, bruised even all to pieces ! Why wouldst thou not suffer me to divert thy death ? why wouldst thou not take pitty of thy kinde and loving mother ? why didst thou shew thy selfe so cruell against thy aged father ? why hast thou left me thus in sorrow ? why hast thou left me comfortlesse, and all alone, *in hac lachrimarum valle*, in this vaile of teares, and shadow of death ?

FINIS

TO THE READER

LO heere thy Celestine, *that wicked wight,*
Who did her tricks upon poore Lovers proove ;
And in her company, the god of Love.
   Lo, grace, beauty, desire, terrour, hope, fright,
Faith, falsehood, hate, love, musicke, griefe, delight,
Sighes, sobs, teares, cares, heates, colds, girdle, glove,
Paintings, Mercury, Sublimate, dung of Dove.
   Prison, force, fury, craft, scoffes, Art, despight,
Bawds, Ruffians, Harlots, servants, false, untrue :
And all th' effects that follow on the same :
As warre, strife, losse, death, infamy and shame.
   All which and more, shall come unto thy view.
But if this Booke speake not his English plaine,
   Excuse him : for hee lately came from Spaine.

287

EDINBURGH

T. & A. CONSTABLE

Printers to Her Majesty

1894